The Faraway Drums

JON CLEARY

The Faraway Drums

WILLIAM MORROW AND COMPANY, INC.

New York   *1982*

Library of Congress Cataloging in Publication Data

Cleary, Jon, 1917–

    The faraway drums.
    I. Title.
PR9619.3.C54F3   823   81-14091
ISBN 0-688-00790-2   AACR2

Printed in the United States of America

First U.S. Edition

1 2 3 4 5 6 7 8 9 10

For Alberto and Jorge

CHAPTER ONE

It was a beautifully clear day for an ambush. Clive Farnol was working his way up from the Satluj River towards the Tibet Road, climbing a steep rocky ridge, when it happened. The first bullet hit one of the four Paharee porters, tumbling him backwards down the slope, and the next three shots sent chips flying from a rock right beside Farnol.

He heard Karim Singh swear and the three surviving porters cry out in fear. Then he swore himself as another bullet whined away off the rock only inches from his face, flicking grit into his face. He tried to roll himself into a ball behind the rock, no easy task for a man as tall as himself, and squinted over his shoulder at Karim. The Sikh was equally tall and he looked awkward and embarrassed as he tried to make himself as small a target as possible. The three porters, all small men, were already sliding back down the ridge, their packs abandoned, their swiftly retreating backs declaring neutrality.

'Coward buggers,' said Karim, spitting down the ridge.

Farnol felt he couldn't blame the porters; it wasn't in their contract that they should die for five annas a day. The shooting had stopped, but he knew that it was not finished. The ambushers, whoever they were, were probably working their way to better positions to pick off him and Karim. But who were they? Why had they chosen to shoot at this small party of travellers? He and Karim were both in hillmen's dress: baggy breeches, faded shirts, goatskin vests and turbans. True, they both carried Lee-Enfield rifles, but the chances were that the rifles firing on them were also Lee-Enfields; stolen British Army weapons were a mark of honour amongst the hillmen, a sort of self-conferred, lethal Order of the Indian Empire. But why waste bullets on what, from a

7

distance, would have looked like nothing more than a small party of villagers moving down from the high mountains to Simla? Any ordinary band of dacoits would have waited till the party had climbed up to the road, then set on them, cut their throats with *kris* and taken what loot they wanted from the packs carried by the porters. And, of course, taken the two rifles.

Farnol suddenly rose up, scrambled up the hill and fell into a depression behind a larger rock; bullets chased him but missed. Karim remained where he was, now lying flat on his back behind a thin spine of rock; he had worked out that the shots were all coming from one direction, a ridge above them and to their left. He was an old hand at ambushes, having seen them from both sides.

Farnol looked around him. In the far distance, whence they had come, he could see the Eternal Snows, the last barrier of the Himalayas; the morning sky was absolutely cloudless and the mountains had the sharp-edged look of white glass. Nearer, the hills fell away as steep ridges, some of them patterned with the corduroy of terraces; he could see the tiny figures of peasants tilling the rocky ground, sowing the wheat that would turn the terraces into bright strips of green in late March. On a ridge up near the road a man and a woman were digging stones and rocks from a new terrace and carting them up to the roadway where they would be used as fill: the ridges were harvested for everything that would bring in a few annas. Still nearer, on a ridge across a deep ravine, Farnol could see a goat-herd and his herd moving, like a small cloud-shadow, up towards the road. The goat-herd had stopped and was looking Farnol's way, a disinterested spectator of the ambush: he looked at the distance as if he were as unconcerned as his goats.

A flash of movement tugged at Farnol's eye: a man ran down from the road to an outcrop of rock high to the left. Farnol turned his head and looked at the ridge on his right. A thick cloak of silver fir that ran up its spine was broken for a few yards by a gully, then continued across to cover the top of the ridge on which he lay.

'I'm going up to the road, Karim.'

'If you say so, sahib.' Karim Singh was that rarity, a

8

cautious Sikh who always weighed discretion against valour; he was no coward but he always thought twice before attempting to be a hero. He would deride others for their instant cowardice, as he just had the porters, but they were Paharees and, being a Sikh, he could not think of them with anything but derision.

'When I reach there, you follow me.'

'If you say so, sahib. But wouldn't it be better to wait till nightfall?'

'Karim, that won't be for another eight hours!' Then Farnol sighed. 'I don't know why I bother to keep you with me.'

'You have become accustomed to me, sahib.'

True, Farnol thought. A man's loyalty was worth more than his bravery. But he wished he had been fortunate enough to have found a legendary Sikh, one of those black-bearded heroes whom Rudyard Kipling was always writing about. Mr Kipling should be here now . . . Another shot rang out, the bullet whining away once more off the rock above Farnol.

'I want you up there on the road five minutes after I get there. Five minutes, less if you can make it. Understand?'

He didn't wait for Karim's usual answer – 'If you say so, sahib' – but all at once rose up and flung himself down the side slope of the ridge. He heard another bullet ricochet away above him, but he kept hurtling down the slope, a tall two-legged mountain goat that, like its four-legged brethren, managed by some miracle to stay on its feet. He reached the bottom of a gully, crossed it and scrambled up to the protecting shadows of the firs. He kept moving, his lungs beginning to ache through moving so quickly in the thin air. Then something hit him and he fell sideways into a tree, all the air going out of him in a great painful gasp. For an instant he wondered why it had not occurred to him that there might be more ambushers here amongst the trees.

Then he saw the big sambhar stag go plunging down through the trees, its head twisting as its antlers struck a tree-trunk, its panic evident in the reckless way it skidded and slid and jumped down the steep slope. Farnol stood up, felt for broken bones, decided there was none and moved on, stiffly

9

now, up through the trees. He had been shooting sambhar for ten years, but he had never been closer than a hundred yards to them. It would be something to tell in the mess, if ever he got back to the mess, that he had been knocked down by a stag as big as a small elephant. Or so it had seemed.

He worked his way up the ridge, stopping only once, to catch his breath and to check he had a full magazine in his rifle. He wore a bandolier of ammunition, but he did not want to get into a protracted battle with the ambushers. He had no idea how many were in the band of dacoits, but he guessed there were no more than three or four.

He came to the edge of the trees, and saw the road running slightly downhill to his left. That meant, with luck, he should be above the enemy, a golden rule amongst hillmen. He had been born in these hills; he had been sent to England, to We'lington and Sandhurst, to be educated; his real education, that needed for survival here, had been bred into him at birth. Four generations of Farnols had fought in India and three of them had been born here; there were instincts inherent in him that still prevailed under the varnish that the years in England had applied. He understood as well as anyone that the tribesmen of these hills, from Afghanistan as far east as Nagaland, knew as much about fighting as any graduate of Sandhurst, probably a great deal more.

He crossed the road at a run, made it to the forest of firs that continued up the slope. He moved swiftly, his experience showing in the way he made use of his cover: like Karim Singh, he was a veteran of ambushes. But on those other occasions he had half-expected them, had known the reason for them.

He came to the spot where, on the opposite side of the road, there was a cairn of stones with a pole of prayer-flags fluttering above it. Pious travellers had built the cairn over the years, each adding a stone to it as he passed; Farnol offered his own prayer of thanks to the religious who had built such a fine redoubt for him. He ran across the road again, took cover behind the big pile of stones and looked down the slope below him. Above him the prayer-flags fluttered like live birds tied by their feet to the pole.

He saw the three men, each crouched behind his own rock,

all three of them armed with long-barrelled rifles; he had been wrong about their having Lee-Enfields and he wondered what sort of guns they were. He looked around for a fourth man, one who should have been left up here on the higher ground as a look-out; but he could see no one. These men below him were either amateurs, new to the ambush game, or they were drugged with hashish, had thrown caution to the mountain wind in the excitement of killing. So far, however, they were not excited or crazed enough to stand up and charge down on where Karim still lay behind his low rock.

Farnol took aim. The men were less than a hundred yards below him, easy targets. He felt no compunction about killing in cold blood; he had learned long ago that one didn't survive if one waited to be hot-blooded about it. Killing was not like making love: one did not work up to it.

He squeezed the trigger, saw one of the men slump down as if all his bones had suddenly melted. He jerked back the bolt, ejected the cartridge, slammed the bolt home again, took aim, fired. A second man, spinning round to face up the slope, stood as if he had been pulled up by a rope, then fell backwards over the rim of a ledge. Farnol aimed the Lee-Enfield a third time, but the third man had slid down below the rock in front of him, got a shot off up the slope as Farnol switched his aim.

Farnol knew at once that he was not going to be able to draw a bead on the man in his new position. He hesitated, scanning the slope; above him the prayer-flags cracked in the rising wind. On the next ridge the goat-herd still stood looking at this duel that was no business of his; Farnol silently cursed him for his disinterest. He was like the bloody villagers who stood on the sidelines of the polo matches down on the plains, careless of who won or lost, showing approval only if one of the players toppled from his pony and broke his leg or neck. That was India: four hundred million bystanders.

He straightened up, sped down the slope, slipping and sliding, heading for a large rock that would give him all the shelter he would need. Then, while he was in full flight, going too fast to drop down, he saw the man rise up, his rifle at his shoulder. Farnol knew he was going to die. A hillman like this one would have spent his life aiming at moving targets: sambhar, gooral sheep, pheasants and men. But the enemy bullet, if it was fired at all, came nowhere near Farnol. As he hit the ground, hurling himself forward to slide down towards the big rock, he caught a lopsided glimpse of the rifleman falling forward, losing his rifle as he did so.

Farnol lay a moment, getting his breath, waiting for the man to reach for his rifle. But he lay still, one arm flung out towards the gun. Farnol got to his feet, aching from the crash of his body against the rocky ground, gravel rash scorching him like sunburn, blood running from a cut above his eye. Moving cautiously, rifle at the ready, he went down towards the hillman. He saw Karim standing up on the next ridge, but he made no sign towards the Sikh; there would be time later to thank Karim for the shot that had saved his life. He paused about ten feet from the ambusher, tensed as the man's arm quivered, trying to grab the rifle just beyond the reach of the weakly clawing hand. Then he moved down, put his foot on the rifle. He recognized it: a Krenk, a very old one, a Russian weapon.

He looked down at the dying man, said in Hindi, 'Why did you try to kill me?'

The man stared up at him out of fierce eyes that were already glazing with death. The rattle was in his throat as he whispered, 'Raj – will die!'

2

Karim Singh came scrambling across from the other ridge. 'Sahib, that was a damned close thing! If it were not for my marvellous accuracy, you would be dead!'

'I am grateful for your marvellous accuracy.' One could hardly tick off a man for his conceit, not when he'd just saved your life. 'Take a look at the other two.'

Karim went across to inspect the other two hillmen, came back to report they were both dead. 'You too, sahib, are marvellously accurate. But haven't I always said so? Such marvellous shots, we are. Our skill leaves me speechless!'

Farnol, deaf to the speechless Karim, was examining the dead man. He pulled his turban down over the cut above his eye and for a moment the flow of blood was staunched. He still felt sore and stiff from his plunge down the slope, but his mind was alert with questions. He went through the man's pockets, but there was nothing in them to identify him. Some dried apricots, a string of prayer-beads: the sustenance of the traveller in these hills. Farnol himself carried apricots in his pocket, but he had never felt the need of prayer-beads.

He lifted the man's arm to lay it by his side; he was a neat man who liked to see even the dead laid out neatly. The ragged sleeve fell back and he saw the marking on the inside of the arm at the bend of the elbow. It was smudged, not a very good tattoo; it looked like a dagger standing in the middle of a jagged circle. He stood up, went down to the other bodies, looked at the right arms: the same marking was there just inside the elbow. One of the tattoos was clearer than the others and he recognized it now for what it was meant to be: a dagger driven into the centre of a crown.

He got slowly to his feet, not wanting to believe the thought crystallizing in his mind. *Raj – will die!* He had taken it as a threat against himself, taking it for granted that the ambushers had somehow known who he was: a political agent, a representative of the British Raj. But the man had meant someone much higher than himself, someone for whom he had no other name but Raj. The word could mean kingdom, a ruler or a great ruler.

Or *The* Great Ruler: George the Fifth, King of England, already down in Bombay and on his way to Delhi where he was to be crowned Emperor of India.

3

'You must remember, Major Farnol, you cannot rule this part of the world forever.'

'We have no intention ever of trying to rule Tibet.' The

13

lama had given himself no name and Farnol knew better than to ask. He knew the etiquette and protocol of these mountains as well as he did those of the messes, the stations and the government offices down on the plains; he took care to respect these customs more than he did those of his own kind. 'Other people covet your country more than we do.'

He was not convinced that what he said was true. Eight years ago Francis Younghusband had led a British expedition up through the passes east of Lue and on to Lhasa; Curzon, the then Viceroy, had dreamed of Britain ruling the Roof of the World as well as the Indian sub-continent. The British influence had declined after Younghusband and Curzon both retired from the imperial service, but Farnol knew there were still men in India and Whitehall who dreamed of enlarging the Empire.

'I am not concerned for my country.' The lama was no more than skin and bone, a shrivelled gourd for the inner peace that kept him alive. Unafraid of death, he waited patiently for its arrival like a passenger at a wayside station waiting for a train that ran to no schedule. 'I speak of India. Time is running out for the English.'

'Perhaps. But it won't run out in my lifetime.' But there were doubts nibbling like mice at all he had been brought up to believe in. 'Not even if I live to your great and honourable age.'

The lama's withered gums did not make an attractive smile; the warm humour was in the faded eyes peering out from its veil of wrinkles. 'I hope you live so long, Major Farnol. But I warn you – there are men in the hills south of here who are plotting to drive the English out of India.'

'Where can I find them?'

But the lama waved a vague hand; it looked to Farnol like a floating leaf. They were seated cross-legged on the terrace that ran along below the southern wall of the monastery; there was no fence to the edge of the terrace and below them there was a cliff that fell sheer for at least two thousand feet. Across the deep valley, an arm's length away on the thin shining air, was the lowest range of the Eternal Snows; Farnol would have to cross it on his way back into India. He had crossed the frontier marked by the cartographers, but it was not marked on the mountains and he knew he would never be asked for a visa.

'Somewhere. Who knows?' The mountains were gods to the people who lived amongst them and the lama would not betray the plotters the gods had chosen to hide. Such a betrayal would need a sign from the gods themselves.

Farnol bit into one of the small Lachen apples that one of the younger monks had brought him and the lama. He had also brought some small barley cakes, an urn of tea and a bowl of yak butter. Farnol had already eaten one of the cakes and taken a sip of the buttered tea; but in all his time in these mountains he had never learned to like the taste of either. The Lachen apple, tart as the small Christmas apples he had once eaten in England, cleansed his mouth.

'Should I fear for my own life going back through the mountains?'

The lama's bones creaked with his shrug; the eighty-one beads of his rosary click-clicked their way between the dry twigs of his fingers. 'Are you afraid of death?'

'Yes.' When you are thirty-two years old, your health is good and your prostate gland is something you don't know you possess, why should one be unafraid of death?

The lama's smile was all gums and wrinkles. 'You should spend more time here with us.'

At the far corner of the terrace where it turned round the monastery wall, a man was seated facing north and east. Farnol guessed the direction of his gaze, towards Kailas, the holiest of all the holy mountains. It was there amidst the Eternal Snows, lying not only in heaven and earth but in the hearts of believers. Farnol could imagine the meditation of the unmoving man at the far end of the terrace, the trance-like contemplation which could make him part of the mountains and the mountains part of him, one with the gods. He himself had always felt the mysticism of these high places, but scepticism had always denied him the transcendental feeling that the true believer could achieve.

The lama saw Farnol looking at the man. 'A seeker after the truth – he comes from the south. He is not one of us but he seeks the same truth.'

'Do many come here from the outside?'

'Not many, but some. We always make them welcome. We should make you welcome if you wished to stay.'

'I must leave for Simla tomorrow.' He smiled. 'But not to seek the truth, not there.' Not amongst the little tin gods.

'As a young man I worked as a bearer in Simla. Are you Church of England?'

'Occasionally.' At Christmas, Easter and on compulsory church parades back at the regiment.

'The Church of England doesn't understand contemplation.' He remembered the vicar's wife for whom he had worked, who had always tried to tell him that cleanliness was next to godliness. He now hadn't had a bath in sixty years and he was sure he was as close to God as any shiny-skinned Christian. 'But then neither does the Englishman, does he? I watched him in Simla. When he was not working he was playing polo or that strange game, cricket – '

'There's time for contemplation there. The spectators often go into trances.'

But the lama, a wise man but unlearned in the wisdom of the west, missed the joke. Or perhaps, Farnol thought, the English sense of humour doesn't translate well into Tibetan. He spoke five languages besides English, but humour was always the note that slipped on the tongue.

'Take care, Major Farnol. Do not spend so much time on the playing fields. I hear whispers – ' Again the leaf of his hand floated in the air. 'The caravans coming back bring us rumours of men in certain villages who will soon be going south to start their work.'

'Tibetans or Indians?' Farnol saw the lama's hesitation and pressed the question: 'You can tell me without offending the gods. You don't want our soldiers coming so far north to seek them out, not again.'

'All I can say is that they are not our people,' said the lama and Farnol knew he would tell only the truth. 'They are Indian. But I can tell you no more than that. The gods will tell you if they wish to.'

The man at the end of the terrace stood up. Farnol, his attention distracted for a moment from the lama, watched fascinated as the mystic, wrapped in a long brown robe, seemed to move in a trance towards the very edge of the terrace, as if he were going to step out on to the clear shining air. Farnol stopped himself from crying out; he knew better than to interfere. He knew how some of these men could put themselves into a state where they achieved the seemingly impossible: to walk through fire and come out unharmed, to sit naked amongst the ice of the highest places and be unaffected. But men did not walk on the air above a valley two thousand feet deep. Christ may have walked on the water but even He had never shown that He could walk on air.

The man abruptly stopped; Farnol guessed that his toes must be curled over the very edge of the tremendous drop. He stood there poised, unmoving, seemingly leaning on the breeze that blew up from the valley; Farnol waited for him to plunge off into the void. Then he turned round; Farnol would swear that for a moment the man actually stepped off the terrace edge, stood on the air. Then he walked back across the terrace, gliding in the long brown robe. As he disappeared past the corner of the monastery wall he looked towards Farnol and the lama. Farnol caught a glimpse of a black beard, a hooked nose and dark deep-set eyes that he was sure saw neither himself nor the lama.

'Were the gods protecting that man when he stood there on the edge?'

'Who knows? We can only put our trust in them. You should put your trust in them, too.'

'I only wish I could.' But that was not the truth: he had the sceptic's false faith in himself.

All that had been a month ago and since then, journeying slowly back through the high passes, working the villages for information like an insurance salesman looking for new clients, he had learned nothing from the gods or any less exalted source. He had heard a rumour or two, but they had been only echoes; nobody knew, or would tell, where the gossip had begun. Once, in a village, a man had pointed a finger, but when Farnol had looked round the man the finger had been pointed at had disappeared; when he turned back the would-be informer had also disappeared. It had always been like that here in the Himalayas: mystery and magic were part of the atmosphere, conjurers, mesmerists and the occasional charlatan were as native to the mountains as the gooral sheep and the snow leopard. The only defence was never to show your bewilderment.

So he had slowly come down from the high places till he found himself on the Tibet Road above the Satluj River and there been ambushed.

He and Karim buried the three ambushers and the dead porter under cairns of stones, mindful that they would wish their own bodies to be treated that way, safe from the jaws of jackals. Then Karim had shouted at the top of his large voice, a trumpet call for the cowardly, despicable, thieving porter-buggers to come back up the ridge and pick up their packs. The porters, who had not yet been paid, a shrewd yoke that generally kept them from running too far, came back, suffered a lash or two from Karim's *lathi* cane, picked up their loads and fell in behind Farnol and Karim. That night and the next Farnol and Karim took turns in keeping guard when they camped, but nobody had appeared to disturb or attack them. Yet Farnol had felt every step back along the Road, through Narkanda, Theog and Fagu, that he was being watched. But whenever he looked back, no matter how quickly, he saw no one.

On the third day after the ambush, in the late afternoon, Farnol walked into Simla. Smoke came up the steep slopes of the narrow ridge on which the town seemed to be plastered rather than built. Down in the bazaar and in the houses where the native population lived on the south side of the ridge, cooking fires had been lit and the smoke rose like an evening mist, drifting into the rear of the Europeans' bungalows built on the upper roads. Maids came hurrying to close the windows, shouting abuse down at the lower life who dared cause this inconvenience. The lower life replied with abuse as thick and pungent as the smoke. It was an evening ritual that each level would miss if ever it were discontinued.

Farnol walked along the road just below the Mall. Indians were not allowed to walk on the Mall, the road that ran along the top of the ridge; that hand-swept, spotless roadway was reserved strictly for Europeans and the Indian nobles. Even they, too, were restricted in that they could not ride in a carriage or motor car; that privilege was reserved for the Viceroy, who, when in residence at the Lodge, would drive the length of the ridge every Sunday morning to church while lesser souls tested their faith with their feet or rode amongst the fleas in a rickshaw.

Farnol, still dressed as a hillman, did not want any run-in with the police till he reached the Viceregal Lodge. Several of the better-class Indians, out for their evening promenade, necks held stiff in their Celluloid collars, looked contemptuously at him, Karim and the three porters; but there was something about the bearing of the tall bearded hillman that stopped them from telling him to get down to one of the even lower roads. Farnol smiled to himself, knowing their thoughts: there was no one more jealous of his station than the Indian who worked for the Indian Civil Service. But then there was no one more class conscious than the English Brahmins of the ICS.

'Snob buggers,' said Karim Singh, who had his own contempt for office wallahs. 'When do we go down to Delhi, sahib?'

'Tomorrow, perhaps the day after. It will depend on Colonel Lathrop.'

A lot would depend on George Lathrop. It was he who had recruited Farnol from Farnol's Horse and, three years ago, sent him into the North-West Frontier as a political agent. Since then there had been other excursions, all of them dangerous, not all of them rewarding; Farnol, a man ambitious for a certain degree of comfort, had had moments when he had wondered why he agreed to work for Lathrop. He had been born in India of a family that had first come here in 1750 to work for the East India Company; his great-great-grandfather had formed Farnol's Horse, a Company regiment, in 1776 and the eldest son or only son of each succeeding generation had been expected to join the regiment. After his education in England Clive had returned to join the Horse, to find his place in the circumscribed life that was the way of the Indian Army. Even if all the blood in him was English, he had been infected by Indian ways: he saw the sybaritic life that the princes lived and he had longed for the opportunity to fall prey to such corruption. He had slept with the daughters of princes and with the wives of several; had he been caught his pure English blood would have run very freely out of his slit throat and down his dress uniform, for princes had a proper sense of occasion even for executions and would not have allowed him to die in regimental undress. But his success with the ladies, by their being clandestine, had not led to any invitations to join the luxury life in the palaces. In the end, bored by life in the regiment, he had instead accepted Lathrop's invitation to be seconded to the Political Service. He had also come to realize that if some prince did offer his daughter in marriage, he would probably back out. He was the sort of man who wished to be corrupted only at a distance or, if closer, then only occasionally.

Three months ago, at the beginning of September, Lathrop had sent him up the Tibet Road to the mythical frontier only believed in by statesmen and cartographers. The word had gone out earlier in the year that on the 12th day of December in this year of grace 1911, George the Fifth of Great Britain and his consort Queen Mary were coming to Delhi to be crowned, at a Great Durbar, Emperor and Empress of India. Farnol had been instructed to find out if the hill tribes were excited by the news, troubled by it or if, indeed, they cared at all. The general attitude, he had found, had been one of bemused puzzlement: King Who? In a region so remote that some villages did not know the name of the headman of the next village fifty miles away on the other side of a mountain, there was little cause for the clapping of hands and shouts of *Hats off, the King!* when someone produced a piece of paper and read to them the news that a Great Raj from over the sea ('What is a sea, sahib?') was coming to let them crown him their Emperor. Farnol knew it would have been different in the Afghan hills where the tribesmen had a political sense that kept their knives sharp and their guns hot. But in the mountain fastnesses kings had held no sway: a man lived and died subject only to his father, his village chief and the gods who ruled them all.

At the gates to the curving drive leading up to the Viceregal Lodge Farnol and his entourage were halted by two guards. The two soldiers prodded the tall dirty hillman and told him to clear out.

'*Nickle-jao!* Piss off!'

'I shall not piss off. I am Major Farnol, of Farnol's Horse, reporting to Colonel Lathrop. Take that bayonet out of my belly.'

The soldiers peered at him, then one said to the other, 'Escort him up to the house, Mick. Let them make up their mind who he is. Give him a poke up the arse if he tries anything. I'll keep this lot down here.'

Farnol walked up the long sloping drive, the guard right behind him with his bayonet at the ready. He did not blame the soldiers for their attitude; one rarely found rankers who were happy in their work these days. A shilling and fourpence a day and a seven-year contract did nothing to make India an attractive tour of duty. Their devotion to duty had not been improved by the policies of the previous Viceroy, Lord Curzon, who had favoured more freedom and rights for the natives; nor had Lady Curzon, an American lady, fired them with enthusiasm when she had said that the two ugliest creatures in India were the water-buffalo and the British private soldier. A poke up the arse with a bayonet was something a man who looked like an Indian and claimed to be a British officer should not find unexpected or even unreasonable.

They came to the junction in the drive where one arm led to the rear of the huge house and the other to the portico over the front entrance. Farnol looked up at the mansion towering against the pale pink of the western clouds. Each time he came here he was amused by the extravagance of it, the incongruity of this massive country house that paid no respects to its foreign location. But it had the most magnificent site in Simla and he always enjoyed walking in its gardens. Ten years ago, when he had been a very junior aide on the staff of Lord Curzon, he had been standing on the south lawn when the Viceroy had come and stood beside him.

'Have you a liking for vistas, Farnol? Are you long-sighted?'

'Yes, sir.' He knew that the Viceroy liked to think he had a poetic imagination.

'I sit here and imagine I can see all of India all the way south to the Coromandel Coast.' Tall though Farnol was, he always felt that the Viceroy was just that much taller. Curzon held his long narrow head in such a way that he always seemed to be looking down on people. It was partly his natural arrogance, but he also had back trouble which forced him to stand very upright: so can minor afflictions set one's image for history. One of the last great imperialists, though neither he nor virtually anyone else saw it that way, he looked upon India as his own domain; he would not have been embarrassed by any modesty if it had been suggested that *he* should be crowned Emperor. 'And I rule it all in the King's name.'

A mere subaltern didn't query such illusions of grandeur. 'A great responsibility, sir.'

Then Curzon smiled, showing the sense of humour that was rarely seen. Or was it something else, a sense of irony at his claim to being long-sighted? 'It is all just in one's imagination.'

Then he had nodded abruptly and gone back to the house and Farnol had been left wondering. A breeze suddenly blew up, whispering through the deodars, and he had shivered, felt the chill of the unknown years ahead.

The bayonet poked him in the buttock. 'Turn right, matey. We're going in the back way.'

'We're going in the front way. Stick me in the arse again with that bayonet and I'll shove it down your throat. What's your name?'

The soldier lowered his rifle, shook his head, then snapped to attention. 'You got to be an officer. No coolie would talk to me like that. Sorry, sir. Can't be too careful.'

'I said, what's your name?'

'Mick Ahearn, sir. Private Ahearn.'

'Irish, eh? Are you with the Connaughts?'

'Yes, sir.'

Farnol knew of the Connaught Rangers' contempt for Indians; their unofficial motto was that those who had been conquered by the sword must be kept by the sword. Since swords were not standard issue, they settled for a jab with a bayonet or a boot up the behind of the conquered. 'In future, Private Ahearn, make sure you have the right coolie before you start blunting your bayonet on him.'

Ahearn followed Farnol up to the big portico and waited while Farnol went up the steps and rang the bell beside the wide front doors. The Indian butler who answered the bell was even more brusque than the soldier had been in dismissing the dirty, ragged hillman. But Farnol pushed him aside, strode into the huge high-ceilinged entrance hall and demanded to see Colonel Lathrop. At that moment a man appeared on one of the galleries that ran around the upper floors of the hall.

'What's going on down there? Who's that ruffian? Have him thrown out!'

Farnol looked up and recognized the man on the gallery. Oh God, he thought, not *him*! But he bounded up the wide stairs, came out on to the gallery and advanced on Major Rupert Savanna, who was slapping his pockets as if looking for a gun.

'Savanna, old chap, how are you? I know you think I'm a ruffian, but you don't have to spread it around amongst the servants. Where's Lathrop?'

Savanna was an unfortunate man. He was plain to the point of anonymity; he would have been more identifiable had he been ugly. Everyone tended to overlook him and so he had made himself more unfortunate: he had become aggressive to be recognized and only succeeded in antagonizing everyone he met. He hated India and everyone on the whole sub-continent; but he knew that if he went back to England he would be even more anonymous and overlooked. He was hard-working, a rare quality amongst the British officers in India, and his diligence, if nothing else, had raised him to a senior staff position in the Political Service, the diplomatic corps of the Viceroy. It was said that he had been promoted on the assumption that a man so disliked would not have any friends to whom he might leak a confidence.

'Farnol? Good God, man, do you have to come up here looking like *that*? Couldn't you have spruced yourself up?'

'I'll do that later. Where am I staying – down at Squire's Hall?'

'Afraid not – the painters are in there. You'll have to stay here.' Savanna looked as if he were offering a pi-dog a room for the night. 'We're all staying here. Got permission from His Excellency, just for the two nights. The Durbar Train leaves tomorrow. I presume you'll be coming down to Delhi?'

'Of course. Where's George?'

'Afraid he's not here. Went back to Delhi yesterday, got tired of waiting for you. You were due here a week ago.'

'Blast!' Farnol leaned against the balustrade, restrained himself from spitting down into the well of the entrance hall. He looked sideways at the portly little man with the very pale blue eyes and the blank face behind the ginger moustache. 'I was held up by a landslide the other side of the Satluj, I had to make a detour. I was ambushed, too.'

'I say! Lose any bearers?' Savanna dreamed of being a hero but was glad he was a desk-wallah. Dreams were safer than deeds and he feared the day when he would have to act. 'Better put that in your report to me.'

'To you?'

Savanna flushed. 'Of course. I'm your superior officer, am I not? George Lathrop asked me to stay on here and bring your report down with me when I go.'

'What I have to report will need to get to him quicker than that. I'll encode it and you can put it on the telegraph line to him tonight.'

'I shall want to know what's in the report before you encode it. I can't authorize its despatch if I don't know what's in it.'

Farnol sighed, scratched himself through his rags. It was always the same when he came back from the hills: as soon as he was within smell of hot water and soap he began to itch. The same irritation affected him whenever he was within smell of a desk-wallah. 'Righto, whatever you say. I'll put it all down in clear first. The gist of it is that I think there is a plot to assassinate the King.'

Savanna gave a half-cough, half-laugh. 'Oh, I say! You expect me to put something like that on the telegraph to Delhi? They'd laugh their heads off. What proof have you?'

Farnol sighed again, scratched himself once more: Savanna, more than any of the other desk-wallahs, always did get under his skin more than the dirt and the lice. 'None. Just suspicions.' He quickly recounted the story of the ambush. 'It ties in with what I heard further up in the hills.'

'What did you hear? Rumours?' Savanna shook his head. 'I'm sorry, old chap. I can't put that sort of clap-trap on the telegraph. It would be one thing to mention it personally to Lathrop, one can bandy suspicions back and forth all day across a desk. But to put it in code on the telegraph – ' He shook his head again, adamantly this time: after all, he was the senior officer, even if their ranks were the same. 'Can't be done. There have been plots and rumours of plots ever since the days of John Company. There's sure to be one about His Majesty – what better way to create a little mischief? You know what these Indians are. But no one down in Delhi would believe it was anything more than a rumour. They're all too busy getting spruced up for the Durbar.'

Farnol knew that plots to kill the British, or their leaders, were not new. Ever since the East India Company, John Company as it was called, built its first trading post in 1640, there had been resistance to the British presence in India and the neighbouring countries. The Indian Mutiny of sixty years ago had not blown up on the spur of the moment; the Afghan Wars had not been riots of sudden bad temper. Conspiracies for independence had been uncovered; one or two princes had rebelled and been firmly put back in their place. But no Viceroy, the King's representative, had died from an assassin's bullet or knife. They had died from cholera or malaria or boredom, but that had been only the climate of the country and not the climate of the population demanding its wage or revenge. Savanna was right: now, especially now, no one would take any notice of a rumour that hadn't a shred of concrete evidence to back it. Farnol had been at the Great Durbar, Curzon's durbar of 1903, and he remembered how for a month before it no one had had any thought for anything but the social events that accompanied it. With the King and Queen due within the week he could imagine the pushing and jostling, like beggars scrambling for coins in a bazaar, that would be going on down in the new capital.

'All right, I'll hold the report till we get down to Delhi.'

Savanna stiffened with six years' seniority. 'You can still write it in clear and give it to me.'

'I'll write it on the train going down.' Farnol straightened up, daring Savanna to command him to write the report immediately. But the other knew his limitations, knew when he sounded petulant rather than commanding. He stayed silent and after a moment Farnol said, 'Do I have to dress for dinner? Are there only you and I?'

'Of course you'll dress! The Ranee of Serog is coming to dinner and also the Nawab of Kalanpur – you know Bertie, a very decent chap. And there will be Baron von Albern and Lady Westbrook.'

'Damn! I think I'll dine in my room.' Then he looked down and saw the girl in bowler hat and riding habit come into the hall below. 'Who's that?'

'Miss O'Brady. An American gel. Evidently she met His Excellency and Lady Hardinge down in Delhi, told them she was coming up here and they invited her to stay at the Lodge. Can't understand why. She's not only American, she's also one of those damned newspaper reporters.'

CHAPTER TWO

Extract from the memoirs of Miss Bridie O'Brady:

I have been to several memorable dinner parties in the course of a long and, forgive my smugness, very rewarding life. Once, when he and his wife had had a falling-out, Richard Harding Davis, that most handsome and dashing of foreign correspondents, took me to dinner at the White House; President Taft himself had to rescue me from the attentions and intentions of the French Ambassador, who had had a falling-out with *his* wife. On another occasion Mayor John Fitzgerald of Boston, known to everyone as Honey Fitz, called me up, knowing I was in New York for the night, and asked me to dinner with him at Rector's with some friends from Tammany Hall. There amidst the cigar smoke, the bubbles of champagne and the giggles of the girls from the Music Hall chorus, I learned more about how a democracy is run than in several months of covering City Hall for the Boston *Globe*. I sometimes feel that one's education can be improved more over the right dinner table than anywhere else, with the possible exception of under the counterpane. I speak, of course, as a lady of mature years whose education in both spheres was completed some time ago.

The most fateful dinner party, in personal terms, that I ever attended was at Viceregal Lodge in Simla in India in December 1911. The guests were as varied as one can only find in outposts of Empire; or *could* find, since empires, if they still exist, are no longer admitted. The acting host was a dull little man named Savanna, but everyone else at the long table in the huge panelled dining-room seemed to me to be an original, even the Nawab of Kalanpur, who did his best to be an imitation Englishman. But the most striking one there in

27

my eyes, even though he may not have been strikingly original, was Major Clive Farnol.

He sat next to me as my partner and through most of dinner I saw little more of him than his profile. He told me later he had only that evening shaved off his beard; that accounted for the paler skin of his lower cheeks and jaw against the mahogany of the rest of his face. He had a good nose, deep-set blue eyes; but his face was too bony to be strictly handsome. He also had a nice touch of arrogance, an air I have always admired in the male sex. Humble men usually finish up carrying banners for women's organizations.

'You are writing the story of Lola Montez, Miss O'Brady?' The Ranee of Serog was dressed as if for a State dinner or a trade exhibition of jewels. Of the upper part of her body only her elbows and armpits seemed undecorated with sparklers; she looked like Tiffany and Co. gone vulgar. She was a walking fortune, several million dollars on the hoof, as they say in the Chicago stockyards. She was dressed in a rich blue silk sari and once one became accustomed to the glare of her one could see that she was a beautiful woman. She was about forty which, from the youth of my then twenty-five years, seemed rather close to the grave. Now I am rather close to it myself I smile at the myopia of youth.

'My grandfather knew her when she was Mrs James, a very young bride here in Simla,' the Ranee said.

'My father always boasted he was one of her first lovers.' Lady Westbrook was an elderly woman of that rather dowdy elegance that the English achieve absent-mindedly, as if fashion was something that occurred to them only periodically like childbirth or an imperial decoration. But, I learned later, she drank her wine and port with the best of the men and smoked a cheroot in an ivory holder. 'But that was only after he learned she finished up as the mistress of King Ludwig of Bavaria. I suppose all men would like to think they shared a woman with a king.'

'Not with King George,' said the Nawab of Kalanpur and spilled his wine as he laughed. 'I understand the Queen sends a company of Coldstream Guards with him every time he goes out alone. She's rather a battle-axe when it comes to morality.'

'I say, Bertie, that's going too far.' Major Savanna was a stuffed shirt such as I had only hitherto seen on Beacon Hill in Boston; I suppose one finds them all over the world, a breed hidebound by what they think is correct behaviour. 'I hope you won't put any of this conversation into your newspaper articles, Miss O'Brady?'

I had come to India to cover the Great Durbar in Delhi, one of the few women correspondents granted such permission. Females were still considered lesser beings in those days, even in the so-called enlightened offices of newspapers; some of the most bigoted male chauvinists I have met in a lifetime of such encounters have been newspaper editors. But I had been taken on as a cub reporter by the editor of the Boston *Globe* who owed a favour to someone who owed a favour to Mayor Honey Fitz, for whom my father worked as a ward boss. I had managed not to blot my notebook and gradually had been given assignments that had, after several years and with great reluctance on the part of the paper's male management, resulted in my being granted a by-line. I had covered stories spread over a great deal of the United States and had attained a certain fame; or in certain circles where anyone who worked for a newspaper, regardless of their sex, was looked upon as a whore, a certain notoriety. Disgusted at the growing cost of Presidential inaugurations, the editor had decided to send me to India to see how the British Empire spent money on crowning an Emperor. It was I who had suggested that I should also do a story on Lola Montez, the Irish-born courtesan who had begun her career in Simla as a 15-year-old bride of a British officer. The editor, thinking of syndication, had readily agreed. There were probably fifty million housewives throughout the United States who were dreaming of being courtesans.

'Quote every word, Miss O'Brady.' Major Farnol up till then had offered only a few words, the crumbs of politeness that gentlemen offer to ladies in whom they are not particularly interested. But now he looked at me full face and I saw his gaze run quickly up from my bosom, over my shoulders and throat and up to my face and hair. I learned later that he was famous for swift appraisals of the landscape

29

and was known amongst the Pathan tribesmen of Afghanistan as Old Hawkeye. 'We must keep on with the good work done by the late King Edward, making our royalty appear human. We have suffered too long from Victorian stuffiness.'

'Oh, I say!' said the stuffed shirt at the top of the table.

'Ach, no.' The one-armed German Consul-General, Baron Kurt von Albern, leaned to one side while a servant took away his plate. He leaned stiffly and with his head seemingly cocked to balance the weight of his one arm; he looked rigid and very Prussian, though he was not a Prussian. He had close-cropped grey hair, a thick grey moustache, wore gold-rimmed spectacles with a silk cord running down to his lapel and looked like Teddy Roosevelt without the bombast. 'Kings should never appear human. They should always suggest a little mystery.'

'Is there any mystery about the Kaiser?' said Major Farnol. 'Other than whether or not he wants to go to war with us?'

The Baron shook his great head sadly. 'Always talk of war. The English and the Germans will never fight. Your own King is almost more German than he is English.'

'More's the pity,' said Lady Westbrook. 'Can't understand why we ever let the Tudors go.'

'Our King is beloved just as he is.' Major Savanna seemed to have had a little too much to drink. He glared down the table in my direction and for a moment I wondered what America had done recently to bring on this aggression. Then I realized he was looking at Major Farnol. 'That correct, Major?'

'Perhaps in England. Here in India no one knows him.'

The King, as Prince of Wales, had visited India in 1905, but he had seen, and been seen by, very few more than the British civil and military brass and the Indian princes. Though England had ruled India for almost two centuries, no reigning monarch had ever set foot in the country. The monarch's surrogates had been the real rulers, the Governors-General and the Viceroys who had had all the trappings of a king and almost as much power, possibly even more. The armorial bearings of all those surrogates hung from the walls above our heads, from the first of them, Warren Hastings, to the present one, Hardinge. Pictures of the monarch might hang in offices and railway stations and jungle bungalows, but everyone knew who was the actual British Raj of the moment.

'I met him once at Lord's,' said the Nawab. 'Came to see the Second Test against the Australians, looked bored stiff. Bally undiplomatic of him, I thought. That's the German in him, I suppose.'

'Being undiplomatic or being bored by cricket?' said the Baron.

The Nawab laughed, a high giggle that didn't go at all well with his appearance. He was rather saturnine, a look that went against the mould of the imitation Englishman he tried to be; when his face was in repose he looked slightly sinister, an image the English have washed from their countenances if not from their hearts.

'Touché, Baron. It's a pity you didn't go to Harrow, as I did. With your physique they'd have made a jolly good fast bowler of you.'

'It sounds a dreadful fate,' said the Baron.

'I don't think the King should have come out here.' The Ranee dismissed His Majesty with a wave of her hand, an explosion of diamond lights. 'Anything could happen to him. He could be trodden on by an elephant, killed by a tiger. Accidents happen in this country.'

'Planned accidents?' said Major Farnol.

Perhaps I was too quick for an outsider; but what should a newspaperwoman be if not quick? 'You mean an assassination?'

I saw Farnol and Savanna exchange glances. The Ranee also saw it: 'What's going on, gentlemen? Have you heard something?'

There was silence for a moment and it was obvious that the two majors were each waiting for the other to reply. Then Major Farnol said, 'No, nothing.'

'Of course not!' But Savanna's voice was not so loud from drink alone; he was far too emphatic. 'Ridiculous! Their Majesties will be as safe here in India as in Buckingham Palace. Correct, Farnol?'

31

I saw Farnol's jaw stiffen, but he nodded. 'Of course.'

Then dinner was finished and the ladies rose to be banished as we always were. The port and the cigars were already being produced, but as we went out the door Lady Westbrook turned to one of the servants. 'I'll have a large port in the drawing-room. Better bring a small decanter.'

I sat with Lady Westbrook and the Ranee for half an hour, then I excused myself and went up to bed. I had been riding that afternoon and was genuinely tired. As I reached the gallery that led to the bedrooms I pulled up startled. Major Farnol sat in the shadows, in a large chair against the wall of the corridor.

'Oh! I thought you were still downstairs with the other gentlemen.'

'I just wanted to say goodnight, Miss O'Brady.' He stood up, towering over me. He wore a tail-coat, the dinner jacket had not become universal with gentlemen, but the suit looked as if he had had it a long time; it was shiny and tight and he looked, well, *caged* in it. 'Will you be going down with us on the Durbar Train? May I have the pleasure of escorting you?'

'Only if you will tell me if you think King George is in danger of being assassinated.' I'm afraid I was rather a direct person in those days. Perhaps I still am.

'I thought you were interested only in Lola Montez?'

'I have all the material I need on her. I'm a newspaper-woman, Major Farnol. A plot to assassinate a king is a story I'd give my right arm for.'

'Both arms?'

We did not use the word *corny* in those days. 'Major Farnol, I expected better than that of you. I'm not some high school girl panting to be taken.'

He smiled, then abruptly sobered. 'All right, no flirting. No, Miss O'Brady, I know nothing about any assassination plot.'

'I think you are a liar, Major.' I gave him what I hoped was a sweet smile.

'All the time.'

'Goodnight, Major.'

I left him then, but I knew we were going to be talking to

each other a lot over the next few days, whether he was a liar or not. In the course of her life a woman will meet a man, or several men if she is fortunate, with whom she feels an instant current of attraction. I had felt that way about Richard Harding Davis, but he was already married; I had also been strongly attracted to a well-known matinée idol, but he was in love with himself at the time and no woman can compete with that. I didn't think Major Farnol would ever be in love with himself but he did strike me as being very self-contained, with few doubts about himself or anyone else, which can be just as frustrating for a woman. My trouble was that, being Boston Irish, I had such little mystery about me that might raise a doubt or two in his or any other man's mind. A woman who loves love as much as I did, and still do, can be too honest for her own good.

But I was not thinking about love that night. I undressed in the big bedroom I'd been given and was brushing my hair when I heard voices in the corridor outside. Moments earlier I had heard voices down at the front of the house; that would have been the Ranee, Lady Westbrook and the Nawab and the Baron going home. Then the big house had been suddenly silent till I heard the raised voices out in the corridor.

I opened my door an inch and peered out. It was not a lady-like thing to do, but a newspaperwoman was not expected to be a lady; it was an implied contradiction in terms. Major Savanna, looking very much the worse for drink, was standing arguing with Major Farnol, whom I could not see.

'You will not mention this ridiculous theory of yours again till we get down to Delhi! There you can do what you damn well please!'

'Keep your voice down, Savanna. This isn't a polo field.'

'Don't tell me – ! You're absolutely insufferable, Farnol, insufferable! You keep *your* voice down – not another word about these rumours, you understand! That's an order!'

He took a sudden step backwards and I realized that Farnol had abruptly shut the door of his room in his face. Savanna raised a fist as if he were about to batter down the door, then suddenly he went marching down the hall towards his own bedroom. *Marching*: it struck me that for a man who a moment ago had sounded drunk he was remarkably steady on his feet.

I closed the door, finished my toilette and got into bed. But I couldn't sleep; I could smell a story like a magnetic perfume, ink brewed by M. Coty. I tossed and turned for an hour, then I made my decision. I got out of bed and put on my red velvet peignoir. It had been bought for Miss Toodles Ryan, the girl friend of Mayor Honey Fitz, but Toodles was annoyed with Hizzoner for some reason and she had given me the gown. Each time I put it on I felt the delicious thrill of being a kept woman, if only by proxy: the safest and least demanding way. Only a year before he was assassinated I mentioned Toodles Ryan to President Kennedy and he, Boston Irish and a ladies' man, winked and smiled. Honey Fitz's hormones were still alive and well in 1962.

I looked at my hair in the mirror, saw that my tossing and turning had made it into a fright wig. I hastily pushed it up, looked around for something to hold it in place, saw the derby, the bowler hat I had worn that day while riding and shoved it on my head. I remembered one of the few pieces of advice my mother had given me when I told her I was determined to go out into the sinful Protestant world and make my own way: 'Always wear a hat, sweetheart. That way you'll always be thought of as a lady, if only from the neck up.'

Clasping my notebook and pencil I opened my door, crossed the corridor and tapped gently on Major Farnol's door. Then I opened it and stepped inside. And felt the pistol pressing against the back of my neck.

The electric light was switched on. Major Farnol was dressed in pale blue silk pyjamas and looked absolutely gorgeous.

'They're not mine – I found them in a drawer. I think they belong to one of the A.D.C.s. Heaven knows what sort of chap wears things like these.'

'You're wearing them.'

'Just as well, if a half-naked woman calls on me in the middle of the night. Do you usually wear a bowler when you go prowling bedrooms?'

I crossed to a chair beside the bed. 'You may get back into

bed, Major. You're perfectly safe. This is a professional call.'

'Do you charge for your services?'

I don't know where Major Farnol learned his badinage with women. I discovered later that he had had considerable success with them, but it could not have been because of his conversational approach. 'Put your gun away, Major, and get into bed. I've taken you at your word that you're a liar and I don't believe you when you say there is no plot to assassinate the King.'

He put the pistol on a bedside table and got beneath the covers. Thinking back, it was one of the strangest interviews I ever conducted. Both of us were aware of the atmosphere around us: he in his glamorous pyjamas, I in my peignoir (even if the bowler did dampen the effect), and the wide bed itself. But I was there on business and I was determined to keep it that way.

'Tell me what you really think is going on, Major.'

He shook his head. 'Miss O'Brady, I am what is called a political agent.'

'Is that something like a ward boss? My father is one in Boston.' I explained what my father did in the interests of democracy and the Democratic Party, which are not necessarily the same thing.

'No, I don't think there's too much similarity. I suppose one could say I'm a cross between your Secret Service and one of your Indian agents from the Wild West.'

'But that's exactly what a ward boss is.'

'Well, I'm sure your father doesn't give away secrets to the chaps from the newspapers. Or even to you, I'll wager.'

'Not unless he's looking for favours.' I saw the gleam in his eye and got in first: 'Please, Major. No more flirting. So you won't tell me what you suspect?'

'No.' There was no badinage there: his voice was flat and emphatic.

'I could write my story without your corroboration.'

'If you did that and I should ever meet you again, I'd tan your bottom.'

'An officer and a gentleman?'

'I make no claim to the latter title. Goodnight, Miss O'Brady. Please turn off the light as you go out.'

I was used to being dismissed, that was part of the game in my profession; but somehow the dismissal by him hurt me. I knew I had brought it on myself, but there are certain occasions when a woman wishes she could retire with dignity. I tried for that as I walked towards the door, but even then I knew that in my peignoir and derby I could not look regal or even viceregal.

I stopped at the door and turned. 'You and I are not finished with each other, Major. I do not give up easily.'

'Nor I, Miss O'Brady. Goodnight.'

I switched off the electric light and opened the door. The club thumped down on my bowler hat and I slumped to the floor.

End of extract from memoirs.

2

Farnol leapt out of bed as the man, masked by a ragged scarf, jumped over the girl and came at him, the club in one hand and a long dagger in the other. Farnol grabbed for the gun on the bedside table, but in the gloom of the darkened room, his eyes still full of the just extinguished electric light, his hand fumbled and knocked the gun to the floor. The intruder dived across the bed at him and he flung himself back, just avoiding the swish of the dagger. He stumbled around in the unfamiliar room, bumped against a clothes-horse. He picked it up and swung it, hitting the assassin full in the face with the wooden shoulders inside his tail-coat. The man let out a gasp and staggered back and Farnol, eyes accustomed to the darkness now, went after him. The thug swung the club blindly and Farnol grunted as it grazed his ribs.

Then the man was past him, jumping over the still prostrate Bridie in the doorway and racing out into the corridor. Farnol scrambled after him, not stopping to waste time in looking for his gun. The man appeared to know his way about the huge house. He ran along the dimly-lit corridor, out on to the gallery and down the wide stairs. Farnol, a blue silk streak, was only a few stairs behind him as they reached the entrance hall. The thug made no attempt to go out the front doors, as if he knew he might run into one of the roving picquets in the main drive. Instead he went straight down towards the ballroom. Farnol grabbed a heavy brass candlestick from a table and chased after him.

The man was tall and thin, as tall as Farnol; and he was swift, just that much swifter than Farnol. His clothes were ragged, but he was recognizable as a hillman: the dark turban wound Pathan style, the blue scarf round his face and the sheepskin jerkin said he wasn't from the plains.

The next two or three minutes were like some bizarre conducted tour of the Lodge. The two men raced through the huge moonlit ballroom, skidding on the polished floor; through into the dining-room where the logs in the big fireplace still glowed; back across the hall to the drawing-room. Here the thug ran headlong into the great velvet curtain that draped its entrance; he dropped his club and tried to slash his way through the heavy cloth with his knife. Farnol caught him and grappled with him, but once again the man got away. He raced back up the stairs and still Farnol pursued him, wielding the candlestick. But the man was frantic now, drawing away from Farnol with every step. He tore down the corridor between the bedrooms. At the far end Farnol glimpsed the open window. The thug went through it without seeming to lose speed. Farnol reached the window, pulled up gasping and looked down, expecting to see the man spreadeagled on the ground below.

But the thug had not committed suicide; once again he had shown he knew the lie of the land around the Lodge. There was a great deodar tree outside the window and Farnol saw the stout branch still going up and down from the weight of the man as he had landed on it. A moment later he saw the man run out from the black shadow at the base of the tree, race across the lawn, vault the balustrade and disappear. There was no point in shouting for the guard; they would never find the thug in the tangled growth down the steep hillside below the lawn. Farnol turned back, still holding the candlestick, and hurried back along the corridor to his room.

Bridie was sitting up, feet spread out in front of her, back against the door, her crushed hat in her lap. She looked at him as he squatted down beside her. 'Did you get him? I saw you gallop past.'

'He got away. How are you?'

'It will teach me not to go uninvited into a man's room.' She stood up, taking his arm; he could feel she was still shaken. 'I'm all right, I think. I'll have a headache in the morning.'

He had to admire her composure. The women who had lived in these hills for years were accustomed to the regular emergency: he would have expected them to recover quickly. But Miss O'Brady was a city girl and an American one at that: he knew little or nothing about Boston or New York but he guessed that ladies there did not have to face emergencies too often. 'I must say, Miss O'Brady, you're not the hysterical sort, are you?'

'I suppose that's an Englishman's compliment, is it? Thank you. No, I'm not the hysterical sort.'

'Jolly good.'

Assured that she was uninjured except for a sore head, he abruptly left her, went along to the gallery and looked down into the entrance hall. Then he came back.

'I wonder where all the servants are? It's late, but I thought someone would have heard me chasing that chap up and down the stairs. Go back to your room and lock the door.'

'No. I'll stay with you till . . . You're worried about something.'

She was still shaken, but she was recovering fast. Her auburn hair hung down over her shoulders in wild disarray, her voice was a little breathless, she held her bowler hat before her like a battered beggar's bowl. She was a damned good-looking woman. He wished he had met her a week later, down in Delhi.

'We'll go and wake up Major Savanna. He's probably dead to the world with all that drink he had.'

They went down the corridor to the room at the end. Its door was beside the open window through which the thug had escaped; the cold night air pressed in against them and

Farnol shut the window. Then he knocked on Savanna's door.

With still no answer to his third knock, he opened the door and went in. He fumbled for the light switch, clicked it on. The room was empty, the big four-poster bed unslept in. On the bed was tossed Savanna's tail suit, his boiled shirt and his dress suit. The wardrobe's doors were open and the clothes were strewn on the floor in front of it.

'Right, go back to your room, lock the door and stay there.' He was already on his way back along the corridor. He still carried the heavy brass candlestick, as if he had forgotten it was still in his hand. He paused by Bridie's door, swung it open and motioned with the candlestick for her to go in. He looked and sounded like a schoolmaster who had found a pupil in some after-lights-out escapade. 'Come on – inside! Lock the door. I'll be back!'

He didn't wait to see if she obeyed him. He went back to his own room, dragged on the clothes nearest to hand, the tail-coat and dress trousers, over his pyjamas, pulled on his shoes; then, still carrying the candlestick but also his pistol this time, he went down to the entrance hall. He switched on lights, found a bell-pull and gave it several tugs that almost pulled it out of the ceiling, creating a carillon effect down in the depths of the servants' quarters. In less than two minutes the butler and two bearers, stumbling with haste, puzzlement and the effects of the sleep from which they had been disturbed, came up from the rear of the house. With them was Karim Singh, the only one who looked fully alert.

'Where's Major Savanna?' Farnol addressed the butler, an elderly Punjabi who had a proprietary interest in the Lodge; he had seen Viceroys come and go, none of them had the tenure that a good servant had. 'Did he say anything to you about going out tonight?'

'No, sahib.' The butler looked bewildered and indignant: it wasn't right that he should be aroused in the middle of the night, in His Excellency's own house, and rudely interrogated by this army officer who was only a major, not even a colonel. 'He should be asleep in his room.'

'He isn't – his bed hasn't been slept in. And I've had a chap in here who tried to kill me.' He didn't mention Bridie. The attack on her had been accidental, he was certain, and he wanted to protect her from any further involvement.

The two bearers hissed with shock, looked over their shoulders, waiting for another attack. The butler said, 'I regret that, sahib. It has never happened before. His Excellency will be most disturbed – '

'I'm sure he will. Karim, get down to the guard-house, get the guard up here on the double – '

'You can call them on the telephone, sahib.' The butler lifted a big red velvet cover, like a huge tea-cosy, from a side-table, exposing a telephone. 'We have every modern convenience.'

Every modern convenience but an effective guard system. Farnol called the guard-house and a minute later there was a banging on the front door. The butler, moving with all the dignity of a State occasion, went to the doors and opened them. Three soldiers came plunging in, a sergeant and two rankers, one of them Private Ahearn.

'How many did you have on picquet tonight?' Farnol demanded.

The sergeant blinked in the light; he, too, had been sound asleep down in the guard-house. 'May I ask who you are, sir?'

'Major Farnol.' He saw Ahearn's eyebrows go up; then he remembered he had shaved off his beard. 'Private Ahearn escorted me up here earlier this evening.'

The sergeant stood to attention. 'Four men on picquet, sir. Did they miss something?'

'They missed a bloody thug who got in here and tried to kill me. He got away, went down the south side of the hill. There's no point in going after him,' he said as the sergeant looked over his shoulder to give an order to Ahearn and the other ranker. 'He'll be halfway to Kalka by now. Have you seen Major Savanna at all?'

The sergeant looked at his two men and Ahearn said, 'Yes, sir. He went out on his horse about half an hour ago.'

'Riding?'

'Yes, sir. I thought it was a bit queer, too.'

'How was he dressed?'

'Why, like he was going on a trip, sir.' Ahearn was a young

40

man, skinny and short, with the long Irish upper lip, thick black eyebrows that looked like caterpillars ready to advance on the potato of his nose and an expression that hinted he had come out of his mother's womb without bothering to bring any innocence with him. 'Breeches, bandolier, the lot. He had a rifle in his saddle scabbard.'

'You don't miss much.'

'No, sir. The Irish can't afford to.'

'That's enough!' snapped the sergeant, Irish too, but careful of his sergeant's pay. A few shillings a day extra could buy an Empire-builder, Farnol thought. 'Do you want me to send someone after the Major, sir?'

'Did he say where he was going?' Farnol looked back at Ahearn.

'No, sir. Didn't say a word, just rode right by me like I wasn't there.'

Farnol now was mystified and worried; but did his best not to show it. 'Righto, sergeant. Double the picquet, stay up here close to the house. I'll see you at six in the morning. Dismiss.'

The soldiers went away, then Farnol dismissed the butler and the two bearers. At last he looked at Karim Singh. 'It was meant to be another ambush, Karim.'

'I should never have left your door, sahib.' Karim was looking around him, shaking his head in wondering disgust. He had a proper respect for surroundings and something was wrong with the scheme of things when some bugger would try to murder a British officer in the Viceroy's own house. 'I should be ashamed that I went down to the servants' quarters and allowed myself the luxury of a *charpoy*. To sleep in a bed is jolly marvellous, but not while your master has his throat cut.'

'Bring your things up to my room and sleep inside my door.'

Karim disappeared towards the depths of the house and Farnol climbed the stairs. Normally a clear thinker, his mind now seemed a mud-heap of confusion. He was no stranger to mystery; that was part of the trade of a political agent. But, had he ever had occasion to give the matter any thought, he would have classified Rupert Savanna as the least mysterious man in India, no more opaque than the air of these mountains on a clear day, every thought, prejudice and remark open to even the simplest intelligence. He tried to run his mind back over the evening, rummaging for a clue that might have hinted at Savanna's intention to depart secretly; but he could think of nothing, Savanna had been as bland as his boiled shirt-front. In future he would watch Rupert Savanna more closely.

At the top of the stairs Bridie was waiting for him. She was still in her peignoir and her hair was still down round her shoulders; but she had run a brush through it and she looked beautiful and composed. He wondered at the mysteries he might find in her if given the opportunity.

'Is everything safe now?'

'I think so. I just hope Major Savanna is safe. He's – '

'I heard. I've been standing up here listening.'

'Well, there's nothing we can do till morning.'

'If he hasn't returned by then, you might ask the Ranee where he is. I was down in the hall this evening when she arrived. I heard her tell him that if he wasn't gone by this morning, he would have her to answer to.'

3

Savanna had not returned by morning. Farnol borrowed two horses from the Lodge stables and he and Karim rode along one of the lower roads to the Barracks. Simla was the summer capital of the Government of India and for eight months of the year the sub-continent was ruled from the over-crowded, stacks-on-the-mill town clinging to its narrow-spined ridge. In late October the government departments moved back to Calcutta where the commercial population, swallowing its sourness at having been deprived of all the summer trade, welcomed them with over-stocked stores and inflated prices, a state of business affairs that lasted only a few days, after which both resentment and prices fell. Next year the government would be moving to Delhi for those months when it was not at

Simla and the merchants of Calcutta were ready to start their own Mutiny for being thus deserted.

Simla had a year-round British population and all the government departments kept on skeleton staffs there during the winter months. The main part of the army battalions went back to the plains with the government, but a company was always kept on duty in the big Barracks.

Captain Weyman, red-faced and red-eyed, pickled in gin and sour cynicism, was the company commander. 'No, I haven't seen Major Savanna in the week he's been up here. He's one of those Lodge blighters, can't see down his nose as far as us barracks-wallahs. Are you a friend of his?'

'No. I'm with Farnol's Horse.'

'Your name's Farnol, too? Oh yes, I've heard of you. One of the club, eh?'

Farnol recognized the type: a British Army officer who had come out to India hoping to transfer to one of the posh Indian Army regiments and had not been accepted. He knew the snobbery attached to such acceptance and did not accept it. but he had never made an issue of it. One either lived with it or one got out of the regiment; of course he had been accepted because he had been born into Farnol's Horse. But, though he would not have admitted it to anyone, he had partly turned his back on the system by becoming a political agent.

'If you like. Then Major Savanna didn't come down here during the night and ask for an escort?'

'Blighter's missing, eh? You want me to send out a search party?' But Weyman showed he had no real concern for the safety of the missing Savanna, the Lodge snob.

'Never mind. Thanks for the offer.'

Weyman smiled at the sarcasm. 'Always glad to help you Indians.'

As they rode away Karim Singh said, 'Why do they dislike us Indians so much, sahib?'

Farnol smiled at the Sikh's implied designation of Indians: he meant the Indian Army, of which he was a proud member. 'Because we are the fortunate ones.'

'You think so?' Karim pondered while he rode; then he nodded. 'I suppose so. We are the best of all, aren't we?'

Perhaps, thought Farnol; but he wondered if all the circles

43

of British life in India rode in their own small circle of mirrors. The lady he was going to see, though not British, spent her life looking in mirrors, cracked though some of them might be.

The Ranee of Serog's small domain began on the first ridge south of the Simla ridge and ran almost down to Kalka, the rail junction at the foot of the ranges. She had a palace somewhere in her territory, but neither Farnol nor anyone else from Simla had ever been invited there; she also owned one of the largest houses in Simla itself. She had never become like her neighbour, the Nawab of Kalanpur, more British than the British; but she liked the social life of this very social town and the unattached men that it offered. It had more appeal than living in the palace with her half-mad brother.

Once the servant who had announced him had left the room, Farnol was greeted by slim arms that wrapped themselves round his neck and a mouth that smothered him with a kiss that had nothing to do with caste or class. 'Darling Clive! You hardly looked at me last night! I wondered if those Tibetan lamas had got to you, converted you to celibacy or something.'

They had been lovers a year ago, but he had thought that was all past history. The Ranee collected lovers as she collected gems; she had once told him that she graded her men as she did her diamonds. She had classified him as a perfect blue-white, which he had thought must be the ultimate till he had found himself superseded by an Italian Consul who was evidently a superior gem in bed, the Ranee's preferred setting. He wondered where the Italian was now, whether he, too, had been replaced by someone even closer to perfection.

Farnol withdrew from her arms and the musky smell of her perfume. She wore no other jewellery this morning than a double-strand necklace of pearls and a heavy gold bracelet that looked like a more expensive class of shackle.

'Come and have breakfast with me like we used to! You are lucky to find me out of bed so early. But I have to catch that train this afternoon and there is so much one has to do!'

She had a large staff who did everything but blow her nose for her. She was the hedonist supreme and when he had been her lover he had enjoyed humouring her. It was almost six months since he had last had a woman, a young lady out on a visit from England who in private had proved to be no lady at all; looking at the Ranee now, still feeling her body against him, he was sorely tempted to forget other things for half an hour or so. But no, he told himself: he hadn't come here to make love to her or banter with her.

'Mala, where is Major Savanna?'

She put her spread hand to her bosom; her gestures at times could be as extravagant as her jewellery. 'Darling, you don't think I've taken *him* to my bed, do you?'

He sighed patiently. He hated arguing with women or interrogating them, either as lover or political agent. 'Did I suggest that? I'm not jealous, Mala, I'm here on business. Do you know where he is?'

The Ranee was not only vain and nymphomaniacal, she was also as shrewd as any trading woman from the bazaars. She had kept her voluptuous looks and she was confident that for some years yet she would not have to do more than lift a finger to have men come to her bed; she had only contempt for any will-power that men professed to have below the navel. But she would never be subject to any of them for, with her, love was a hunger of the body and not the heart.

'Don't be sharp with me, Major Farnol. I don't keep track of minor government officials.'

'Your Highness – ' He hadn't called her that in private since their first meeting. 'You know Major Savanna is more than a minor government official.'

'Oh? What is he then?' Through the windows of the large morning-room in which they stood he could see a hawk planing on the breeze, ready to pounce: it struck him that her voice was suddenly like the hawk's flight, lazy but alert.

'You know he is like me, a political agent, a senior one.' He didn't mention the Secret Service, though that was not its official name; nothing was secret if it was talked about. 'You were heard last night to tell him that if he wasn't gone by this morning, he would have you to answer to. How is it that a British officer, who isn't seconded to your service, has to answer to you?'

The hawk had dropped out of sight, fallen on some

invisible prey. A monkey clambered up and sat on the window-sill and the Ranee walked towards it and snapped at it. It looked at her with its decadent child's eyes, clicked its teeth at her, then disappeared below the sill. The Ranee leaned out of the window, as if she were actually interested in where the monkey had gone. At last she turned back into the room.

'Whom do you have spying on me, Major? One of the servants up at the Lodge? I think His Excellency would be interested in that.'

'You're free to complain to him, Your Highness.' They were now exhibiting the cold formality of ex-lovers, which has the same chill as that of diplomats about to declare war on each other.

'I'm afraid your spy, whoever it was – Was it that beautiful Miss O'Brady? But you'd never met her, had you? And the Americans, I'm told, are such poor spies anyway. They think everything should be open and above-board. So naïve.'

'Why not take an example from them?'

'Ah, Major – ' She softened for a moment, but he was not yet *Darling Clive* again. 'What secrets have I ever kept from you? No, your spy has a ringing in his ears, I'm afraid. All I said to Major Savanna was that I'd see him on the train this afternoon. I was just being polite. I'd rather not spend the journey with him down to Kalka and Delhi. He's a frightful bore. I wonder what Mrs Savanna sees in him?'

'There is no Mrs Savanna, as far as I know.'

'I'm not surprised.' The Ranee had only contempt for wives. She had been fortunate enough to inherit her domain, her fortune and her position direct from her father and she had never had to pay homage to any man but him. Marriage was a state of disgrace into which no woman should ever allow herself to fall.

'Then you can't tell me where he is?' He did not call her a liar, as he might have a village woman he'd been interrogating. After all she was, in theory if not in practice, a sovereign ruler, even if she was at present out of her territory.

'No, Major, not at all.' She gazed at him blandly, her dark eyes as unrevealing as the monkey's had been. 'Let's hope he is on the train when we leave at one o'clock.'

46

'Let's hope so, Mala. Otherwise I may have to come back to you.'

'Do that, Clive. Do you still snore when you lie on your back?'

He left her on that less formal note and went out to where Karim waited for him with the horses. All up and down the road he could see gharrys and tongas being loaded with trunks and suitcases; the Durbar Train this afternoon looked as if it would be packed. Residents who had not been down to Delhi in years were making the journey; many had never been there, being only acquainted with Calcutta or Bombay or some army cantonment. But they'd have gone to Timbuctoo if His Majesty, God bless him and the Queen, had invited them. Their invitations to the receptions and levees were more carefully packed than their frocks and suits and dress uniforms.

Farnol and Karim walked their horses down to the road that ran through the bazaar. Storekeepers offered them everything from food to elixirs; the smell of curry and fried cakes thickened the thin mountain air; voices, the bleat of a goat, the piping of a musician, the chorus of a bazaar, impressed themselves on the ear. Two men, shoulder to shoulder, a four-legged beast with a two-humped back, came down the narrow street and the crowd fell back; the men carried a tree-trunk twenty feet long and two feet thick; Farnol and Karim dragged their horses into a side alley and the men went past, faces set like stone, trance-like under their massive burden. A small band of Tibetans sauntered down the road, long hair falling down to their shoulders, sheepskin jackets hanging to their knees; dirt cracked on their faces as they smiled and waved their long wooden pipes at the storekeepers, who forgave them their ragged and filthy appearance because they knew these Tibetans were truthful and honest and not thieves like some of their own kind. Two government messengers in scarlet and gold strutted down the middle of the road, self-important as bantam cocks; monkeys sat on roof-tops and mocked them. Farnol and Karim moved through the press of the crowd and as ever Farnol felt the pleasure he always did when he was in a bazaar. If you were to understand India, this was where you had to come.

47

Then up ahead, surrounded by beggars and storekeepers, he caught a glimpse of Miss O'Brady.

Karim shouted to the crowd to let the sahib through and began whacking about him with his *lathi*. The horses shied and Farnol had his attention distracted from Bridie as he tried to quieten his horse. When he looked back towards her he did not immediately see her; instead he saw the two men pushing through the crowd on the far side, one of them faintly familiar. Then he recognized the blue scarf and the sheepskin jerkin the man wore; he let go his horse and fought his way through the crowd, shouting to Bridie. His voice carried: Bridie suddenly popped up, as if she had been squatting down to look at something. And behind her the two men suddenly halted, looked across the heads of the crowd at Farnol. For just a moment he saw the dark eyes above the mask of the blue scarf on the taller of the two men; it was the man who had tried to kill him last night. Then abruptly the two men turned and bolted.

Farnol tried to thrust his way through the thick press of bodies, but one had to be as slippery as a bazaar thief to move quickly through a bazaar crowd. By the time he got as far as Bridie the men had disappeared from the far edge of the crowd, were gone down one of the steep alleys of steps to a lower level.

'You shouldn't have come down here!' His voice was more curt than he intended, but he was concerned at how close she had come to being either murdered or kidnapped.

'What's the matter? I came down here to buy some last-minute things – '

He took her by the arm, more roughly than was necessary, pulled her behind him through the crowd as Karim, now dragging both horses, followed him. The crowd, sensing tension between the sahib and the memsahib, always glad of a free show, moved up the narrow road with them. He had always been at home with a bazaar crowd; all at once now he hated them and struck out with his free arm. The crowd fell back without resentment, or at least any show of it; they silently mocked the Europeans who always wanted space around them, as if they were some sort of holy men. When Farnol finally dragged Bridie into the clear he was more angry with himself than with the mob that had impeded him. He had once thought of himself as a champion of these people.

'For Heaven's sake – !' Bridie, too, was angry with him. She straightened her hat and jerked down her sleeves. 'What's wrong with a little shopping? I was down here yesterday – '

'Yesterday was yesterday,' he said, sounding even in his own ears obvious and pedantic, as if he were talking to a child. 'The man who tried to kill me last night was in that crowd. He was either going to harm you or kidnap you.'

The crowd now stood at a respectful distance, but still close enough to have their ears cocked. Voices were hissing for everyone to be quiet so that nothing would be missed of what the sahib and the memsahib said to each other. Farnol realized he had said too much and, once again angry at them, he turned on them and told them to clear off. Karim added his larger shout to that of his boss and the crowd reluctantly retreated.

Farnol and Bridie climbed the hill, with Karim bringing up the rear with the two horses. Bridie had regained her composure, though she was worried now rather than annoyed. 'You really think he'd have kidnapped me? Or – ?' She couldn't bring herself to go on. She was not new to violence, she had reported on two murders and a strike battle; but she had always been at least one remove from it, a reporter and not a victim. She shied away from the thought of herself as a possible victim. 'Why me?'

'I don't know. Perhaps they wanted to trap me into coming after you.'

'Would you?' It was not coquetry: she suddenly felt alone and didn't want to be. She looked back down the steep hill to the bazaar; backs were turned, the crowd was no longer interested in them, a living had to be made. But she saw the press of people, the river of bobbing heads between the banks of the ramshackle stores, and she saw the India in which one could so easily be lost.

'Of course.' He looked at her with sudden sympathy; and something more. 'I say, I'm awfully sorry I was so rough with you. I tend to act a little quicker than I think.'

'Trust to your reflexes.' She managed a smile. 'But I'll know what to expect in future.'

'How's your head this morning?'

'Just a small ache, not much. Have you been to see the Ranee? I asked for you at breakfast – '

They were walking along the road that led to the Lodge, under the overhang of the tall deodars. Far below he could see the train at the terminus, already being loaded for the afternoon's journey down to Kalka. He counted eight carriages and twelve wagons; he couldn't remember ever seeing such a long train and he wondered how it would handle the very narrow gauge track; it could be a long slow trip. Especially with the elephants, standing in the station yard, that would be later loaded on to the wagons. He guessed they would not be experienced train travellers and if the train got up too much speed, swaying on the numerous bends, they might go berserk.

'The Ranee said she knew nothing about Major Savanna and that nobody could have heard her say that he was answerable to her.'

'She's a liar.'

He was not accustomed to women being so direct, not even the Ranee. 'That's what I think.'

'Does she know it was me who overheard her?'

'No, she thinks it was one of the servants. We'll meet her again on the trip down, so watch you don't give too much away.'

She paused and looked directly at him. 'We're in this together now, aren't we?'

He hesitated, then with a mixture of apprehension and yet pleasure he said, 'I'm afraid so, at least till we get to Delhi.'

Behind them Karim, ears as finely tuned as those of the bazaar crowd, twisted his mouth as if he had suddenly sucked on something sour. A woman's place was not with men, they were nothing but trouble outside the bedroom or the kitchen. Was not the black deity of death a woman, Kali? He wondered if some poison had got into the sahib that he should show such weakness. He knew the sahib liked women and spent a lot of time in their bedrooms. But he looked and sounded different in his way with this American woman.

They came to the gates at the bottom of the Lodge drive. Half a dozen soldiers stood outside the guard-house, amongst them Captain Weyman, who looked distracted and angry.

'What's happening, you ask?' he snapped at Farnol. 'Everything, it seems. You tell me Major Savanna has disappeared. Now I've lost one of my men, just packed his kit and up and left.'

Farnol ran his eye over the soldiers, guessed who had deserted even before he asked, 'Who's gone?'

'Chap named Ahearn, one of the detachment from the Connaughts. All the same, these damned Irishmen. Sorry, miss.' He looked at Bridie twice, as if not appreciating her looks the first time.

In the background Farnol saw the soldiers, all Irishmen, look at each other as if they knew no apology would be handed to them.

'There's something else,' said Weyman, peeved at the world, Irish or otherwise. 'The telephone line and the telegraph wire down to Kalka have been cut.'

'Cut? You mean someone actually *cut* the lines?'

'Well, I don't know if it's actually that. Most likely a landslip somewhere has pushed some of the poles down a hill. I've sent a party down the lines to check. It's a damned nuisance, though. Sorry, miss. But a day like this is enough to make any gentleman forget his manners.'

'Yes, I'm sure.' But Bridie could see that Farnol was troubled by more than Captain Weyman's lapse of manners.

CHAPTER THREE

I

Extract from the memoirs of Miss Bridie O'Brady:

I had never seen such a train. I had travelled on campaign trains in the United States and they have a bizarre enough air to them, like a travelling fair, with political promises being sold like snake-oil and rhetoric streaming out from the rear platform thicker than the smoke from the locomotive up ahead. The Durbar Train made any campaign caravan look like a commuters' drab streetcar. The carriages were festooned with ribbons and flags; that made them only imitations of American campaign cars. But no Presidential candidate had ever been trailed by wagon-loads of elephants, not even the Republicans in their wildest extravaganzas. There were twelve elephants, two to each of six wagons; there were two dozen horses, four to each of six wagons. And there were three flat-cars, two of them piled high with howdahs like wrecked fancy coracles, rolls of striped tents like rock candy, and a great sheaf of flags and pennants, the silver tips of their poles and lances glimmering in the afternoon sun. The third flat-car carried the Ranee of Serog's state coach.

The British passengers on the train were sensibly dressed for the long dusty journey; there would be plenty of time down in Delhi for them to bring out their finery. But excitement and anticipation made their faces bright and I'd never heard such a chattering amongst a group of English; they sounded like the Italians I had heard down on Mulberry Street in New York, except for the vowel sounds. Their children, usually so well-behaved (whatever happened to well-behaved children? They now appear to be an extinct species), raced up and down without restraint. I wondered what the King, who was reputed to be a notoriously strict parent, would think of this wilfulness that his coronation had brought on. If Major Farnol thought there was still too much Victorian stuffiness prevailing, the Simla residents seemed determined to leave it behind them in the hills, at least for this journey.

The Ranee of Serog and the Nawab of Kalanpur, with their entourages, had arrived at the same moment, coming down opposite roads to meet at the junction just above the station in a traffic jam of rickshaws, tongas and doolies, those swaying contraptions carried by two or four bearers in which the passenger swung and bounced as on bumpy currents of air. Doolie passengers knew turbulence long before jet planes were invented. There were shouts and screams of argument between the drivers and bearers, then some British soldiers, who would be travelling on the train as an escort, rushed up and sorted out the jam, prodding beasts and humans alike with their bayonets. The colourful procession flowed like a slow rainbow-shot waterfall down the final incline to the station.

The Nawab, dressed for travelling but still looking like a peacock beside the sober English turkeys, came up to me, all charm and a mile-wide smile. 'Where do you travel, Miss O'Brady, in which carriage?'

'I don't know. Wherever I can manage a seat, I suppose.'

'Miss O'Brady! Don't you know the precedence here in India? I am at the top, of course, being a prince. But the English have so many classes. Where will you fit in amongst them, a stranger and an American? Will you be with the *pukka* Brahmins of the ICS, the Indian Civil Service? Don't you know Simla is known as the Heaven of the Little Tin Gods? Or will you be lower down the scale, with someone from the army perhaps? Or even further down, down there amongst the bally commercials, the bank managers and other low life? Travel with me in my carriage, Miss O'Brady. You need not sit with my wives but can keep me company: We'll be jolly good company for each other.'

'Your wives? Plural? You look like a bachelor if ever I saw one, Your Highness.'

He waved at his *zenana* of half a dozen wives. 'What better way of being a bachelor than having more wives than one? I have more freedom than any bachelor who keeps a mistress. One woman is one too many, half a dozen is not enough. I should like several dozen, but the blighters cost money.'

He was laughable, a joke really; but something about him told me it would be dangerous to laugh at him. Perhaps he really did want to be English, but I found it hard to believe; he enjoyed being a prince too, even if only an Indian one. He would believe in precedence as much as any of the English he had just been maligning. Don't we all? Hollywood didn't invent the star system, it just followed historical custom.

Then there was a commotion some distance away and Lady Westbrook came sweeping down on to the platform. She was followed by a single servant toting a trunk and a suitcase, but she gave the impression that she was trailed by a whole retinue of bearers. She also gave the impression that she had decided to wear everything she hadn't been able to pack into the trunk and suitcase. She was wearing *two* large-brimmed hats, one felt and the other straw, a tweed suit over which she had pulled on a long cardigan and an Inverness cape; over one arm she carried two more cardigans and round her neck was thrown a thick cashmere scarf. Nothing she wore matched anything else; she was a dazzling clash of colours. Everything about her suggested she had just come from a better sort of English bazaar. But she was a true eccentric, as distinct from today's exhibitionists who try to pass as eccentric, and one knew she really had no idea how she looked nor did she care.

'I am not sitting in there!' she trumpeted at the station-master as he tried to usher her into the carriage immediately behind the engine. 'You know blasted well where I'm entitled to sit! Give me my proper accommodation!'

The station-master, a mixed blood, a *chee-chee* as the English called them, was harassed and out of his depth. He tried to squeeze his painfully thin face in behind his toothbrush moustache. 'Memsahib, all the other carriages are full – '

'Then some people have seats to which they're not entitled! Look at all those children! They should have been left at home with the cats and dogs – Ah, Bertie!' She had sighted the Nawab, came barging along the platform like a runaway

54

junk stall. 'Do you have a spare seat in your carriage? Of course you must with all those wives. They can sit on each other's laps. In there!' She waved a hand to her servant and he struggled into the Nawab's carriage with her trunk and suitcase. 'Is Miss O'Brady travelling with us, Bertie?'

To my surprise the Nawab did not seem annoyed at Lady Westbrook's intrusion. Instead he laughed and shook his head at me. 'Ah, do you not love the English? They walk all over us and expect us to love them.'

'Wrong, Bertie,' said Lady Westbrook, taking out a cheroot and fitting it into her ivory holder. 'We never look for love, that's not an English need. What about you Americans, m'dear – do you look for love?'

'All the time.'

'Foolish – you're due for so many disappointments.' She puffed on her cheroot, looked up and down the platform. 'Well, we're going to be a jolly little party, aren't we? If only they can keep those damned children quiet . . . Be off!' She slapped at some children who were chasing each other round us. 'Ah, here comes Major Farnol. My, how handsome he looks!'

She looked at me as soon as she said it and I recognized her as another of those banes of the lives of young presentable girls. She was a woman who, with too much time on her hands, exercised herself by playing match-maker. I looked away from her and at Major Farnol as he approached. Unlike most military men he moved with considerable grace; West Pointers, for instance, tend to walk like flagpoles. He was dressed, as he had been this morning, in his field uniform of khaki tunic, breeches, highly polished riding boots and topee. It was drab in its colour but somehow he gave it a dash of glamour, though we did not use that word in those days. He saluted me and Lady Westbrook and winked at the Nawab, with whom he seemed on intimate terms.

'Are we all sorted out? Am I still riding with you, Bertie?'

'Of course, old bean.' The Nawab seemed eager to play the genial host. 'But I thought you'd be riding down with Mala.'

'Nothing ever escapes the gossips up here, does it?'

'It's food and drink to us,' said Lady Westbrook. 'Are you

having another affair with her? The Ranee's a man-eater,' she explained to me. 'Destroyed more men than any tiger.'

'But not me.' Major Farnol smiled, winked at the Nawab, then, as an afterthought, winked at me. 'I've reformed, Viola. I'm positively monkish.'

'Like those monks in *The Decameron*.' But Lady Westbrook gave him an affectionate smile.

Then the station-master blew his whistle and the assistant station-master blew his and the engine-driver blew his; we were whipped aboard the train by a chorus of thin blasts. The train drew out past a packed mass of smiling faces and waving hands, the Europeans left behind standing in the front of the crowd, the Indians bringing up the rear. I had noticed on my journey up from Bombay and then from Delhi up to Simla that railroad stations in India are never empty, that even in the middle of the night there were always people standing, sitting or lying fast asleep on the platforms. They came there for company, for shelter, for some distraction from their poverty; but they always looked to me as if they were waiting to be asked aboard, to be given a ticket on a journey to anywhere but that spot where they waited so patiently and hopelessly. I sometimes wept at the hopelessness one found in India and I understand it has got no better, is even worse now than then.

We all settled down in the Nawab's private car, which was far more luxuriously decorated and furnished than any Pullman car I had seen back home, even that of the President. The wives sat at one end, cramped together on two couches covered in red silk; three of them, the younger ones, kept their veils up across their faces, but the three older ones sat and watched us with bare-faced curiosity. I looked for some resentment in their stares, but there was either none or I was not sharp-eyed enough. The Nawab seemed oblivious of them, which, I suppose, is a good defence when you have six of them.

Though it was only 65 miles down to Kalka, the journey was going to take us at least five hours. The railroad track wound its way in a series of loops down through the hills, with never a stretch of straight track longer than a hundred yards; coming up, I had been struck by the number of tunnels we passed through and then had seen the numbers painted at the entrance to each one; the final number had been 103. The train went round its first long curve and I looked back through the window and saw the open wagons and the flat-cars at the tail. The elephants and horses stood swaying in the wagons, backs to the smoke from the locomotive blowing back over them. On the last flat-car, their backs also to the smoke, were the dozen soldiers who were our escort. That, I guessed, was the order of precedence, the British Tommy right back there behind the elephants and horses.

I turned back and looked at Major Farnol. The Nawab and Lady Westbrook had got up and moved to the front of the car where a bearer was serving them tea and biscuits. 'Still nothing on Major Savanna?'

'He's disappeared completely.'

'Are the telephone and telegraph wires still cut?'

'I checked just before we got aboard. The wires are still dead. Captain Weyman is now worried about what has happened to the men he sent down the line.' He looked out at the hillside dropping away like a cliff right beside us. The tops of the pines and cedars were just below us and it was as if we were riding on a rattling magic carpet above the forest. Monkeys swung along the tree-tops, keeping pace with us like urchins, and the children in the train hung out of the windows and screamed encouragement at them. 'We have just two stops, at Solan Brewery and Bangu. Don't get out, stay here in the carriage.'

'Is that an order?' I said with a smile.

'Yes.' But he didn't return my smile.

We had been travelling for no more than half an hour, had gone perhaps no more than five or six miles, when the train abruptly began to slow, the wheels screeching on the rails and the cars battering each other with a loud jangling of iron buffers. I put out a hand to steady myself and it fell on Major Farnol's knee opposite me. He put his hand on mine, pressed it, then rose quickly and went to the door that led out on to the rear platform. I saw that he had taken his pistol from its holster as he stepped out the door.

'Damned trains!' Lady Westbrook was on her second cup of tea; or rather it was on her. She wiped herself down where

57

the liquid had spilled on her. 'Never a journey without something going wrong!'

'They are still better than making that dreadful journey up here by *tonga*, all those painful weeks by cart. You don't really want the old days to come back, Viola.' But the Nawab was not paying any real attention to her. He handed his cup to a servant, brushed past his wives, snapping something at them in Hindi that stopped their chattering in an instant and went out on to the rear platform to join Major Farnol.

I stood up to follow him, but felt Lady Westbrook's hand on my knee. I was surprised at the strength of it; it was like a claw. 'Stay here, m'dear. Leave it to the men.'

I sank back on my seat. 'What's going on?'

She let go of my knee, sat back, rattled her cup and saucer and handed them to the servant as he jumped forward. 'I don't know. But in these hills, when the unexpected happens, you learn it is better for women to stay out of the way.'

Then the Nawab came back, no longer genial, looking decidedly worried. 'I'm afraid this is as far as we go. There's a bally great landslide up ahead, completely blocking the line.'

End of extract from memoirs.

2

Farnol jumped down from the carriage, followed by Karim who had been riding on the rear platform. As they began to walk up towards the front of the train they were joined by the sergeant of the escort of soldiers. 'Don't look good, sir.'

They were walking on the cliff side of the railway line. The track curved round one of the many tight bends and they looked across at the tumble of rocks and earth and trees just ahead of the grunting, steaming engine. As they passed the Ranee's private carriage, she came out on to its platform right above Farnol. He was surprised to see Baron von Albern, the German Consul-General, standing in the doorway behind her; he had not known her to be particularly friendly to the Baron. But he made no comment.

'Are we going to be delayed long, Major?'

'I don't know, Your Highness. But from the look of it from here, I'll be surprised if we get through at all.'

Other than the two private cars of the Ranee and the Nawab, all the carriages had box compartments. People were leaning out the windows, voluble and curious. Farnol, Karim and the sergeant walked on past them, careful not to miss their step on the rough permanent way and go plunging down the hillside into the trees below. Trees cloaked the steep hillside above the track and Farnol, on edge again, recognized the situation for an ideal ambush. He had instinctively chosen to walk along the outer edge of the permanent way, with the train itself as a barricade against any gunfire that might come from up there in the trees.

He stopped, said quietly, 'Sergeant, go back and deploy your men along the other side of the train. Tell them to keep low, in against the bank. And see that no one gets out of the train.'

The sergeant looked surprised, but he was an old campaigner and he took off at once on the order, running back towards the rear of the train. Immediately above Farnol a voice said, 'Something wrong?'

A man was hanging out the window of one of the compartments. He was hatless and his thin blond hair hung down in a fringe round his long-nosed, long-jawed face. He had the adroit eyes of the ambitious or the survivor, and Farnol wondered how acute his hearing was.

'Nothing.' He wanted no panic starting up amongst the passengers.

'But I heard you tell the sergeant – '

Farnol stared up at the man. 'You heard me tell him nothing, sir. You understand what I'm saying?'

'Of course,' the man said after a moment. But other heads were hanging out of windows close by and as Farnol walked on he saw the heads withdraw and he felt, if he did not hear, the murmurs inside the compartments.

The engine-driver and his fireman were standing at the front of the train with the conductor. Farnol introduced himself and the driver, a *chee-chee* with a plump face and a thick moustache, looking like a coal-dusted walrus, shook his head resignedly.

'Never get past here in a month of Sundays, sir.' The landslide was a sixty-foot-wide mound of rocks, earth and trees that covered the track and ran down to disappear into the trees below. 'I don't understand it, sir. There ain't been any rain for a fortnight, that's what usually causes the slides.'

'Karim, go up to the top of the slide. Keep your eyes peeled.'

Karim caught the warning in Farnol's voice, unslung his rifle and went clambering up the slope beside the landslide. Then the sergeant came back and with him was the Nawab.

'My men are in position, sir. I tried to tell His Highness he oughta stay in the train – ' The sergeant was a 12-year man, his dislike of India and Indians of all ranks, but particularly princes, burned into his dark, wizened face.

'If something's going on, Clive, I think you can do with my help.' The Nawab sounded less British, less an impostor. 'My bodyguard is back there, six men with rifles.'

'I'm hoping we shan't need them.'

Then Karim came sliding down the slope. 'Oh, I don't like it, sahib. Some bugger has used dynamite up there – '

'Righto,' Farnol snapped, 'everyone back behind the engine! Sergeant, get down and warn your men. Better get the Nawab's men, too. Tell them to take as much cover as they can. And tell all the passengers to keep away from the windows on your side of the train.'

The sergeant went round the front of the engine and raced down the track below the trees. Farnol and the others remained on the outer edge of the track, the train crew all squatting down to make themselves smaller targets.

'Is it an ambush?' the Nawab said.

'I don't know, Bertie. It could be dacoits. I suppose Mala herself must be carrying a fortune in jewels with her. You too?'

'One is expected to put on a show. I'm afraid I've brought the bally lot. The wives, y'know. They're all looking forward to dazzling the English ladies. God knows how much the blighters would get if they did rob us. A couple of million pounds' worth at least.'

'I can't understand why they haven't already put in an appearance, or fired on us.' Farnol looked around him, puzzled. 'At least one shot, just to let us know they're here.'

There was no sound but the hissing of steam from the engine's boiler. A chill breeze blew up the narrow tree-shrouded valley below them; an eagle hung in the air like an ominous leaf; clouds seemed to form out of nothing to cover the sun and turn the green pines black. Then Farnol caught a glimpse of movement and round the next bend up ahead came a small flat-bed trolley-car, two men working the see-saw lever that propelled it and a third man sitting on the front of the trolley. The two men suddenly stopped pumping as soon as they saw the landslide and the trolley slid to a stop just short of it.

'Stay here!'

Farnol left the Nawab and the others still sheltered beside the engine and scrambled across the slide, expecting a bullet at any moment to hit him or slap into the dirt beside him. Twice he missed his footing and he had to grab at a fallen tree as the earth slipped away beneath him; once he just managed to jump ahead as the tree he had grabbed also slid down; out of the corner of his eye he saw it plunge over the edge and a moment later heard it crash into the trees below. He had just reached the far side of the slide when there was a rumble behind him. He turned to see the rocks and earth and trees slipping away, taking a section of the track with it. The rumbling deepened, then faded; dust rose up in a brown cloud and when it cleared there was a wide gap in the ledge that carried the railway line. It was going to take a month of Sundays, as the driver had said, before any train would be running on this part of the track again.

The three men on the trolley were Post and Telegraph workers. Two of them were Indians, the two who had been doing the hard work on the lever handles, and the other was a *chee-chee*, one who might have passed for European but for his slightly bluish gums and the blue marks in his finger-nails. He was grey-haired and in his fifties, his gullied face a network of lines and pockmarks.

'No, sir, we didn't see no soldiers down the line. Nobody. We been looking for breaks in the telegraph line, I dunno nothing about the telephone wires. We found four breaks between here and Solan, sir, cut by snips. I don't like the looks of it. These buggers here wanted to go home right away.' He nodded to the two Indians standing in the background; then he winked at Farnol, man to man, us whites sticking together. 'You know what they're like soon's they get a sniff of trouble.'

Who can blame them? thought Farnol; but he said, 'Gibson, I want you to go back to Solan, get on the telegraph and ask the Railway Superintendent at Kalka to send up another train immediately. You can leave your two fellows here and I'll send two soldiers with you. It's all downhill so you should make pretty quick time.'

The sergeant brought up two soldiers, who cautiously made their way across the slide above the gap. Farnol gave them instructions; they looked at him dubiously but scrambled aboard the trolley. They took up their positions on the front of the trolley, their rifles at the ready, and Gibson got up behind them.

'It could be midnight before they get a train up here, sir.'

'Just so long as they get here. I may have to take this train back up the line, but I'll leave someone here to meet the Kalka train. Good luck.'

The two soldiers looked sourly over their shoulders at him when he said that, but Farnol had given the trolley a push and it went rolling down the track, gathering speed on the slight decline that led to the next bend. It disappeared round the bend and Farnol stood for a moment wondering why the dacoits, or whoever had caused the landslide, still had not shot at him and the train. He felt that eyes were watching him, but there was no way of guessing how close the watchers were. He clambered up the slope into the trees above the slide and worked his way across through the thick forest. He was stiff with tension, his breath hissing as he forgot to breathe steadily in the high thin air; for a moment he seemed to have lost all the animal skills that had been natural to him for so long. He was no stranger to danger, but he had never before been responsible for a train-load of civilian men, women and children. He watched every tree as if it hid an assassin, but no one jumped out at him with gun or knife and at last he slid down on to the railway line.

'Driver, could you reverse the train as far back as Simla?'

'Not with all these carriages and wagons, sir. If they was empty, yes, but not with all them elephants and horses. It's a pretty heavy load for an old engine like this one.'

Farnol nodded, glancing up at the ancient engine that looked as if it had had trouble getting the train this far *downhill*. Then the Nawab said, 'There's the trolley, across there on that far bend. I say, they're going fast!'

Farnol looked beyond the near bend round which the trolley had disappeared a few minutes ago, saw it now in view on a far shoulder of the mountain that towered above the railway line. The foreman was working the driving lever up and down as fast as he could, speeding the trolley along, as if once he was out of range of Farnol he was as determined as the soldiers with him to get out of the danger zone as soon as possible. The trolley was a hundred yards short of the far bend when the foreman fell forward over the see-sawing arm of the lever. It swung up, lifting him sideways, and he toppled off the trolley and went hurtling down the sheer cliff-face below the track. One of the soldiers straightened up, then he, too, fell off the trolley, hit the permanent way and rolled over the edge of the cliff and followed the foreman down into the green surf of trees far below. The other soldier just lay back as if going to sleep and as the sound of the three rifle shots reached the watchers beside the engine, the trolley disappeared round the far bend, its see-sawing driving lever still going up and down in a stiff-armed farewell.

Farnol acted at once. 'Back into the train! Get us back as far as you can, driver! Hop to it!'

But the driver couldn't budge the old engine. It gasped and wheezed and its wheels spun with a thin screech on the rails; but none of the carriages or wagons behind it moved even a yard.

'Ain't no use, sir. She'll just bust her boiler.'

Farnol, still standing beside the track, looked at the Nawab. 'I'm afraid all your animals have to come off, Bertie. Mala's too. Will you organize it while I tell the passengers

63

what's happening? I'm going to have to send them all back up to Simla. They'll be safer there than down here.'

'What are you going to do?'

'I'm not sure, but I think I'll try to get down to Kalka somehow. I have to get on the telegraph to Delhi. Now hop to it, will you?'

The Nawab went hurrying down the train and Farnol followed him, stopping beside each carriage and telling the curious passengers what he intended doing. They had heard the echoes of the shots and most of the faces that hung out of the windows and doors were frightened and puzzled. One didn't expect this sort of thing in the hills south of Simla, this wasn't the Khyber Pass or the North-West Frontier.

There was also chagrin and disappointment. 'But we may never get to the Durbar in time! We can't possibly go back up to Simla!' She was a formidable woman who filled a window of her own, like an oversized portrait in a too-small frame. 'We shall wait here till they send up another train!'

'You'll do nothing of the sort, madam. I can't be responsible for the lives of all of you. I'll have a man stay here and bring a message up to Simla when a relief train arrives.'

But he had no faith that that would happen. When the Durbar Train did not arrive down in Kalka on time there would be worried questions, especially since it was known that the telephone and telegraph lines had been cut. He could imagine the argument and indecision that would occur as to whether another train should be risked.

He left the woman and went on down the train.

'I'm not going back up to Simla,' said the Ranee. 'Have them take my elephants and horses and coach down to the cart road down there. I'll go down to Kalka by road.'

'Mala, you can't –'

But one of her servants was already helping her down. 'Clive, don't tell me what I cannot do – as I told you before, I'm not one of your little base wallah wives. Coming, Baron?'

'Of course.' The Baron, heavily-built and one-armed, also had to be helped down to the ground.

Then the Nawab came back. 'Shouldn't be long. I'm having my chaps take everything down to the cart road – Hello, Mala old girl. Where are you going?'

'She's going down to Kalka by road, so she says.'

'I say, what a topping idea! Why didn't I think of that?'

'Bertie, for God's sake – ! It'll take four or five days at least, those blighters could take pot-shots at you all the way – '

'Perhaps, old chap. But what's the alternative? Leave everything here and have them pick my chaps off one by one and then steal the lot? What sort of show would I be able to put on down at the Durbar then?'

But Farnol saw behind the smile, knew that Bertie was concerned for something more than his vanity, his image as a prince in the parade of princes. He looked to the rear of the train, saw the first of the elephants already being led back between the railway tracks to the path that led down to the narrow road cutting through the trees several hundred feet below.

'All right, get everything down there. See that your guards have their rifles loaded, keep two of them on the alert all the time. I'm coming with you.'

'I hoped you'd say that,' said the Ranee right behind him.

'Be jolly glad to have you,' said the Nawab.

'You'll be excellent company, Major,' said the Baron.

Farnol looked at the three of them, suddenly uneasy again; but this time he was not looking for some distant rifleman to take a shot at him. He was surrounded by hospitable smiles, but all at once he trusted none of them. Especially the Ranee's, the widest smile of all.

'Get everything down to the road, Bertie. I'll join you as soon as I've got the train under way.'

But his arguments were not over yet. Bridie O'Brady and Lady Westbrook were on the platform of the Nawab's carriage and as soon as Farnol told them what was happening they said they would be travelling down to Kalka by road.

'Miss O'Brady and I can ride in the Ranee's coach. For twenty years I travelled up and down this road by *tonga* – I know every bump and dip in it. We'll go down in style, Miss O'Brady, pretending we're princesses. We may even throw a penny or two to the peasants – '

'Lady Westbrook – '

'No more discussion, Clive. Just see that my bearer gets my things off the train. What *is* going on, anyway?'

Farnol was unaccustomed to arguing with women. He came of a long line of Farnol men who looked upon women as one of God's more pleasant afterthoughts, like rainbows and other trivia of nature. His own father had never quite accepted Queen Victoria as his sovereign and had been surprised the Empire had survived under her. He himself had progressed to the extent that he allowed women equal rights in the bedroom; at least in a bedroom there was no other man, one's true peer, to see him occasionally playing second fiddle. In public he took it for granted that a woman knew her proper place.

'Viola, there are dacoits covering the railway line and the road. If you persist in going down that road, you could be shot. You, too, Miss O'Brady. I'm ordering you both to get back on the train.'

Lady Westbrook sniffed, looked at Bridie. 'Do you allow the men in America to talk to you like that?'

'No,' said Bridie. 'I'm sorry, Major Farnol. I'm accompanying Lady Westbrook.'

'Damn!' said Farnol and didn't apologize.

Twenty minutes later the wagons and flat-cars were empty. The elephants and horses were down on the road, the elephants saddled with their howdahs; half a dozen of the Ranee's men were struggling with her coach as they eased it down the steep path to the road. There had still been no more shots and Farnol had the feeling he was working in a vice that would close as soon as the train had disappeared. But he knew he had to stay with the party going down by road, more for his own reasons than for theirs. Somehow he had to get on the telegraph to Colonel Lathrop. He was certain that Lathrop would take heed of his warning of a plot against the King's life.

He spoke to the sergeant of the escort. 'When you get back to Simla tell Captain Weyman I suggest he has everyone on twenty-four-hour stand-by. I'll have the telegraph line repaired as soon as possible.'

'You think they'll try coming up to Simla, sir?'

'I doubt it. This isn't some sort of uprising, sergeant – we'd have heard about it before this if anything had been stewing. I think they are just dacoits and nothing more.'

'Puzzles me why they haven't opened up on us. Them buggers usually don't waste no time.'

'It puzzles me, too, sergeant.'

'You think they're waiting to pop them off down there?' The sergeant nodded down at the small caravan gathering on the road below. 'Maybe I'd better give you some of my blokes, sir – '

'No, they're needed to guard the train, just in case. Hop aboard, sergeant, there's the whistle.'

The train creaked its iron joints, the wheels gave faint squeals, then it started to ease slowly backwards up the slight incline. Farnol stood beside the track, nodding to the heads hanging out of the windows as they went by above him. The stout woman would have fallen out of her window if she could have squeezed through; she could see the social climax of her life disappearing as the train took her backwards away from it, all the unwritten letters to her less fortunate friends in England never to be written at all; her tirade at Farnol drifted back, harder on the ear than the clang and screech of the iron wheels. Two little girls hung out of a window crying, deprived of the biggest picnic they would ever have seen. Finally the engine went past, puffing and grunting and wheezing like an old bull elephant coaxed out of retirement to push its way through a teak forest; the conductor stood on the step, ready to drop off and take cover further up the line where he could hide and wait for the arrival of the relief train, if and when it came. The engine went by, Farnol waved to the driver, then turned to walk down the path to the road. And stopped.

On the other side of the line, between the tracks and the steeply rising hillside, stood a man and a woman, two suitcases beside them.

3

'Awfully sorry to trouble you, Major.' It was the long-nosed, long-jawed man who had spoken to Farnol earlier. He had put on a deer-stalker cap and it only seemed to accentuate the long thinness of his face. 'My name is Monday. This lady is my wife.'

She was pretty in a vague sort of way, as if her looks came and went with shifts of light. She was dressed in a brown travelling suit and brown hat and she reminded Farnol of a good-looking field mouse. She smiled sweetly.

'We're coming with you, Major. I'm sure you'll be able to find room for us.'

All at once Farnol suspected she might be a field mouse with very sharp teeth. 'Sir, just who are you that you think you can invite yourself to travel with me?'

'Please don't misunderstand me, sir. We are not forcing ourselves on you.' For the first time Farnol noticed that the man had a slight accent. 'Perhaps we should not have got off the train without requesting your permission. But here we are and I trust you will not leave us here.'

'I may do just that, sir. You still haven't told me who you are.'

'I am the Asian representative for Krupps.' Both he and his wife stood very still, as if the name *Krupp* sounded like the single note of a leper's clapper bell even in their own ears.

'You have an English name, or so it sounds.'

'My grandfather was English. My wife and I are Hungarian. But we always stand for *God Save The King.*'

'Bully for you,' said Farnol and started walking down the path towards the road. When he stopped and looked back the Mondays were still standing on the far side of the railway line, their suitcases still on the ground. 'Righto, you'd better follow me. But I warn you – I shan't be responsible for you.'

'You are a sweet man.' Magda Monday followed Farnol down the path, leaving her husband to struggle with the two suitcases. 'So gallant.'

Farnol just bowed his head, then looked up past her at her husband whose arms looked as if they were being pulled out of their sockets by the weight of the suitcases he carried. 'Cannonballs, Mr Monday?'

Monday managed a Hungarian smile, which can be read a dozen ways. 'We shall enjoy the Major's company, my dear. The English sense of humour is famous.'

Mrs Monday put her hand out for Farnol to help her down a steep part of the path; she went past him on a wave of perfume that suggested she might have upset a bottle of it all over herself before getting off the train. He noticed that the buttons of her brown jacket were undone; her bodice was low-cut, exposing more bosom than one expected to see in India in the daytime. She saw the direction of his gaze and looked directly at him, turning her body slightly towards him. He knew a whore when she smiled at him.

'Englishmen never treat their women with any sense of humour, do they, Major?'

'Only when we bury them, madam. Our graveyards are full of husbands' wit.'

Bridie O'Brady, Lady Westbrook, the Ranee of Serog and now this one: Farnol could feel his latent misogynism rising sourly within him. He led the way down to the road, getting well ahead of them, and walked up to Baron von Albern, who stood beside the Ranee as they waited for horses to be hitched to the Ranee's coach. The other horses were being saddled; final adjustments were being made to the howdahs on the elephants' backs. None of the servants looked enthusiastic about the journey ahead and kept glancing over their shoulders up at the surrounding hills.

'Herr Baron, those people coming down the path are Hungarians – the gentleman says he is a representative of Krupps. Do you know anything about him?'

'Not much, Major.' The Consul-General was straightforward, which may have explained why he had never risen to being an ambassador. 'They only arrived two days ago. They stayed at the Hotel Cecil. Herr Monday paid a courtesy call on me.'

'Was he intending to sell arms to anyone in Simla?'

'I couldn't say. He told me nothing about his business.'

Then the Mondays came down on to the road. Zoltan Monday dropped the suitcases and began bending his arms as if he were trying to push them back into their sockets. Bridie and the others looked at the pair curiously, then all looked at Farnol. Curtly he explained who the newcomers were, saw the Ranee look at them with sharp interest when he mentioned the name Krupp. The Nawab, standing in front of

69

his six wives, gave a bright smile of welcome to Madame Monday, but ignored her husband. Lady Westbrook sniffed loudly and Bridie made mental notes for her as-yet-unthought-of memoirs.

'I am delighted to meet you all,' said Magda, who would have introduced herself in the same way to every circle of Hell. At fifteen she had walked the Fisherman's Bastion above Budapest looking for men; at twenty she had found Zoltan in the chandeliered lobby of the Astoria Hotel. She had trained herself for rebuffs as a boxer builds the muscles of his midriff to absorb punches. 'I'm sure we shall have a very good journey together.'

'It won't be for want of your trying.' The Ranee had already decided there were too many women in her caravan; she also recognized a possible mischief-maker. She got up into her coach. 'Get in, Viola. You, too, Miss O'Brady.'

'Thank you, Your Highness, but if I may I'd like to ride one of your horses with Major Farnol.'

'As you wish.' The Ranee, not trained for rebuffs, made no attempt to sound gracious. She turned her head away and looked down at the Hungarian woman. 'Perhaps you had better ride with us, Madame Monday.'

'Monday?' Lady Westbrook had donned her two hats again and looked like a war-torn pagoda. She looked Magda up and down as the latter got into the coach and sat opposite her. She decided that Magda was riff-raff. 'Is that your name or the day you are available?'

Magda's smile had the bright shine of a razor turned to the sun. 'I have just been complimenting the Major on the English sense of humour.' She moved sideways on the seat to make room for the bulk of the Baron. 'We appear to have taken sides, Herr Baron. You and I against the British Empire.'

The Baron put on his glasses, looked across at the ladies of the Empire. 'I should never take sides against such a formidable force.'

The procession got under way. Karim and two of the Nawab's armed men rode up front on horses, with Farnol, Bridie and the Nawab immediately behind them. Then came the Ranee's coach, the twelve elephants, their howdahs stuffed with the Nawab's wives and all the luggage, and finally the rest of the horses ridden by Zoltan Monday and the Ranee's and the Nawab's escorts. All over India similar caravans were making their way towards the Great Durbar, but none of them had been forced to make their march in the way this one had been.

There was no scabbard on Farnol's saddle and he rode with his rifle slung across his shoulder. The procession eased its way down the narrow sloping road, its pace geared to that of the elephants. Farnol was already resigned to the fact that they would probably have to go all the way down to Kalka by these means. He had little faith that a relief train would be sent up; all the regular drivers would be working on the extra trains going down to Delhi for the Durbar; any relief driver would fall sick as soon as he learned he had to take a train up into the hills where dacoits were operating. If he and the others made the journey safely, he estimated that it would take them five days to get down to Kalka; from there it was only an overnight trip by train to Delhi. That would give him still a day or two before the King was due to arrive in the capital, time for him to see George Lathrop and convince him that extra protection should be provided for the King-Emperor. That is, *if* he could convince Lathrop: so far he had no more evidence than the attack on his own life. The King himself, if offered such evidence, might brush it aside. An attempt to kill a sovereign's subject did not necessarily mean the ruler himself was next on the list. The King might feel that was taking democratic precedence too far.

'I think they've done a bunk, Clive,' said the Nawab looking around.

'Perhaps. But I'm still puzzled, Bertie – why go to all that trouble to stop the train, then just buzz off?'

Bridie had been silent ever since she had got off the train. She was aware of the tension in Farnol; it was reflected in herself. In the course of her job as a reporter she had once or twice been threatened by hooligans, but she had never felt that her life was in danger. She was not a cowardly girl, but she did not know yet if she was brave; for the moment she was glad of the men riding on either side of her, no matter how inadequate their protection might be. She was not helped by the restive horse she was mounted on; she wished now that she had not been so quick to decline the Ranee's invitation to ride in the coach. She was riding side-saddle, as she had seen all the women in Boston doing; it was the way ladies were expected to ride and in certain matters she tried to pass for a lady. That was her Irish mother's influence; it had never been Sheila O'Brady's ambition that her only daughter should grow up to be the biddy of some Boston ward boss, as she had done. Bridie had been on a horse no more than half a dozen times and her discomfort added to her tension. She sat the horse like a wooden doll.

'You don't look comfortable, Miss O'Brady,' said the Nawab. 'Would you prefer to ride one of the elephants? I can give you a howdah to yourself.'

Then the bullet zipped past Farnol's head, ricocheted off a rock and whined away. The sound of the shot followed immediately, as did the second bullet. It hit Farnol's saddle just as he dropped down out of it; the horse shied, but the bullet had hit the thickest part of the saddle and hadn't gone through. Farnol pulled the rearing horse down; the Nawab had grabbed the reins of Bridie's horse and was swinging it and his own mount back towards the shelter of the elephants. Karim and the two guards up front were already off their horses and returning the fire; it came from halfway up the steep slope above the road, from the midst of a thick stand of deodars. Farnol had quietened his horse, had unslung his rifle and was scanning the dense forest above him.

'Cease fire!'

Karim and the two guards ceased firing, tried to soothe their nervous horses. Then Karim said, 'You want me to send these two chaps up there, sahib?'

Even in the tension of the moment Farnol had to smile. Good old Karim, who knew when to sacrifice someone else's valour for his own discretion. 'No, stay where you are. I think they're already moving out.'

He had caught a glimpse of movement up through the trees: two, maybe three men going swiftly up the slope. He thought he recognized one of the men, but he was too far away; perhaps his imagination was playing tricks, conjuring up the man in the blue scarf. There had been no more shots after the first two. And those two had been aimed at him, at no one else in the caravan.

'Righto, remount. Keep your eyes peeled.'

Leading his own horse he went back to the coach, where the driver, with the aid of his assistant, was just getting the coach's two horses under control. In the coach itself Lady Westbrook was trying to revive Magda Monday, who had fainted. Her husband had ridden forward from the rear and was gazing anxiously down at his wife, who lay with her head in the Baron's lap. The Ranee ignored the unconscious Magda and looked out at Farnol. She had raised a parasol against the afternoon sun and looked sedate and regal.

'Well? Have they gone?'

He didn't know whether to admire her or suspect her: her coolness was almost too perfect. 'I think it's safe to go on. Those shots were meant for me, not the rest of you.'

Lady Westbrook, who had been waving a bottle of smelling salts under Magda's nose, abruptly sat up straight. 'Why should they only shoot at you, Clive? Are you something special?'

Lady Westbrook knew what he was; she knew what everyone in the Punjab States was. 'Political agents are often targets, Viola. You know that – your husband was one.'

'No one ever tried to pop him off in this part of the country.' She gave her attention again to Magda, who was now beginning to stir. 'Come on, gel – wake up! Does she often go off like this, Mr Monday?'

'I don't think she has ever been shot at before,' said Monday, still anxious about his wife.

'Nonsense, she wasn't shot at. It was Major Farnol they were after. They'd have mowed us all down in a moment if they'd wanted to. Sit her up, Baron, put her head down between her knees. There, that's better.'

'I should have brought another coach.' The Ranee was wasting no sympathy, a property she had in only small supply. 'Let's move on.'

'May I ride with my wife?' said Monday.

'There's no room,' said the Ranee and poked her parasol into the back of her coachman. 'Drive on!'

Magda lifted her head from between her knees and looked

73

at the princess opposite her. The two women stared at each other and Lady Westbrook, eyes as alert as those of a Pathan scout, saw the battle lines drawn. She gave herself a sniff of the smelling salts and sat back to enjoy the rest of the journey.

Monday reached across, patted his wife's shoulder and rode back to the rear of the procession. Farnol mounted his horse and went up to the front again. After a moment Bridie followed him, but the Nawab remained to ride beside the coach.

'What sort of story will you write about all this?' said Farnol.

'It isn't over yet, is it?' Bridie was slowly learning how to control her horse, but she knew she would never make a good rider. She wondered if she would ever make a good foreign correspondent.

Farnol hesitated, then shook his head. He felt reasonably certain that no one else was in any real danger, unless another bullet aimed at him should go astray. He was still puzzled as to why the assassins, whoever they were, should be going to such lengths to kill him; and where had Rupert Savanna disappeared to and what was his connection with the Ranee? Why had an arms salesman, and a salesman for a German firm at that, suddenly appeared in these hills? His puzzlement increased his suspicion: he looked back up the road and saw a caravan of potential enemies.

'Do you mind if I stay close to you?' said Bridie.

'That may not be healthy.'

'Maybe not. But I'd still feel safer.'

He smiled at her, wondering why women always used such an obvious weapon as flattery. 'You honour me, Miss O'Brady.'

'And I give you a pain in the neck, too. You don't fool me, Major.'

'I don't think any man has ever done that, has he?'

'If a woman never let a man fool her occasionally, her life would be very dry and unexciting.'

'Stay close to me, Miss O'Brady, and we'll fool each other.'

'Thank you. Now we've both been warned.'

The road wound down through a forest of blue pine. Farnol could see ahead to where the forest petered out and

74

the southern slopes of the hills began their sparsely cloaked descent to the plains. Down there he would find little cover if they should be attacked again and he began to wonder if there was an alternative route.

They came round a bend and suddenly they were in a small village. They passed down the main street, which was also the bazaar; but business was slack and storekeepers came to their doors and shouted invitations to come in and buy. Then they saw the Ranee and abruptly shut up and bowed their heads; this was her domain and they knew she was no customer. Children stared wide-eyed at the modest magnificence of the procession; above them, on the roof-tops, monkeys stared with eyes just as big but shrewder. The Ranee reached into the silk handbag she carried, took out a handful of small coins and tossed them out; the children, thrashing about them with closed fists, just beat the monkeys to the money. One monkey did manage to grab a coin and retreated to a roof-top where it bit on the coin, found it inedible and, imitating the Ranee's benevolence, tossed it back down to the children.

The caravan passed through the village, then the pines started to thin out. The sun dropped behind the mountain above them and the air abruptly turned cool. Farnol pulled his horse to one side and waited till the coach came up to him.

'We are going to make camp soon, Your Highness. This is your territory – where do you suggest?'

'My dear Clive, when I'm this close to home, I don't camp out. We shall detour and call in at the palace.'

'I say, old girl, do you think that's wise?' The Nawab was on the other side of the coach; he looked across at Farnol. 'Mala's brother, Mahendra, doesn't make visitors welcome.'

Farnol had never visited the palace of Serog, but he knew of it. It had stood since the 16th century and once had been one of the glories of northern India. He had also heard of Mala's mentally unstable brother, known as Mad Mahendra and discreetly ignored by every arm of the British Raj. The palace did not suggest itself as a hospitable inn for the night.

But he knew better than to attempt to change the Ranee's mind; that would be like trying to alter the course of the Ganges with a shovel. The procession moved on, came to a side road which cut away through the last of the now thin forest. The lead horsemen, on a cry from the Ranee's coachman, turned off the main road and led the way through a narrow ravine that abruptly grew into a high-walled gorge. It was a natural gateway, Farnol saw at once, an ideal spot where intruders could be turned back.

Armed tribesmen, four on either side of the narrow road, materialized out of the rocks at the foot of the gorge's walls. Farnol called a halt and rode ahead, spoke in Hindi: 'The Ranee comes home. Let us pass.'

They looked at him with hostile suspicion; he imagined he could see their fingers curling on the triggers of their rifles. Then one of them looked towards the coach, saw the Ranee and instantly shouted to his colleagues. All eight jumped down from the rocks and rushed to pay their respects to their mistress. Farnol breathed a sigh of relief and moved the procession through. Then he fell in beside Bridie.

Bridie was curious: 'But this place is only a few miles from Simla – doesn't she ever come down here? Is it hers or her brother's?'

'Hers. She belongs to one of those families where the eldest child, girl or boy, inherits everything. Her brother is more than half-mad – I gather he's something of a handful. So she leaves him here and prefers to live up in Simla or, in the winter, down in Bombay. She likes her social life and – ' he glanced up at the towering walls of the gorge ' – I don't think there would be much around here.'

Then the gorge opened out and the procession came into a narrow valley that was almost lush after the rocky barrenness they had passed through. The slopes of the mountains on the northern side were sparsely timbered; erosion scars showed like old yellow wounds on the rocky earth. But the slopes on the southern side and the floor of the valley were thick with pines, rhododendrons, laurels; meadows of autumn-yellowed grass stretched away on either side of a narrow tumbling river. Farnol knew such pockets of near-lushness could exist in these hills; he had seen such valleys even further north and at higher altitudes. They were oases protected from the fierce sun that, aided by the searing winds from the deserts of the western Punjab and Rajputana, killed all young vegetation on the mountains' southern slopes. The people who lived in this valley might never see the majesty of the Himalayas, but they would never have to scratch for a living as did those who lived on the mountain-tops and were surrounded by the most breath-taking views in all the world. But even those who lived on mountain-tops did so only because it gave them the opportunity to see an approaching enemy. He had never met a peasant hillman who chose his home because of the view it gave him.

The procession came round the end of a ridge running down from the southern wall of the valley and straight ahead, on a low bluff above the white-wealed river, was the palace of Serog.

'Oh my!' Bridie pulled her horse to one side while she paused to stare at the magnificent castle. 'It's like something out of a fairy tale!'

'Its history is as full of blood and gore as most fairy tales.'

The palace, or castle, for it was both, towered above the river in rising terraces on which marble-domed guard-towers, delicately decorated with pierced grilles, looked as fragile as pavilions of candy. Inside the thick outer walls the main buildings of the castle merged into each other through corner towers that rose from the ground to be topped, a hundred feet high, with blue domes that seemed to be nothing more substantial than mirages on the blue light of the late afternoon. The castle dominated the entire valley, but the effect was of a great blue-and-white cloud that had floated down to the valley floor rather than a threatening mass of rock and marble.

Farnol was a hundred yards from the castle before he recognized the huge dark rocks on either side of the great gateway. They were rows of fighting elephants, thirty or forty of them, their tusks tipped with metal and each beast chained to a stake at a safe distance from those on either side of it. He wondered how often Mad Mahendra came out on to his castle walls and ordered the elephants to be let loose to fight each other in a welter of blood.

He halted the procession and waited for the Ranee to bring her coach forward. 'You'd better go in first, Your Highness. Your brother may not welcome us.'

'He knows better than to disagree with me,' said the Ranee

and her tone suggested that everyone should know better.

'Perhaps we'd better get out,' said Magda Monday.

'Stay where you are,' ordered the Ranee and rapped her driver on the back with her parasol.

The coach went in under the great decorated arch of the gateway and Farnol and the rest of the party sat and waited. The fighting elephants began to raise their heads and trumpet as they became aware of the elephants in the caravan; the latter became restless, began to back off, wanting nothing to do with the hoodlums beneath the castle walls. The Nawab and Zoltan Monday rode up beside Farnol and Bridie.

'How long do we stay here, Clive?' said the Nawab.

'Just for the night. I want to be down in Kalka by Wednesday evening at the latest.'

'I think we'd have been safer camping by the roadside. I take it you've never met Mahendra? Sometimes he can be as charming and sane as you and I – ' He smiled at Bridie to let her know how charming he, at least, could be. 'But other times . . . One of his ancestors was the biggest butcher in our history. Mahendra composes songs to his memory.'

'He must be charming,' said Bridie.

A man came to the gateway and beckoned to Farnol. The procession slowly made its way into the great courtyard of the castle. Farnol was surprised at the size of the courtyard; there seemed to be room enough for a small army. The coach was drawn up beneath a high portico attached to the main building; the Ranee and the coach's three other passengers stood on the steps that led up to the tall, wide doors studded with big brass spikes. Nothing about the castle of Serog suggested any welcome to visitors.

Prince Mahendra was standing on the steps above his sister. He was a slim young man, younger than Farnol had expected: he could not have been more than twenty. He wore a pale blue silk *achkan*, the long tight-fitting coat that came to his knees; his head was wrapped in a pink turban and he had a magnificent ruby in the lobe of one ear. Round his neck was a double strand of spinel rubies, each as large as a small pigeon's egg, and his thin left arm seemed held down by the weight of the diamond-encrusted bracelet on his wrist.

'He must have seen us coming and got dressed in a hurry,' the Nawab whispered to Bridie. 'This family is so bally vulgar.'

Today appeared to be one of Mahendra's days of charm and sanity. He greeted all the women, with the exception of the Nawab's wives, with a bow and a smile. He shook hands with all the men and Farnol was impressed with the strength in the thin brown fingers. He could see now that *thin* best described the prince. He was almost skeletal, as if his flesh had been worn away by the fever of his occasional madness.

'Do come in, how splendid of you to visit me! My sister insists that I always have the palace ready for her, but she never comes.' He kissed the Ranee's cheek. 'Mala my dearest sister, welcome home.'

'Don't be so melodramatic, Bobs. Take us inside and see everyone is settled in. We'll all be down for dinner, except Bertie's wives. Put them in the *zenana* and see they're fed.'

The Political Service had a dossier on Prince Mahendra, as it had on all the princes, great and small. Farnol had read it and he knew that Mahendra's full name was Roberts Akbar Mahendra Kugar of Serog. At the time of his birth the Commander-in-Chief in India had been Sir Frederick (later Lord) Roberts; the baby prince's father had been a great admirer of Bobs and had named his son after the general. The boy, as he grew older, had been labelled with the C-in-C's nickname. Farnol was to wonder what the now retired field-marshal would think if he knew that a young madman now answered to the famous nickname.

The guests were led into the main entrance hall, which looked like a great roofed cloister with colonnaded arcades on three sides. The floors were blue-and-white marble, laid in an intricate Persian pattern; the domed roof was a diminished reflection of the floor, the pattern being the same but smaller. Everything looked as if it had been washed every day for centuries and Farnol wondered in surprise if cleanliness was one of Mahendra's fetishes.

Mahendra put a brown claw on Farnol's sleeve as he was about to follow Bridie up the wide stairs to the bedrooms. 'Pray stay a moment, Major Farnol.' He had a soft sing-song voice, that of a man who might talk or sing to himself for hours on end. 'Have you seen your Major Savanna lately?'

The Ranee, the last to ascend the stairs, turned back. 'What about him?'

Farnol stayed silent, letting the subject of Rupert Savanna lie between the brother and sister. He saw Mahendra's eyes widen slightly, then narrow, and he wondered how long the prince's charm was going to last. It was obvious that Bobs did not believe in wasting charm on his sister.

'He sent me a message that he would come down here last night. He didn't turn up.'

'Does he come here often?' said Farnol.

'Of course not,' said the Ranee quickly. 'Bobs doesn't encourage visitors. The Major has disappeared, Bobs, but don't worry about it. He'll turn up.'

'I wasn't worried about him,' said Mahendra and again Farnol saw his eyes widen, then narrow. 'I don't worry about anyone, not even you, Mala my dear.'

'Darling Bobs,' said his sister, put her hand on his cheek and Farnol waited for the blood to flow under her long nails. But she just patted him, then took her hand away and held it out to Farnol. 'Come on, darling Clive. I'll show you to your room. It's next to mine.'

'How jolly,' said Farnol for want of something else to say.

'Whore!' Mahendra's eyes remained wide this time.

'Perhaps, darling. But I'm a selective one.' Which, she seemed to think, was some sort of compliment to herself.

She led a reluctant Farnol up the stairs and along a marble-floored corridor to a door. 'I have a suite next to this room. I'll send for you when I'm ready.'

'Mala, old girl, that's all over. You kicked me out a year ago, remember? You said I was never there enough to be – I think you called me your Constant Lover.'

'Darling Clive, I'm not asking you to be my Constant Lover. This is just for tonight, to keep ourselves amused. What's the alternative? Playing bridge with Viola and those other dreary people.'

'You don't really think they're dreary. You're just afraid you may have some competition from Miss O'Brady and Madame Monday.'

'And shall I?'

'Mala, in the past few days there have been three attempts to kill me. That sort of thing does nothing for a man's potency.'

She smiled, ran the back of her hand across his cheek; he felt the sharpness of her diamond rings. 'You've changed, Clive. Or you're lying.'

She left him and went along the corridor to where a tall bearded Sikh stood outside a door. The guard opened the door for her, closed it behind her, then resumed his post, feet wide apart, hands folded on the hilt of a long heavy sword that looked as if it could take off the head of a buffalo with a single blow.

Farnol opened his own door and went into his room. Sitting on his bed was Private Ahearn.

CHAPTER FOUR

I

Extract from the memoirs of Miss Bridie O'Brady:

I believe that the palace of Serog had five hundred rooms. Three hundred bedrooms, one hundred reception and withdrawing rooms, kitchens, storerooms, quarters for the staff of two thousand; but no bathrooms. I presently live in an apartment with four bedrooms and four-and-a-half bathrooms; I have never quite understood what a half-bathroom is and presume it was invented by an architect for a client who believed in less than full hygiene. I mention this to point the difference between a 400-year-old castle in India in 1911 and an apartment in America today. Our present society has as much skulduggery, murder, rape, theft and other assorted crime as there was in British India of that day, but we have far less body odour.

The bedroom I had been shown to was out of the *Arabian Nights* rather than *House and Garden*. It seemed large enough to have held a small ball in; I can only assume it was the bedroom of one of the more favoured wives of a past prince of Serog. There was the largest bed I had ever seen; it was not a popular pastime in 1911, but one could have held a group sex orgy in the bed and still had room for voyeurs. Scattered about the room were more *chaises longues* than I have seen on the floor at W & J Sloane at sale time; the princess for whom it had been furnished could have flung herself down anywhere and never hit the floor. Two facing walls of the room were floor-to-ceiling mirrors; the canopy over the bed was also a mirror; if one stood in the middle of the room and looked at a mirror wall one could see oneself reflected into infinity. It was like looking at a regiment of oneself in single column of march, as I think Major Farnol would have called it.

In one corner of the huge room, where no carpet or rug covered the marble floor, servants had brought in a big copper tub and filled it with hot water. I was soaking in it, the servants having retired at my request, when the bedroom door opened and Major Farnol and a soldier stepped hurriedly in, shutting the door behind them. They both took one look at me in the bath, which fortunately was high-sided and hid all of me but my head, then Major Farnol grabbed the soldier and spun him round. They both stood facing the door.

'Forgive this intrusion, Miss O'Brady – '

'Goddam!' I swore occasionally in those days, though nothing like the young girls and actresses of today. 'What's the meaning of this?'

'I want you to allow Private Ahearn to stay in your room for an hour or two. Miss O'Brady, this is Private Ahearn – There's no need to turn round, Ahearn!' The soldier had been about to pay his compliments to me, but Major Farnol roughly turned him back to face the wall. 'He can guard you while you're protecting him.'

'Protecting him from what?'

'He can tell you himself. I must go back to my room. Behave yourself, Ahearn. You're on your honour as an Irishman and a gentleman.'

That did nothing to reassure me. Coming from a long line of Irishmen, I didn't think the two titles were compatible. Judging by Ahearn's smirk, neither did he; but he nodded and said the Major had nothing to worry about. He didn't mention whether I had to worry or not.

Major Farnol opened the door a crack, peered out, then disappeared so quickly it was almost as if he had squeezed himself into a thin wraith and slid through the crack. Private Ahearn closed the door and continued to face it.

'There's a dirty great Sikh down the hall, miss, outside the Ranee's room. That's why we had to duck in here in a hurry – the Major didn't want him to see us. Will you be long taking your bath, miss?'

'I had intended having a nice long soak, Mr Ahearn, but I don't suppose that's possible now. Do you have any sisters?'

'Seven of 'em, miss.'

'Any of them nuns?'

'Five of 'em, miss.'

'All right, imagine that you're in the convent and I'm one of your sisters who is a nun. Keep your back turned.'

I got out of the bath with some difficulty, slipping once and falling back into it with a loud splash. Private Ahearn turned instinctively to help me, but I snapped at him to remain where he was. I managed to get out, dried myself quickly with one of the threadbare towels the servants had brought me. I put on my peignoir but left off my hat; after all I was in my own bedroom. Or at least the bedroom allotted to me for the night, public though it may have suddenly become.

'Turn round, Mr Ahearn. You may sit over there on the blue sofa.' I sat down on a purple sofa some twenty feet from him; if he was to spend the night in here there must be no hint of intimacy. 'Now tell me what this is all about. Are you the soldier who deserted this morning?'

'Yes, miss. I'm not exactly person gratis with the Major, if you know what I mean, yes.' He had a habit I'd noticed with certain Irishmen of finishing a sentence with *yes*, as if confirming their own statements. 'But he's put me on trust on account of what I know.'

'What do you know?'

'Major Savanna is here in the palace, yes.'

'Major Savanna? What is he doing here?'

'I dunno, miss.' It was obvious that he was not accustomed to being asked questions while sitting down; his feet were planted firmly on the floor, but he sat forward as if about to rise at any moment; his hands kept moving from the sofa to his knees and back again. Private Ahearn, a born rebel, had probably spent half his time in the army being interrogated, always standing at attention. 'I seen him this afternoon when I first come in here.'

'What are you doing here?'

'Hiding, miss. I got lost coming down through the hills. I was heading for Kalka but I had to stay away from the road or the railway line, and I come here into the valley and seen the palace. I sneaked in here, the guards are pretty lazy, I suppose they never get anyone around here anyway, and I hadn't been in the place ten minutes when I see Major

Savanna. He looked pretty angry, if you know what I mean.'

'Did you speak to him?'

'Why should I want to speak to him, miss? I'm leaving the army, not joining it. I just turned my back and did a bunk.'

'Why does Major Farnol want you to hide in my room?'

'I was hiding in his room when he come into it. I come up here and I just picked one at random, if you know what I mean. I didn't know youse were all coming here – '

'Neither did we. Major Farnol has probably told you what happened to our train. But you still haven't explained why you have to use my bedroom to hide in. Why not the Major's?'

'It's because of the Ranee, miss. She's a bit of a – if you know what I mean. Even us blokes in the ranks know all about her.' Private Ahearn screwed one hand into the other, kept looking intently at them as if he were trying to construct some Chinese puzzle out of them. The Irish are always embarrassed whenever anything relating to sex, no matter how peripheral, is mentioned. I think if Dr Kinsey had conducted his research in Ireland instead of Indiana he'd have been reduced to interviewing the donkeys. 'The Major is afraid she'll come into his room some time tonight, yes.'

I felt a slight pang of jealousy at that; then told myself it was premature on several counts. 'Is Major Farnol going to ask the Ranee about Major Savanna's presence here?'

Ahearn's hand was now trying to peel his potato nose. 'I dunno, miss. He does seem a bit put out by it all, I think.'

'What's he doing about you? I suppose you're a deserter?'

He nodded. 'I dunno, miss. I could do another bunk, I suppose, but from what the Major told me, it don't look too healthy in these hills just now. He's told me to stick around, so I think I will.'

'Why are you deserting?'

He looked at me in surprise. 'Miss O'Brady, you're Irish, ain't you? Would you be wanting to serve in the British Army?'

'I'm American, Mr Ahearn, and I'm female, so I hardly think the opportunity would arise. Why did you enlist? Or were you press-ganged or whatever it is the British Army does?'

'Miss, I didn't know what I was letting m'self in for. If you come from where I come from, you'd be joining even the Zulus. I dunno nobody in the army out here who don't want to get out of it, except the officers and them fellers who've gone soft in the head from the heat and the dysentery and the fever, yes.'

In certain ways I was very innocent in those days. 'But if you wanted a life of adventure, then you have it, haven't you?'

'Miss, who said anything about a life of adventure? That wasn't why I come out here.' He sighed, all at once looking very sad and small. 'You sign up for seven years and if you're a bit soft in the head and they talk you into signing up again, you're out here for another five years. We get just over a bob a day, take away the stoppages – sometimes they stop you an anna for blowing your nose at the wrong time. They stop you for this, they stop you for that – sometimes I've gone a month without drawing a penny. Everywhere is out of bounds – they want you to live in the barracks, like you was in a convent. Well, I mean a monastery, you know what I mean. You never get to talk to a woman like I'm talking to you now – a native bint comes around and some officer or the sergeant-major, he shoos her off like she was a leper or something. It's parades, parades, parades – parade for mess, parade for drill, parade for church. And me a Catholic amongst a lot of Orangemen. And when you ain't parading you're marching from one end of the blooming country to the other, yes. You ever been down the Great Trunk Road, miss? You oughta see that. Us poor blighters on the line of march up and down it, passing each other, going nowhere like only the army can send you. Then there's the fever and the rash and the terrible food . . . If I had my way I'd give India back to the coolies and tell 'em to – ' He broke off, looking embarrassed again. 'Sorry, miss. I got a bit carried away then.'

'Where will you go if you manage to get away?'

'America, Australia, somewhere where you can be something else but a ranker in an army that thinks you're only half-human. Most of the officers don't care about you and the officers' wives are even worse – '

'Is Major Farnol like that?' I hoped to God he wasn't.

'I dunno, miss. I think he's a bit more human than some of 'em.'

I stood up and he also rose. I looked past him at our reflection in the mirror-wall; we were reflected again and again. We looked ridiculous, I in my peignoir and he in his torn and dirty uniform; a battalion of soldiers and their camp followers? I just wondered how reliable a protector he would turn out to be. I shouldn't blame him if he was concerned only for himself.

'I must get dressed to go downstairs, Mr Ahearn. I shall have to ask you to turn your back again, please. No, don't face the mirror. Go back and face the door.'

I dressed carefully, even though there was a strange man in my room. I don't wish to go into my *affaires d'amour*, but there had been occasions when I had dressed with a man in my room, though none of them had been strangers. But I did not allow Private Ahearn's presence to hurry me. I was preparing myself to compete against the Ranee when I got downstairs.

When I was ready I allowed Private Ahearn to turn round. 'You look beautiful, miss. A real credit to the Irish.'

'Thank you, Mr Ahearn. There is some fruit in a bowl over there. I'll try and smuggle up some hot food to you later. Perhaps Major Farnol's bearer, Karim Singh, can do that.'

'Major Farnol's already thought of that, miss.'

'Major Farnol seems to think of everything.'

I went downstairs, stopping twice to ask directions of a servant; it was like being a guest in Grand Central Station in the early hours of the morning. The Ranee had described the palace as *home*; but one couldn't describe it as homely. I finally came down into the entrance hall and there was Prince Mahendra at the foot of the stairs. He was dressed for the evening, in colours even more gorgeous than those he had worn that afternoon.

As I discovered a little later, all the gentlemen were in evening dress. In those days in India, even on remote out-stations, gentlemen always dressed for dinner; it was called 'keeping up appearances' and I must say that it appealed to me. It was probably foolish, sometimes uncomfortable and often inconvenient; but the gentlemen kept up their standards. Younger readers may laugh at such social snobberies, but every generation has its idiosyncrasies. I find it amusing that the world today has been captured by four grown young men who affect Buster Brown haircuts and swear like longshoremen.

Prince Mahendra was certainly dressed for the evening; in sunlight he would have blinded one. He wore pink silk: long *achkan*, tight ankle-length breeches, silk slippers; his turban was pink-and-purple stripes. He appeared to be wearing so many rings, necklaces and bracelets I wonder that he was not bent over under the weight of them all. Then his sister came down the stairs and beside her he paled into a piece of paste jewellery. There is a point beyond which vulgarity has its own splendour. Some sunsets are vulgarly splendid or splendidly vulgar and the Ranee could have taken her place with them.

'What lovely pearls, Miss O'Brady!' She squinted as if she were having some difficulty in seeing my single strand. 'A present from an admirer?' Her tone implied that he must have been an impoverished one.

'No, I bought them myself.'

'American women are so independent. I treasure my own independence . . .' Then she looked at her brother. 'Bobs, you've been at the treasury again. I've told you before – you must ask me before you go in there and start decorating yourself.'

Bobs pouted. 'I did it for you. I thought you would want to impress your guests.'

She gave him a forgiving smile. 'Dear Bobs. Of course. Thank you.'

I mentioned in an earlier chapter of these memoirs that the most fateful dinner party I ever attended was at Viceregal Lodge at Simla. The dinner at the palace of Serog was almost as fateful and not a little bizarre. The dining-hall was immense, with fluted columns rising out of the walls to support a domed ceiling so high that it was lost in shadows above the glow of the oil lamps hung along the walls. There were four huge fireplaces in which log fires blazed; one needed their warmth in that vast hall. It was rather like dining in Canterbury cathedral, though there was no feeling that anyone had ever knelt down there to say a prayer or two.

All the plate and cutlery was solid gold; the wine goblets were gold and encrusted with rubies. The wine was French, the absolutely best clarets and champagne. The food was a mixture of English and Indian cooking at its very worst. The soup was an offering that was a desecration of the golden bowl in which it was served; the fish, had it still been alive, could have swum contentedly in the water which flooded my plate; the curried camel, for it could have been nothing else (I am sure I got part of the hump as my serving) was just a plateful of yellow jaundice. The sweet was an English trifle, a concoction of stale cake set by a bricklayer in a mortar of custard. Admittedly it was pot luck for unexpected guests, but with two thousand staff it could have been expected that at least one or two of them could have whipped up a decent meal.

Everyone but Prince Mahendra had been drinking more than their proper share of wine, obviously intent on washing away the taste of what they were eating. Some could hold their wine; others could not. One of those who could was the Nawab; he and the Ranee evidently ignored their religion's ban on liquor. One of those who could not was Magda Monday, who, I'm sure, had no religion but herself.

'I have played in England with Ranji.' The Nawab was trying to explain to her the pleasures of cricket. 'Prince Ranjitsinhji. To see him step down the wicket and drive the rising ball – Ah! It is like making love to a beautiful, responsive woman!'

'Really?' Magda, even if she had been totally sober, did not look as if she could imagine the pleasure of being made love to by a cricketer who could drive a rising ball, whatever that is. She looked across the table at Baron von Albern, who was sitting on the Ranee's left and on my right. 'Do you understand this English cricket, Herr Baron? Do they play it in Berlin?'

'I do not know,' said the Baron. 'Did you play any cricket there this summer, Bertie?'

Major Farnol was sitting across the table from me, on the Ranee's right. He had been about to drink from his goblet, but he abruptly paused; above the mask of gold and rubies I saw his quick sideways glance along the table at the Nawab.

Bertie himself suddenly seemed to have lost all his enthusiasm for cricket.

'What were you doing in Germany?' said Farnol. 'I thought you always spent all the summer in England, playing cricket every day?'

'It rained for a few days, washing out any cricket. I just popped over to Berlin to buy some Dresden figurines. I collect them, you know.' It was such an obvious spur-of-the-moment fabrication that even I could see it.

'No,' said Farnol. 'I didn't know that. I thought you collected only cricket bats and balls.'

The Nawab laughed heartily; one could almost see him forcing the laugh out of himself. 'You're so droll, Clive.'

'I've heard,' said Lady Westbrook from where she sat between the Nawab and Prince Mahendra, 'that Har Dayal was in Berlin this year.'

'No,' said the Ranee from the top of the table, 'the last I heard he was in California, at some place called Berkeley.'

'Who is Har Dayal?' I asked.

There was silence for a moment. It struck me even then that only Magda Monday and I did not know who he was; even Zoltan Monday, sitting on my left, had stiffened when Har Dayal's name was mentioned. Magda, quite tipsy now, slurped in the silence as she took another sip of champagne.

Then Prince Mahendra said, 'He is the leader of our principal revolutionary movement. He was at Oxford five or six years ago and since then he has hated the English.'

'He should have gone to Cambridge,' said the Nawab, in control again. 'Look at me – who loves the English more than I?'

'What would he be doing in California?' I asked.

'He is there trying to corrupt the Sikhs who emigrated to America some years ago.' The reputedly half-mad Mahendra seemed remarkably well-informed about a world from which he had cut himself off. He was better informed about parts of America than I was; I didn't know there had been any Sikh immigrants into California, though I learned later it was true. He looked along the table at his sister and smiled. 'Am I talking too much, dear Mala?'

'Dear Bobs, of course not.' She ducked her head under its

skullcap of diamonds, bent over her trifle in a glitter of hard light.

Farnol was looking across the table at Zoltan Monday. 'You appear to know Har Dayal, Mr Monday. Has he ever tried to buy arms from you?'

'I once met him in Constantinople. He was not in the market for arms then.'

'A pity,' said his wife, in the market for more wine; she tapped her empty goblet and looked over her shoulder at the servant who stood behind her. Each of us had a uniformed servant standing behind his or her chair and Magda had kept her man busy pouring champagne. 'Krupps sends poor Zoltan nasty little notes when he doesn't sell his quota of guns. Would you care to buy half a dozen howitzers, Your Highness?'

I'm sure everyone thought she was addressing the Ranee; instead she looked sideways at the Nawab. I thought for a moment he was going to hit her with his wine goblet; then he lowered it slowly to the table and smiled. He was not the best actor I'd seen, but he wasn't bad.

'I'm a peaceful man, Madame Monday. All I shoot are tigers and one doesn't need howitzers for that. Isn't that so, Bobs? You were the only man who could shoot more tigers than I.'

'Bobs never goes shooting now.' The Ranee was too quick with her intrusion; I saw Mahendra stare furiously at her. I saw with horror the madness about to break through the thin dark mask; but the Ranee saw it too. She rose abruptly, finishing the meal. 'We'll have coffee in the Peacock Room.'

It sounded as if we were dining in a hotel, were about to repair to some side room with one of those fancy labels so beloved of hotel managements; but I don't think I remarked it at that moment. I was still sitting watching Mahendra. He jumped to his feet, sending his chair back with such force that it almost knocked over the servant standing behind it. He whirled (there was no other word for it; I should not have been surprised if he had spun right round like a Dervish) and literally ran out of the room. The Ranee lifted a hand and four servants disappeared after the fleeing prince. I noticed that the four servants were her own men who had been at her end of the table, not the palace servants who had been serving the rest of us.

She gave us all a smile as bright and hard as the blaze of diamonds on her head. 'Bobs is having another of his little attacks. Excuse him.'

Only Magda and I seemed to be surprised by Mahendra's queer behaviour. It could not have been British phlegm, *sang-froid*, call it what you will, that kept the others discreetly polite, as if they had seen nothing out of the ordinary. Perhaps Major Farnol and Lady Westbrook could have claimed such a social asset; but not the German, the Indian and the Hungarian. The Baron, the Nawab and Zoltan Monday acted as if they had spent all their lives in Mahendra's company and knew that the only way to live with his madness was to ignore it.

As we went out of the room Lady Westbrook said, 'I shall come in for coffee in a moment, Mala. I think I should like a little walk first to settle that beautiful dinner. What about you, Miss O'Brady?'

I am not slow to catch an invitation, especially one accompanied with a stare that dared me to refuse. 'A very good idea, Lady Westbrook.'

'Call me Viola,' she said as she led me down a wide corridor away from the rest of them. She put a cheroot in her holder and began rummaging in her huge handbag, which would not have been out of place carried by a Pony Express rider, for a box of matches. 'You and I may have to be allies. Do you mind if I call you Bridie?'

'Do by all means. And please tell me, what's going on in this place?' I felt as if I were on some sort of loom, slowly being woven into a pattern that, because I was part of it, I couldn't see.

She got her cheroot lit, puffed on it. 'I only half-understand it all myself. I don't know if you should try to find out. Perhaps it would be better if you confined yourself to Lola Montez and went no further.'

'I'm afraid I haven't given a thought to Miss Montez in the past twenty-four hours.'

The corridor seemed to stretch for miles ahead of us, a long gloomy tunnel lit by yellow oil lamps. It was cold in here after the warmth of the dining-hall. Archways led into side galleries and as we walked along servants, some of them armed with long swords, materialized like dark djinns out of the shadows, then faded back into them. Somewhere out in the moonlit gardens a peacock screeched. Then I heard a harsh coughing sound.

'A leopard,' said Viola. 'I haven't been to this palace since I was a gel. I came here once with my husband. But I remember Mala and Bobs' father had a large menagerie – leopards, tigers, those fighting elephants you saw outside the gates. I suppose Bobs still keeps the animals.'

We at last reached the end of the corridor and turned to retrace our steps. As we did so a man stepped out of the shadows of an archway, stumbled across the corridor, walked straight into the wall and slid down it. He crouched there on his knees, his face against the wall, then he slowly turned round and sat down, his face turned up to us, his staring eyes showing no recognition of Lady Westbrook or myself.

It was Major Savanna.

End of extract from memoirs.

2

Farnol put down his coffee cup and said quietly to the Nawab, 'You'd better tell me about Berlin, Bertie.'

'I don't think it is any of your business, Clive.' The Nawab kept his voice low. The two men were sitting slightly apart from the others in the Peacock Room, a magnificent salon hardly designed as a coffee annexe. The Nawab, who had a modest fifty-room palace, had been looking around enviously at what Mala and Bobs possessed. Every time he came here he entertained the idea of proposing marriage to Mala.

'Perhaps none of mine, Bertie. But it could be the business of the Government – you know how they feel about the Germans. It used to be the Russians, but now it's the

Germans. Did you meet Har Dayal while you were in Berlin buying your Dresden pieces?'

'You're not your usual amiable self, Clive.' He patted at his white tie with a nervous hand. Unlike Mahendra he was dressed English style for dinner; it occurred to Farnol that he had never seen Bertie in an *achkan* or any other style of Indian dress. He wondered what Bertie's subjects thought of their prince who so assiduously aped the British. 'Do relax, please.'

'Bertie, someone's trying to kill me.'

The Nawab had been smiling, trying to keep the conversation on a light plane; but now he sobered. 'You really do think you're the only target?'

'Yes.'

'Why?'

But Farnol no longer trusted the Nawab. He had never been a close friend, they never saw enough of each other for such a friendship to develop, but he had always looked upon him as one of his more likeable acquaintances. But it was six months since he had last seen the Nawab and a change had taken place in him. A change brought on, perhaps, by a visit to Berlin?

'You're not going to tell me anything about Berlin?'

'No, Clive.'

Then Bridie, breathless from running, appeared in the doorway. 'Major Farnol -, come quickly! It's Major Savanna!'

Though Farnol was on his feet at once he missed nothing of the reactions of the others in the room. Everyone but Magda responded to the name *Savanna*, even Zoltan Monday. The Ranee put a nervous hand to her throat, covering up a lode of diamonds in the choker she wore. The Nawab seemed to go grey under his dark skin; his cup rattled in its saucer as he put it down. And the Baron looked across at Monday and gave just the slightest shake of his head.

Then everyone rose to follow Farnol as, holding Bridie's arm, he hurried down the long corridor. He shouted for Karim, his voice echoing and re-echoing down from the high vaulted ceiling, and by the time he and Bridie reached the end of the corridor the tall Sikh had come running, his *kris* at the ready.

Lady Westbrook stood up from where she had been kneeling beside the semi-conscious Savanna, her bones creaking as she did so. She rubbed her knees, gasped for breath. 'I was never one for being on my knees, even when I was young. He's in a bad way, Clive. He looks as if he's been drugged.'

'Karim, get a couple of the servants to take him up to my room – '

'There are plenty of other rooms.' The Ranee had arrived. She was somewhat breathless, unaccustomed as she was to moving at anything above a graceful walk; she could make love for hours, but that was another form of exercise altogether. Her breathlessness made her look flustered, something Farnol had never seen before. 'There's a room opposite my suite – '

'No,' said Farnol flatly. 'He goes into my room. He's my responsibility. Lady Westbrook, Miss O'Brady – would you come with me? I may need your help.'

'Perhaps I could help?' said Zoltan Monday. 'I was once a medical student – '

'No, thank you.' One part of Farnol's mind cynically waited for the Nawab and the Baron to offer their help; but they both held back. 'I'll let you know, Mala, if I need any more help.'

Up in Farnol's room Savanna was laid out on the big bed. Farnol dismissed the two servants and told Karim to undress the now almost unconscious man. As if careful of their modesty, he led Bridie and Lady Westbrook across to the windows, careful to keep their backs to the bed where Karim, not very carefully or gently, was pulling off the major's ragged clothes.

'He looks as if he's been through hell,' said Lady Westbrook.

'I think he probably has been. He's been pumped full of God knows what. I've seen tribesmen in these hills who looked just as he does.'

'What happens to them?' said Bridie.

'They start to come out of it, or so you think, then all of a sudden they become uncontrollable and in a minute or two they're dead.'

'We must prevent that,' said Lady Westbrook. 'Get Karim

to get me some mustard. I'll mix it up and feed it to him, it will make him vomit. Clean out his stomach.'

Farnol looked across at the bed where Karim was now pulling up the sheet over the undressed Savanna. 'You can't give him that while he's unconscious. If he comes round, we'll try it. Go down to the kitchens, Karim, and ask for some mustard. On your way tell Private Ahearn to come across here from Miss O'Brady's room. Tell him to make sure he's not seen.'

'Private Ahearn? Who the devil's he?' said Lady Westbrook. 'I wish you'd tell me what's going on, Clive.'

Without hesitation and very succinctly Farnol told her everything, about Private Ahearn and about his own suspicions of a plot to assassinate the King. She was a far from stupid woman and she did not dismiss his suspicions as rubbish. She was seventy years old and she had lived in this country for fifty-two of them, ever since she had come out as the bride of Lieutenant Roger Westbrook. She had missed the Mutiny by only two years; she still remembered the aftermath of bitterness and suspicion. Her husband had spent most of his adult life doing just what Farnol was doing, ostensibly advising the princes and hill chieftains on how best to get along with the Raj but always with a finger in the political waters to note a change in temperature or in the current. Four times she had nursed him when he had come home wounded by would-be assassins; he had never had to tell her that the British Raj was not universally loved. Nowadays she lived amongst tea parties and gymkhana picnics and dances in Simla, sustained by her port and cheroots and gossip, but she had never lost her perspective or her memories of the hatred that still simmered in India after the Mutiny. There was a blind ex-sepoy in Simla, no older than herself, who had seen the bloody revenge taken by the British and one afternoon, sightless eyes staring down the years, had told her all about it in a sing-song voice devoid of any emotion. She believed every word Farnol now told her and did not think of deriding him.

'Do you think Bridie is in danger, too?'

'Yes. I don't know whether they mean to kill her or kidnap her and try to get at me through her.' He looked at Bridie. 'In future don't go wandering off like you did tonight after dinner.'

Bridie nodded. She was tense and nervous again; she looked across at the limp figure of Savanna and saw herself lying there in his stead. 'Do I stay in here with you all night?'

'I think it will be safest. Will you stay too, Viola?'

'Oh God, I've always hated playing chaperone. I always feel I'm spoiling the young people's fun. Do you really think any of those downstairs will care if you two spend the night together? That Madame Monday is probably already asleep, she was so tipsy – can't stand women who can't hold their drink. As for Mala, she wouldn't know what one meant if one mentioned moral decorum.'

'It's Mala I don't want in here. If I'm left alone with Savanna, she'll insist on keeping me company. I don't trust her and it has nothing to do with moral decorum, as you so nicely put it.'

Then the door opened and Karim Singh and Private Ahearn slipped into the room. Karim looked around at everyone, then at Farnol. 'Getting jolly crowded, sahib.'

'The more, the safer,' said Farnol. 'What's going on outside?'

'Nobody's there, not even that chap outside Her Highness' door.'

Ahearn was looking at Savanna in the bed. 'Is he dead, sir?'

'No. But he may be before we can get him out of here. What's the matter?'

Ahearn had made a sour face. 'I'm wishing I'd stayed up in Simla, sir.'

'I'm glad you didn't, Ahearn. I may need you.'

'That's what I'm afraid of,' said Ahearn and sounded like the sad Celts of all time.

Farnol sat down on the bed beside Savanna, turned the slack grey face towards him. The only patch of colour in it was the ginger moustache, which looked now like some clown's crude make-up. 'Rupert – it's Clive Farnol. Why are you here?'

But the pale blue eyes were even paler than Farnol remembered, clouded pools of idiocy; they stared at Farnol without any recognition of what they saw, if they saw anything at all. Savanna's breathing was so shallow that Farnol, suddenly fearful, leaned forward to make sure that the man was not dead. But Savanna still lived, if only just.

'Was there anything in Major Savanna's clothes, Karim? Any notebook, a piece of paper?'

'Nothing, sahib. Someone tore all the pockets of his tunic. They turned his trouser pockets inside out. They were jolly thorough.'

Farnol stood up. 'Viola, mix up the mustard. Give it to Savanna only if he regains consciousness – send Karim for me as soon as he does. Karim, you and Private Ahearn are responsible for the two ladies and the Major. Don't let anyone in the room – *anyone*! Use your *kris* or even your guns if you have to.'

'Jolly good, sir,' said Karim, but he didn't look happy and neither did Ahearn. 'I shall try to use persuasion first – '

'Naturally. I don't want you chopping up the wrong people by mistake.'

'I'll tell him to chop them up if they're the wrong people.' Lady Westbrook was not bloodthirsty but she was not averse to the spilling of it in a good cause. 'We'll be all right, Clive. Go and do what you have to.'

'What do you have to do?' said Bridie.

'Try and get to the bottom of all this. I'm not going to learn anything by turning my back on it – all I'll probably get is a knife in it.' Then he thought his tone was too harsh and he softened it. 'I'm sorry. I shouldn't be so blunt.'

'It's the only way,' said Lady Westbrook. 'Pussyfooting never won wars. And I think we may have a small war of our own right now.'

When Farnol got out into the corridor he paused for a while, put out a hand and leaned against the wall. He was not the sort of man who thrived on danger; he was satisfied if he survived it. He was no coward, but he did not relish the thought of being killed; three attempts to kill him meant that the odds were shortening. Sooner or later a bullet or a knife was going to strike home and he could not bring himself to be fatalistic about the prospect. He could feel the shifting in the foundations of himself, courage turning to sand.

As he started to walk down the corridor he was surprised at

the quietness and the utter absence of anyone, even a servant. It was as if there had been a general desertion and he wondered who had ordered it. His heels clicked like bone against bone on the marble floor; the oil lamps glowed dimly like lamps for the dead. He had the sudden strange impression of walking through catacombs; he looked for skeletons but there were none. He walked on to a thick rug without seeing it and the sudden silence of his footsteps was like the shock of a pistol shot. He went down the wide stairs, feeling the night chill taking hold of the palace. He wondered if he would find any of the other guests still in the palace.

But if the others had, indeed, departed in a hurry, Baron von Albern was still on hand. He sat in the Peacock Room, which he had not left even after Bridie had raised the alarm about Savanna's dramatic re-appearance. He was smoking a cigar and drinking port and thinking of other, greener hills than those that surrounded the palace, the hills of Thuringia. He would be going home there next year and he wondered how many peaceful years he would have left to enjoy them.

He looked up as Farnol came into the room but, contrary to his usual punctilious politeness, he did not rise. 'Forgive me, Major. I am a tired old man this evening.'

Farnol sat down, poured himself a glass of port. 'Where is everyone?'

Kurt von Albern gave a sort of facial shrug. With only one hand, he was limited in his gestures. He expressed everything with his face, keeping his one hand only for essentials. He had lost the arm forty years ago in the war against the French and, when alone, still bitterly regretted its loss. It had been his sword-wielding arm, his love-making hand: there had been no conquests after its loss. Only magnanimous apologies from men with whom he would have otherwise fought a duel and ball-destroying love-making from women who took him to bed out of pity. He stubbed out his cigar and picked up his port.

'I fear everyone has retired, even the servants. The decanter is almost empty, but no one has come in to see if I want any more. Perhaps you would care to bang that gong?'

'Not yet, Baron. I'd like you to tell me if you know anything about what's going on. I don't think you've been entirely open with me.'

'I could plead diplomatic immunity.' But the Baron smiled. 'Major, you and I should be friends. I'm German, but I'm not your enemy.'

'Not yet.' Then it was Farnol's turn to smile, to take the edge off that remark. 'I mean the Kaiser. Nobody knows what he has planned for the future.'

The Baron nodded morosely. He put down his port and took off his glasses; he looked older without them, as some people do. He let them hang by their black silk ribbon while he picked up his drink again. 'We're all at the mercy of those who rule us. A cliché, but so true.'

'But even at our level we can occasionally change the course of events.'

'Perhaps you, Major. But I'm too old.' Or felt too old, which can be worse.

Farnol put down his glass, leaned forward, kept his voice low. Whispers could be magnified in such a room as this; the palace had been built by a Mogul prince who, surrounded by intrigue, had wanted nothing kept secret from him. The room, round with a domed ceiling, had no corners to absorb sound; in the mosaic gardens of the tiled walls peacocks stood alert listening. Farnol wondered how many men had condemned themselves with their own voices here in this room.

'Baron, how did you know the Nawab had been in Berlin this summer?'

'A friend in Berlin sent me the information. The Nawab was there without any official invitation.' He did indeed feel old tonight, old enough not to want to be burdened by minor diplomatic secrets. 'It was as much a surprise to me when I learned of it as it was this evening to you. He has never shown any sympathy for Germany.'

'I'm more worried that he might be showing sympathy for Har Dayal or some of the other revolutionaries. There are Germans who are very sympathetic towards Har, colleagues of yours in the Foreign Office in Berlin.'

'Why do you always suspect us so much?' It was a rhetorical question and the Baron knew it; but it was heartfelt, because he admired England and things English, if not all the English themselves. 'You should worry about the Russians. Look at what they are doing in Persia this very minute, doing everything they can to put it under their thumb. They have forced the Persians to get rid of their American economic adviser, Shuster, some name like that – ' He sighed, feeling suddenly very tired as well as old. His memory could no longer cling to minor details; names, unless they were linked to a face, slipped away like drops of water off the waterproof skin of a diplomatic wallet. 'How do you know about the meddlers in Berlin? It isn't official policy to stir up trouble here in India.'

'Baron – ' Farnol smiled. He liked the old man, wished he knew him well enough to have spent more time with him. 'You know as well as I do that subversion is never official policy. When Lord Curzon sent Younghusband up into Tibet, it wasn't official policy. It was something decided upon by Lord Curzon and London only sanctioned it when it was too late to stop it. It's been like that ever since governments were invented and it will go on being like that. As you said, we're all at the mercy of those who rule us. But we're also at the mercy of meddlers at a lower level. I've been guilty of it myself on a very low level. It's called historical anticipation or, if you like, don't let's leave everything to our stupid rulers.'

Kurt von Albern put his glasses back on, smiled, perked up a little. 'You should not spend so much time out in the field, Major. You would have made my time in Simla much happier if you had worked there. One doesn't get much appealing cynicism up there, except occasionally from an Indian.'

'The Mondays – ' Farnol did not want to be sidetracked into a discussion on cynicism. 'You must know more about them than you've told me.'

The Baron shook his head. 'Truly I do not. What little I saw of them in Simla, they were delightful company, especially Frau Monday . . .' He had reached an age when women, even those full of pity, no longer took him to their beds; so he looked at young women and dreamed of what he had once enjoyed. 'I don't think she is quite of his class, but she knows how to make an old man feel younger. Or wish he were so. There's no political harm in her, Major. Sexual harm, perhaps, but nothing else.'

'And Herr Monday?'

'Ah – ' He drained the last drop from his glass of port, looked at the empty decanter, decided it would be too much bother even to strike the gong for a servant to bring more port. 'No diplomat ever really welcomes an arms salesman coming to his door wanting patronage. It contradicts diplomacy. Herr Monday brought a most comprehensive catalogue with him. He is trying to sell more than hunting rifles.'

'To whom?'

'If I knew, Major, I should let you know. I do not want us falling out. Not just you and I. England and Germany.'

Farnol stood up, knowing the Baron was telling the truth and he would get no more from him. As he did so he saw Albern suddenly look past him. 'Ach – a servant at last! Get me more port. We'll have a last night-cap, Major.'

'I am sorry, sahib, I am not one of the palace servants – I do not know where the drink is kept. I am one of the Ranee's men. She has sent me here to ask Major Farnol to come to her rooms.'

The old diplomat got slowly and heavily to his feet. 'Oh, I envy you, Major. Or should I?'

Farnol still had enough humour in him to be able to smile. 'Not tonight, Baron. I'll see you in the morning. We'll be leaving early, I hope.'

He followed the servant through the silent halls and corridors, came at last to the door of the Ranee's suite. The giant Sikh stood outside it again, the point of his big sword between his feet, his hands resting on the hilt. He lifted the sword and Farnol, still on edge, tensed, thinking he was going to be struck by it; but the Sikh was only raising it in salute as he stepped aside for Farnol to go into the room. The door was closed behind him and for some reason that amused him, Farnol waited for the turning of a key in the lock but there was none.

The Ranee's bedroom could have accommodated a small durbar; arches opened into two other large rooms for any overflow. Farnol had spent nights in several bedrooms with the Ranee, but the size of this room, he felt, would have made him impotent; it would have been like making love in a theatre with the audience likely to file into their seats at any moment. The Ranee, dressed in diaphanous pink, was reclining on a divan at the foot of the great canopied bed. She looked almost comical in her seductiveness but Farnol knew better than to smile. Mala saw no humour in any role she played.

The room, Farnol noticed at once, was unusually warm. Rooms of such size, with their tessellated floors and high ceilings, were difficult to heat in the cold months in these mountains. Then he saw the giant ceramic-fronted stoves in the four corners.

'A present to my father by the Russians,' said the Ranee. 'From Tsar Alexander the Third himself. Those were the days when the English were afraid that the Russian bear was ready to come down into India and gobble them up. Sit here, Clive darling. Come on, I'm not going to gobble you up.'

He sat down on the end of the divan like an apprehensive schoolboy. Then abruptly he smiled and relaxed, let his eyes enjoy the Ranee. She wore nothing under the smoke-thin gown; she was naked in a pink mist. She had taken off all her jewellery except a wide diamond bracelet and her rings: there had to be a limit to one's nakedness.

'What are you smiling at?'

'Mala, are you trying to seduce me?'

'Clive darling, if you're willing, so am I. That's why I had all the stoves lit, so you wouldn't feel the cold when you took your clothes off.'

He shook his head. 'You can dampen the fires – and yourself. I'm not taking anything off. Mala, what is Major Savanna doing here in the palace?'

'Why don't you ask him?'

'I'm sure you already know that he's drugged and may be dying.'

She put her foot, in its purple silk sandal, into his lap, moved her heel into his groin. He took hold of the foot and, gently at first, then tightening his grip, slowly twisted it. He had always believed that every man, and every woman (or at least every woman he had made love to), had a streak of sadism in him or her. He allowed the streak in himself to widen.

'You'd better tell me what you know, Mala, or I'll cripple you. You'll never be half as attractive hobbling around on a crippled foot.'

He had not expected her to cry out, to surrender at once: that wasn't Mala. But he had also not expected her to endure the pain as long as she did; she stared at him, only a tightening round the full mouth hinting at the pain she was feeling. He could feel the tendons stretching, the bones ready to grind against each other; then he felt the strength draining out of his own hand. He let go her foot, found himself sweating.

She drew up her foot, massaged it, then stretched her leg back towards him again; but this time the foot rested beside his thigh, not in his lap. 'You had better take off your tie and coat, Clive. You're sweating like some little office-wallah from Calcutta.'

He undid his white tie, slipped off his tail-coat. His starched shirt-front seemed ready to pop out of his waistcoat. 'You should not tempt me, Mala.'

'Tempt you to hurt me? Was I doing that?'

Abruptly angry, he jumped to his feet and walked away from her. 'Dammit, don't let's beat about the bush! Tell me what's going on or I'll have it arranged that you'll be barred from the Durbar, that you won't even get near the King!'

'You're not that important, Clive – you don't have that sort of influence. If you knew the men I'd slept with, you wouldn't make such a foolish threat. I'll attend the Durbar, whatever you think you can do. But you really don't think I'm planning to kill the King, do you?'

It took him a moment, in his anger, to get his thoughts together. Then: 'Who told you I think there is a plot to assassinate him? Major Savanna is the only one who knows what I suspect.'

'No, darling.' She stood up, tested her foot before she walked on it, then came towards him. Beneath the gossamer veil of her gown he could see the body he had once known so well. But he could resist it now: or so he told himself. 'You as much as told me yourself, at dinner at the Lodge last night And someone has not been trying to kill you just because you're a political agent. I suppose they've tried that before, but not three times in four days. You may be right – someone may well be planning to assassinate the King. But it's not me, darling.'

He didn't know whether to believe her or not. Her tongue could be as devious in lying as in loving. 'All right, I do think there is a plot of some sort. But I have no evidence of it and nothing may ever come of it, it may just turn out to be a brainstorm of mine. But that doesn't alter what's happened to Rupert Savanna. So you'd better tell me what you know, because I'm not going to let it rest. I'll keep at you all the way down to Delhi and then there I'll have Colonel Lathrop take over. I know *he* hasn't slept with you. His wife takes care of him too well.'

She sighed, lifted her arms above her head: the breasts rose up under the gown. He waited for her to yawn; she looked ready for bed, to dismiss him just by turning her back. Then she lowered her arms, crossed to a chair and sat down, drawing the gown about her in a flimsy show of modesty (though he knew she was incapable of modesty).

'Clive, Major Savanna has had his own little plot. He's been trying to turn Bobs against me.'

Farnol pulled up another chair, sat down opposite her. All the seductive posturing was out of the way now; they were getting down to brass – no, in her case, golden tacks. He might even get the truth from her.

'Why should Savanna want to involve himself in your affairs? You're the rightful ruler of Serog and you're the one the Government recognizes. Why should we British want to bother ourselves with someone as – as unstable as your brother?'

'Clive, the English have been trying to topple kings and princes for centuries – it's their principal overseas sport. Not cricket, as foolish Bertie seems to think. I know I'm not popular with my people. It doesn't worry me. I don't believe in the Hereafter, so I'm not going to trouble myself by

building up any heavenly credits amongst a lot of ignorant
peasants.'

He smiled. 'Why are you honest only when you're so
despicable?'

'Don't try to flatter me, Clive.'

His smile widened and he shook his head. 'All right, no
flattery. But you are dodging another question. Why do the
English want you moved out and Bobs moved in?'

'I didn't say they did. I said Major Savanna did. Now
whether that means the same thing, I don't know. Perhaps
you'd have to ask my brother.'

'I'll do that.' But he had no faith that he would get an
honest answer, if one at all, from Mahendra. 'How long has
this – this plot of Savanna's been going on?'

'I'm not sure. I only learned of it two days ago. Last night I
told Major Savanna what I knew. That was when I said he
would have me to answer to.'

It all sounded truthful enough. Then: 'It wasn't you who
had the train stopped, so that we'd have to come down this
way? No, you're a plotter yourself, Mala, but that would be
too elaborate. It was just sheer chance, was it?'

'Yes. You see, the gods do smile on the wicked occasionally.
They love their little ironies, just like the rest of us.'

'Were you going to go on down to Delhi and wait till after
the Durbar before you did anything about Savanna and your
brother?'

'No. I knew that Bobs is also coming down to the Durbar.
He was planning to kill me in Delhi, but now he has the
chance to kill me any time between now and the Durbar. He
told me tonight he is coming with us in the morning.'

3

Lady Westbrook, declaring that she would be safe since no
one was interested in killing off an old bird like herself, had
gone back to her own room. Private Ahearn was sent across to
Bridie's room to sleep; Karim Singh made himself as

comfortable as he could outside Farnol's door and settled down to guard his master. That left Farnol and Bridie alone with the still unconscious Savanna.

'Did you try to feed him any of the mustard?' Farnol said.

'No. He might have vomited and choked. We'll just have to be patient.'

'We?'

'I'm as interested in the mystery of all this as much as you are. Not just from a story angle, either. It's personal now.' She was surprised at how concerned she had become for his safety, though she was not yet prepared to tell him so. 'How did you fare with the Ranee?'

'How did you know I'd been with her?'

'I could smell her perfume on you when you came back in here.'

'There was much less of that faring, as you put it, than you suspect. Mala had her designs on me – '

'Oh my God!' Her reaction was a defensive one, against letting her feelings get away from her. Attack the man if you don't want to be too attracted to him . . . 'Do you have any modesty about your charms?'

He considered for a moment. 'No, I don't think I have. Modesty is only an inferiority complex raised to being a virtue.'

Well, she had always told herself she liked a man with an air of arrogance about him. 'Go on,' she said resignedly.

'One must face facts and I take it that, as a journalist, that's all you're interested in? She had designs on me and I declined her offer. May I go on further?'

'Do.' She glanced at the still form of Savanna, glad that he could not hear this conversation. She knew that the conversation, flippant and trivial as it was, was a dance in which she and Farnol were trying to fit their steps together. They were life-and-death partners who didn't yet know each other well enough for things to be taken for granted.

'I learned quite a lot from Mala, but all it seems to have done is deepen the mystery.' He told her of Savanna's attempt to drive a wedge between the Ranee and her brother. He did not tell her that the Ranee suspected Mahendra might try to kill her on the journey down to Delhi. He kept that information to himself in order to protect her from further worry, if from nothing else. He would have to see that she did not keep close company with the Ranee, though, knowing Mala, he thought that possibility would be remote. 'I don't think I'll get to the bottom of it all until Major Savanna comes out of his coma.'

'If he comes out . . .'

He looked at Savanna, grey and still as an effigy of himself. 'Yes. If . . .'

Bridie sighed, sat back in her chair, all at once tired by the long frightening day. 'Is it always like this for you? Is this what running an Empire means?'

'I don't run the Empire any more than you run your newspaper. I'm only a cog, just as you are.'

'I didn't mean you personally. I meant the whole British Raj. You're masters of, what, four hundred million people? And how many are there of you?'

'Not as many as you would think. A hundred thousand of us at the most, including the army. The whole of the Indian Civil Service, those who make India work, is run by only thirteen hundred British civil servants – they've learned how to delegate minor authority to the Indians and *chee-chees* who work for them. You must have noticed, India isn't over-run with the English.'

'Do you think of yourself as English? Lady Westbrook told me how long your family has been here.' It struck her that she was far less American, by several generations, than he was Indian.

It was a question he had pondered on over the years, ever since he had come back from his schooling in England. 'No, I don't think I really am.'

'Indian, then?'

'No, not that, either.'

'Then what happens to you if India ever demands its independence, as we Americans did? They will, you know, some day.'

He surprised her by nodding. 'Of course they will. But when they do, it will be the intellectuals and the money-makers who will take over and the peasants and the coolies in the cities will be no better off, they'll be just as poor as they ever were. My father once told me that no one will ever solve the economic problems of India. All the Raj has done, he said, was to make chaos work.'

'Will they demand their independence soon?'

'Men like Har Dayal are already demanding it. But how do you get an ocean of people to follow you?'

'You English appear to have done it.'

'No, they're not our followers and we're not their leaders. We couldn't have done as much as we have without the co-operation of the princes. And they will never band together for independence – they'll have too much to lose.'

'So you use the selfishness of all these petty rulers like the Ranee and the Nawab and the bigger maharajahs to keep India under your thumb?'

He smiled. 'I'm surprised you Americans don't burst with your self-righteousness. Some day, when America decides to have an Empire you people will do exactly what we're doing.'

'I hope I never live to see the day.' But even in her own ears she sounded as if she was talking from a pulpit.

Farnol glanced at Savanna, saw the pale blue eyes wide open and looking at him. He got up hurriedly, crossed to the bed, excited by the thought that at least he would be able to question Savanna. But as soon as he leaned over the bed he saw the eyes were blind, unmoving. Savanna was dead. He let out a curse and straightened up, thumping his fist on the bed.

Bridie knew from the curse what had happened. She got up at once, went to the door and opened it. 'You'd better come in, Karim. Major Savanna has just died.'

Farnol remained standing beside the bed; his stare was almost as intense as that of the dead man. Savanna was beyond all the wages of Empire now; he no longer cared about whatever prizes he had hoped to achieve with his intrigue. His place in the order of precedence would no longer be a worry to him; and anonymity might after all be a joy in Paradise. He had died relatively young, as most men did in India; Farnol knew as a fact that one rarely saw old Europeans in the country; his own father at sixty-five was looked upon as a survivor. Farnol was a man in whom pity ran deep and, though he had never liked Savanna, all at once he felt sorry for the dead man. To die from poisoning somehow took all the dignity and honour of one's dying.

'Wrap him up in the sheet, Karim,' he said. 'We'll bury him first thing in the morning. Get some of the servants to dig a grave.'

Karim bundled up the body, slung it across his shoulder; in such a country as his he was accustomed to the dead, they were part of the landscape. 'I'll put him across in Miss O'Brady's room, sahib. That Irish chappie can keep an eye on him till morning. You get some sleep.' He had the tact not to say *You and Miss O'Brady get some sleep*: but he nodded at the bed. 'I'll wake you early, sahib, so you can say the prayers for Major Savanna.'

Across the hall in Bridie's room Ahearn looked with horror on the sheet-wrapped bundle Karim brought in and laid on the floor. 'Holy Jay-sus, I can't sleep with him in here!'

'He can't hurt you,' said Karim contemptuously. He could never understand some of the lower levels of the British Army, especially the Irish. They seemed to be full of more fears and superstitions than a child. 'He's dead. You don't have to salute him or anything any more. Just let him lie there and ignore him.'

'Ignorant coolie bastard,' said Ahearn after Karim had gone out and shut the door. He looked down at the body in the sheet, then lay down again on the bed and turned his back on it. 'Jay-sus, Mary and Joseph . . .'

In his room Farnol was saying, 'Do you mind sleeping in the bed after a dead man's been in it?'

'I think I'd rather sleep here on this couch.' Bridie had her sensitivities if not her superstitions. 'My mother thought every bed should be blessed with holy water after someone had died in it.'

Farnol handed her two blankets and a pillow. 'I'll turn my back if you want to undress. You may find it uncomfortable sleeping in your stays.'

'I don't wear a corset when I'm travelling, thank you. But if you would turn your back, I should like to undo a few buttons.'

Farnol lay down on the bed, pulled the remaining blankets over him, undid a few buttons of his own. 'I wish we had met somewhere else. In England, perhaps at some country house party. I once spent a very pleasant weekend – ' Then he smiled. 'But you don't want to hear that.'

'No. Goodnight, Major.'

But Bridie, too, wished that they had met in other circumstances. She felt that if they had, he would not be sleeping in the bed alone.

CHAPTER FIVE

I

Extract from the memoirs of Miss Bridie O'Brady:

Burials, even in the most mundane surroundings, always have their awkward air for us Caucasians, as if we have still not accepted them as part of the routine of living. Grief does take the stiffness out of some, but most of us, those there only to pay respect to the dead, are rigid with disquiet, selfishly aware of who might be lowered into the grave. In that early December morning in that narrow valley in the Himalayas, as we buried Major Savanna, none of us was limp with grief; but we were as awkward as gate-crashers at the wrong party. Not so the hundreds of palace staff who, despite the early hour, materialized to stand in a circle round the newly-dug grave as Karim and Private Ahearn lowered the body into it.

'Can't you shoo them away? Listen to them. It's indecent, all that chatter.'

'There's no privacy in India, m'dear,' said Lady West-brook. 'There are always onlookers. Curiosity is a healthy habit with them. Just ignore 'em.'

I tried to do that, but it was not easy. I stared at the body, still wrapped only in a sheet and with no coffin, as it disappeared into the hole in the brown earth; Major Farnol had said a prayer, in a stiff formal voice that suggested he did not say many prayers in any circumstances at all. Karim and Ahearn stepped back and the two palace coolies who had dug the grave began to shovel dirt in on the body. The chatter in the crowd increased as it turned away and began to stream back towards the palace. The show was over and it was time to go to work.

I drew my collar up against the chill morning air, looked up gratefully at the sun as it slipped in through the gap at the end of the valley. The dawn blue of the valley suddenly gave way to greens and browns; retreating shadows made quick sketches of the contours; the thin air sparkled for a moment or two as if full of tiny translucent insects that lived and died in an instant. Mist rose out of the river like steam, turned into wraiths that fled before the sun. On a high peak snow had fallen during the night and it glittered like a silvered mailed fist held in the sky.

As we walked back towards the palace I heard barking and roaring and screeching. 'That's the menagerie,' Clive said. 'Quite a clamour, eh?'

'Do the animals know someone is dead?'

'If they do, I don't think they care.'

'Do you? I mean about Major Savanna.'

'He was an English officer, so I care about the way he died. But on a personal level, no. Not if you mean shall I miss him. We were never close. As a matter of fact, we detested each other. But – '

'But?'

'I'm not going to forget how he died. And I'll do my best to find out why.'

'I should let him rest, Clive.' Lady Westbrook was smoking her first cheroot of the day, spoiling the morning air. 'You have enough to worry about with the possible plot against the King.'

'What if it should all be linked?'

Lady Westbrook looked surprised, a reaction I hadn't seen in her up till now. 'Your imagination is running away with you. Are you trying to play Sherlock Holmes?'

So far this morning Clive (for that was what I was calling him in my mind now, not Major Farnol) had looked very stern; but now he smiled. Some people have a smile that can alter the whole set and character of their face; his was one of them. I wondered what he had been like as a younger man, before he had had to shoulder the burden of other men's deaths: what he had been like at the country house party weekend, for instance. Some women are selfish and jealous, resentful of what they can never fully know, the years of a man's life before he came into their own life. I was one of them.

'I don't think I should ever make a good detective, Viola. One needs patience to follow clues and I'm not a patient man.'

'You have been warned, Bridie,' said Lady Westbrook, a matchmaker even at seven o'clock in the morning.

The air now was full of the cries and roaring of animals. We came up the road to the main gates and I saw the fighting elephants moving restlessly at their stakes, lifting their heads and trumpeting challenges that chilled the blood. Down towards the river the caravan elephants were tied to their stakes, but they were quiet, they knew better than to advertise in a tough neighbourhood. The whole palace was coming alive, turning into the small town which it really was.

Then through the gates came Prince Mahendra on a splendid black horse. Behind him were two mounted servants and behind them a small cart drawn by two horses. In it were two more servants and, in a cage behind them, two masked leopards.

Mahendra reined in his horse. 'Out walking so early? The English do so love to exercise, don't they?'

'We have been burying Major Savanna,' said Clive and pointed back along the valley to where the new grave was already lost in the brightening sunlight.

'Oh yes.' Mahendra's mocking smile hadn't changed. He was a man whose smile didn't alter anything about him: it held the world at a distance. He was dressed this morning in khaki drill hunting clothes and the drab colour seemed to accentuate his thinness. 'Well, I shall see you later. I am going hunting *chinkara*. My pets haven't had a run lately.'

I looked at the two leopards, could hear them growling softly in their throats. Pets?

Clive said, 'Your sister told me you were coming with us this morning when we leave.'

'I am. You will wait for me.'

'No, Your Highness. We go when I give the word. And that will be in, let's say another hour.'

'The caravan belongs to my sister and me. It will leave when we give the word, not you, Major.'

He rode off and as the cart started up again the leopards' growling increased. One of them turned its head in my

114

direction and the sharp teeth showed under the black leather mask that stopped it from seeing me. It knew prey when it could smell it.

'What's a *chinkara*?' I said.

'A small deer.' Clive was staring down the road after Mahendra, who had galloped ahead of his small retinue, disappearing in a cloud of dust. 'He lets the leopards go, taking off their masks, when his bearers sight one. The *chinkara* hardly stands a chance with two leopards after it. But I think that would be Bobs' idea of sport.'

'I feel the whole Kugar family is a damn menagerie,' said Lady Westbrook. 'They should all be wearing masks, including Mala.'

Clive's stern, angry face relaxed again as he smiled. 'I should not let her hear you say that, Viola. You can't run as fast as a *chinkara*.'

She snorted, threw away the butt of her cheroot. 'I'm going to have breakfast. I hope it's a little more civilized than that muck we had for dinner last night. Porridge, bacon and eggs, toast and marmalade, tea. How does that sound to you, m'dear?'

'Wonderful.' We really gave meaning to the word *breakfast* in those days; we broke the fast to smithereens instead of just damping it with a cup of coffee. 'I'd like some pancakes and maple syrup instead of the porridge.'

'Ugh,' said Clive. I think that the English don't put in their sweet tooth till mid-morning.

The Ranee must have been as disgusted as we were at last night's dinner and had issued instructions that a good breakfast had to be provided. It was as good as the one I'd had at the Lodge, a real English breakfast. We ate, not in the dining-room, which was no place for breaking a fast, but in a small room that looked out through arches on to the river. Everyone met for breakfast at the same time, as if nobody wanted to miss anything of what might be said about last night's happenings.

'A burial?' Magda Monday was a woman obviously accustomed to champagne; she might not be able to hold it while she was drinking it, but it didn't hold her the next morning. 'Before breakfast? Poor Major Savanna.'

'What did this – this Major Savanna die of?' said Zoltan Monday.

'Poison,' said Clive.

I glanced up from my porridge and saw him look casually round the table as he dropped his small bomb. He looked and sounded casual, but I was now coming to recognize how alert he could be under that relaxed exterior. None of the others, except Lady Westbrook and the Ranee, looked relaxed; or if they had been, they had all at once stiffened. Even Magda lost her bright gaiety.

'Or he was overdosed with drugs. One or the other killed him.' He was spreading the shrapnel from his bomb. 'Or murdered him, if you like.'

The Nawab was the first to recover. 'You haven't told us why he was here.'

'I don't know.' Clive pushed his empty porridge bowl away, signalled for a servant to bring him bacon and eggs. 'I thought one of you might be able to help me.'

'Murdered?' Magda seemed to take a while to recognize the word, as if she had suddenly forgotten all her English.

'He was here to see Bobs,' said the Ranee, ignoring Magda as she might have one of her servants. 'I told you that last night.'

'So you did.' Clive's face might be able to hide his true thoughts but it could never feign innocence. He must have realized it, because he suddenly smiled, then attacked the bacon and eggs that had been put down in front of him. 'But Sherlock Holmes examines every avenue.'

'Sherlock Holmes?' Monday, too, seemed to have recovered. 'Are we supposed to be characters in some Conan Doyle mystery, Major?'

'The butler did it,' said the Nawab, distributing that wide, insincere smile round the table. 'You must have a thousand butlers here in the palace, Mala.'

'You know your household protocol as well as I do, Bertie – there can only be one butler. And I'm sure Mohammed didn't do it, did you?' She smiled at the grey-haired butler who stood behind her chair supervising the other servants. He just returned her smile, as he might have handed her a clean napkin. 'I think it would be good manners if we dropped the whole subject.'

So the death, or murder, of Major Savanna by poisoning or an overdose of drugs was dropped as a matter of etiquette and we all got on with breakfast.

Prince Mahendra did not return till mid-morning. In the meantime Clive paced up and down the corridors and terraces like one of Mahendra's menagerie eager to escape. With a reluctant Private Ahearn as my bodyguard I, too, paced the terraces but at a more leisurely speed. Despite the threatening atmosphere of the palace I began to wish I could spend a few more days here.

'Would you stay in India, Mr Ahearn, if you could live like this?'

'Like the prince or like them?' He nodded down towards the servants we could see in one of the many courtyards. Men were chopping wood with small axes, their strokes almost as slow as the growth of the tree that had supplied the wood; it seemed to me, and it was an heretical thought for an American, that these people knew the proper value of time. Women, graceful as stalks in a gentle breeze, walked from a well with tall jars balanced perfectly on their heads. 'I shouldn't want to be a coolie, miss. Even a ranker's better off than them. But a prince, yes. Yes.' He paused a moment and imagined Prince Mick Ahearn, Rajah of the Bogs. 'Yes, I'd stay here then.'

Then Zoltan Monday came along the terrace, tipped his deer-stalker hat and asked if he might accompany me in my stroll. 'We foreigners perhaps should stick together, Miss O'Brady. I feel very much an outsider, don't you?'

I did, but I was not going to confess it to him. I was suspicious of Mr Monday for no other reason than that I did not like his trade. 'Don't you always feel something of an outsider, Mr Monday? I mean, selling arms?'

Perhaps because he had always been an outsider, Monday managed to hide any offence he might have felt at my remark. He had developed a thick skin, he wouldn't have been stung if he had fallen into a beehive. 'If arms were not available, do you think the world would be a better place?'

'Of course.'

He shook his head at my naïveté. 'Miss O'Brady, when

Cain killed Abel he hadn't bought his club from an arms salesman. If my employer and others were not here to supply what the kings and princes and governments and revolutionaries want, all those people would try manufacturing their own. And they would kill as many of their own side as the other because they would manufacture such faulty stuff. Man is a fighting animal, just like those elephants of Prince Mahendra's, and all we do is give him a professional supply of what he needs to survive.'

'Or kill, as the case may be.'

'The balance of human nature.' I waited for him to smile, but he was serious. 'I make no apology for my profession, Miss O'Brady. You are a newspaper reporter. Don't newspapers demolish governments and people, only you do it with the written word? The law of libel is only another name for a shield.'

'I don't think I have ever demolished anyone with a story of mine.'

'I have never killed anyone. I have never fired a shot in anger.'

'You're incorrigible, Mr Monday.'

'I am Hungarian, Miss O'Brady.' He must have heard all the jokes about Hungarians; but I was to learn over the years that Hungarians had a sense of humour that allowed them to laugh at foreigners' jokes about them. We Americans still don't have such tolerance, something I have lately been told by some Poles. 'Don't let's quarrel. We may have to form our own little international cartel to survive this journey down to Delhi. You, me, my wife and Baron von Albern.'

'What would you say was the inside cartel?' If Clive was to play Sherlock Holmes, I decided I might attempt Dr Watson.

But if Monday had any clients in the palace, he was protecting them. 'I don't sense any co-operation at all amongst the rest of our friends. Except perhaps between Major Farnol and Lady Westbrook.'

'Do you suspect they might be up to something?'

'In my profession one never takes anything or anyone at face value. I once sold two dozen machine-guns and five hundred rifles to some Orthodox priests in Turkey. They said prayers for the quick delivery of the consignment.'

Oh, I tell you, I was being exposed to cynicism and corruption that fine morning. 'I think I can vouch for Major Farnol and Lady Westbrook.' I tried the direct approach: 'Was Major Savanna a client of yours?'

'No . . .'

But there were dots after his answer and I read them. 'But he was buying for someone else?'

'Ah, here comes Prince Mahendra!' We were on a terrace that overlooked the main gates. He looked past me down towards the road. 'Perhaps now we can start on our way.'

Very politely he had shut a door in my face. He was going to answer no more questions by an inquisitive reporter bent on demolition. I gave up, watched Prince Mahendra as he came up the road and in under the archway of the big gates. The leopards, unmasked now, were in their cage on the cart; across the rump of a horse was slung the bloody, mangled carcase of a small deer. Mahendra looked up, saw me and waved a hand at the carcase.

'You should have come with me, Miss O'Brady. It was a marvellous hunt.'

'Some other time, Your Highness.' But I knew now that I wanted to be gone from the palace as soon as possible.

End of extract from memoirs.

2

The caravan got under way immediately, as if Mahendra was no longer interested in creating any delay. It was now a sizeable procession, a slow train on its way to pomp and ceremony. Mahendra brought his own additions: six more elephants, none of them fighters; carts and a small victoria; twenty servants and a dozen mounted escort. He himself was astride a magnificent black stallion and he rode up to the head of the line and raised his arm for the order to proceed.

'I don't think the Nawab's wives are all aboard yet,' said Farnol.

The wives, two to an elephant, were still scrambling into their howdahs. They were laughing and chattering amongst themselves, schoolgirls ready for another holiday picnic. It was as if their veils did indeed cut them off from the world: they appeared ignorant of, or unconcerned by, Savanna's death and burial. Yet Farnol knew how quickly news and gossip reached the *zenana*: it was food and drink to the women.

Mahendra did not even look back down the procession. 'I don't wait for women. We move now.'

Farnol, still looking back, was relieved to see the last of the wives settle herself into a howdah. He was no supporter of women's rights, but he had always felt that Indian women deserved better treatment than they received. One didn't necessarily have to give women the vote and equal rights, but they should be treated as near-equals and not as privileged, and more often unprivileged, prisoners.

'They're all aboard.'

Once they had begun to move Mahendra looked at Farnol riding just behind him. 'You may be my second-in-command, Major.'

'That wasn't what I had in mind. We may run into trouble and I think I'm more experienced than you at handling it.'

'I would remind you that we are still in the State of Serog and this is still a princely State. Under the treaty with the English, we princes may not make war on each other – ' He paused a moment, as if sipping chagrin at what the interfering English had forbidden. 'But within our boundaries we are still entitled to keep order in our own way. I am descended from a long line of warriors, much longer than yours, Major – it's in my blood. I think I can handle any trouble that may occur.'

Farnol made no reply nor did he look at Bridie and the Nawab riding beside him. Like a professional soldier he did not like having command taken away from him, especially when he knew he was more competent than this half-mad youth who was taking over. But now was not the time to start any small war between himself and Mahendra.

As they came to the bend in the road that would hide the palace of Serog, he drew his horse aside and waited for the procession to pass. He looked back at the palace, towering like some fantasy from the past above the cascading river. It had been the home and spawning bed of a long line of warriors; more than one murderer had lived there under the title of prince. But now a thought struck him: who would inherit it all? Neither Mala nor Mahendra, as far as he knew, had an heir. Had Rupert Savanna been thinking of that when he had begun his interference in the affairs of the Kugar family?

He cantered after the procession, glanced at the Ranee as he passed her carriage. She was riding with Lady Westbrook, Magda and the Baron, but she might have been riding alone, so little notice did she seem to be taking of them. She looked up at Farnol and smiled from under her parasol.

'Do you have any children, Your Highness?' He might as well ask the question in public as in private: he doubted that she would give him a truthful answer anyway.

The parasol wavered above her in a coy display. 'What a question to ask a maiden lady! And in front of my guests, too!'

'Take no notice of us, Mala,' said Lady Westbrook, as if her hostess had not already been doing that. 'I'm trying to imagine you as a mother.'

'No, Major, I have no children. Do you have any, Madame Monday?'

'I hope to,' said Magda, but she made it sound as if having children were an inconsequential pursuit like having tea or getting her hair done. 'What about you, Lady West-brook?'

'I had three. My two sons died, one from the fever and the other from a Pathan bullet. My daughter lives in England with her husband and evidently is dying slowly from the climate, so she writes me.'

Farnol noticed how the Ranee had turned the question of children away from herself. She glanced up at him from under the parasol, gave him a mocking smile; he was sure she knew why he had asked the question. He gave her a smile in return, winked and rode on up ahead again. So far their small war, as Viola Westbrook had called it, was still civilized.

The procession passed through the narrow gorge that was the gateway to the valley and soon they were back on the cart road. This would not meet the main road to Kalka for at least another two days and Farnol knew he would not feel safe till then. And even then, not entirely so.

Every so often the river from the valley came close to the road, then disappeared through a cut in the hills. The vegetation on the slopes was changing; scattered cacti could by now be seen among the thinning pines. In another day or two the air, too, could change; Farnol wrinkled his nose at the thought of the dust-laden, ammoniac smell that lay below. After his first experience of the high air, when his parents had taken him to Simla as a small boy, he had never again felt comfortable with the smell of the plains.

Occasionally he saw game bounding or fluttering away through the scrub or trees above the road: deer, partridge, once a small arrowhead of ducks shooting up from a hidden pond. But he did not want to pause to re-stock the larder. There could be someone on the higher ground still intent on hunting *him*.

They passed through another village and the villagers came to the doors of their huts and stores and looked fearfully at the procession as it came down the narrow street. Was this an army of tax-collectors? Was the Ranee or the Prince demanding more money to pay for the pleasures that the villagers never shared? Then they recognized that there was an air of ostentation about this caravan that told them they were safe till another day: taxes were never collected with swagger such as this. The horses and elephants proceeded down the street and the villagers pressed their hands together and bowed their heads as first the Prince and then the Ranee went by. Above the villagers' heads monkeys bared their teeth in sardonic grins and scratched themselves in what could only be described as derisive places.

'Oh, I should love to have been a ranee or a princess!' said Magda and waved to the populace, who squinted at her above their clasped hands and wondered who she thought she was.

'Keep your hand down,' said the Ranee. 'They only become confused if they have too many to pay homage to.'

'What will they all do when there are no more kings and princes?' The Baron knew what he would do: retire and be content. He had met the Kaiser only once and did not like him.

'We must ask Miss O'Brady,' said Lady Westbrook, who, though no republican, had never really felt the need of kings and princes. 'Think of all those Americans waiting to pay homage . . . May I wave a hand, Mala? I see a little boy there staring straight at me. He probably thinks I'm the Dowager Ranee.'

'Do, by all means,' said the Ranee graciously, but didn't extend the favour to Magda or the Baron.

Up front Prince Mahendra rode looking straight ahead, uninterested in his sister's subjects. He had not spoken since his few words with Farnol at the start of the trek from the palace. It hurt him that the villagers were not paying homage to him, but even if they had been he would still have ignored them. Half-mad, he knew how to lock the doors of himself.

'When your sister dies, these people will bow down before you, Your Highness.' Farnol had guessed part of the reason for Mahendra's sullen silence.

Mahendra unlocked himself. 'Is she going to die?'

'Sooner or later. It's a habit with us all.'

Bridie shivered. 'Do we have to talk of dying? We started the day with a burial. That's enough.'

Still a discomforted rider, exhausted by the tensions that had warped her in the past thirty-six hours, she had lost, if only temporarily, all her enthusiasm for the adventure. She had been inspired to be a newspaperwoman by the deeds and excursions of Nelly Bly; she was beginning to appreciate that Nelly had had an intrepidity that she doubted she wished to emulate. The Boston *Globe* would, if the worst happened, give her a glowing obituary, but obituaries were bequests from the living that the dead could never cash. She began to think of easier assignments, such as covering another of the testimonial dinners, Catholic feast days in a double sense, to Mayor Honey Fitz. To sit on a comfortable, unmoving chair, to eat good American food and to hear Toodles Ryan relay all the latest gossip . . .

'They say,' said the Nawab, 'that Mala is running short of funds. Is that true, Bobs?'

'I'd heard the same about you, Bertie.' Mahendra was fully open now, almost amiable.

'We're all feeling the pinch. Everything is so bally expensive nowadays. Have you tried to buy an elephant lately? Pretty soon we shall all have to get rid of our elephants and horses and ride in a single motor-car and nothing else. The world is going to pot.'

'The tortoise must be sinking,' said Farnol.

They all looked at him blankly. 'We were talking of elephants.'

'You haven't read your Warren Hastings. The world is supported by an elephant, who stands on a tortoise, who stands on water.'

'That is one of our sayings,' said Mahendra. 'General Hastings stole it, as you have stolen everything else.'

'Oh, I say, don't let's start that, Bobs old chap,' said the Nawab. 'Even with the price of elephants what it is, we haven't done too badly.'

Bridie had heard the rich of America, riding in their Pierce-Arrows and Rolls-Royces, complain of what the government, their *own* government, had stolen from them. The rich, it seemed, were more put upon than the poor.

In the late afternoon the road wound down through a thick stand of bamboo, then straightened up suddenly as if to mirror a traveller's surprise. Ahead of them, as if the road were a driveway running up to its compound gates, was a large *dak* bungalow, a bare flagpole standing on the ragged lawn in front of it like an exclamation point.

'Home,' said Lady Westbrook in the coach, gazing up past the riders ahead of her.

'Home?' said the Baron, riding backwards, twisting awkwardly to look over his shoulder.

'I lived here thirty, no forty, years ago. When my husband was political adviser to Mala's father.'

'It's so close to Simla. Do you come down here at all?'

'Never. It was like all the *dak* houses, they were never really homes. One was always being moved on. We carried our gardens with us, in pots. I've carted chrysanthemums and geraniums from one end of India to the other. One carted a lot of other things, too, of course . . .' She meant memories, but she did not feel sentimental enough to mention them.

Servants came running out of the house as the caravan, concertina-ing together, came to a halt before the low-fenced compound. The road, it could be seen now, turned at right angles and ran along the front of the compound, to disappear into some ragged pines.

A butler, in white coat and red turban, welcomed the visitors. No, there was no sahib in residence. As His Highness knew, this bungalow was for sahibs of the Raj on circuit; but as he also knew, no sahibs came on circuit on this road any more. The butler sounded critical and regretful, but it was all said with bowed head. And it was said to *him*, Mahendra, because so far the butler hadn't noticed who was in the coach further down the caravan.

'Prepare rooms for eight people,' said Mahendra. 'The biggest two for myself and the Ranee.'

'The Ranee! She is with you?' The butler raised his head, saw his mistake and went scuttling down to the coach, where he pressed his hands even more tightly together and bowed his head even lower to make up for his lapse.

'Bloody crawler,' said Ahearn and looked around for rebel support but there was none.

Mahendra got down from his horse, dropping the reins for some bearer to pick up and, stiff-legged as a stilt-walker, strode up on to the wide verandah and into the house. Farnol helped Bridie down from her horse, studiously averting his gaze as she rubbed her sore rump.

'Would you rather ride in the coach from here on? Perhaps I can get Mahendra to let you use the victoria.'

'We'll see.'

The bungalow was no palace, but it had its comforts. Lady Westbrook got stiffly down from the coach and looked at the rows of flower-pots that lined either side of the drive like up-turned fezzes left behind by beheaded Turks. 'Nothing in them. You could often tell what sort of family you were going to visit by what they grew in their pots. I can remember one family who grew nothing but small cacti, just like their children.'

There were not enough rooms to give everyone a room of his own. The Ranee, Mahendra and the Nawab each had one. Bridie shared with Lady Westbrook, Farnol with the Baron. The Mondays, recognized even by the butler as the genuine outsiders, were given the last and smallest room. The butler looked at Karim and Ahearn, not quite sure where he should put them.

Farnol told him. 'They will eat in the kitchen with you, Buhandar. When we go to bed, they will sleep in the hall here, one inside the front door, the other inside the back door.'

Buhandar, the butler, looked troubled. 'Someone is coming during the night, sahib?'

'I hope not. Karim, make sure that the Ranee's and Prince Mahendra's escorts sort it out amongst themselves – No, I'd better do it.'

He knew Karim was no diplomat and would take it for granted that his place in the Indian Army, a member of Farnol's Horse, one of the elite regiments, gave him rank over any buggers in some ranee's or prince's small force. Farnol went out to where the *mahouts* were feeding and watering the elephants and the *syces* were unsaddling and watering the horses. He found the Ranee's corporal and also the Prince's, found also that each resented the other.

'All right, you take one side of the compound, *Naik* Mahbub Ali. You, *Naik* Chota Lal, take the other side with your men.' One was a Muslim and the other a Hindu, but he knew that with this particular pair religion had nothing to do with their animosity towards each other; they were only reflecting what the mistress and the master felt for each other. Christ, he thought, why don't I just jump on a horse and ride pell-mell for Kalka and the train to Delhi? But then, of course, he would arrive in Delhi with nothing but his suspicions. He might still arrive there with nothing more, but at least he would have tried. And been tried, as he was by these two uncooperative *naiks*. 'I want a double picquet on both sides of the compound and keep an eye on the rear.'

'Are these the Ranee's orders, sahib?' said Mahbub Ali.

'Yes. And His Highness', too,' he told Chota Lal. He knew they knew he was lying, but so long as he gave them both the same lie they were prepared to accept it. It was a way of saving face in front of the other.

Tents were being put up for the Nawab's wives within the

compound. The Nawab had not stopped to see to their comfort; there were enough servants to look after them; wives should be supported but not coddled. One of the wives, perhaps the youngest, though it was difficult to tell because of the veil, had paused and was looking in Farnol's direction. Several times during the day when he had ridden up and down the procession, he had noticed her staring at him. Moderately vain, like most men, he had taken it for granted that she had been attracted to him because he was a contrast to her husband; he had ridden taller in the saddle and given her his best profile. But there was no coquetry in the dark eyes showing above the veil and he wondered now what was her interest in him. She saw him looking at her and she abruptly turned and lost herself behind the other wives who, with no husband at hand to berate, were taking it out on the servants, whose only sin was that they were male.

Farnol went back into the house to his shared room. The Baron was already soaking in the big copper tub in the small bathroom that opened off the bedroom. It was a primitive bathroom: a stone floor, mud walls and a ceiling of drooping hessian that, more likely than not, held a snake or two. There was a wooden lavatory box over a hole in the floor, the copper tub and water that was only running when bearers came scuttling in with buckets of it. The bedroom seemed to be full of bearers coming and going.

'Such a multiplicity of servants,' said the Baron, lifting a big sponge above his head and squeezing water over himself. 'I shall miss all this when I go home next year. I think we Germans made a mistake establishing our colonies where we did. Tanganyika, South-West Africa, New Guinea – blacks never make good servants, not like these fellows.' He waved a soapy hand at the two bearers pouring more hot water into his tub and they smiled and nodded their heads in acknowledgement of what they took to be praise. 'I envy you, Major. Having India, I mean.'

'What about Berlin? Does it envy us, too?'

'Probably,' said the Baron, but said no more, concentrating on washing the useless stump of his arm.

Everyone dressed for dinner again. Though Farnol was a rebel against some social customs, it did not occur to him to flout this particular custom, particularly when ladies were at table. His clothes were laid out on the bed, his dress shoes shone like black ice; he never had to worry about how or when his laundry was done, so that there was always a clean dress-shirt waiting for him. He and the Baron went down the short hallway together, shirt-fronts white and full as sails on a galleon.

The meal would have been better served to diners in sackcloth, someone doing penance. Mulligatawny soup, curried chicken (or, as Bridie wrote later in her notes, curried bones), blancmange for dessert: but everyone was hungry. The empty plates left the cook with the impression that he was, as he had always thought, indeed a great chef, a word he had once heard a visiting French consul use. Conversation was desultory, mainly because of the mood of the Ranee and her brother, who appeared not to be speaking to each other.

But Bridie managed to engage Mahendra's attention. Perhaps he was unaccustomed to having a good-looking woman seated on his right; or perhaps it was that he knew little or nothing about Americans. His sullen mood warmed under her approach and Farnol, seated on the opposite side of the table, on Mahendra's left, had to admire the way she handled him. Neither the Indian nor the Englishman was to know that she had honed her approach in interviews with City Hall politicians, whose variety of moods could be as mercurial as those of any unbalanced prince. Indeed, there were one or two who thought of themselves as princes, which was a measure of how unbalanced they were.

'Americans want to know about Indian princes,' she told Mahendra. 'They wouldn't want to live anywhere else but in our republic, but they secretly admire kings and princes, especially exotic ones.'

'Are we exotic?' Mahendra didn't seem to think that amusing.

'I don't know any of our politicians who dress quite as beautifully as you do.' She laughed to herself, then explained: 'I was thinking of President Taft in blue silk and pink turban. He was something like sixty inches round his waist. But your slimness suits it.'

Mahendra was unused to flattery; he preened himself

under the obvious compliment. 'One has to keep up appearances. Our people expect it.'

'I'm sure they do,' said Bridie, and Farnol, watching her closely, saw the republican cynicism in her eye. 'I'd like to do a story on the way you live, Your Highness.'

'I live very simply,' he said, unconscious of the treasure in pearls which hung round his neck. He had, indeed, dressed very simply this evening; he had put on the pearls only because his valet had already got them out of their box. He lived an ascetic life by his own standards. 'It is true I am surrounded by servants, but for whom else would they work if not for me? I only employ them to keep them from starving.'

He really believes it, thought Farnol; and saw how Bridie allowed him to believe it: 'It is just like life in America, Your Highness. We employ so many bureaucrats only to keep them from starving.'

'We have much in common then,' said the Prince, silkenly smug in his concern for the starving masses of the world.

When the meal was finished everyone repaired to the front verandah, since there was no drawing-room in the bungalow. Mahendra did not sit with the others but went down the steps and strolled up and down the driveway, head bent and hands clasped behind his back. Farnol, declining coffee, went down to join the young prince.

'Your Highness, you haven't told me why Major Savanna was at the palace.'

Mahendra did not stop walking, just turned his head as Farnol fell into step beside him. 'Should I, Major? Am I responsible for the comings and goings of English officers?'

'Where did you go to school?'

'The Bishop Cotton School in Simla.'

'No more than that?'

'I was going to go to Oxford, but I decided it would not suit my temperament.' Did that mean he knew he was mentally unstable? Farnol remembered a line from a favourite poet, Dryden: *There's a pleasure sure in being mad, which none but madmen know.* But Mahendra did not look as if he knew any pleasure at all.

'Didn't they teach you at Bishop Cotton that we, the English and the Indians, must respect each other?'

'It always seemed to me that we were taught to respect the English. I can't remember anything being said about the reverse. They may have implied it, but I fear I must have been a little dense. I'm still accused of that by my sister.' His smile did nothing to warm the chill night air.

Somewhere on the hill behind the bungalow a leopard coughed and outside the compound the elephants and horses stirred restlessly. The Ranee and the others on the verandah called out goodnight and went into the house. Mahendra turned to follow them, but Farnol put a hand on his arm. The prince stiffened, looked down at Farnol's hand. He was of a rank that should not be touched by people of inferior rank and he considered an English officer an inferior.

Farnol knew what he had done, but he was not going to apologize. 'Your Highness, I think we'd better talk. Major Savanna died in your palace from an overdose of drugs or some poison. Now if I don't get the story of why he died and what he was doing there, you could receive a visit from someone with much more authority than I. He might come with troops, more than your little army could handle.'

'Take your hand away, Major.' Farnol did so. 'Don't ever put a finger on me again.'

'If you respect me, as I'm trying to respect you, there won't be any need for me to lay a hand on you.' Farnol wondered if he should have begun this interrogation. He was tired and he would need all his wits about him to keep Mahendra calm and sane. He could not tell the prince what the Ranee had told him, that she was certain her brother intended to kill her. But he had to take risks: 'Major Savanna came to see you, Your Highness. I know that much for a fact.'

'Who told you that? Mala? You were one of her lovers, weren't you? I suppose she tells lots of fancy stories in bed. Bedtime stories.' He smiled again, looking pleased this time, as if he was not accustomed to any humour from himself.

'I haven't shared any bedtime stories with Mala for a year, Bobs.' He took another risk using the nickname; it was almost as bad as laying one's hand on him. But he had to get this conversation on to an informal basis, he was never going to get Mahendra to talk while it remained *Your Highness* and *Major*. He was relieved to see that the prince did not

130

seem to mind the sudden intimacy. 'I found some papers – '

'Where? I thought – ' Then Mahendra realized he had made a slip. 'You're clever – Clive, isn't it?'

'You thought you'd taken all his papers from him? All his pockets had been cut off.'

Mahendra shook his head. 'I didn't do that nor did any of my servants. Nor did I poison Major Savanna.'

It was too dark to read his face and the soft sing-song voice gave nothing away. Yet Farnol thought Mahendra was telling the truth. 'Who did, then? He did come to see you, didn't he?'

'Yes.' He walked in silence, head bent again. In the giant oak beside the bungalow a night bird cried, like a troubled child, and a monkey chattered grumpily at being awakened. 'There was someone else in the palace – I don't know who. The place is so big, so many rooms – I have never been in them all.'

'Can you make a guess who it was? No? All right then – why did Savanna come to see you? Why was he trying to get you to turn against Mala?'

'Did his papers say that? What a foolish man, putting things on paper.' It did not seem to occur to Mahendra that Farnol might be lying about the papers. 'But I suppose he had to report to his superiors. He told me that the English saw my point, that Mala is not worthy of being the ruler here in Serog.'

Farnol doubted that Savanna had been acting under instructions from his superiors, certainly not from George Lathrop. 'She's not popular, I know that. But did Savanna promise to make you ruler?'

'I did not need his promises.' The head came up. 'I could rule Serog without his help. There are others – '

'Who?'

But now Mahendra became crafty. They had come to the foot of the steps; an oil lamp on the verandah cut his face into thin planes of yellow and black. His eyes narrowed with suspicion and anger: he was being tricked by this Englishman. 'It is none of your business, Major! Go to bed, leave me alone! Go to bed with my whoring sister, let her tell you what she knows – if she knows anything at all!'

I've pushed him too far. He had had no experience with anyone as mentally unstable as Mahendra. With the dim-witted, yes, plenty of times, and with mystics on a plane that he had found almost unreachable. But never with anyone as unpredictable as this half-mad prince. He realized that Mahendra could be driven to murder without any conscience . . . 'Mala will tell me nothing because I no longer go to bed with her. I am trying to keep the peace here in Serog – '

'Who said I wanted peace? You English – you think you always know what's good for us!' He was straining to keep a hold on himself, as if he knew the crack in him was widening. His voice was rising, thin now, no longer sing-song: 'We'll do what we want – !'

'Bobs – ' The Nawab stepped out of the shadows on the verandah. 'Bobs!'

Mahendra swung round and looked up in puzzlement at the Nawab. Then with something like an animal whimper he stumbled up the steps and disappeared into the bungalow. The Nawab looked after him, then down at Farnol.

'You should treat him more carefully, old bean.'

'I wish you'd mind your own business, Bertie. How long have you been standing there?'

'Long enough. We must take care of our own. The Princes' Trade Union, you know.'

Farnol went up the steps to the verandah. 'You're hiding something, Bertie. I think you may even know who's trying to kill me. If you did, that wouldn't be cricket.'

The Nawab looked pained. 'Don't let's joke about holy subjects, Clive.'

'Me or cricket? You're the one who's joking.'

The Nawab stared at him, then he turned, saying over his shoulder as he went, 'All the jokes may be over, Clive. And no one will be sorrier than I.'

3

When Farnol woke in the morning he could hear the movement and shouting outside the compound. The Baron, in cream silk pyjamas, was standing at the window.

'I think we must hurry. Prince Mahendra is already out there. He's not planning to go without us, surely?'

Farnol pulled on trousers and jacket over his pyjamas, went out on to the verandah. The Ranee, dressed for travelling, was standing at the top of the steps. 'What's going on, Mala? It's only – ' He took out his watch. 'Dammit, it's only half past six! Where the devil does your brother think he's going?'

'He's going back to the palace. He's no longer interested in the Durbar. I say good riddance!'

For a variety of reasons, all of them a jumble in his mind at the moment, Farnol knew he could not allow Mahendra to go back to Serog. Mahendra was involved in some major mischief; his threat to kill his sister was only part of it. But he knew that the prince would not listen to any plea or demand from himself, not after last night.

Then Bridie, dressed but looking as if she had done so in a hurry, came out on to the verandah. Farnol grabbed her by the arm and almost pulled her down the steps. He walked her up and down the drive while he quickly explained why he had to keep Mahendra with them in the caravan.

'Go down and flatter him some more, please. Tell him you need him for your story, tell him you're going to make him its hero, anything you like. But keep him with us!'

'I don't know that he'll listen to me. He suspects women – I think he even hates us – '

'I'm sure he's not the first woman-hater you've met. You'll convince him he must stay with us.'

'Who's flattering whom now?'

'You can flatter me when we get down to the Durbar. You haven't seen me in my dress uniform. I'm truly exotic.' His smile was only fleeting. 'Don't let him go back!'

Bridie went on down the driveway and out of the compound to where Mahendra stood waiting impatiently beside the road. Farnol went back up to the verandah and the Ranee.

'What are you doing, Clive? Having Miss O'Brady offer herself to Bobs? It won't work, you know. He's a dedicated celibate or he's asexual, I'm not sure which. Sometimes I can't believe we came from the same father.'

'Did you have the same mother?'

'No. Perhaps that explains it.'

'Miss O'Brady isn't going to offer to get into his bed. There are other ways of winning a man, Mala.'

'Really?' The Ranee smiled, as if she knew that the other ways, whatever they were, could so often be a waste of time.

The others had now come out on to the verandah, the Nawab, the Baron and Zoltan Monday half-dressed, Lady Westbrook and Magda in their dressing-gowns. Magda's gown was not meant to be worn outside a bedroom, but Lady Westbrook's was a sensible, all-purpose blue woollen gown that came right up to her throat. She also wore one of her hats, which set the seal on her decorum.

'What's the hullabaloo? Clive, you said nothing about such an early start. Breakfast isn't ready yet!'

'I'm sorry, Viola, it's not my doing. Prince Mahendra is planning to return home. Miss O'Brady is down there trying to persuade him not to.'

Then the Nawab, who had been uncharacteristically silent, said, 'Miss O'Brady's coming back. And so is Bobs!'

Farnol watched the prince and the reporter come up the driveway, chatting amiably; he half expected them to hold hands, so friendly did they appear towards each other. He glanced at the Ranee. 'You see, Mala. There are other ways.'

She seemed not to have heard him. She was staring down at her brother and Farnol saw the odd expression on her face; it took him a moment to recognize it as relief, a weakness he had never seen in her before. Then she turned her head and smiled at him.

'You must teach them to me some time, Clive.'

Mahendra took Bridie's arm and helped her up the steps.

He smiled at the group on the verandah, as innocent as a child who had wandered away for an early morning walk. 'Did I waken you? I am so sorry. I am always an early riser, I forget that some people like to stay in bed. Is breakfast ready?'

'Bobs – ' The Nawab, too, looked relieved. 'Don't get up so early again. None of us is as young as you.'

Farnol was looking at the Baron and Monday; but if they were relieved, they did not show it. Everyone went back into the house, Farnol following the Baron to their bedroom.

'You have a problem with that young man,' said the Baron.

Farnol washed, combed his hair; then remembered he hadn't shaved. That took another five minutes and all the time he cursed for letting himself get out of his routine. He had found from long practice that keeping to routine, especially first thing in the morning, gave him a firm base for the rest of the day. And, God knew, he needed a firm base for the next three or four days.

He finished dressing, put on his Sam Browne belt, checked that he had full chambers in his pistol. He looked up and saw the Baron watching him.

'Wearing a pistol to breakfast?'

'Baron, from now on I'm going to wear it to bed, too. I have quite a few problems, not just the one with Mahendra.'

'Am I one of your problems, Major?' The Baron paused as he stood in front of the cracked mirror tying his tie. He looked at Farnol beyond the reflection of himself; he remarked that in the fly-blotched mirror he himself looked old and tired. With a sharp pang he wondered if Thuringia would now remain just a memory, if he would ever go home again. 'It would disturb me if you thought of me as one.'

Farnol all at once felt sympathy for the old man. He had worked for his country with honesty and dignity, but Farnol was sure there had been times when Berlin's instructions had meant that those virtues had to be sacrificed for expediency. It was the same with all diplomats, he guessed, and remembered the expediences he had had to deal in.

'No, Baron. I think you know more than you have told me. But I trust you.'

The old man bowed into the mirror. 'Thank you, Major. Do you know our poet Goethe? He came from my region. He once wrote: *Whatever you can do, or dream you can, begin it.* That sounded so inspiring when I was young. *Boldness*, he said, *has genius, power and magic in it.* Now I'm not so sure. I dreamed of being another Metternich, a Bismarck. But . . . Ach!' He looked in the mirror again at himself. 'Diplomacy has no room for conscience. It is even worse than politics.'

'I don't think I've given a thought to conscience since we started this little trip.' He buttoned the flap of his holster. 'That's another problem altogether and I hope it doesn't arise. Shall we go in for breakfast?'

The caravan got under way at eight o'clock before the sun had risen above the steep mountains to the east. The staff of the bungalow came out and stood in line, heads bowed and hands pressed together as first Prince Mahendra and then the Ranee passed them. Then they went back into the compound to sit and wait for perhaps months before any more visitors came to the bungalow. Lady Westbrook, who had once called it home, did not bother even to look back as the coach rolled down the road.

'I never enjoyed it,' she told the Ranee. 'I was too often left alone there. Your father was always calling my husband up to the palace for advice. So far as I know, he never took a damn bit of notice of anything Roger ever told him.'

'That would be Father,' said the Ranee, every inch her father's daughter. She knew the dangers of taking advice from the English: her father had advised her of that.

Farnol left Bridie to ride with Mahendra and the Nawab, to flatter one and be flattered by the other; he was sure she could handle both. She was another of his problems, a more personal one; he was becoming attracted to her, more interested in her than he should be at this time and in these circumstances. He had had several love affairs, some might say many: that depended on the tally-keeper's experience or lack of it. But he had been in love only once. She had been one of the Fishing Fleet, one of those British girls who came out every year at the beginning of the cool weather as guests of relatives or friends, went to parties and balls and gymkhanas and never took an eye off the men, young or middle-aged, who, they had been told, were in the market for a bride. His love had been one of them, but after six months of India she had decided she could not live there and had gone home, one of those labelled Returned Empty. It had taken him a year to get over her; but he had been pleased to learn that she had found a husband in a safer clime, a wool merchant in Bradford. He could not see Bridie O'Brady wanting to stay in India and he could not see himself living anywhere else. So the problem of falling in love with her should be put right to the back of his mind. Which, as any 80-year-old priest will tell you, is easy.

He rode always with an eye on the slopes that towered above the winding road. An eagle planed lazily on the morning air and he wondered what the sharp-eyed bird could see. Would men ever be able to spy from the air? It was only eight years to this very month that those American brothers, the Wrights, had actually got a flying-machine to stay in the air. Yet last year Louis Blériot had flown right across the English Channel! There was talk that, if and when the next war came, the battles would be fought by aeroplanes. He could not bring himself to believe that, partly because he was a cavalryman and he would not want to see horses relegated to drawing carts for the supply corps. He did not wish to see war break out, not a major war as some people were already talking about, but if one had to fight, then it was better to enjoy it. His father had fought in the Second Afghan War and told him of the thrill of leading a cavalry charge. Still, he looked up at the sky now and wished he could see what the eagle could see.

He rode at the rear of the procession with Zoltan Monday. Immediately behind them were Karim and Ahearn, mounted on two of the Ranee's spare horses. Ahearn was one of those Irishmen who seemed a natural horseman, as if some ancient Celt jockey had spread his seed indiscriminately through the bogs and slums of Ireland. He had never been on a horse's back till he left Belfast and even here in India only rarely; but now he rode with the same ease and grace as the tall Sikh beside him. For the first time in his life he had a small air of dignity about him, as if he did not want to shame the magnificent chestnut he rode. The Ranee, taking her best horses down to the Durbar for her own advertisement, had elevated Ahearn, if only temporarily.

'I'm beginning to enjoy this,' he told Karim.

'Major Farnol and I, we have ridden right across the top of India.'

'I've done it on foot. It ain't the same bloody thing, I can tell you.'

'You should not always be so bloody unhappy.'

'I'm Irish, ain't I?' There was an Irish happiness in being unhappy. But he patted the horse's neck and did look happy. 'If I could join the cavalry, mebbe I'd sign up again.'

Farnol heard the remark and looked over his shoulder. 'Do your job properly on this trip, Ahearn, and we might get you a horse.'

'What's my job, sir?'

'Seeing the sahib isn't shot or stabbed in the back,' said Karim Singh as if he thought Ahearn should know.

'Holy Jay-sus.'

Farnol grinned, confident that Karim knew *his* job, and turned back to Monday, who was looking at him curiously. 'Are you not afraid, Major?'

'Of course. Just as you are.'

Monday did not deny it. 'It is part of the job. But I try to hide that from my wife.'

'Why did you bring her with you on this trip to India?'

'She comes with me on every trip.' There was another fear, that he might lose her if he left her at home; but he did not confess that. He knew she loved him, but there was always the nagging doubt. 'She is a great help. Men respond to her.'

'They buy howitzers because of a woman's smile?'

Monday himself smiled. 'It has happened.'

'When we get to Delhi, Mr Monday, I am going to ask the Political Service to look into you. You won't mind?'

'Not at all, Major. My business is legitimate. One of my best friends is the Vickers' representative. We exchange Christmas cards every year.'

'If ever we should go to war, will you still exchange cards?'

'Of course. He and I will not be at war with each other.'

Farnol was not enjoying the conversation. But short of

holding a knife at Monday's throat, how was he going to learn the real purpose of the Krupps man's visit to the Himalayas? He could only hope to trap him into a slip of the tongue. He looked up, saw the Nawab's youngest wife riding in the howdah on the last elephant. On an impulse he smiled at her, expecting her to pull her veil higher and turn her head away. But she didn't, just shook her head and only then looked away.

'Will the Nawab mind that?' said Monday. 'You flirting with one of his wives?'

'Only if you tell him. Perhaps you pass on bits of gossip like that to your clients?'

But Monday was too smart for that one: 'The Nawab is not a client of mine. You said yourself he only collected cricket bats and balls.'

They stopped for lunch beside the river, which now tumbled down, like a giant's writhing hang-rope, out of a narrow defile in the hills. A sward of long grass ran from the road down to the riverbank; half a dozen elephants were marched up and down to flatten the grass and banish any snakes. A small grove of pines stood beside the river, their dark brown bark looking as if it had been applied by hand in small slabs to the slender trunks. It seemed a splendid place for a picnic and the cooks were soon lighting the fires and preparing lunch.

Farnol dismounted and stood close to the elephants who were carrying the Nawab's wives. As the youngest wife got down and moved apart from her companions, seemingly casually yet deliberately towards Farnol, he said softly, 'Do you wish to speak to me?'

One advantage of the veil was that one could speak without appearing to. 'Not now, I cannot. But tonight, if it is possible.'

Then she moved away after the other wives across to where a tablecloth was being laid out for them on the crushed grass. It struck Farnol that he did not know her name, who she had been before the Nawab had married her or where she came from. Or why she felt she had to speak to him.

'Clive,' said the Nawab right behind him, 'are you ogling my wives? Are you thinking of cuckolding me *en masse*?'

'Not if you continue to keep them in *purdah*. When are you going to let them free to run around, Bertie?'

'Dear boy, why don't you ask Bobs when he's going to let his menagerie free to run around? I'm a very solicitous husband – I know what's best for them.' The Nawab was smiling as always, but Farnol suspected he was not joking when he said, 'Clive, don't compound your troubles by looking at my wives. You have enough to trouble you with Mala and the delectable Miss O'Brady. And Mrs Monday too, I'm sure, if you give her an ounce of encouragement.'

'The only one you've left out is Viola.'

The Nawab, the smile still on his face, looking as if he had forgotten it, glanced across at the old lady making herself comfortable in a camp chair. 'Viola, I think, is the only one who can look after herself.'

'Not even Mala?'

'Not even her.' Then he turned full away and looked at the frail wooden bridge that spanned the river. 'Do you think that bridge will hold? Mala and Bobs really should spend some money on maintaining their roads and bridges. That one looks as if it was built by Akbar himself and hasn't been touched since.'

Farnol walked across with Karim Singh to inspect the bridge. As he did so he noticed that the Nawab moved over to speak to his wives. When he got to the bridge he manoeuvred himself so that, while appearing to be carrying out an inspection, he was looking back at the Nawab. Bertie was talking to his youngest wife, laying down the law more like a tyrannical father than a solicitous husband. The girl stood very still and, from a distance and with her face hidden behind her veil, it was impossible to tell whether she was frightened or defiant.

'Sahib – look here!'

Karim had slid down the bank and was perched precariously on a jumble of rocks above the raging river. Farnol, reluctantly leaving the Nawab to the disciplining of his youngest wife, clambered down the bank. And pulled up short, shocked at what he saw.

A water-logged bundle was caught between two rocks that jutted out into the river. The sheet that bound it was ripped and almost torn from the body; the body itself looked as if it had been smashed by hammers and ripped by knives. But the smashed and battered face was recognizable as that of Rupert Savanna.

4

Farnol was no stranger to shocks; but the sight of Savanna's mutilated body made him tremble. The dreadfully battered face bobbed and dipped in the swirl of water round the two rocks that held the body. One eye was still intact and it stared, like a dead fish's eye, at the bright sky overhead. The ginger moustache, dark with water, looked like an ugly blood blister above the broken-toothed mouth. Farnol's shock gave way to anger at this final indignity to Savanna. The man had been buried, he should have been left to the hidden worms.

'Bring it – him ashore, Karim.'

But as Karim edged out on to the rocks, a wave of white water swept over the rocks, grabbed the body and tore it loose. The sodden bundle went on down the river, hitting another rock and bouncing high into the air, then plunging back into the water like an armless diver. Then it was gone from sight.

Karim straightened up, looked up at Farnol. 'Who would do such a thing, sahib?'

Then Farnol saw that the Sikh was looking up past him, though the question had been addressed to himself. He turned and saw Mahendra standing on the bank above him.

'Did you see who that was, Mahendra?' This was no time for *Your Highness*: anger made him brutal and direct.

'Major Savanna.'

'You don't seem surprised.'

'Only that his body came so far. I told my servants that when we left Serog they were to dig up the body and put it in the river.'

'You *what?*' Farnol scrambled up the bank.

'You did not ask my permission to bury him, Major. I do not want any English officer buried in Serog. I'd have told you that if you had consulted me before you put Major Savanna in his grave.'

I *am* dealing with a madman, Farnol told himself. He had begun to think that perhaps Mahendra was perhaps no more than emotionally unstable, was subject to fits of temper that his detractors had swollen into insanity. But there was no temper in Mahendra now, just a coldness that was terrifying.

'This will be reported when I get to Delhi.' Farnol knew how limp and ineffectual that sounded: he was only saved from sounding ridiculous by managing not to splutter. Which, God rest ⁺he poor bugger, Rupert Savanna would have done.

'What do you think the Government will do, Major? They'll be so busy bending their knees to the King, wondering who's going to get a knighthood, that your report will just be pigeon-holed and forgotten.' He was that worst sort of madman, one who thought intelligently. 'Don't fret yourself, Major. The body will finish up at the bottom of the river eventually. What's the difference whether it is buried under water or earth? It's the soul that counts, isn't that what you Christians teach?'

Farnol shut his mouth, deciding to say nothing further. Whatever he said would not matter: Mahendra would only laugh. The prince stared at him, challenging him, then he turned and walked away, his thin arrogant back offering one last insult.

Then Karim, still down on the rocks above the river, called out. 'Sahib – come down again! Look!'

Farnol, still trembling with anger and frustration, slid down the bank again. He looked up under the bridge to where Karim was pointing. One of the timber supports of the bridge roadway had been sawn through; a second was sawn halfway through. The saboteurs, whoever they were, had been interrupted by the arrival of the caravan. Or, macabre irony, had been scared off by the sudden appearance of Savanna's body.

'The buggers could be somewhere close, sahib.' Karim

looked up at the surrounding slopes. 'You think they are going to take another pot-shot at you?'

Farnol was scanning the steep hillsides. They were only sparsely cloaked with trees. A few scrubby pines, some cactus trees that looked like dead signallers propped up, their raised arms semaphoring messages that had no meaning: he could see no worthwhile cover for a sniper. But then he had known Pathan tribesmen who had fired on him from behind the cover of a rock no bigger than their heads and he had not seen them till they had shot at him. He felt a tightening of his nerves, a creeping itch in his back.

'Karim, get Private Ahearn and half a dozen men. Chop down two of those pines over there, trim them and shove them up here beside those two supports. And Karim – ' The Sikh paused, looked back. 'Say nothing about Major Savanna's body. If anyone saw it, I don't think they recognized what it was. So mum's the word.'

'Of course, sahib. Mum's the word.'

Karim scrambled up the bank. Farnol looked up again at the sabotaged supports, wondered who seemed so intent on his not getting down to Delhi; for he was certain, even if he was self-centred in his concern, that he was still the target. Then he wondered if he should attempt to shore up the bridge at all. Perhaps he should have waited to see if any of his fellow-travellers would have hung back from crossing the bridge. But that would mean exposing the innocent to danger and he couldn't risk that.

He went up the bank and across to the picnic. The Ranee, sitting in a camp chair, turned her head sharply as she heard the sound of the axes cutting into the pines. 'Why are they cutting down those trees?'

Why should she be concerned with what the servants are doing? But Farnol told them curtly of the sabotage Karim had found under the bridge. 'I don't know if those extra supports I'm putting in will be enough, but we'll have to risk it. We'll go across one by one on foot, then one horse at a time, then the bearers pulling the coach and the victoria and the *tongas.*'

'What about the elephants?' said the Nawab.

Farnol had been watching him, the Ranee and Mahendra:

if anyone in the party had any connection with the saboteurs, they were the three main suspects. But none of them gave anything away. The Nawab and the Ranee appeared as concerned as himself that the journey should continue, and safely; Mahendra, Savanna apparently forgotten, seemed careless of whether they went on or not. Farnol felt he was touring with a troupe of actors far more experienced and talented than himself.

'Do you have to take the elephants with you?'

'Of course!' The Ranee was not going to sacrifice appearances at the Durbar for the sake of safety here at the bridge.

Farnol shrugged, though he did not like the thought of putting the elephants at risk. The generations of India-born Farnols had not bred that English trait out of him: he hated to see any animal hurt, even those he hunted. And he truly loved elephants.

'Well,' said the Nawab, 'don't let's spoil lunch.'

Farnol sat with Bridie and Lady Westbrook in the camp chairs that had been set out for the party. They were a little apart from the others and Bridie said quietly, 'You look worried, Clive.'

He had debated whether to tell her about the discovery of Savanna's body and decided against it. 'I feel I shouldn't be sitting here with you. Just in case someone has me in his sights.'

'He'd have shot you before this if he was going to,' said Lady Westbrook, munching on cold chicken, boiled egg and a tomato. She had learned long ago never to let anything spoil her appetite; she believed that one's mind worked better on a full stomach than an empty one. She looked up at the hills, but her eyes were no longer good enough for distant viewing and all she saw was a blur of yellow and grey-green slopes. Once she had stood on a mountain-top on the Tibet Road with her husband and seen the edge of the world; or so she allowed her memory to tell her. Her memory was as sharp as her eyesight had once been, but she knew the pleasure of letting it slip occasionally into imagination. 'You'll just have to watch out when you get to the other side of the river. What's that on that plate there, m'dear?'

'Caraway seed cake,' said Bridie. 'Would you care for a slice?'

'Two,' said Lady Westbrook.

Farnol finished his lunch, having eaten slowly, stretching out the minutes till he could no longer delay the crossing of the bridge. Karim and Ahearn had supervised the propping up of the supports of the bridge and now the journey had to be continued.

He walked across the bridge, his nerves tightening again as he appreciated how exposed he was. He glanced up and around him but still could see no one; but he was as certain that someone's eyes were on him as if they had reached down and put a hand on him.

The bridge was little more than a wooden roadway slung across the river. It had thick ropes along each side as handrails, but they were more a warning than any sort of protection; anyone missing his step on the rough planks would slide under the ropes and into the water and would quickly follow Savanna's body down the tumbling river. The bridge was built on the suspension system, with twisted cables of rope that came from anchors of rock at either end up over an arrangement of thick tree-trunks and down to meet in the middle of the span. It was a type of bridge that had been useful and safe for years. But now all at once it felt flimsy beneath Farnol's light tread and he wondered if he should risk sending even the horses across, let alone the elephants.

He made up his mind quickly, before doubt could strike again. He reached the far side and shouted back to Mahendra: 'Come on over, Your Highness! The rest of you follow one at a time!'

He saw Mahendra mount his horse. Furious, he was about to shout to the prince to come across on foot; then once again he shut his mouth. If Mahendra was foolish, *mad* enough, to test the bridge on horseback, then dammit, let him. If he crossed safely, then it would prove the bridge would hold while the others crossed singly on foot.

Mahendra rode on to the bridge without hesitation, kept his horse on a tight rein while it picked its way across the rough flooring. Then he was sitting above Farnol, face stiff but eyes mocking.

'You may tell the others to come across, Major.'

So the party strolled across the bridge one by one: if there were any watchers hidden on the slopes, they must have been laughing their heads off. When the first half-dozen had crossed and he was satisfied that the bridge would hold under the foot traffic, Farnol went back to the opposite side, slid down the bank and inspected the supports again. The new poles looked firm enough. He came back up to the road.

'All right, the horses now. One at a time, one *syce* to each horse.'

The horses crossed safely, their grooms more nervous than the animals. Then the coach, the victoria and the *tongas* were hauled across, each of them pulled by only two men. Farnol went down below the bridge again. The sawn-through support had shifted, but the extra poles had settled in more firmly against the beams that carried the roadway.

He decided to stay down here and watch the supports as the elephants went across. 'Righto, Karim – send the first elephant across! Tell the *mahout* not to ride it – walk with it!'

He had already instructed the *mahouts* what to do if he shouted a warning and the expressions on their faces told him they had no enthusiasm for the venture. But he knew they would do what they were told. They were prepared to risk the collapse of the bridge in preference to risking the wrath of the Ranee, the Nawab or Mahendra.

Farnol stationed himself so that he could see under the bridge and yet follow the progress of each elephant as it made the crossing. The first *mahout*, an older man than the rest, hesitated before setting his thin bare foot on the first plank of the bridge. He looked down at Farnol and his fear was as clear as another feature on his thin dark face. Then the elephant nudged him with its forehead and he stumbled forward, the elephant moving after him. Farnol, alternately glancing under at the supports and up at the man and elephant on the bridge, saw the *mahout* putting his feet down so cautiously that one might have thought it was *his* weight that would bring the bridge crashing down. He minced his way across and the elephant lumbered after him; slowly they made their way across what had now become in Farnol's eyes a frail catwalk. But the supports held and the old *mahout* and his charge safely made it to the other side, to a loud cheer from those already there. But the *mahouts* still on the wrong side of the bridge could not bring themselves to join in the cheering. Each one knew when he'd be ready to shout with joy and relief.

The next half-hour was the longest thirty minutes Farnol could remember. After each elephant and its *mahout* had crossed he went in under and checked the supports of the bridge. The sawn-through support had shifted still further and the new pole beside it was now taking all the weight.

He clambered out from under the bridge and looked up at the last elephant and its *mahout*. This one was only a boy, no more than fourteen; he smiled down at Farnol, but it was an old man's grin, forced and hopeless. Farnol clambered up the bank and patted the boy on the back.

'What's your name?'

'Mahmoud, sahib.'

'You run on across the bridge. I'll bring your elephant.'

The boy hesitated, then shook his head. 'He will not move for anyone but me, sahib. He worked for my father, who is dead, and now he works only for me.'

Farnol looked up at the great beast, which seemed to him to be the biggest of all the elephants in the caravan. A small eye returned his look, then the animal lifted its head and raised its trunk. He waited for it to trumpet, but it didn't: it just waved its trunk from side to side as if dismissing him. He knew of elephants such as this, who could be rogues in the hands of anyone but their regular *mahouts*. This rickety bridge would be no place to try to prove he was the beast's master.

'Whom do you work for?'

'The Ranee, sahib.'

'I think you'd better go back, Mahmoud. I'll tell Her Highness.'

'Oh no, sahib. I must take my elephant across.'

Farnol did not know whether it was loyalty to or fear of the Ranee that decided the boy on his duty. He knew that the Ranee did not treat her house servants well; but she would have very little if anything at all to do with her *mahouts*. But evidently fear of her temper had filtered down from the house servants and the boy would rather face the risk of a tumbling bridge than her wrath.

'All right, Mahmoud. Go very slowly and keep to that side of the bridge. I'll come behind you.'

The boy nodded, tapped the elephant with his stick, and it lowered its trunk and he scrambled up it and sat on its neck with his legs tucked in behind the huge ears. He looked down at Farnol.

'He understands me better if I am up here, sahib. He trusts me.'

Farnol hesitated, then nodded. 'All right, go ahead.'

The boy gave a soft-voiced order and the elephant, as if suddenly aware that all was not well, put a tentative foot on the first planks of the bridge. For a moment Farnol thought it was not going to go any further; then it stepped on to the bridge and began to lumber slowly across. Farnol slipped down the bank again, peered in at the supports; the new poles slipped a couple of inches even as he looked at them. Then they settled, appeared firm against the rocks. He scrambled back up to the road, started off across the bridge after Mahmoud and the elephant.

He could feel every nerve-end pressing to burst out of him, every sense heightened. The periphery of his vision had widened: it seemed that on one look he took in the hills above him, the raging river below, the anxious group standing at the far end of the bridge. He could feel the vibration of the elephant's tread coming back at him through the planks; or so he imagined. He found himself treading lightly, as if trying to draw his own weight up into the air above the fragile roadway. He had once had a delicate encounter with the Calcutta top brass and had described the experience as *walking on eggshells*; he felt he was now literally doing that. His whole body was drawn in as if to make it weightless; his muscles ached with the effort. His hearing had become even more acute than usual; the noise of the river seemed a roar just below his feet. He looked down, half-expecting to see the water seeping through the cracks between the planks. And saw the roadway beginning to tilt back towards him.

He heard the shout from those up ahead as he looked back. The end of the bridge was sliding slowly down the bank, the roadway rippling into a graceful curve as it fell away behind him. Everything seemed to happen in slow motion; but he knew it was all happening too fast. He yelled to Mahmoud and began to run. He could feel the roadway falling away beneath his feet; he was running up a hill that kept moving away. He threw his feet at the retreating, buckling planks; flung himself forward and fell headlong to grab at the side ropes of the bridge as they swung in over him. He looked up ahead and above him, waited with horror for the elephant to come sliding back down the bridge and take him with it into the river.

It was the river that saved them, if only for the moment. The suspension ropes on the far side snapped under the strain and that end of the bridge fell into the water. The current grabbed it and swept it round like a tightly curved whip. The suspension ropes up ahead suddenly twisted into a net that caught the elephant and Mahmoud; they hung there above the raging white water in a basket of ropes and planks. Below them Farnol, up to his waist in water, clung to a rope and fought the river as it tried to drag him under.

The elephant was screaming with fear, struggling to break out of the ropes and planks; the *mahout* clung desperately to its back, bound there by the web of ropes. There was pandemonium on the bank; panic seemed to have taken hold of everyone. Bridie had rushed to the bank's edge and, though hampered by her long skirt, was scrambling down over the rocks, shouting to Karim to follow her. But the Sikh was one of those who had not panicked.

He came down over the rocks, bringing a long rope with him that he had snatched from one of the *tongas*. Ahearn came with him, slipping on the glass-like rocks and almost tumbling into the river; Karim shot out an arm and pulled him back just in time. Bridie, wet through from the spray flung up by the trailing bridge as it whipped back and forth in the boiling water, recklessly reached out a hopeless hand towards Farnol, but he was too far away.

His head was still above the tumbling surface of the river, but the spray was blinding him, choking him as he opened his mouth to gulp in air. His arms felt as if they were being torn away from his shoulders; a moment ago he had tried to be weightless, now his body felt as heavy as one of the black rocks that bordered the river. He was no longer afraid of the elephant's falling on top of him; it no longer mattered how he died. If it was quick, and it would be, one way of dying was as good or bad as another.

Karim balanced himself on a rock while Ahearn held on to his belt. He flung the rope out towards Farnol; the wind caught it and it sailed away in a mocking curve. Karim tried again; this time the rope hit Farnol across the face. He grabbed at it, desperately clutched it for the lifeline that it was. Then Ahearn ranged himself beside Karim and both of them settled their legs like stanchions. Bridie, feeling useless but knowing she would only be in the way if she tried to help with the rope, resorted to prayer. She gabbled a *Hail Mary*, rushing through it in one breath.

By the time she was halfway through it, Farnol was in the water, clinging with both hands to the rope and kicking his legs to drive himself across the fierce current. The water was icy but so far he had not felt it; he felt nothing but the strain on his arms and the terrible urge to survive. Slowly, fighting the river with all their combined strength, Karim and Ahearn dragged him across the current. He hit a rock, felt his hip and knee strike it, then Karim was reaching down and pulling him up on to the jagged bank.

He lay across a black rock, arms and legs widespread as if just dropped from a cross. He felt, rather than saw, the drenched Bridie bending over him. At last he looked up through the water that still ran off his face and was warmed and surprised by the anguished concern she showed. He raised a bleeding hand, took hers and found the strength to squeeze it. For a moment they were as intimate as if they were wrapped together in love-making.

Then he heard the screaming of the elephant, laboured now and not so continuous. He raised himself, saw the great beast still trapped in its basket of ropes and timber, looked for Mahmoud and saw the boy, seemingly unconscious, still pinned to the elephant's back by the ropes. He got to his feet, still sore and exhausted, and Karim and Ahearn helped him up to the roadway.

The Nawab and the others crowded round him. 'Are you all right? Are you hurt? My God, we thought you were done for, old chap!'

Farnol straightened up. Deep within him exhaustion and relief at his own rescue tugged at him to turn away from the river, to take the easy way out: let someone else worry about the young *mahout* and the terrified elephant. But he knew he couldn't do that; and it was not just a sense of duty as an army officer. He could not turn his back on anyone in danger of losing his life. Life, they said, was cheap in India. But he had always put more than the market price on it.

The elephant, too, was exhausted; it had stopped struggling. It hung in its basket, made ridiculously pathetic by its size: one almost wanted to laugh. Mahmoud was still unmoving, the ropes tight across his back and neck; Farnol had a horrifying thought that the boy might already be dead, strangled by the ropes. He started giving orders, was glad to see that none of the servants or escorts stopped to query his authority.

Four elephants were brought to the end of the bridge and a rough harness of ropes attached to them. Then Farnol looked at Karim. 'Will you come out there with me?'

He knew that if they had been alone Karim would have queried the wisdom of such a move. But he was a Sikh amongst lesser breeds and after a moment's hesitation he said, 'If you say so, sahib. What are we going to do?'

'We're going to put ropes round that section of the bridge and have these elephants here drag it up on to the road. But before we do that we're going to cut the *mahout* out from those bridge ropes, otherwise they're going to slice him in half.'

The Ranee said, 'You don't have to risk your life, Clive. There are enough bearers here – let them go.'

'I'd rather do it myself, Mala.'

He was not curt with her, but he turned away at once and made his way out on to the tangle of ropes and timber. His wet clothes were chilling him now; he badly wanted a leak. But he was ashamed to be feeling any discomfort: it was nothing to what the boy bound to the elephant must be feeling.

He and Karim worked their way carefully down the hanging bridge. It was still moving, its bottom end dragged by the current; it moaned and squeaked like a living thing. Up on the bank Ahearn was supervising the feeding out of the long harness ropes and the Nawab had cleared the roadway. There was no pandemonium now but an organized effort to prevent the *mahout* and the elephant being swept to their death.

'Mahmoud!' Farnol hung in the rigging above the boy and the elephant.

The boy stirred, tried to turn his head but was too constricted by the rope across his neck. 'Sahib?'

'We're going to get you out of this, Mahmoud. Hold on just a little longer.' *Where the hell do I expect him to go*? But Farnol knew the banalities that were uttered in moments of crisis: it was the sound of a voice, not the words, that comforted.

It took them ten long minutes to get the harness ropes down round the elephant. It took another twenty, even longer minutes to chop through the planks of the roadway hanging below the elephant; the weight of the trailing length of bridge in the water would be too much for even a dozen elephants to pull up on the bank. At last there remained only the skimpy basket, supported by the harness ropes, in which hung the elephant and Mahmoud.

'Right.' Farnol looked across at Karim on the other side of the big rough basket. 'Do you want to go back up on the road? When I cut this rope to free Mahmoud the whole lot may come unstuck.'

Karim, like Farnol, was hanging like a mountaineer from the web of bridge ropes, his feet wedged in above a splintered plank. Below him the elephant, tiny eyes red with fear and exhaustion, was grunting and heaving in huge gasps. Mahmoud still couldn't move, but he was conscious and tensed, ready to be saved.

'I think I had better stay, sahib. It may need the two of us.'

Farnol nodded his thanks; Karim had been with him too long for words always to be necessary. He took out the knife he had brought down with him, sawed at the rope across the boy's neck. It snapped and fell apart; Farnol saw the bloody wound across the thin brown neck and almost wept for the boy. But he didn't linger on the *mahout*'s injuries, instead he went on to the other two ropes that bound him. The elephant, as if sensing that something was about to happen, began to struggle weakly; its trunk came out of a gap in the web and thrashed like a dark handless arm. The ropes creaked, a plank splintered and fell away into the water and was gone from sight immediately.

'Tell him to be quiet, Mahmoud! Be still!'

The boy beat a weak fist on the elephant's head, shouted at it. The animal quietened, but it was still terrified; Farnol could see the great grey hide trembling under the ropes like volcanic mud about to erupt. He slashed at the last rope that trapped Mahmoud, grabbed the boy as he slid down into his arms. The elephant, feeling the boy slide from its back, feeling itself abandoned, let out a terrible scream and began at once to struggle frantically.

'Pull!' Farnol yelled. 'Pull!'

Up on the road the four elephants began to strain against their harness. Slowly the end of the bridge was drawn up; the stricken elephant came up in its basket of planks and ropes like meat being delivered to some upper storey. The elephants strained forward and the ruined bridge came up over the edge of the bank, bringing with it its mixed cargo.

A loud cheer went up and even the Ranee beamed and applauded. Only Mahendra remained unmoved by it all.

CHAPTER SIX

Extract from the memoirs of Miss Bridie O'Brady:

I don't know if I joined in the cheer when Clive, Karim Singh, the *mahout* and the elephant were at last drawn safely up on to the road. It seemed to me that I had been holding my breath ever since Clive had gone down to put the harness ropes in place; if I did cheer it could only have been a silent one. My legs were suddenly just sticks of jelly and I sat down without really looking to see if there was anything behind me. Fortunately there was a rock, a hard rough seat that I barely noticed against my bottom.

I was wet through. My hair had come loose and was hanging down about my face. I felt weak and almost ill; yet I was thrilled and full of admiration. I had just seen the rescue of the man I was coming to love, though I had not yet admitted that to myself; but I had also seen what made the British Raj work. It was the beginning of my education in the British in India.

Up till then all I had seen, possibly because it was all I wished to see, was a master-servant relationship, with all the advantages to the master. Like most Americans, but not all, of that period, I was anti-colonial, a firm, if unsworn, enemy of imperialism. So far I had sent home two despatches and both of them had been tinged with my American distaste for the British presence in India; it was the sort of story that the Boston Irish readers, and particularly my father and Mayor Honey Fitz, would relish reading. Like all nationalities we Americans have convenient memories and eyes that can turn blind on a whim. Our occupation of the Philippines wasn't really imperialism, though of course there were some Americans who were honest and stupid and proud enough to claim that it was and what was wrong with it, anyway? Too, even as I had written my despatches, American bankers had, with their acquisition of the National Bank of Nicaragua and the state railroads, virtually been allowed to buy Nicaragua. Imperialists are like certain seducers: it is only rape when the other fellow does it.

Now, beside the wrecked bridge on the banks of that remote river in the Himalayan hills, I had seen what made the Raj work. It was leadership, the quality that impelled a man like Clive Farnol to risk his life to save that of a young *mahout* and an elephant. He could have stood safely on the bank and sent several of the hundred or so servants, the easily replaceable, out to risk their lives on the bridge. But he hadn't; and I saw that all the servants, the ordinary Indians, respected him for what he had done. They might not love the British nation and its institutions, as the Nawab professed to do, but they could admire and sometimes love the individual Englishman. Of course, in the end, individuals do not prevail.

While the caravan got itself organized again, I found a secluded spot and changed out of my wet clothes. Clive Farnol, in another spot, may I point out, did the same. We met again at the head of the procession as it moved off.

There was an intimacy to our relationship now that neither of us was yet quite ready to mention frankly. We were hamstrung by several factors. Even though I was, and still am, emotionally impulsive, I had already told myself that I was in the wrong place for allowing myself to fall in love with a man. India was not for me; and I was sure America was not for Clive. There was also the matter of our careers: I could not see myself giving up my job as a newspaperwoman to be the wife of an Indian Army officer. I had already paid short visits to army posts and seen the boring life that army wives led. They were no more than walking decorations for their husbands' tunics, and they were always under the command of the colonel's lady, made as conscious of their inferior rank as if they wore pips instead of posies on their dress fronts. I could not see myself as Mrs Major Farnol.

All these reservations did not, of course, come to me at once. But the glimmerings of them were there as we resumed our journey down the cart road to Kalka. We rode alone at the head of the procession. The Nawab and Prince Mahendra were at the rear of the caravan and that did not strike me as odd till I saw how alert Clive was. Sitting tensed in the saddle, as if ready for some sudden buckjumping by his horse, he was looking up and around him, his eyes never still.

'Are you still expecting to be shot at?' Without thinking, I allowed my horse to drop a pace or two behind his.

He looked over his shoulder. 'That's a good idea. In fact, it might be better if you went right down to the back, rode with the ladies in the coach. Yes, they could take another pot-shot at me. I'm just wondering why Bertie and Mahendra decided to leave us up here on our own. Especially Bobs. He wanted so much to be leader of this little parade.'

I kept my distance behind him, but I didn't want to go back to join the ladies. I wasn't thinking of being brave; I just wanted to remain with him. I was not indulging in any Irish recklessness; there is also an Irish caution that tends to be overlooked. So I kept a good horse's length behind him, a safe distance measured against the accuracy of those hillmen snipers, and kept my own eye out for any movement on the surrounding slopes.

'What about the Nawab?'

'I'm not sure about him. He may be back there just keeping an eye on his wives.'

'Why should he suddenly start worrying about them?'

'Not all of them. Just one.' He rode in silence for a while and I thought he was concentrating on scouting the hills up ahead. Then he looked back over his shoulder again. 'The youngest one. She wants to tell me something.'

'Something about Major Savanna, do you think?'

'I haven't the faintest idea. But Bertie interrupted us and I'm not sure if he suspects her. I must try and see her tonight somehow.' He twisted even further round, looked directly at me. I suddenly realized that he had just made a decision to take me fully into his confidence from now on. The thought warmed me, even if it frightened me a little. 'Perhaps you'd help.'

'How?'

'Could you keep Bertie occupied for ten or fifteen minutes this evening?'

'Occupied?' It was a term Toodles Ryan used to use. 'You don't mean – ?'

For a moment he looked blank; then he burst out laughing, the snipers in the hills forgotten. 'Good God, no! Do you think the Political Service uses ladies that way?'

Mata Hari hadn't been heard of then; but I knew of Belle Boyd and other female spies and I had no wish to emulate any of them. 'I'll distract the Nawab's attention, if you like, but I shan't keep him *occupied*.'

He smiled and again I was aware of the new intimacy between us. 'Bridie,' he said, 'when we get to Delhi, save me every night you're there.'

The exchange seemed to relax him; or perhaps he thought we had moved far enough down the road to be beyond the range of any snipers who had been watching what went on at the bridge. He pulled his horse back, to ride beside me and keep me enthralled for the next hour with his adventures in the Indian Army and later the Political Service. It was like listening to Mr Kipling's stories come to life. I began to appreciate what sheltered lives ward bosses led, but I knew I would never embarrass my father by telling him so. He thought he led the most exciting life of any O'Brady since an uncle of his had retired, stuck with arrows, from being a Pony Express rider.

Several of the carts had been sent on ahead before the bridge had collapsed. There were no oxen drawing the carts, as would have been normal; they were pulled by horses. Loaded down as they were with tents and camp gear, everything that the Ranee and the Nawab and Mahendra would need when they set up their establishments down in Delhi, the carts' progress was necessarily slow. So by the time we started off they were already several miles down the road ahead of us, the several butlers riding with them and scouting for a place to set up camp for the night. Back in America I had covered several stories on the rich, on the people such as the Fishes and the Lorillards and the Flaglers, but I had never experienced their way of life. Now, as an outsider, I was coming to appreciate the advantages of having squadrons of servants when travelling. All one had to do, it seemed, was to *arrive*.

So in the late afternoon we arrived at the latest camp site. The road still ran close by the river, but here the water ran more smoothly. Tents had been set up and there was a canvas bath in each one, with hot water, as it were, on tap. I bathed, changed and, putting on a coat against the dusk's chill, went out to occupy the Nawab. I was not inexperienced in getting men's attention and holding it; I think there is a courtesan somewhere inside me who never quite managed to get out. Most men, when flattered by a woman's attention, can be as simple and unguarded as the boys most of them really are; but I was not so sure that the Nawab was ever unguarded behind that smiling, 'dear boy' front of his. Cricketers may live in a fantasy world (Rudyard Kipling had once called them 'flannelled fools'), but Bertie, the Nawab of Kalanpur, well aware of the real world, was no fool, flannelled or otherwise.

He, too, had bathed and changed and was sitting in a canvas chair down on the river bank. On a table beside him were glasses, bottles of gin and tonic and some limes. 'My dear Miss O'Brady! A drink? Do join me – I feel so sinful when I drink alone. My dear pater wanted to cut me off without a rupee when he learned that I took alcohol. Fortunately he died before he could disinherit me.'

The bottles and glasses were right beside him and he could have poured me a drink without effort. But, without looking round, he clicked his fingers and a bearer appeared out of the dusk and poured me a drink. The Nawab raised his glass to me and I knew I was going to get all his attention, at least for a while. I could not see Clive, but I hoped he could see me and was taking advantage of what I was doing for him.

'You have had so many adventures here in India – will you write a book about it all when you go home to America?'

'Maybe. But I think Mr Kipling has cornered the market on stories about India.'

'Ah, how he maligned us up there in Simla with some of his stories. But then sometimes he could write the most marvellous tale. Have you read "The Man Who Would Be King"?'

'Yes.' I sipped my drink, tried to sound, oh, so casual: 'Would you like to be King of the Himalayas?'

He gazed at the river a while and I waited for some sharp answer that said he had not been taken in by my innocent question. A kingfisher, late going home, skimmed the water, looking for an evening snack; then suddenly it was gone, disappearing into the blue shadows on the opposite bank. I remembered the old legend, that the kingfisher came out of the Ark as a dull grey bird; not knowing which way to fly, it flew directly into the setting sun, which burnt its breast red but left its back reflecting the green-blue of the evening sky. I noticed that the Nawab, moving closer to Delhi and the expected magnificence of the Durbar, was changing his colours. This evening he did not wear the white shirt and black tail-coat he had worn previously, but was in a pale blue *achkan* and breeches. He wore no jewellery, but perhaps he was holding that back for the final display.

At last he said, 'No, I should not like to be King of these mountains. There are too many nooks and crannies where enemies might hide. I am a lazy man, Miss O'Brady. All I want is a quiet life.' He looked at me then and smiled. 'A quiet, rich life. To play cricket all day and spend my nights with beautiful women.'

'Would your cricket leave you any energy to spend on the beautiful women? I'm told our baseballers do all their mating in the off-season.'

'I field in the slips – one doesn't have to expend much energy there.'

This was all too esoteric for me: what the devil were *the slips*? I hoped that Clive was working fast questioning the youngest wife from the *zenana*; I was not going to be able to keep going very long on the subject of cricket. But I dared not look back towards the tents where the *zenana* was quartered.

'Will you still play cricket when the British finally leave India?'

The light had almost gone now, but even in the falling darkness I sensed him stiffen. 'Who told you they were going to leave?'

'They must go eventually, mustn't they? Someone once wrote that the beginning of the end for the British Raj was the Mutiny. I did a lot of research before I came out here, Your Highness.'

'Call me Bertie. I don't think you did enough research – or you read the wrong sort. The Mutiny was over fifty years ago – the English are still here. Do you see any evidence of their leaving?'

I realized I had taken too sharp a tack. I might learn something more about him than what he presented to the world; but the chances were I should soon be out of my depth. I had indeed done some research reading on the ship coming out to Bombay, but since my arrival I really had not seen any evidence that the British were ready to pack up and leave. Indeed, the coming Durbar might be just the reverse, a raising of flags and flourishing of trumpets to let the world know that they intended to remain in India.

I was saved by the approach of Magda Monday. She was the right one for the moment. Had the Ranee or Lady Westbrook come on the scene I fear the Nawab would have lingered only a moment, then politely left us. But another pretty woman, even if her looks could now hardly be seen in the gathering dark, would keep him interested. I wondered what beauties were hidden behind the veils in the *zenana*.

Magda lavished perfume on herself. Though she sat on the other side of the Nawab from me, I still got a very strong whiff of her. 'What a lovely perfume!' said the Nawab, sniffing as if he had a cold. 'Is it French?'

'Bulgarian,' said Magda, and seemed to send out another wave of it. It was like being down-wind from a rose-syrup factory. 'My husband has it specially made for me. Do you like your ladies perfumed, Your Highness?'

Oh my God! But the Nawab seemed to revel in the direct assault. 'Of course. I noticed you aren't wearing any, Miss O'Brady.'

'I couldn't find my eye-dropper.'

Magda laughed. She was like her husband: you couldn't dent her with an axe. 'Miss O'Brady prefers the subtle approach. But one only needs that with men who are afraid of women. And you're not afraid, are you, Your Highness?'

Suddenly, perversely, I liked her. She was an old campaigner from the battles of the sexes; she had won her medals, perhaps by losing her honour, but she had certainly won them.

160

I wondered how Clive, who did not have a subtle approach with women, was faring with the Nawab's youngest wife. Then we heard the shot from over behind the *zenana* tents.

End of extract from memoirs.

2

Farnol had seen Bridie go down to sit with the Nawab and at once he had made his way discreetly, using the long line of tethered elephants as a screen, towards the *zenana*. The two tents housing the wives had been set well apart from those of the main party; two armed men from the Nawab's escort guarded them. But a latrine shelter had been put up in a stand of bamboo behind the tents, and Farnol, standing by the last of the elephants, had seen one of the older wives go towards it without any interference from the guards. He stood and waited and two or three minutes after the first wife had emerged from the shelter the youngest wife came out of one of the tents and walked towards the bamboo. Once behind the screen of bamboo she moved quickly across to join Farnol.

'My name is Ganga, but you mustn't mention it to my husband.' She spoke in Hindi, her voice just a whisper behind her veil. 'I do not know what he would do to me if he knew I had spoken with you. He can be very cruel with his tongue sometimes.'

'What is it you wanted to tell me?'

'The other Englishman – Major Savanna?' The girl was trembling; Farnol could smell the fear in her. 'The gossip is that you do not know why he was at Prince Mahendra's palace.'

Farnol did not wonder how the gossip had reached the *zenana*: Indian ears, he knew, could hear whispers in a cyclone. 'Do you know why he was there?'

'To see Prince Sankar.'

It took Farnol a moment to understand whom she meant. 'Your husband's cousin?'

'Yes. The Rajah of Pandar. He was there at the palace the night we arrived. I saw him with Major Savanna.'

'Was Major Savanna all right when you saw him? I mean, was he ill?'

'I don't think so. He was very angry. He and Sankar were arguing – it was a very fierce argument.'

'Could you hear what they were saying?'

'Only a word or two. They were in a courtyard below our rooms, but on the other side of it. I heard Major Savanna say your name.'

'Did you hear what he said about me?' Jesus God Almighty, could Savanna have been in the plot to assassinate him?

'No. I said, they were too far away. But once Major Savanna almost shouted your name, he was so angry.'

'Did any of the other wives see them?'

'No, I was at the window on my own.'

'Why are you telling me this?' He wanted to believe her; but she could be lying to him for her own ends. Or someone else's.

She was silent. In the darkness she was a presence rather than a shape; it struck him that if she passed him in daylight without her veil he would not recognize her. All he knew of her was her eyes and her voice; the voice sounded like that of someone very young, a schoolgirl. Behind them the wall of elephants stirred restlessly; a *mahout* called out for them to quieten down. The night breeze rustled drily through the bamboo and over by the kitchen tent a cook screamed at some bumble-footed coolie. Dinner would soon be ready, he must be getting back to join the others before he was missed.

'I do not like being one of the wives – '

'Your husband must love you – ' He didn't really believe that.

'He tells me he loves me more than the others. But he tells that to all of us – '

He wanted to laugh. It was like some joke from *Punch*, if *Punch* went in for jokes like that.

'I want to leave the *zenana*.' He had to lean forward to hear her; she smelled of some musky perfume that her sweat of fear heightened. 'Perhaps you could help me – '

Farnol saw the tiny red flash in the darkness in the instant that he heard the shot. Ganga fell forward into his arms and he dropped to the ground with her, waiting for the second shot. Behind him an elephant screamed and out of the corner of his eye he saw the long line swaying against the stars like a mountain range heaving in an earthquake. *Christ, they're going to break loose and stampede!* Careless of whether there would be a second or third shot, he scooped up Ganga, got to his feet and staggered away from the elephants, plunging blindly into some bamboo and crashing through it as if it were no more than sticks of celery. He could hear the *mahouts* shouting as they tried to quieten the elephants, but the huge beasts were screaming and trumpeting and, faintly behind their clamour, there was also the terrified neighing of the horses.

He stumbled through some bushes, avoided a cactus tree more by instinct than because he saw it, and staggered out into the open beside the *zenana* tents. The panic was subsiding in the elephant and horse lines, the *mahouts* and *syces* gaining control. He stopped and laid Ganga on the ground, knowing as he did so that she was already dead. He was kneeling beside her when the Nawab loomed over him.

'What happened?'

Farnol stood up slowly, feeling for the first time the scratches and cuts from his crashing through the bamboo. People were crowding in behind the Nawab; the other wives, servants; but so far he had seen none of the Europeans nor the Ranee and Mahendra. For the moment he was in the Nawab's territory, like someone trapped in an alien embassy.

'She is dead. Someone shot her.'

A bearer raised a paraffin lamp on a stick as the Nawab dropped to one knee beside his dead wife. It was as if he had not recognized the limp shape at Farnol's feet; but now the yellow glow of the lamp showed her face with its veil torn away. Farnol was surprised how young she looked; she could not have been more than sixteen. Young and beautiful, but dead; the Nawab suddenly bent his head and gave a strangled sob. The other wives all began to weep then, as if they had been waiting for their husband to lead them by example. The servants looked neither sad nor curious, as if a death in the *zenana* could never touch any of them.

'I'm sorry, Bertie.'

163

Farnol walked quietly away, the wives and servants opening up their ranks to let him through. He came out into the open to see Bridie and the others standing in a group outside the dining-tent.

'One of Bertie's wives has been shot,' he told them.

There was a gasp from the women and murmurs of concern from the men. But Farnol was watching Mahendra, the only one who showed no expression at all. In the pale yellow light from the paraffin lamps in the dining tent, the young prince looked as if he might have been alone, lost in contemplation that had nothing to do with the tragedy of a moment ago.

'Who shot her?' said the Ranee. She sounded angry; but she could have been afraid. 'Why?'

'Clive –' The Nawab had come up, stood on the edge of the group. 'I'd like to talk to you. Alone.'

Farnol glanced at Bridie, wondering how successful she had been in distracting the Nawab's attention before the shooting. But the light was not good enough for him to read any glance she gave him; he turned away and followed the Nawab down to the edge of the river. He was sickened and shocked by what had happened to Ganga, the effect doubled by the thought that he, and not she, had been the real target.

'What were you doing with Ganga?'

There was no point in lying: the girl was safe from any punishment Bertie might inflict on her. 'She wanted to see me about Major Savanna.'

'She should have minded her own business. She'd still be alive if she had. What did she know about Savanna?' But the question seemed rhetorical; his voice broke. 'She was the one I truly loved, Clive. But she never believed that.'

That's always a problem when you have five other wives: but one couldn't say that without sounding flippant. Still, he was surprised at the sincerity of Bertie's grief; the man had never shown himself to be anything but self-centred. 'How old was she?'

'She would have been sixteen next week.'

A child, by his own standards: but then he had always been more interested in older women, whether English or Indian. 'I never dreamed I was exposing her to any danger by talking to her. Except from you – I thought you might be angry with her if you knew.'

'I'd never have hurt her.' Bertie waved a hand at the night: 'But who would kill her?'

'Bertie – I think whoever it was, was trying to kill me. In the dark I think he was off target.'

'You should not have talked with her,' the Nawab said stubbornly, as if there were some hope that death could be rescinded.

Below them the river hissed and whispered and out in midstream a fish splashed, a large one, perhaps a *mahseer*. It seemed to Farnol, his mind still askew, that the sounds were sinister. Abruptly he wondered if Bertie had brought him down here to make him an easier target for that second shot. The moon came up over the valley's rim like a yellow explosion in slow motion and he knew how clearly he must be outlined against the suddenly bright river.

'She told me your cousin Prince Sankar was at Mahendra's palace the night before last, that he was with Savanna before Savanna became ill.'

The Nawab stared out at the river, sighed heavily. 'I did not know that. I haven't seen Sankar in, oh, almost a month.'

'What has he to do with all this?'

'All what? Nothing, as far as I know. Why should he?' But Farnol knew the Nawab was lying.

He had never met the Rajah of Pandar. The State of Pandar was neighbour to the States of Serog and Kalanpur; once it had been the only State in this region, till tribal chieftains, long before the British came, had fought the ruler of Pandar and set up their own principalities. But Pandar was still the biggest and richest of the three States and till six months ago had been ruled by an elderly recluse who had never encouraged visitors, least of all officers of the British Raj. Perhaps Savanna had visited him on courtesy calls, but Farnol would have to wait till he got down to see George Lathrop before he could check that. The ruler had died and his only son and heir, Prince Sankar, had come home from Europe, where he had lived for ten years, to become Rajah. The State had had a reputation for stability and the British, not wanting to stir quiet waters, had never interfered more than was necessary.

Farnol himself sighed, decided he was going to get nowhere with the Nawab. And it was time he found a background other than the silver river, made himself a much less exposed target. 'Righto, Bertie, we'll leave it at that. I don't believe you and I want you to know it. So we'll both know where we stand from now on. But with the murder of your wife, I thought you might be forthcoming. Just for her sake.'

'Goodnight, Clive.' The Nawab went up the bank and across to his tent.

Farnol was left alone, outlined against the bright silver background. He shivered, waiting for the bullet to hit home; then he went up the bank and across to the dining-tent. It took great effort not to run.

No one ate much, the talk was desultory and Farnol was glad to escape from the table. Bridie followed him out into the night and at once he was concerned for her.

'You shouldn't be near me. You saw what happened to that girl.'

'I can't keep avoiding you all the way down to Delhi. Let's sit down here.' There were two canvas chairs outside Farnol's and the Baron's tent. 'I'll sit apart from you, if it'll make you feel any easier.'

He went into the tent, turned out the paraffin lamp so that they would not be silhouetted against it. Then he came back and sat down beside her, not bothering to move his chair apart from hers. He felt comforted, which was something he had not felt with a woman in a long time. He had certainly never felt comforted by Mala.

'Bertie seems genuinely upset. He says he loved her.'

'How old was she? She was very young, wasn't she?'

'Not quite sixteen.'

'Oh my God! And he's – what? Forty?'

'They marry young in this country.'

'But the difference in their ages!' She knew of elderly men back home who had young mistresses; but that was different. The girls were always free to leave, they would have laughed at the thought of marriage unless a huge settlement was written into the marriage contract.

'I thought it happened a lot in Ireland. Old men marrying young girls. I remember reading once that Sir John Acton, who was the Prime Minister of Naples in Nelson's day, was sixty-four when he married his thirteen-year-old niece.'

'Disgusting!'

But they were both just making words. He put out a hand and took hers, forgetful of targets and snipers. 'It's better, of course, if you're much the same age. How old are you?'

'Old enough.' She turned her hand over, linked her fingers in his. 'But I still say, that poor girl. Bertie's wife. Not just that she died the way she did, but that her life was already decided for her. Women should have more – more freedom than that.'

'I agree.' But he would have agreed with anything she said that evening. Anything to be comforted.

3

The youngest wife, Ganga, was cremated early next morning beside the river. Farnol insisted that the caravan move on, but he stayed behind with the Nawab and the four escort guards. A pyre had been built and the body already laid on it before the sun came up. The caravan moved off and only Magda and the Baron, riding backwards in the coach, looked back.

'Don't cremate me, sweetheart.' Magda shivered and looked up at her husband riding beside the coach. But she couldn't resist torturing herself, singeing herself with flames not yet lit. She said to the Baron, 'Do you want them to make ashes of you, Herr Baron?'

'I am a Catholic, Madame. We only burn our sinners.'

'Catholics,' said Lady Westbrook to the Ranee. 'They think they own Hell as well as Heaven.'

By the river Farnol divided his attention between the pyre and the surrounding hills. He knew he was exposing himself once again to risk, but he felt he owed it to Ganga to be there. She had lost her life because of him.

'I should take her back to my palace,' the Nawab said. 'But

that bridge going down – it would mean going back up the main road, it would take so many more days – I'd miss the Durbar – '

'You'd be excused. It isn't a command performance, is it?' But all at once the Nawab's grief and love for his dead wife looked spurious.

And he seemed to realize it: 'It's not just being there to honour the King. I have business – there are things I must do – '

Now was not the time to interrogate him. Later perhaps, but not now. He said sympathetically, 'I don't think she would mind going all the way down to Delhi. Not if you take her ashes home afterwards.'

'I'll do that.' The Nawab nodded absently, as if the idea had not occurred to him. 'But it takes time for the body to become just ashes. You mustn't stay, Clive.'

He seemed to bear no animosity this morning; or perhaps he was still genuinely wrapped in grief. His face was pale and strained, his eyes red-rimmed. Farnol could not imagine his weeping all night, but it looked as if it might have been so. He took a torch from one of the guards and put it to the paraffin-soaked dead wood of the pyre.

The flames leapt high and at once some of the branches fell in on themselves; the body slipped, seeming to flinch away from the flames. Farnol had witnessed dozens of cremations, but he could never reconcile himself to the sight of the fire devouring the body. He closed his eyes, tried to imagine what the girl had looked like alive; but he had seen her face for only a moment and she had been dead then. He smelled the sweet, sickening odour of burning flesh and he tried to shut his nostrils against it. He opened his eyes and saw the shroud turning to flaking ash, saw the lovely face for an instant, then the flames wrapped it hungrily and he shut his eyes against the horror.

He turned away, keeping his eyes averted. 'I'm going on, Bertie. You should catch us up when we stop for lunch.'

The Nawab nodded, but said nothing, just continued to stare at the fire devouring what might have been his one true love. Farnol went across to his horse, mounted it and set off at a canter down the road. He put the thought of any sniper out of his mind; if he were going to be murdered this morning, the shot would already have been fired. He reined in the horse a quarter of a mile down the road and looked back. The pyre was a mass of leaping flames, bright red and yellow in the early morning light; a wreathing column of smoke climbed straight up through the still air. He had noticed that the smoke from pyres almost invariably turned black, as if the bodies flew their own mourning flag. He wanted to weep for the dead girl, but he hadn't known her well enough for that sort of grief. But he felt sadder for her than he had for Rupert Savanna.

He caught up with the caravan several miles down the road, fell in for the moment beside Karim and Ahearn riding at the rear. 'That sniper is still with us. He was trying for me last night, not the Nawab's wife.'

'You are sure of that, sahib?'

'Of course.' But then he was not so sure. Once a target, always a target: a man's conceit could run away with him. What if Ganga had been the target, if someone had wanted her silenced before she told him too much? Could Bertie have suspected her and arranged for her to be watched and disposed of? Was all his grief a sham?

'How much longer before we get to Kalka, sir?' said Ahearn.

'What?' His mind was spinning like a lottery barrel. 'Two nights, I should think.'

'What happens to me then, sir?' Ahearn was thinking of doing another bunk. Things were too bloody dangerous around here. He'd be far better off on his own, yes.

'That's up to you. I can turn you over to the provosts in Kalka or you can come on down to Delhi with me and I'll see what I can do about having you transferred to my regiment.'

Karim Singh looked sideways at Ahearn, wondering why the sahib would want a deserting Irish bugger in Farnol's Horse. The Indian Army was meant for better men than that.

'I think I'll be coming down to Delhi, sir,' said Ahearn, who had had experience of being handed over to the provosts.

Farnol rode on up ahead and the Irishman and the Sikh were left to themselves. The Ranee's escort were riding immediately behind them, but neither Karim Singh nor

Ahearn thought of getting into conversation with them. Each had his own standards for the proper company he should keep.

'You think I'd be doing meself a favour if I joined His Nibs' regiment?'

'His Nibs? You mean Major Farnol?' Karim sounded as disapproving as a governess. 'You'd have to smarten yourself up. We're a very posh regiment, as good as The Guides or the Bengal Lancers or Probyn's Horse, or any of them. We only take the best chaps.'

Karim's father and grandfather had served in Farnol's Horse, always as bearer to a Farnol. Sikhs preferred to be soldiers of the line, but the Singhs had never considered themselves as being anything less by being a bearer to a Farnol. They were never expected to do menial tasks, there were always coolies to be found to carry the water, make the bed, clean the boots; but when they were alone together in the field, camped in the hills, Karim took as much pride as a family butler in caring for his master. He and the sahib were part of the regiment and, in Karim's eyes, everything they did was in the name of the regiment. The top brass in Calcutta or Delhi might not think so, but Karim Singh's second religion was the regiment and one of his gods was the sahib and he never gave a thought to the brass. The only judges, in his eyes, were the other posh regiments.

He was 35 years old and he hoped he would grow old in the regiment. He had a wife and two sons in a village in the Punjab and, more often than he would confess to the sahib, he longed to see more of them. To his secret shame, he had found he was also a family man; he kept it hidden, as if it were a venereal disease. But the pox would be forgiven; but not love of a wife and kids. His trouble was that he did not know his sahib as well as he thought: Farnol would not only have forgiven him his love of his family but been delighted by it. Farnol, too, had his secrets.

'Do you have a wife?' Karim said.

'Me?' said Ahearn and almost fell out of his saddle laughing. 'Jay-sus, man, who'd have me? Some coolie girl?'

'Some coolie women make good wives.' His own wife was not a coolie: not to him, though maybe to the English.

'No offence, man. But if I married a cool – an Indian woman, I'd be trapped here in this bloody country for life. Yes. I could never take her home to Belfast with me when me time was up. Not to Belfast, they'd never let her in.' He could not take himself home, either: he knew that now for a fact, yes. He dreamed of America or Australia, where there were opportunities for the Irish, so long as there wasn't an Englishman or a Scotsman ahead of them for a job. The trouble was, the bloody English and Scots were everywhere. The Welsh left home, too, but wherever they went they disappeared down the coal mines and were never heard of again. 'She'd die in bloody Belfast, if they let her in at all. So would I.'

'There are women going to waste in this country.' Karim was glad he had no daughters, though his wife always wished for one.

'I know. I been looking at them wives of the Nawab. Five of 'em. Six of 'em in another week or two, I suppose – he'll get a replacement for that one he's burning back there. Them fellers run their *zenanas*, they can always get reinforcements. I'd like to reinforce one of them wives, make her pregnant, up the duff.' He looked up ahead at the howdahs swaying like coracles on the tide of the elephants' backs. A wife looked back at him and he dreamed that she was smiling at him behind her veil. He raised a hand and waved, but she turned her head away disdainfully. He said bitterly, and he meant Mother India as well as the contemptuous wife, 'Bitch.'

'You watch out,' said Karim. 'You get too close to those wives and the Nawab's chaps will put a bullet in you. Or cut off your balls.'

'Jay-sus,' said Ahearn, who had never heard of an Irish eunuch and did not want to be the first.

It was mid-afternoon before the Nawab caught up with the caravan. Farnol did not question him as to what had delayed him, but it did seem as if the cremated Ganga's ashes had taken a long time to cool. The ashes were in an Army and Navy Stores' biscuit tin and were under the care of the eldest wife in one of the howdahs; as if the Nawab still thought the youngest wife was safe only within the *zenana*. He was quiet and sober-faced as he joined Farnol, Bridie and Mahendra at the head of the line. He was no longer Bertie, the flannelled fool.

'Will you report her death?' he asked Farnol. 'I'd rather you didn't, you know.'

'Are we still in Serog?'

'I think so. Are we, Bobs?'

Mahendra, quiet and sober-faced as his fellow prince, nodded. 'Our boundary is the next bridge.'

'Where shall we be then?' said Farnol.

'In Pandar.'

Oh Christ, thought Farnol. It struck him that he had worked the wrong side of the Simla hills, always to the north and never down here where they sloped towards the plains and British rule. But that was where he had been ordered to go; the English always had a blind eye for trouble close to home. They treated the Scots and the Irish and the Welsh that way and it worked; so, they had evidently thought, with the States of Serog, Kalanpur and Pandar. But now trouble could be on the very doorstep and he knew nothing of the lie of the land.

'All right, Bertie, no report. Bobs can report it if he wishes.'

'It is Mala's business, not mine,' said Mahendra.

'Why don't you just scatter the poor girl's ashes to the winds and forget all about her?' Bridie was burning, but she would leave no ashes.

'That is not in very good taste, Miss O'Brady,' said the Nawab stiffly. He had taken on another character altogether, but it didn't fit him. He had played the second-hand Englishman too long, the plummy Oxford accent kept asserting itself as if mocking him.

'I know,' said Bridie. 'But I don't think any of you are in good taste. You are all trying to pass the buck. The poor girl's death should be investigated.'

'By whom? Sherlock Holmes?'

She looked at all three of them and saw that they were allies, if uncomfortable ones. 'Oh my God! Doesn't anyone care for the girl?'

'I do.' The Nawab looked genuinely hurt and Bridie was instantly sorry for her remark.

'We have our rights,' said Mahendra. 'We, not the English,

rule our own States. We have power over life and death, so they say.'

That sounded a little melodramatic, Farnol thought; but he knew it was true. He was ashamed that Ganga's death could be put aside; yet it suited his purpose for the time being. He had to stay on speaking terms with the Nawab and Mahendra. He would learn nothing if he cut himself off from them. In a land where the population, especially the educated minority of it, loved talking as much as breathing, one always stood the chance of catching a slip of the tongue.

'So no one will do anything about her death?' said Bridie. She might have been harrying some District Attorney due for re-election.

'We did not say that.' The Nawab moved his horse up beside that of Mahendra, showing Bridie his back and the horse's rump, closing the subject.

Bridie looked at Farnol and he shook his head, silently asking her to be silent. She shut her lips tight and he remarked how plain even a good-looking woman can be when she is disapproving.

Back in the coach, with Zoltan Monday riding beside it like some better-class postillion, the three other women and the Baron had been very quiet, each for his or her own reason.

Magda, bored and drowsy, glanced lazily out at her husband, wishing they were in bed together. She did not enjoy these excursions to the outlands of the world; she was a woman for pavements. She did not mind accompanying Zoltan out of Europe if it meant they stayed in some hotel like the Perapalas in Constantinople; she would have enjoyed the stay in the palace at Serog had the circumstances been different. But the dreary, dusty trips to meet clients were a dreadful bore; lately, the trips seemed to be getting longer and drearier, as if the customers for armaments were retreating to the outposts of the world they hoped to conquer. She was no student of revolutionary politics, she longed only for the journey in which clients came with their lists and their cash to hotels like Shepheard's in Cairo or the Grande Bretagne in Athens.

'Not much longer, my love,' said Zoltan in Hungarian, as if reading her thoughts.

'I think it would be much better manners if we all spoke English,' said Lady Westbrook, coming out of her own torpor.

'My husband was making love to me.' Magda smiled, coming awake. She delighted in verbal thrusting, just as she did the other sort. 'Would it be good manners if he spoke in English?'

'It would be entertaining and perhaps enlightening,' said Lady Westbrook, forgetting her own manners.

'Is love-making so different in England and Hungary?' The Ranee languidly sat up straighter, glanced at Zoltan, wondered if she had missed something there under the deer-stalker cap and the tweed knickerbockers.

'Ladies, please,' said the Baron. 'Spare my blushes. I'm still capable of them, even at my age.'

Zoltan Monday smiled indulgently at his wife, but not before he had seen the Ranee glance towards him. He had heard of her reputation before he had come up to Simla; he gathered intelligence even more thoroughly than the clients who used the weapons he sold them. He wondered what she would be like in bed, if she thought the *Kama Sutra* just a primer or an advanced study book; but he would never attempt to find out. Afraid of losing Magda, he never allowed himself to be unfaithful to her. But there was another hunger in the Ranee besides her sexual hunger: he recognized the lust for power. After all, he had been selling to that vice all his business life, it was as familiar to him as the catalogues in his suitcase.

They passed through several small villages, where the villagers came out to pay their homage and the children hoped for a coin or two from the Ranee or Prince Mahendra, which they didn't get. In the late afternoon the caravan crossed the river again, this time over a solidly constructed bridge; now they were in Pandar. The countryside didn't change and only a few in the caravan appreciated that they had crossed a boundary. But Farnol felt it, like an itch in his back. He knew, more than most, that crossing a state boundary meant entering another state of mind.

'Do you have to request permission to pass through, Bertie?'

'My cousin and I are the best of friends.' But the Nawab's tone was not reassuring. 'Our families haven't fought in two generations.'

'Bertie's family was on the English side in the Mutiny,' said Mahendra. 'Sankar's grandfather backed the sepoys. The English have never forgiven them for that. Nor have the princes.'

'What about Sankar? Is he for the English?'

'Of course,' said the Nawab, cutting in ahead of Mahendra.

'Did you see him often in England?'

The Nawab seemed to hesitate; or perhaps he was just steadying his horse. 'He lived on the Continent.'

'Where?'

'Clive, how you do ask questions!'

'Yes, I'm afraid I do. Where did he live?'

The Nawab's horse was restive again. 'In Germany, at Baden-Baden. He loves to gamble.'

'He must wish for a casino at Simla. He'd find the whist or bridge parties rather dull. He must dislike us English for being so staid.'

'He is one of us, dear chap. We princes are realists. We know the Raj and ourselves are complementary. We shouldn't exist without each other.'

'We know how much the English depend on us, all 562 of us.' Mahendra suddenly seemed to have a passion for detail; or anyway selective detail. 'The big ones like Kashmir and Hyderabad, the medium-sized ones like Dholpur and the small ones like us.'

'There are many smaller than you,' said Farnol. 'Don't cry poor.'

Then they turned a corner in the road through the hills and there was a large village and, just outside it, a guard post. Four armed soldiers came out of a grass hut and stood hesitantly in the middle of the road, nonplussed by this army coming down on them.

'Move aside,' said Mahendra at the head of the column.

'Your Highness – ' The senior soldier kept his rifle slung over his shoulder; he knew when belligerence was foolhardy.

'There is a road tax for travellers. His Highness the Rajah has just declared we must collect it.'

'How much?' said the Nawab.

'One anna per person, Your Highness.'

'Ridiculous,' said Mahendra.

'Write him an IOU,' said Farnol, sitting easy, amused at this display of fiscal banditry. He wondered just how recently Sankar had decreed that tax must be paid. An hour ago, perhaps?

'It is not a joking matter,' said Mahendra. 'I should not dream of taxing Sankar if he rode through my territory.'

My territory: Farnol noted the possession, even if it was only illusory.

'Perhaps I'd better take over for a moment.' He pushed his horse forward, assuming authority, certain that Mahendra and the Nawab would not want to lose face by disputing it in front of the four soldiers in the roadway. He looked down at the senior soldier. 'I am Major Farnol, a British officer. I am escorting Their Highnesses and Her Highness the Ranee of Serog down to Delhi as the guests of the Government. As such they do not have to pay taxes. You will let us through.'

'Yes, sahib.' The man knew a real soldier when he saw one. He called himself one of the Rajah's soldiers, but he knew it was a joke. His rifle was his uniform; without it he looked like everyone else. But he knew how to stand to attention. 'Yes, sahib. But you will explain to His Highness the Rajah if you see him – ?'

'Of course.' Then Farnol looked at the two princes: 'As you said, we're complementary. We have our uses for each other. I've saved you all of six or seven rupees.'

They passed through the village, which spread out on the narrow stretch of flat ground on either side of the road and climbed in terraces up the sides of the hills. Clouds hung like kapok on the mountains and there was a smell of rain in the air. Smoke from the evening fires had flattened out till it looked like a floating roof above the village. The main street became crowded as the caravan moved down it and Bridie, riding at the head with Farnol and the two princes, felt like an American queen. Perhaps, when she got back to America, she should look for some politician who might one day be President... Unlike certain others in the caravan, she did not crave power, but she found she liked all the benefits that went with it. Power corrupts everyone, even consorts and ladies-in-waiting. And newspaperwomen, she admitted wryly.

Camp was already set up by the advance guard a quarter of a mile down the road from the village. Hawkers were squatting around it like beakless vultures; children held out the tiny begging-bowl of their hands and asked for *baksheesh*. The escorts cleared them away with loud authority and they went uncomplainingly, with that resignation that Bridie, becoming familiar with it now, found distressing.

'If only they'd protest,' she said to Farnol. 'Why do they let themselves be pushed around like that?'

'If we stayed here, they'd be back tomorrow and the day after and the day after that. They win, in the end. You finish up buying from them just to get rid of them. They know that.'

A merchant came into the camp with a cart drawn by two camels, having bribed two of the escort to turn their backs. He looked about him and saw a tourist.

'Memsahib!' He pulled back a tarpaulin and exposed rolls of silk in the cart, in colours so rich they challenged the dusk. He whipped out a roll and flung an end over Bridie's shoulder and looked at Farnol. 'Buy a sari for the lady, sahib.'

'No,' said Bridie. 'I'd feel an impostor, a fake.'

'You're right.' But Farnol could see her in a sari and the image excited him. Saris came off so much more easily than dresses and petticoats and all those damned things women wore. 'The English ladies in Delhi would blackball you. East is East and West is West and never the togs should meet . . .'

'Do you wear a turban with your dress uniform, like the Bengal Lancers?'

'Of course. It's the way we chaps in the Indian Army distinguish ourselves from the British Army. Men are allowed to dress up. The ladies excuse it because they like us to look dashing. We all looked dashing before the Victorians spoiled everything.' Then he spoke to the merchant: 'Does the road go past the Rajah's palace?'

'No, sahib.' He was a portly man with a waxed moustache and the slyly friendly eyes of a man who never sold on credit:

he had to convince one of his own honesty while he suspected yours. 'The palace is further back in the hills. The side road to it is blocked by guards.'

'Do you ever see His Highness down here?'

'Never, sahib. We have never set eyes on the new Rajah. Nor on the old one, either. Life is very quiet here, except for the new taxes.'

'There are other taxes beside the road tax for travellers?'

'Oh yes, sahib. Taxes for this, taxes for that. They say it is because of the Durbar. It was like that at the other Great Durbar, eight years ago. The people have to pay so that our masters can look princely and magnificent.'

'You're a socialist?' Farnol smiled, agreeing with the man but not prepared to let him know.

'A socialist – me? Sahib, I'm an entrepreneur.' He had once hawked books around army barracks, getting an education while he made a living. He had a vocabulary that he rarely had the opportunity to use. 'Some day I shall live on Malabar Hill in Bombay. Could a socialist do that?'

'But you resent paying taxes?'

The merchant looked over his shoulder. 'What merchant does not, sahib? Do Mr Fortnum and Mr Mason pay willingly?' He lit a lamp, hung it on the side of his cart, beamed and winked in its light. He was a man of the world, here on a back road in the hills. 'I'll come again in the morning, sahib, bring you some wonderful presents for the memsahib. Which is your tent?'

Farnol smiled again. 'I'll be up, watching for you. Bring some jewellery, some stones. But good stuff, if you have any.'

'I have everything, sahib.' The waxed moustache seemed to move with a flourish under his hooked nose. 'I am an entrepreneur.'

He went away, taking his evil-smelling camels with him, and Bridie said, 'I shan't allow you to buy me an expensive gift.'

He smiled. 'I told you, you finish up buying from them just to get rid of them. Otherwise he could follow us all the way down to Delhi.'

CHAPTER SEVEN

Extract from the memoirs of Miss Bridie O'Brady:

I was saddle-sore and longed to be riding in an automobile. In 1911 there were 500,000 automobiles on the roads of America, but in India they were still few and far between. Sitting in my canvas bath that evening, easing the soreness out of my bottom, I began to think of travelling the rest of the journey down to Kalka in Prince Mahendra's victoria. But even as I luxuriated in the thought of that comfort I knew I'd be back on my horse tomorrow morning, riding beside Clive. I fear women like a little masochism in their love for a man.

Not that I had yet admitted I loved him, even to myself. I kept reminding myself of the circumstances, that I was past the age for infatuation (as I grew older I realized, of course, that there is no limit to the age for infatuation). The test would be if and when I went to bed with him (can this be a lady of 79 writing this? Call it the truth of senility). In those days that *was* a test; even fast girls did not fall into bed as quickly as they appear to today. Listening to my grand-daughters talk about some of their friends I wonder why some of them ever bother to get dressed. A bath, a peignoir and clean sheets and they're set for life.

'May I come in, m'dear?' said Lady Westbrook outside the tent flap. 'I shan't look.'

She came in, sat down with her back to me and lit a cheroot. She had already had first use of the bath and was dressed for dinner. She was wearing the same dress she had worn each night I had dined with her and I wondered if it was the only gown she owned and what was in her trunk, which was brought in each night but never opened. I had come to have some affection for her, which was unusual, for I think that women do not make friends of each other easily. We were compatible, perhaps because we knew the acquaintance would not last beyond Delhi.

'*Entre nous* – ' I had soap in my ear and it was a moment before I realized she had used a French phrase. She had been reading Henry James in the coach this afternoon, her lorgnette moving up and down like a pair of loose eyes to accommodate the movement of the coach. '*Entre nous*, m'dear, I think the plot has thickened. And your dear Clive is not taking us into his confidence any more.'

'He's not my dear Clive, Viola.'

'We'll see. The point is, I think he must be frank with us. There are two sides in this matter and Clive is acting like the typical English officer, not taking his troops into his confidence.'

'You and I are his troops?'

'Of course. Oh, and Karim Singh and that Irish fellow.'

'Who are the other side?'

'Bertie, Mala and that awful brother of hers.'

'What about the Baron? And the Mondays?'

'I think the Baron is neutral. Strange, a German being neutral. I think Magda and her husband are first reserves for the other side. Or perhaps they are the ball-boys. Isn't that what they call them?'

'It depends what game they're playing.' I got out of the bath and began to dry myself. 'Viola, are you trying to tell me you and I are in danger?'

'Not me, m'dear. They won't bother with me. But yes, I think you may well be. And that's why I think Clive should tell us everything he knows or suspects.'

'I'm not sure that I want to know.' My editor at the *Globe* would have sacked me on the spot if he'd heard me. A newspaperwoman not wanting to know . . .

She turned her chair round, ignoring the fact that I was in no more than my drawers and was just drawing on my chemise. 'Are you afraid, Bridie?'

'Yes.' Women are more direct and honest about being afraid.

She nodded and pondered, as if wondering if, at her age, it was worthwhile being afraid. 'I suppose I am, too. For you, I mean. Well – ' She stood up, pulled her crocheted shawl about her bony shoulders. She would never have been beautiful, but in her young days she would have been handsome and men would have looked at her twice. Which is enough, with the right man. 'We must buttonhole Clive tonight and pry everything out of him.'

'Prise,' I said pedantically, without thinking.

'Pry, prise.' She went out of the tent and I heard her say to the evening, 'An American trying to teach me English!'

Dinner that evening was no better than we'd been having. Mulligatawny soup again, curried venison (the *chinkara* that Mahendra had caught a couple of days ago?), stewed fruit with bright yellow custard that looked as if it had been coloured and flavoured with a little curry powder. My taste buds must have been blunted; I actually enjoyed what I was served. Subconsciously, perhaps, I made allowances; the dining-tent was not meant for *haute cuisine*. We sat at a trestle table that kept rocking from side to side; bearers were continually crawling under the table-cloth to shove flat stones under the trestles' legs; it was like dining with one's legs in a kennelful of dogs. Children from the village crowded one opening of the tent, eyes, bright points in their thin dark faces, stabbing at one's guilty heart.

'Ignore them,' said Lady Westbrook. 'The cooks will give them the scraps later.'

'Are you sure?'

She looked along the table at the Ranee. 'Mala, will you settle my conscience and tell your bearers to feed all the scraps to the children?'

The Ranee was casually dressed for dining in the bush, wearing no more this evening than perhaps a hundred thousand dollars' worth of diamonds. 'I thought you didn't like children, Viola?'

'I only dislike the well-fed ones. They are always the cheekiest and noisiest.'

'Hungry ones can be cheeky, too.' Magda sounded unexpectedly, uncharacteristically serious. Perhaps she, too, had once been hungry.

The men were all quiet and, looking at them, I realized that none of them, with the possible exception of Zoltan

Monday, would ever have known real hunger, the sort of hunger that stood outside the door of the tent now. They all belonged to the ruling classes, even Clive.

So we dined there in comparative splendour in our tent, under the paraffin-lamp chandeliers, with the servants bustling in and out with plates of food that must have tortured the senses of the children in the doorway. I'm ashamed to say I did no more than sit there and feel sorry for them. Without realizing it, I was falling into the defence of those confronted by India for the first time. The size of its poverty is so huge one begins to accept there can be no solution. The problem is probably worse now even than it was then.

End of extract from memoirs.

2

When dinner was over Bridie said, 'Lady Westbrook and I would like a little chat with you, Clive.'

He had risen from his chair when the women stood up from the table, but he didn't move to follow Bridie. 'Later. I have to have a chat with the men first. They've put the port out. It would be rude to leave now.'

'The Nawab and Prince Mahendra are leaving.'

'Ah, but they always have the excuse that they're not supposed to drink.'

Bridie, showing her displeasure, left the tent and Farnol sat down again opposite the Baron and Zoltan Monday. He could only guess at what Bridie and Viola Westbrook wanted to discuss with him. He did not believe that they had information that would be new to him: what would be their source? He could only think that they wanted to offer suggestions on what he should do. Despite the fact that certain army brass thought he was too nonconformist in his approach to certain military and intelligence tasks, he was still too much a soldier. Sandhurst and then the Staff College at Quetta had, by studied omission of any mention of them, never encouraged the idea that women had anything to contribute to a soldier's profession. Women's thinking was too emotional, it muddied what should be clear-cut issues. He was not so unintelligent that he thought women unintelligent; Bridie, Viola Westbrook and Mala were present evidence of sharp, wide-awake minds; even Magda was not, as he had heard Bridie use the word, dumb. But intelligence did not make them experienced. And, though the stakes were higher than he had ever known before, he was the only one experienced in the murderous intrigue that was entangling them like weeds at the bottom of a dark pool. He would reject their suggestions and would be abused as a stubborn, blinkered male; which, perhaps, he was. But everyone knew how blinkered was the stubborn logic of women.

'Who brought the port?' said the Baron.

'The Ranee. She always thinks of men's comforts.'

'Does she provide many of them?' said Monday. 'One hears gossip – '

Farnol and the Baron smiled at each other, the one from experience, the other from forlorn hope. Farnol said, 'It's not good form to talk of a lady in the mess.'

'Are we in a mess?'

'A nice play on words,' said the Baron, savouring his port. 'The Hungarians are always so much wittier in English than the English.'

'And so are the Irish,' said Monday, trying to be modest.

Farnol, careless of an Englishman's reputation for wit in English or any other language, said bluntly, 'Yes, we are in a mess, Mr Monday. I think you are contributing to it.'

'Do we have to spoil a pleasant evening?' But the Baron knew it was already spoiled.

Monday retreated behind the small mask of his port glass. 'You are wrong, Major. I have contributed nothing, not even a lady's pistol.'

'Then I can only think you are still waiting to meet your buyer.'

It was a wild shot, but it nicked the target. Monday took a long time to swallow the sip of port he had taken; it was good port but it didn't call for such long savouring. At last he said, 'That's the truth of it, Major. Until I do meet him and sell him something, am I breaking the law?'

'Who is your buyer?'

'Ah, Major, I can't tell you that!' Monday smiled, trying to shorten the interrogation by friendly unhelpfulness.

'Mr Monday, tomorrow we shall be moving out of Pandar into the Punjab. British rule applies there. I'm sure I can find some law you've broken and I'll have you locked up. You may be in jail for a week or a month, because I understand every magistrate in the country is on his way to Delhi for the Durbar. There's a rumour they are all going to be decorated by the King. You have no idea how far civil servants will go for an honour.'

'You're pulling my leg, Major.'

'You can't be sure of that, Mr Monday. Ask the Baron how conveniently we can stretch the law here in India. I'm sure he's reported on it to Berlin. All colonial powers like to learn from each other.'

'All but the French and the Belgians,' said the Baron, intent on keeping the club exclusive.

'Ah, the French,' said Monday, trying for any diversion. 'They tell themselves they have nothing to learn from anyone.'

'I hope the Hungarians have more sense than that,' said Farnol. 'Especially you, Mr Monday. I warn you – if you don't tell me who your buyer is, you won't get past Kalka. You'll be held there at least till the Durbar is over.'

Monday put down his empty glass and the Baron leaned across and re-filled it. 'I'd advise you to be honest with the Major, Herr Monday.'

The Hungarian sighed, picked up his glass, then put it down again. 'I went to Simla to meet a man named Mr Brown. I waited three days for him, but he never appeared.'

Farnol looked at the Baron. 'You've spent more time in Simla than I have. Have you heard of this chap Brown?'

'It's not an uncommon name. There are half a dozen Browns in the government offices in Simla.'

Farnol nodded. 'It's obviously a *nom-de-guerre*, a rather obvious one, I think. Don't smile, Mr Monday – I'm not trying to be witty. With what you sell, all your clients are in a war of some sort. How was he going to contact you?'

'I was to stay at the Hotel Cecil till he got in touch with me.

I waited three days and I thought that long enough. My wife wanted to get back to Delhi to see the Durbar.'

'You put your wife's pleasure before Krupps' business?'

Monday's face tightened. 'Don't insult my wife, Major!'

'I apologize. I didn't mean to insult her. But it does seem strange to me that you would make the journey all the way to Simla from – where did you come from?' Monday sat rigid inside the role of an offended husband. 'Come, Mr Monday. Where did you get your invitation to come to India? You didn't come out here on the chance of picking up some business.'

Monday crumbled slightly. He suffered more for Krupps than Krupps knew or cared. He tried not to concern himself with the morals of what he did; all he wanted was to make a good living, with opportunities for travel. He sometimes wondered if the workmen back in Essen ever gave a thought to the end result of what they manufactured, if they thought of the shell bursting and the shrapnel hitting home and some stranger, man, woman or child, dying in agony, even if only the swift agony of knowing that life was over. He was only the salesman, he often told himself, not the maker. But he could never sell himself that line, not entirely.

'I met an Indian gentleman in Constantinople. He was on his way to study in Berlin.' He looked guardedly at the Baron, who ignored him.

'His name wasn't Har Dayal, by any chance?'

'No. I don't think I have to give you his name, Major. Constantinople isn't in British territory. Yet.'

Farnol gave him a weak smile, like a card that had been trumped. 'I don't think the Turks would welcome us. They have always been more hospitable to Germans. And, I suppose, Hungarians who work for German firms.'

'Business is business. The Turks want to buy only the best.'

'Well said,' said the Baron, stirring up the sediment of his pride. He came of a school that found it hard to believe that trade had anything to do with national pride.

Farnol felt he was losing control of the conversation. His voice took on an impatient note: 'So you met this Indian gentleman and he told you to come to Simla and see Mr Brown on the off-chance of picking up some business?'

'I don't do business that way, Major. I was given a down payment of five thousand pounds as evidence of faith. Mr Brown was to give me the details of the order and where and when it was to be delivered.'

'A big order?'

'Initially it would be half a million pounds, then possibly more.'

'All field guns?'

Monday hesitated, then nodded. Then the Baron said, 'I don't think so, Herr Monday. You not only work for Krupp, you are also an agent for Mauser and Deutsche Waffen Munitionsfabriken.'

Farnol was learning much more than he had expected. What sort of revolutionary movement was it that was already thinking of ordering field guns? And how many rifles and machine-guns could be bought, even after the purchase of the field guns, with the sort of money Monday had mentioned? He had seen the Mauser-DWM 198 rifle and the DWM MGO-08 machine-gun used by Pathan tribesmen on the North-West Frontier and he knew how effective they were. Most rebellions began with a few captured rifles and machine-guns. But this was someone, a madman perhaps, who was already thinking in terms of a war rather than a rebellion.

'How could they bring so many guns, especially field guns, into the country?' The Baron was as disturbed as Farnol. 'It would be impossible to do it without their being intercepted.'

'Oh, they could do it, Baron. They could bring them in over the old roads, down through Persia and Afghanistan. It's been the way in for centuries.'

The Baron looked at Monday with genuine disgust. 'Anything for profit, Herr Monday. Whatever Major Farnol does with you, I shall certainly report your activities to Berlin.'

Monday looked at him almost sympathetically. 'I think Berlin already knows, Herr Baron. For your own sake it would be better to turn a blind eye.'

The old man sat very still, as if only his will kept him from slumping in dejection. He glanced at Farnol and the latter nodded understandingly: the man in the field so often never entered into the calculations of the plotters back home. But the Baron knew more than the Englishman did: that German embassies and consulates were expected to act almost as foreign offices for Krupps salesmen. He had had that indignity forced upon himself when he had been the consul in Shanghai. Only God and the Kaiser knew what went on these days between Berlin and Essen. A soldier, he thought, should never become a diplomat; and once again cursed the loss of his arm.

'It is despicable.' His voice seemed on the verge of breaking. He should never have come here to India, he had always been too sympathetic towards the English. But he had had connections, he had asked for the post and he had got it. Yet all the while, he supposed, they had been laughing at him behind his back in Berlin. He took out his fury on the Hungarian: 'Coming here as a visitor, to sell arms to a pack of revolutionaries. Like – like some Levantine hawker – '

'I never question what the arms are needed for, Herr Baron. When I first started with Krupps I was assistant to their agent in Italy. We sold guns to the English to use against the Boers in the South African war. Nobody in London questioned that – '

'Don't make things worse for yourself by spreading lies,' said Farnol.

'It is the truth, Major. The English needed certain types of guns for the war in South Africa and they didn't have them. They bought them from us. They know all about it in Whitehall and the English gunners who fired the guns would know. But not the Englishman in the street or officers like yourself. No, you wouldn't be told, Major. You English felt enough shame about the Boer War – you wouldn't have wanted anything else to think about.' The outsider, the Hungarian, was showing uncharacteristic anger; one might have thought he was the one who had been wronged. He had learned to live with his own hypocrisy, he did not have to live with other people's. 'Not all revolutionaries are dishonourable men, Major. You don't despise Cromwell, I'm sure – '

It was true, Farnol thought. History was a corridor of mirrors, the good and the bad mingled in the reflections on the walls. But all he could say was, 'You are under arrest, Mr Monday. If you behave yourself, you can continue the journey just as you have been, without any interference. If not, then I'll have to put you in the care of Karim Singh and Private Ahearn.'

'I am still in the State of Pandar.'

'You are in a State of Illusion, if you think that means anything to me. I can bend a boundary as well as a law. Just try me.'

Monday looked at his glass for a moment, then he raised it and smiled at Farnol. Experience had taught him that, with certain nationalities, the image of being a good loser had its advantages. The English loved a good loser in sport, as if winning was something to be ashamed of; what mattered was to have taken part in the game, or so they said. He had never found them good losers in business, but perhaps they were another breed of Englishmen; the most successful pirates had always been Englishmen. Soldiers, of course, had no preference for winning or losing. The war, like the game, was what mattered.

'You have my word of honour that I shall behave myself, Major. Now that you have put my business aside, perhaps I can relax and enjoy myself.'

'Do that. Perhaps the Baron can give you a hint or two.'

'Really?' But the Baron, who had a sense of duty and a conscience, had forgotten how to relax.

Farnol stood up, walked to the door of the dining-tent, then turned and said sharply, 'Who came and told you that Mr Brown wouldn't be turning up in Simla?'

Another wild shot, but right on target this time. Monday spilled a little of his drink, took time to mop it up with his napkin. 'What makes you think that? I told you, I just grew tired of waiting.'

'No, Mr Monday. You'd have waited a month for a half-million pounds' order, no matter how much your wife wanted to see the Durbar. Who came to see you instead of Mr Brown?'

Monday said quietly, 'It was Major Savanna.'

Farnol kept control of his surprise. 'Did he tell you who Mr Brown was?'

'No. He was very abrupt – he was with me for only a couple of minutes. He said he'd learned why I was in Simla and I had to be on the train for Kalka the next day, the Durbar Train, or he'd have me arrested. I didn't question him. I just decided to leave.'

Farnol went out into the evening, feeling he was trying to break free of thick cobwebs. The air was still, and warmer now; they were below the mountain winds here. Up the road the lamps of the village hung like motionless fireflies in the dark; a sad thin song came from a flute, as if the player did not look forward to the morning. A line of villagers squatted on the edge of the camp, like an audience waiting for some entertainment to begin. Poor blighters, Farnol thought. The emptiness of a peasant's life always distressed him: he knew how bloody awful the simple life could be. He walked towards the line of villagers, spoke a few words to them in Hindi, got a few smiles in return. It was an easy form of charity but it made him feel a little better. They would be the losers if any revolution started here in their region.

He was interrupted by Karim Singh, who appeared at his back. 'You should be more careful, sahib.'

He nodded. 'I forgot, Karim. In the meantime I want you and Private Ahearn to keep an eye on Mr Monday. He is under arrest. He can move about the camp, but he mustn't leave it. Sleep close by him tonight, so that you can take care of *him*.'

'He is a bad chap, this Mr Monday?'

'He's not dangerous, if that's what you mean.'

'Good. I should not like to shoot a chap in front of his wife.'

'No shooting at all, dammit!' Then Farnol took a deep breath. 'Sorry, Karim. I'm tired.'

Karim was all solicitousness. 'You get a good night's sleep, sahib. The Irishman and I will take care of things.'

Farnol headed towards his tent, but was waylaid by Bridie and Lady Westbrook. The latter snapped, 'Well? You've kept us waiting long enough.'

He had forgotten them. 'I'm sorry, ladies. Can't it wait till morning?'

'No, it cannot. What's up, Clive?'

He was tired, too tired for explanations; but even so, he

would not have told them everything. He had tended to forget that Bridie was a newspaperwoman; he lived in a country where white women rarely worked and certainly never as a reporter. He knew that, like most Americans, she was anti-imperialist; her newspaper would probably welcome any stories that put the British Raj in a bad light. He had no guarantee that, in the privacy of her tent, she had not already written a despatch on the possibility of an assassination attempt on the King; if she had, he could do nothing about it. If he forcibly took her story from her, she would only re-write it when she got to Delhi, Bombay or on the ship going home. If there *was* an assassination attempt, then the story must be published; but he could not assist her in a story about a *rumour* of a plot. He wondered if Rudyard Kipling, in his days as a newspaperman in India, would have written a story based on such a rumour.

'I'll tell you when we reach Delhi.' He was still sorting out in his own mind the information Monday had given him about Savanna.

'Don't you trust us to keep it, whatever it is, to ourselves?' Lady Westbrook's cheroot glowed in the darkness like an angry eye.

'No.' It would save time to be blunt.

'Well!'

'Goodnight, ladies. We'll be making an early start.'

He moved on, but hadn't gone twenty yards before the Ranee called to him from the doorway of her tent. He was being ambushed by inquisitive women; he looked around for Magda and the Nawab's wives, but they had already retired. He followed the Ranee into her tent, knowing, with that sinking feeling that men get when they know their actions will be misunderstood by a woman, that Bridie and Lady Westbrook had stopped outside their own tent to watch him.

He heard Lady Westbrook say, and he was sure he was meant to hear her, 'Our trouble, m'dear, was that we were wearing too many clothes.'

But the Ranee was dressed sensibly for sleeping in a tent, though she did look out of character in her woollen night-dress. 'I'm tired, Mala – '

'Clive darling, relax. I'd never attempt to make love on a

camp bed. The Army and Navy Stores never sell anything that would encourage sex – that would lose them the Archbishop of Calcutta's custom.' She sat down in a camp chair and waved to him to do the same. 'Are we going to finish the rest of the journey without any more trouble?'

'How can I promise you anything like that? I'm surprised Bobs has been as quiet as he has.'

'I think there are things happening that have him puzzled. I wish I knew myself what's going on . . .'

He shook off his tiredness, determined to add a little more information to the little he already had. 'Mala, what do you know about Prince Sankar?'

'I've never met him. Bertie tells me he's not interested in women.'

'He spent, what, ten years in Europe?'

'From what Bertie has told me – he got religion or something in his last year.' She made it sound as if Sankar had got the pox or something.

'Sankar was at your palace the night we stayed there. Has Bobs got religion, too? He doesn't appear too interested in women.'

'Oh, he'll marry some day, if he lives long enough. I think. he dreams of founding his own dynasty if he can get rid of me. Who knows what mad dreams he has?' She ran a hand through the raven lushness of her hair, looked with distaste at the frail camp bed. 'I hope there is something more comfortable for me when we get to Delhi. I ordered a double bed to be sent up from Calcutta or Bombay. Perhaps – ?'

'Perhaps,' he half-promised. He hated the traitor in his loins; it had memories of her that the rest of him wished he could forget. He would have to make love to Bridie as soon as she would let him; it would be the best way of exorcising Mala from himself. 'But what if your tent is next to the King's? Everything is going to be under canvas down there.'

'Then the King should find it interesting listening to us. I'm told he's rather stuffy, not like his father at all. Good old Edward. Did you know that I met him once when I went to London?'

'Don't tell me – ?'

'Clive darling, would I tell you if I had? That would be *lèse-majesté* in the worst possible taste.'

He stood up. 'You have a certain sense of honour, Mala. You have never told me the names of any of the men you've slept with.'

'I can never remember their names, darling.'

He stopped at the tent-flap. 'Incidentally, I've put Mr Monday under arrest. He came up here to sell guns, field guns, to some mysterious buyer who never turned up. You may have a rebellion on your hands very soon.'

'Perhaps.' She sounded unperturbed. 'But I'll see that other people are deposed before I am.'

'Bobs? Bertie and Sankar?'

But she wasn't to be drawn. 'It's a matter amongst ourselves, Clive. I'll attend to it when it happens.'

'It could happen while you are down in Delhi.'

She shook her head reassuringly. 'Not while the others are all down in Delhi with me. Rebellions need leaders on the spot. I thought you'd know that. Goodnight, Clive.'

He went across to his own tent, glancing first towards the tent of Bridie and Lady Westbrook. It seemed to him that there was someone standing just inside the closed flap of the tent, but he couldn't be sure. He felt like a guilty husband creeping home, and the thought suddenly made him laugh and feel better.

The Baron, in his pyjamas, sat down heavily on his bed. 'I am getting too old for these discomforts. When I first came to India I would go tiger shooting, living under canvas – '

'How did you – ?'

'Hold a rifle? I didn't. It was all make-believe. I'd choose the best shot in the party, sit beside him and imagine it was my shot, not his, that had got the tiger. Does it sound pathetic?' He tied a knot in his empty pyjama sleeve; though he needed no reminder. 'I still enjoyed it, Clive. In any hunting party, it's not the shooting but the talk afterwards, amongst men, that is the real enjoyment. We'd sit there, with all those noises around us that you hear only in the jungle, and – ' He sighed, lay down and pulled a blanket over himself. 'Diplomacy was forgotten. One could be honest.'

Farnol undressed, got into bed and almost at once fell

asleep. When he woke he had no idea whether he had been asleep for five minutes or five hours. But even in deep sleep he had heard the faint crack of a twig trodden on; he had learned, like an animal, to keep one ear awake. He lay tensed, watching the unlaced tent flap; the flap behind his head was laced tightly. The inside of the tent was black; he could not even make out the shape of the Baron on his bed opposite. But the glow of a dying camp fire threw a faint glow on the open flap; he saw the opening widen as the figure slipped in. He waited for the man to come towards him, readying every muscle to spring up from the bed. But in the darkness he abruptly lost the man; then he realized with horror that the intruder was heading for the Baron. He threw back his blanket, came up off his bed and dived across the tent. He hit the man in the back and they both fell forward on to the Baron. The bed collapsed beneath the weight of them all and the Baron cried out in German and threshed wildly with his one arm.

Farnol felt the intruder's arm coming back at him and sensed, rather than saw, the knife. He jumped back, pulling the man with him; grabbed the arm and jerked it up behind the man's back. There was a gasp and a grunt of pain; but the would-be murderer was strong and wasn't going to give in easily. He kicked Farnol in the shins, drove his other elbow into the Englishman's midriff; then he broke loose and Farnol felt the knife slice down his pyjama sleeve, just missing his arm. He knew he had to get the assassin out of the tent; the darkness was too much of a handicap. The man seemed covered in grease and Farnol recognized the smell: it was cheetah's fat. It was an old trick to scare away any camp dogs that might raise a warning: dogs were frightened to death of cheetahs and the mere smell of them sent a dog scurrying away.

Farnol broke away from the man, stumbled backwards towards the opening, hit the tent-pole and almost brought the whole lot crashing down. Then he was out in the open and the man was coming after him, long knife upraised. Farnol fell back, looking for more space, and tripped over a tent-rope. He went down in a heap and the assassin stood above him.

Then the shot rang out and the man fell forward over Farnol. The latter rolled to one side and the knife missed his head by inches. He crawled out from beneath the body of the man and saw the Baron, pistol in his one hand, standing in the tent doorway.

'Thank you, Baron. Thank Christ you can still fire one of those.'

He went into the tent, lit the lamp and brought it out as Karim Singh, Private Ahearn and four of the guards came running up. He kicked the dead man over on his back, reached down and pulled the turban-end away from the man's face.

It was the merchant, the entrepreneur who had everything, including, it seemed, knives for assassination.

3

'This bugger would not have got into your tent, sahib, if I had been guarding you instead of Mr Monday.'

'He might have killed you before he got to me, Karim.' Farnol looked down at the dead merchant; the waxed moustache was flattened against his upper lip like a big black moth. 'The point is, he's dead and not you or me.'

But Karim Singh was still unhappy and said so to Private Ahearn as they called bearers to pick up the body and take it away. 'We have to be in two places at once from now on. We have to look after the sahib as well as that other chap Monday.'

'I'm beginning to think I oughta stayed in Simla. Whose bloody trouble is it, anyway? It's got nothing to do with me.'

But Ahearn was less disgruntled than he sounded. The closer he stayed to Major Farnol, the more he put the officer in his debt, the bigger his chances of being transferred to Farnol's Horse.

A horse, not American or Australian horizons, had become his dream. He could not remember being as happy as he had been these past few days, riding instead of marching, watering and attending to his borrowed mount each evening as if it were a favourite child. India, from the extra height of a horse's back, had taken on a whole new aspect.

The whole camp had been disturbed by the shot, but Farnol, curtly and with no respect for rank or sex, ordered everyone back to bed. Bridie and the others wanted to ask questions, but he was in no mood for them. He was still recovering from the shock of how close he had come once again to being murdered; he was not about to display the cracks he could feel in himself. He could be arrogant, but he was not vain: he never thought of himself as a hero nor did he strive to be one. But he did believe in keeping up appearances and right now he needed to appear to be a competent British officer, in command of himself as well as the situation. So he acted like a competent British officer and sent everyone to bed, as he might have dismissed a company of Farnol's Horse. He was a little surprised that everyone did go, though Lady Westbrook made a fighting retreat.

'You should tell us what's going on, Clive. We could all be killed in our beds.'

'I promise you that won't happen, Viola. Now go back to your beauty sleep.'

'Who needs a beauty sleep if one's throat is cut in the morning?' But she was more concerned for him than she was for herself and he recognized it and was grateful.

Four bearers were putting the merchant's body on to a pallet when Farnol went back to them and pulled up the dead man's sleeve.

'The mark is there, sahib?' said Karim Singh.

It was there, on the inside of the elbow. 'The crown and the dagger. This one is a better tattoo than those other chaps had.'

'This bugger had more money for a good tattoo. He's not a coolie, this chap.'

'No. We'll find out in the morning who he really is.'

He went into his tent, got into bed and felt suddenly cold. He knew it was not just from the fact that he'd been outside in only his pyjamas; he knew what sort of cold it was, the shiver of fear. He looked across at the Baron and wondered what reaction the old man was feeling.

'You've just declared whose side you're on, Baron. I'll have to see they don't try for you next.'

'Perhaps.' The Baron seemed unworried. 'I am sorry, Clive, if all this is directed from Berlin.'

'I don't think it is. Not *directed*. Assisted, perhaps. This is a local movement.'

'Aah!' It was a long, sad sigh. Wishful thinking made Thuringia suddenly so much closer; he would resign immediately after the Durbar and go home. He would read Goethe and, like the poet, look around for a mistress, one old enough not to waste pity on him. But not *too* old: there were limits to what one should have to put up with in a woman, even a mistress. He could not, for instance, imagine Lady Westbrook's making any man comfortable in his old age. 'Why must everyone be so ambitious?'

'Weren't you ever ambitious?'

The Baron turned his head and smiled as he reached across with his one hand and turned out the lamp. 'Of course. But at my age one wonders why.'

In the early morning Farnol, accompanied by Karim Singh, went up the road to the village. A small group of elders waited, as if they knew he would be coming. 'We have seen the dead man, sahib. He is a stranger.'

'You have never seen him before?' Farnol kept the surprise out of his voice; he had assumed that the merchant had had a store in the village. 'Not even yesterday before we arrived?'

'No, sahib.' The spokesman peered at Farnol out of cataract-dimmed eyes; he could have been an honest man but his eyes would never bear witness. 'We want nothing to do with the stranger. You must bury him yourself, sahib.'

The body rested on the camel-drawn cart, on the cargo of bright silks. Someone from the village, knowing the stranger was dead, had stolen the tarpaulin during the night but left the silks; the latter would be too easily identifiable. The cart had become a gaudy hearse, but the camels looked as indifferent as ever and smelled just as badly.

'I shall pay you to dispose of the body.'

'With respect, sahib, we want nothing to do with an enemy of the Raj.'

Oh, pretty soon, whether you like it or not, you may have a great deal to do with an enemy of the Raj. He looked at the five faces around him, but it was impossible to tell the thoughts behind the dimmed eyes and the veils of wrinkles. 'Thank you for your respect. All right, I shall have the body burnt.'

'Will you burn the man's goods with him, sahib?' The eyes were not so dim that they couldn't see the value of the silks.

'I present them to your village for your loyalty to the Raj.'

'We are most honoured, sahib.' Their feet scraped the dirt as they itched to be at the gift.

So for the second time the caravan's bearers had to build a pyre and burn a body; but this time there was no call to wait for the ashes. The caravan moved on after a breakfast at which there was very little conversation. Farnol watched the Nawab and Mahendra for their reaction to last night's attempted murder of himself, but other than a quiet question from the Nawab as to how he felt this morning the night could have been uneventful.

But as they started off at the head of the caravan Mahendra said, 'Will you be leaving us at Kalka, Major?'

'That will depend on how I'm to get down to Delhi. Does my presence worry you?'

'Not really. But you do seem to carry bad luck with you.'

'Not for myself. I've been very lucky so far.'

It was a quiet day: no incident, and very little talk amongst those most concerned with the safe arrival of the caravan at Kalka. The escort and cooks and bearers chattered amongst themselves; they had their own problems and the possibility of a dead sahib would make no difference to their lives. In mid-afternoon the procession came down through a defile on to the main Simla-Kalka road and at the first village Farnol reined his horse in before the store that was also the post office.

'Is the telegraph working?'

The postmaster's tunic had been inherited from a predecessor, who had been a much larger man. He kept losing his hands up his sleeves, so that half the time he appeared handless. 'Oh yes, sahib, working very well to Kalka. But not to Simla. Something is very wrong up there, I fear.'

'The telephone?'

'Oh sahib, this is a poor village. We have no telephone. I

shall be dead and gone before there is a telephone here.' He beamed, as if neither death nor the absence of a telephone worried him.

'I want to send a telegraph message to Kalka. Urgent.'

'Everything is urgent priority from here, sahib. Nobody uses the telegraph, everyone is too poor.' A generous hand appeared out of a sleeve like a crab. 'The telegraph line is all yours, sahib.'

Farnol sent the message to the O.C. of the Military Depot at Kalka. He requested that a detachment of troops be sent up the Simla road to meet the caravan and that a special train be ordered for the guests of the Government, the Ranee of Serog, her brother Prince Mahendra and the Nawab of Kalanpur. The answer came back in an hour. *Am aware of situation on Simla-Kalka railway line. Escort will meet you. Will do best with special train but jolly short supply.*

They camped that night in the lower hills, within sight of the plains. Farnol walked out on to a low bluff and gazed south. He could see the long low haze of smoke and dust hovering over the villages; he sniffed and imagined he could smell the acrid air that stretched south a thousand miles from here. The setting sun turned the haze into golden shields above the villages, but one had to be here on the slopes, far away, to appreciate the beauty of it. He doubted that anyone in the villages was raising his head to look at the colours above him.

'I'll be glad when this journey is over.' Bridie had come and stood beside him. 'But I'm not looking forward to Delhi, despite the Durbar and all the spectacle that's promised. I think I've fallen in love with the mountains, the high ones up beyond Simla. I only saw them from a distance, when I'd go riding down at Annandale, but they were so beautiful . . .'

'You have to live amongst them to appreciate them.'

'Will you be going back to your regiment to stay?'

The regiment was stationed on the plains. He remembered the polo matches, the pig-sticking, the practice charges across the *maidan*: there had been pleasures in being a cavalryman. But he also remembered the formalities that had irritated him, the small world of the mess and the parade ground and the tight, precedence-bound social circle that surrounded both. He had known a freedom in the past three years that had spoiled him for the regiment.

'It depends. My father feels I should go back – he'd like me to command it, as he and his father and my great-grandfather did.'

'Does family tradition mean much to you?'

'Yes and no. I don't think I'd feel much for myself if I broke the tradition. But I'd feel for my father. The regiment for him is *family*.'

'Then you'll be expected to go back to it.'

'They're not going to give me command while I'm away in the Political Service. I think I may have been away too long.'

'You don't sound as if you do want command.'

He'd had that ambition once; but he doubted it now. 'It's cavalry. I wonder if they'll use horses in the next war – '

'You think there'll be another war?'

'They are talking about war in Europe now. There have been enough flare-ups this year – the Germans rattled their swords at Agadir in June. Oh, there'll be another war some time, sooner or later. There'll always be wars while men are still alive to fight them.'

'You're talking like a soldier. *Hoping* there'll be one – '

'No. I don't want a war. It won't be fought here in India if there is one. Perhaps some skirmishes with the tribesmen, perhaps even something bigger with the revolutionaries. But it won't be *the* war – that will be fought in Europe. And I don't think there'll be a place for cavalry there. They'll be using motor cars and lorries – '

'Is that what the generals think?'

'I don't know. But all the generals are old now – they won't last long with their old ideas. Then the new men will take over. I don't think I'd want to fight a war in a motor car.'

'You think it should be some operatic exhibition, all your horses charging and you waving your sword?'

'Yes.' But he smiled; then was sober. 'But I don't think the next war will be like that. Not with the guns I hear Krupps are making . . .' He looked back towards the camp for Monday, as if expecting the Hungarian to produce a sample. 'I think I may emigrate to America. You will be neutral in all future wars.'

'Why should we be?' In her own ears she sounded like William Randolph Hearst, eager to provide yet another war for newspaper copy.

'Why shouldn't you be? You have all that water, the Atlantic and the Pacific, on either side of you.' But he knew that West Point and Annapolis would be disappointed if he were right.

She changed the subject. Or changed to a detail of the same subject: she wasn't sure which. Till she had crossed the Atlantic she had not known there was so much talk of war in the chancelleries of Europe. When she had left Boston at the end of October the newspapers had been full of the Philadelphia Athletics' World Series win against the New York Giants; the comments of Connie Mack and John J. McGraw had had far more importance than the warnings of statesmen in foreign capitals. She began to wonder who would listen to Mr Mack and Mr McGraw if America went to war.

'I wish you'd tell me more of what's going on here.'

'If I did, you'd write an article for your newspaper. And it might all be based on rumour. I promise you – I'll tell you everything when we get down to Delhi. Or as much as I can.'

'We were partners when we started out from Simla. That's what you led me to believe.'

'It's become much more complicated since then. Be patient, Bridie, it'll only be another day or two.' He put out a hand and after a moment she gave him hers.

'I worry for you, Clive,' Bridie said. 'Last night I was so sick I couldn't sleep – '

He knew then that he wouldn't be able to say goodbye to her in Delhi. But he didn't know what else he would be able to say.

Then Magda came storming towards them. Zoltan had kept from her the news that he was under arrest, but at last she had noticed that he had been accompanied all day by the bearded Sikh or the glum Irishman. A few minutes ago she had learned why they were keeping so close to him.

'Major Farnol, how dare you arrest my husband!'

'Mrs Monday – '

'*Madame* Monday!' It sounded better: she had taught herself all the nuances of social elevation. 'You have no right to do such a thing! My husband is no criminal. People are being killed and all you can do is arrest my husband for going about his business!'

'Is he really under arrest?' said Bridie. 'That's something you didn't tell me.'

He wanted to tell her it was none of her business. Why did she have to keep putting on her reporter's hat? 'Mr Monday knows the reason,' he told them both. 'I think it would be best, Madame Monday, if you left the matter to us men.'

'Oh my God!' said Bridie, putting on her feminist hat.

'Horseshit!' Magda lost all her social elevation: she was back on the Fisherman's Bastion in Budapest. Then she remembered where she really was, tried to recover a few rungs in the ladder. 'Excuse me. I get so angry and excited when someone insults my husband. Dear Zoltan – all he is trying to do is make a happy life for me.'

Farnol had the grace not to laugh. 'Madame Monday, I'm sure Mr Monday is a devoted husband and a good man. Unfortunately, he happens to sell arms . . . I shall see that he is put to no indignity. But I also have to see that for the time being he is out of business. Just look at it as a holiday, a vacation. Sit back and enjoy the rest of the journey.'

'What happens when we reach Kalka?'

'There, I'm afraid, things will be taken out of my hands.'

She went back to the camp. Women don't walk gracefully when they're angry, especially if they are wearing high-heeled boots. Bridie, looking after her, decided that if ever she had to make an angry exit she would not hurry. Then she looked at Farnol.

'Are you two-faced?'

'Possibly.' But it hurt to be thought so. 'I'm in good company – Janus was a god, you know.'

'You're not only two-faced, you're insufferable.'

'It's a family virtue.' Then he took her hand again and lifted it to his lips. Magda, sneaking a look back at him, thought he looked very dashing and Hungarian. But she wouldn't tell Zoltan that. 'In the job I've had for the past three years, if one doesn't look both ways at once, one doesn't survive. Being two-faced isn't always a nasty fault.'

She pressed her hand against his lips. 'I'd love my father to meet you. He'd have you in the US Senate in no time.'

The camp that night was quiet. The atmosphere at the dinner table was strained, but no arguments arose. Everybody went to bed early and everybody rose early, as if eager to get the last day of the caravan over and done with as soon as possible. Prince Mahendra appeared at breakfast with a smile, which he displayed as if it were a birthday gift for everyone. The Nawab, his grief for his young wife now put aside (or perhaps inside: grief, like the heart, becomes shabby if worn on the sleeve too long), told a cricket joke that no one but Farnol appreciated. The Baron replaced the straw hat he had been wearing with a white topee and looked younger and quite dashing. The Ranee, Lady Westbrook and Magda took their places in the coach and raised their parasols against the morning sun as if they were running up celebration flags. Bridie, her bottom becoming more accustomed to the saddle, took her horse up to the head of the column beside Farnol. The Nawab and Mahendra rode at the very front of it and Zoltan Monday, flanked by Karim Singh and Private Ahearn, rode at the rear, just behind the coach and ahead of the last escorts. The caravan crossed the border from Pandar to the Punjab, but not even Farnol noticed any difference in the air. He could not imagine the revolutionaries, if and when they surfaced, stopping to mark the boundary.

The detachment of troops from Kalka met them on the road in mid-morning. A platoon of infantrymen, khaki uniforms dusty and sweat-stained, topees pushed back from their flushed faces; two camels drawing a water-cart, another two camels harnessed to a kitchen-cart; half a dozen bearers; and a pink-cheeked lieutenant on a horse. The soldiers were whistling *Soldiers of the Queen* and somehow managed to make their whistling sound satirical and even obscene. The whistling died away when they saw the caravan bearing down on them.

'Christ Almighty, it's Hannibal and his fooking elephants!'

'Don't get too close to 'em. You ever seen them dark spots on an elephant's foot? That's all that's left of slow coolies.'

The troops were recently arrived from England and today's march was the longest they had so far made. They were hot, footsore and already hated the young officer who had his horse to prevent his being footsore. He was Lieutenant Lord Bunting and his father, so they said, was a bloody belted earl.

'Freddy Bunting, Major. Northern Fusiliers. Jolly warm, isn't it? The ladies must be feeling it, eh?' He sounded bluff and confident, but he was actually shy. He was just twenty and India pressed down on him with more than just the heat of its sun. His troops stood easy and contemptuously behind him and he wondered how long it would be before he could gain their respect. He longed for action, to take the Khyber Pass on his own and prove himself. 'I'd like to rest my men for an hour. Then we can start down again.'

'Did the O.C. manage to get us a special train?'

'Afraid not. The Railway Superintendent's almost off his rocker, poor chap. We got a message through from Solan about the landslide that stopped the train from Simla. The Superintendent's sent a train up to meet them, but they're going to be rather squashed. Only two carriages, it'll be rather stacks on the mill.'

But Farnol knew that everyone from Simla would get down to Delhi, if they had to build pyramids on each other's shoulders.

Mahendra said, 'The Superintendent will have to find a train for us.'

The second son of an English earl and the Indian prince stared at each other. Freddy Bunting had been told how arrogant some of these rajah blighters could be. 'I think you'll have to take that up with him, old chap. I don't work for the railways.'

'Then how do we get down to the Durbar, old chap?' said the Nawab. 'We have to be there, y'know. We can't insult His Majesty by not turning up.'

Bunting wished he could be there himself. As a six-year-old boy he had seen the Diamond Jubilee parade of Queen Victoria. *Look at it, my boy,* his father had said, *that's the glory of the Empire.* It seemed to him that the whole world had ridden through the streets of London on that shining day. And heroes, too: Roberts of Kandahar, Wolseley of Tel-el-Kebir: they brought the blaze of Empire with them. He had looked forward to the Durbar, but as soon as he had arrived at Bombay he had been shunted up-country. The old hands had grabbed the Durbar for themselves, it was theirs and no Johnny-come-lately was going to share it with them.

'You had better see if one of your own chaps can help,' he said. 'There's a special being got up today in the yards at Kalka. It belongs to the Rajah of Pandar, I think.'

4

They reached Kalka just after dark, into an evening still warm from the day. The station was crowded, as if everyone in the Punjab had decided he would try for a seat on a train to Delhi. But only some of them were travellers and most of those were not interested at all in going to Delhi: they only wanted to get home, to Moradabad, Lucknow, Allahabad; but all the trains via Delhi were booked by the damned sahibs and the *chee-chee* desk-wallahs and the princes with their damned elephants. The rest of the crowd in the station, the majority, was made up of hawkers, thieves, beggars, spectators and the homeless who came there every night to sleep under the corrugated-iron roof of the platforms.

Farnol went with the Nawab and Bunting to the Railway Superintendent's office, picking their way carefully over the shrouded figures that were already stretching out for their night's sleep. The station was a cauldron of chatter, a shriek occasionally bubbling to the top as a boy tried to steal a fried cake from the portable stove of a woman vendor. A grey-white cow nosed its way down the platform and the shrouded figures, seemingly without seeing it, rolled gently to one side to make way for it. In the yellow-lit smoke under the roof sparrows swooped and darted as if day and night no longer meant anything to them. An engine whistle blew out in the yards and the would-be travellers, recognizable by their cardboard suitcases or their bundles, stood up and looked expectantly into the darkness. But nothing appeared and they subsided again with a laugh, as if amused by their own foolish hope.

'They'll annoy the hell out of you half the time,' Farnol told Bunting. 'The other half, you'll finish up admiring them.'

'There are so *many* of them. At school one read about them, but *millions* don't mean anything when one reads of them in a schoolbook – '

'Where did you go to school?' The Nawab turned his head, his attention distracted; he trod on a sleeping form, walked over it as if it were a bag of rubbish. 'Harrow? I say! You must come up to Simla some time. Do you play cricket?'

The Superintendent's office was crammed with complaining travellers who looked as if they might not travel for at least another week. Fists were raised and tickets waved like empty grenades: they were just as useless. A *chee-chee* minor official yelled that there would be no refunds, everybody would have to wait till there were trains available. A stout Parsee, wife and three children clinging to him as if he were some beast of burden, turned and shouted at Farnol and Bunting, the two Englishmen, that it just wouldn't do, it wouldn't do at all, the Government should be ashamed of itself, it wouldn't have been like this under Lord Curzon.

The Superintendent was a Scot, a hunk of Grampian granite dumped down here in northern India. He picked up a long cane and swished it round him and the crowd fell back against the walls. He ran a hand through the barbwire of his red curls and grinned balefully at the newcomers.

'To think I could've gone to bloody Canada!'

Bunting introduced Farnol and the Nawab. 'I've explained, Mr Morton, that you had to let the special go that was intended for them.'

'I've got no bloody engines, that's the trouble. Get me an engine and I'll give you a couple of carriages and some wagons, but that's all I can do for ye.'

The Nawab said, 'I understand my cousin, the Rajah of Pandar, has a special train. Has it gone yet?'

'No, it's still out in the yards. If His Highness doesn't mind hitching the extra carriages and wagons on . . . Ask the mon himself. He's over there in the corner.'

Farnol turned towards the corner where, despite the crush in the rest of the room, there was a clear space. A man sat there on a rickety chair that his very presence turned into a throne; two tall, muscular guards stood behind him, swords hanging from their belts. He was dressed in a dark blue *achkan* and pale blue turban and he was smiling at the surprise on the face of his cousin, the Nawab.

'You and your friends are welcome to travel with me, Bertie.'

Farnol had seen him only once before and then only fleetingly; but there was no mistaking the hooked nose, the deep-set eyes and the black beard. He was the brown-robed mystic who had been on the terrace of the monastery in the high mountains on the day Farnol had talked with the lama.

CHAPTER EIGHT

Extract from the memoirs of Miss Bridie O'Brady:

The Rajah of Pandar's special train did not get away from Kalka till midnight. He did not invite any of the women aboard his own carriage and we were left to make ourselves comfortable in the single carriage, instead of the two promised, that the Railway Superintendent was able to make available to us.

'The engine just won't be able to pull any more,' he explained. 'Not with all your wagons loaded with elephants. You're lucky as it is that the track is downhill all the way. Well, have a good trip.'

It was a car that Pullman or Wagon-Lits would have used for the transportation of criminals, if they had been in that business. The windows were barred, both those on the corridor and those on the outside of the compartment; the door was stout teak with heavy bolts on it and a sign above it, *Beware of Dacoits*; the seats, which doubled as bunks, were smeared with cracked leather rather than covered with it. It was a mobile slum.

'I'm sorry about this,' said Clive, inspecting the accommodation. 'I'm afraid things are better for us men.'

'I'm sure,' said Viola Westbrook, who had lived a life that was always better for men.

'It's nothing luxurious. Sankar seems a rather austere chap. There's just more room.'

'I'd settle for that,' I said. 'I'll take the top bunk, Viola. Goodnight, Clive. Enjoy being a man.'

He grinned at both of us, backed out into the corridor and bumped into the Ranee. 'Clive, have you seen this carriage? I can't travel in something like this! I'm sure it hasn't been used since the Mutiny!'

'That's what we should do,' said Viola. 'Mutiny!'

Backed up behind the Ranee in the corridor were Magda and the Nawab's five wives. Beyond them was the train's conductor, a thin Hindu wearing an ill-fitting uniform and an equally ill-fitting expression of authority.

'Allow me passage, ladies. Stand aside, ladies – ' He reached the Ranee. 'Allow me, Your Highness – '

She hit him across the face with her jewelled handbag, a several-thousand-dollar thwack; he staggered back with blood instantly spurting from a cut across his nose. She didn't even look at him, but continued to glare at Clive. 'Tell Sankar I wish to see him – at once!'

'I'm here.' The women stood aside for *him*. The conductor disappeared, holding his bleeding nose. I noticed that Prince Sankar, like the Ranee, didn't give the conductor even a glance. 'What is the trouble?'

The Ranee told him in Hindi and it sounded to me as if there was a lot of swearing in it. He just gazed at her superciliously and I realized that here we had a man who had only contempt for women. I am never quite certain how to deal with such men. Misogynists are usually torn in a love-hate relationship with women; the majority of men, who love and need women, try to keep us in our place because they treasure the security of being amongst their own sex; bars and clubs and lodges are only symbols of men's cowardice and never worry me. But contemptuous men? I have never been able to handle contempt from either men or women.

'You are welcome to get off the train. I shan't be offended if you do.' He had a soft voice, that of a man who didn't use it much. He spoke in English, as if his message was meant for the rest of us as well. He was handsome in a, yes, *cruel* way; as I said before, I like arrogance in a man; but not cruelty. He had the coldest face I had ever seen; compassion would only have disfigured it. 'But beggars can't be choosers. Ask any of the beggars out there on the platform.'

I thought for a moment that the Ranee was going to hit *him* with her handbag. But she whirled abruptly, pushed her way through the Nawab's wives and disappeared into a compartment down the corridor. The compartment door was slammed to with a crash. The wives looked at each other, nodded and went back to their own compartments; perhaps they were more used to contempt than I was. Or Magda.

'Your Highness, the least we deserve is some bedding and blankets. Please see that the servants bring us bedding from the carts.'

Sankar looked at Clive. 'Who is this one?'

'Madame Monday.'

Then Clive introduced Viola and me, but Sankar did not even glance at us. He just looked at Magda. 'Everything is packed and on the wagons, we can't waste time unpacking. I'll send you your husband. He will have to comfort you.'

Then he turned and left the car. Viola said, 'Clive, are you going to let him treat us like that? Dammit, this is an *English* train! Kick him off and let him see whether beggars can be choosers or not!'

'Viola, he has precedence, even if he is out of his own State. I'm afraid you'll have to put up with what he's offered you. I'll send Karim Singh and Private Ahearn to take care of you. And some bearers.' He looked at Magda. 'I'll tell your husband to travel with you, Madame Monday.'

'If you were a gentleman,' I said, 'you'd also travel with us and share our discomfort.' What I meant was that I should feel safer if I knew he was close at hand. I was coming to need him, which is another step to falling in love.

'I wish I could. But I have some business to attend to.'

I followed him out on to the platform. The crowd stood at a respectful distance, curious as ever and, some of them, resentful. Under the corrugated-iron roof of the platform the clamour gave us privacy: no one would hear what we said.

'Clive, who is that man Sankar? Is he the one who has been trying to kill you?'

In the dim illumination of the station it was impossible to read anything from his shadowed expression. Then, very quietly, he said, 'Yes, I think so.'

'But why?' I must have cried out, because he put a soothing hand on mine. 'For God's sake, Clive, tell me what's going on!'

He looked around at the crowd, a thousand pairs of eyes watching us with a sort of animal patience. Then he took my arm and led me along to the end of the platform. We were beyond the platform lights here, lit only by the moon on which scudding clouds seemed to shred themselves like dark hessian. A few yards from us a large cow stood like a white rock monument.

'Tell me, Clive, please – for our sake!'

He sighed: Secret Service men hate to reveal secrets. I often wonder what CIA men talk about in bed with their wives. 'There's a plot to assassinate the King. I have no definite proof – '

I suppose the suspicion of something like it had been there in my mind ever since that first evening in Simla. So I didn't gasp or have an attack of the vapours; and I felt no excitement at the news scoop that now lay in my hands. No, I just felt sick. Assassination is almost as old as murder: how long after the killing of Abel was the first tribal leader done to death by treachery? I was fifteen years old when President McKinley was shot and I remember I was sick: I grieved for the man but more for my country. Just two years ago as I write this, I was so sick that I had to take to my bed: but then I grieved as much for President Kennedy as I did for America.

'What do they want? Independence? Isn't there some other way – does a man have to be assassinated?'

'The man happens to be a king. Read your history, Bridie – kings have always been expendable – ' He held my hand. 'Kings are so – so *visible*. Revolutionaries have nothing to gain by killing nobodies – '

'They've been trying to kill you!' For love a woman will reduce a man to nothing.

He smiled, kissed me for my gaffe. It was so natural that I thought nothing of it: we *were* partners now. 'I think I'm out of danger now. We're too close to home, as the saying goes.'

'Clive, please – do take care.'

'I shall – I promise. But you must promise me you'll mention this to no one. This is not for the newspapers, yours or anyone else's.'

I hesitated; but with the taste of him on my lips there was nothing else I could say: 'I promise.'

We went back to the train. He put me into my carriage, pressed my hand and went on up to Prince Sankar's car. We women's car was at the very rear of the train, behind the wagons of horses and elephants. Which, I suppose, was some consolation: we could have been behind a wagonful of camels.

Mr Monday came down to join his wife and five minutes later the train pulled slowly out of Kalka. I stood in the corridor while Viola got undressed and looked out at the crowd on the platform. The sleepers did not stir, just lay there like the dead. But the would-be travellers, those without a train to carry them where they wanted to go, stood and watched as we slowly pulled away. A group of young men stood opposite my window and they stared at me till I could feel embarrassment flushing through me like a fever. One of them took a step forward and I thought he was going to spit at me. But all he did was smile and say, 'Be sure that the elephants and horses have a pleasant journey, memsahib.' I think I'd have felt better if he had spat at me.

I went into our compartment, got undressed, said goodnight to Viola and climbed into the upper bunk. I used my travelling bag as a pillow and covered myself with my topcoat and tried to tell myself that I was so exhausted I should sleep anyway. But I have never been a good subject for auto-suggestion; Celtic pessimism never allows you to expect too much. The train wheezed and jolted its way through the night and it seemed as if I heard and felt every mile of the 200-mile journey. I wondered how the King was sleeping this night; but of course he would not know what I knew. Once I heard Magda in the next compartment cry out: she could have been dreaming or making love. Whatever, she was enjoying the journey much more than I.

End of extract from memoirs.

2

The Rajah of Pandar's private carriage was not a corridor car with compartments. It was what the Americans call a day-coach. All the seats had been removed, some rugs put on the floor and half a dozen cane chairs, with cushions, placed by the windows. Some camp beds had also been brought aboard for the comfort of the Rajah's guests, plus some blankets. The carriage was, in effect, a men's club on wheels, even if a less-than-luxurious one. It was still a good deal better than the women's club at the tail of the train.

Farnol reclined in one of the chairs and studied the Rajah. Sankar had not offered his guests a night-cap and Farnol, remembering the man's devotion to religion, had not expected any; but he had, with a sort of cold politeness, offered them cups of tea. Farnol sipped his and wondered if it had been poisoned. But it was unlikely that Sankar would want so many witnesses to another attempted murder.

'I have the feeling I've seen you before, Your Highness,' he said, trying a line like a fisherman casting.

'I doubt it, Major. I am not a social person.'

'Oh, this wasn't a social occasion. Somehow the memory is of us being alone together.' It was difficult to feel comfortable and even-tempered while drinking tea with a man who had tried to murder you. 'It's hazy, but you know how hazy memory can be sometimes.'

'I have an excellent memory.'

'Well, I'm sure it'll come to me sooner or later.' Or should he come out with it now, tell Sankar he had seen him at the monastery in the mountains, at the Viceroy's Lodge and in the bazaar in Simla? He wondered if there was a good or poor quality tattoo inside the elbow in the silk *achkan* sleeve.

'Sankar, I notice you have no elephants on the wagons behind,' said the Nawab.

'I shall be riding a horse in the parade. There will be enough ostentation without adding to it.'

'A little pomp and ceremony never hurt anyone, old chap.' Farnol had noticed that the Nawab looked nervous and uncomfortable as if he had just questioned an umpire's decision at cricket. 'I've brought a golden howdah with me.'

Farnol waited for Sankar's lip to curl; but the man was not so obvious as that, at least not in his facial expressions. 'What about you, Bobs? Do you have a golden howdah, too?'

'I have to ride with Mala in her coach.' Mahendra was sulky and withdrawn; but, Farnol noticed, also a little deferential. 'She is the ruler of Serog. I am invited only for the ride.'

'What about you, Baron?' Sankar hadn't spoken to the old man since the latter had come on board the train. 'Is there going to be some German pomp and ceremony?'

'No, Your Highness. We Germans will just be spectators at this coronation. He is your Emperor, not ours.'

Farnol waited for a reaction from Sankar but there was none. He was convinced now that the Rajah of Pandar was the leader of the plot that had the Nawab and Mahendra in its web and that had, somehow, entangled Savanna. But he was no closer to knowing the whole plot, nor if the King was still to be assassinated.

'And you, Major? Are you to be just a spectator?'

'I shall be riding with my regiment.'

'And adding to the pomp and ceremony, no doubt. There is no one who does it quite so well as the English.'

'I understand the Kaiser puts on a good show. And Emperor Franz Josef does it very well in Vienna, I'm told.'

'I saw them both while I was in Europe. Operetta, nothing more. The English are the only ones who can make a pageant of it.'

'Would you like all that to finish?' Another line thrown.

'Oh, it will all die out some day, Major. Money can't go on being wasted on such vanities.' He took out a watch, a golden one; he allowed himself a small vanity or two. 'It is one o'clock. Perhaps you gentlemen would care to turn in.'

He got up and went out on to the rear platform of the carriage, closing the door after him. Farnol hesitated, then, avoiding the looks of the Nawab and Mahendra, he followed

Sankar out on to the platform. The Rajah did not seem surprised to see him.

'I like to look at the peace of the stars before I go to sleep,' he said.

'What do you do on stormy nights?'

'You English are so down-to-earth. How could you have produced all the poets you have? On stormy nights, Major, I trust to memory.'

'Of course. You told me what an excellent memory you have. My own has suddenly improved. I remember where I saw you – at a monastery on the Tibet Road, beyond Jangi.'

'It is possible. But when I go away to meditate, I leave memory at home.'

Behind them the open wagons rattled in the black box of the night. Dimly Farnol could see the elephants swaying like badly packed cargo; horses gazed backwards into the night like carousel steeds going the wrong way. In other wagons the escort guards, *mahouts, syces* and bearers slept packed in on each other, human livestock. At the far end of the train was the carriage where the women rode. If Sankar chose to attack him now, to throw him off the platform, he would be chopped to pieces before Bridie rode over the top of him. He felt the coldness in his spine and he leaned back against the door of the carriage.

'My cousin told me you had an adventurous trip down from Simla.'

'We down-to-earth English thrive on adventure.'

For the first time Sankar smiled, a thin blade in the starlight. 'Of course. That was what brought you to India in the first place, wasn't it?'

'Adventure and profit.' One had to be honest. Idealism had never been encouraged by the East India Company, but a sense of adventure did pay dividends.

'But you're not interested in profits?'

Some John Company men had made huge fortunes; but never the Farnols. There was Farnol money invested in England and there were tea plantations in the Assam hills; but the family wasn't rich, not the way the princes were. 'Not personally. Neither, I suppose, are you. But you do have the advantages of taxes. Travellers' tax, for instance.'

'My collectors asked you for that?' Again the thin smile. 'That is not for gain, Major, just for privacy's sake. Taxes are often better than fences for keeping people away.'

'You seem to have studied economics. You're ahead of your time, Your Highness, at least for India.'

'No, Major. I am exactly right for my time. Goodnight.'

3

The train grunted, puffed and clanged its way through the soft plains night and at last sighed its way into Delhi at ten o'clock in the morning. Fifty miles north of the city it passed through a rainstorm and Farnol, gazing out at the rain falling as silver spears against the distant sun, wondered if the Durbar would turn into nothing but the greatest, most splendiferous mud-bath of all time. But by the time the train reached Delhi the sun was shining and the clouds were as innocent as lamb's wool.

Thirty miles north of the city the train had been halted at a wayside platform and Farnol had gone back down the train to the last carriage. He called Karim Singh and Ahearn out into the conductor's space at the rear of the carriage and asked the conductor to go elsewhere for a few minutes. The latter did so without a word, but his expression said enough about what he felt on the subject of being ordered out of his space on his train.

'That chap Mr Monday,' said Karim, 'he's been no trouble, sahib. I think Private Ahearn and I are wasting our marvellous skills just keeping an eye on him.'

'That's what I'm thinking, too, yes,' said Ahearn, trying to look possessed of marvellous skills. He could lie and cheat and malinger with the best of them, but he had an idea those talents would not get him far in Farnol's Horse.

The train started off again, but Farnol decided to remain where he was. He wanted to make sure that he would be seeing as much as possible of Bridie during her stay in Delhi. Sankar's plot, of course, permitting.

'I think you can forget Mr Monday now. Get back into your hill dress, Karim, and when we get to Delhi I want you to shadow Prince Sankar everywhere he goes. Keep as close to him as his shadow, but don't let him know you're following him. Has he had a good look at you?'

'I don't think so, sahib.'

'Well, don't let him. Stay on his tail. I'll send Private Ahearn out each evening to meet you at the main gate to the Red Fort and you'll give him your report.'

'Am I going to miss seeing the regiment in the parade, sahib?'

'That will depend on whether Prince Sankar wants to see the parade. I'm sorry, Karim, but I'm afraid we're going to Delhi for more than just a social visit now.'

Then he went down the corridor and knocked on the door of Bridie's compartment. 'It's me, Clive.'

Bolts were slid back and Bridie and Lady Westbrook looked out at him. They had the pinched, irritable look of women who hadn't slept well and wanted the fact known. Bridie said, 'My, how refreshed you look!'

'You both look wonderful,' he said, tossing the ball back.

'All right, that's the end of the sarcasm,' said Lady Westbrook. 'Did anything happen up your end of the train during the night?'

'Nothing. I think our troubles may be over.'

'I think you are lying,' said Lady Westbrook.

He shrugged. 'You'll have to put up with that for a while yet, Viola. Perhaps I can give you a bit more of the truth after I've seen George Lathrop.'

She snorted. 'George Lathrop has spent his life trying to hide the truth. You political agents are all the same. If ever I wanted Roger to tell me he loved me, I had to have him swear it on a bible.'

'In the meantime, will you both be my guests this evening? Unless the programme has been changed, my regiment is having a reception.'

Bridie looked at Lady Westbrook and the latter said, 'I think we should accept, m'dear. You may never have another opportunity to see British peacocks on display. And the gossip will do my heart good.'

Farnol and Bridie smiled at each other, each listening to the gossip in their own hearts. Love was happening, if nothing else was.

Zoltan Monday came out into the corridor, stretched, saw Farnol and looked embarrassed.

'Ah, good morning, Major. Checking on your prisoner?'

'You're now on parole, Mr Monday, free to do whatever you wish. I'd just like you to report to me this evening at a reception my regiment is holding. Don't bring your catalogues.'

Monday smiled. 'You have an almost Hungarian sense of humour.'

'It must be a marvellous defence.'

'Oh, it is, Major, it is. That's all that holds the Austro-Hungarian Empire together, though the Austrians would never admit it.'

'You sound very chipper this morning. Are you expecting to meet Mr Brown in Delhi?'

Monday's face clouded. 'I am no longer interested in that business, Major, not even for half a million pounds. There are other clients.'

'I'm sure there are. But where?'

'My wife thinks she would like to see Singapore.'

Then a little later, before the Ranee, Magda and the Nawab's wives emerged from their compartments, the train was pulling into Delhi.

George Lathrop was waiting for Farnol at the top end of the platform. 'I got your telegraph message from Kalka, but I had the most awful bloody job finding out which station your train was arriving at. Then when I got that information nobody knew which platform. They've built Christ knows how many new stations around Delhi. Look at this one, Salimgarh. Ten platforms, every one of 'em three hundred bloody yards long. This is where the King comes in tomorrow. Well, how are you, dear boy?'

George Lathrop was bluff and hearty, with prematurely white hair, a bristling white moustache and a monocle stuck in his right eye. He stopped just short of giving the impression of being a buffoon; only when he dropped the monocle from his eye did one see the penetrating shrewdness of his gaze. He had been in military and political intelligence for thirty years and he never scoffed at rumours of murder.

'I'm worried,' said Farnol.

'I thought something must be on your mind, sending me that wire. Where's Rupert Savanna?'

Farnol told him without elaboration. 'I'll fill you in later.'

'Jesus Christ!' Lathrop whacked his leg with his swagger stick. 'Righto, keep it till we're in a quiet place to talk. Whom did you come down with? That lot, eh? A nice bloody assortment. Well, come on. That's all your kit? Good chap, you travel light.'

As they walked down the long platform Farnol looked at the bright new station festooned with banners and bunting. 'I've never seen a station looking as clean and deserted as this.'

'Within three months it'll look like all the rest. Coolies under your feet everywhere, dirt and shit all over the place –' Lathrop loved India and the Indians, but he could never be accused of being sentimental about either. 'Hello, who's this pretty gel?'

Bridie was coming towards them. She was tired and creased from the long journey; but her smile showed she was still a pretty gel. Farnol introduced her and Lathrop snapped his heels together and saluted her. He was happily married, but the story was that he wore his monocle only to hide his roving eye from his wife.

'I'm staying with Lady Westbrook,' Bridie told Farnol. 'I don't fancy being cooped up in the tents reserved for the Press.'

'Sensible gel,' said Lathrop. 'Those newspaper chaps are cads and bounders, every one of 'em. Old Viola will take good care of you.'

'Old Viola indeed! You make me sound like some musical antique.' Lady Westbrook had come down the platform behind a screen of bearers. 'How is old George Lathrop?'

Lathrop shook hands with her and kissed her on the cheek. 'You look bloody marvellous, old gel. Now we can start the Durbar.'

'Has Clive told you all the trouble we've had getting here?

And don't swear in front of Bridie – she has some illusions that all Englishmen are gentlemen.'

Lathrop apologized to Bridie. 'Didn't realize I was swearing, thought I was on my best behaviour.' He had the reputation of having the filthiest tongue in India; he could be obscene in four languages and seven dialects. The apology enabled him to ignore Lady Westbrook's question, guessing it was going to lead to more questions: he had caught Farnol's swift warning glance. 'Well, must be off. Enjoy yourselves, ladies.'

He whisked Farnol away down the platform, leaving Lady Westbrook indignant and Bridie off-balance at Clive's abrupt departure. Lady Westbrook said, 'Blighter hasn't changed. Everything takes second place to damned business! Well, where's someone to take care of our luggage? Bearer!'

As they got into a military gharry outside the station Lathrop said, 'Sorry I had to whisk you off like that, dear boy. Saw the princes and the Ranee coming down and didn't want to be trapped by them before you'd talked to me. I once spent two nights with the Ranee. Dreadful bloody woman, didn't know how to say no to her without getting my throat cut. Don't mention it in front of the good wife, though.'

I was wrong, Farnol thought. George Lathrop *had* slept with Mala: she's had her claws into all of us. He made no comment, instead looked out at the city of Delhi growing, actually growing while he watched, around him. He had not been in Delhi in five years and he was amazed at the transformation.

'All this, George, just for the Durbar? This used to be nothing but waste land – is that *grass*?'

'It ain't green paint, dear boy. Yes, it's grass. Parks, polo fields, cricket pitches. I came up here during the summer with His Excellency – this is all H.E's baby, y'know. Over there – ' he waved a hand – 'there must have been a couple of thousand coolies, all squatting on their haunches in ranks. They were planting grass. Then the rain came and now – hundreds of acres of lawns!'

'What's it all going to cost? A fortune for one week's celebration? No wonder there – '

'Keep it to yourself, old chap.' Lathrop nodded warningly

at the back of the gharry driver. 'Just sit back and enjoy it all.'

'That's not going to be easy.'

He looked out at the almost unrecognizable city. Delhi had known other glories than what would be enacted here in the coming week. It was not one city but a whole history of cities; but, as he had remembered it, it had been little more than dusty, overgrown ruins, overgrown with poverty-stricken coolies who had no memory of history. Anang Pal had been here, built the Red Fort nine hundred years ago; Kutb-ud-din had made it into a capital; Tamerlane had sacked it, as he had sacked so many other cities; Baber, the first Moghul emperor, had captured it. Shah Jehan had built it into the greatest city in India; inside his palace he had ordered the inscription, 'If Paradise be on the face of the Earth, it is this – it is this, it is this.' But Paradise had proved less eternal than the Earth: in less than a century Nadir Shah had sacked the palace and carried off the Peacock Throne to Persia: the city began to crumble into the ruins on which it had been built. All that had remained, but for the Red Fort, some mosques and some tombs, had been the people, the most durable element in history.

Then the gharry was driving into the tented city that had mushroomed in the past week. Farnol had never seen such a vast encampment; the sun blazed on what might have been an arctic ice-field, the white tents throwing off a glare that seemed to dissipate the brown dust in the morning air. Flags flew everywhere from a forest of flagpoles, a silent battle of colourful challenges; regiments and clubs and institutions were proving their right to a place in the Durbar sun. Above it all the shite hawks hung in the sky, waiting patiently for the city to be demolished and the pickings, as always, left for them and the beggars from the crumbling Old City to the south.

'Forty-five square miles of it,' said Lathrop. 'An extra quarter of a million people. All of it, as you say, for just one week. There were objections in Cabinet in London, I'm told, to the cost. Especially after the famine we had this year – ' Then he nodded again at the driver's back. 'Tell you about it later.'

They turned off the main road, drove up a red dirt road on

which the dust had been settled by a camel-drawn water-cart. They pulled up in front of a large tent flanked by four smaller tents; Farnol noticed that the pole outside the Political Service's headquarters was bare of any flag; Lathrop believed that if one did not advertise, one might not be asked questions. As they got out of the gharry Lathrop pointed up the road.

'That's the King's camp. Jolly nice, too. I went through it yesterday with the Security chaps. Rather exotic. Don't know how the King will take to it. He's not much for silks and satins, I gather.'

Lathrop led the way into the big tent, casually returning the salute of the Ghurka on guard at the entrance. He and Farnol passed through an outer office where four NCOs sat at desks, and into the rear of the tent. The office staff greeted Farnol with nods, but they knew the real greetings had to wait while the O.C. got his report from this man who had the reputation of being the best field man in the Service.

Lathrop waved Farnol to a chair and took his place behind a desk. Coloured photos of the King and Queen hung on one wall of the tent; on the opposite wall hung a photo of the real Raj of India, His Excellency the Viceroy, Lord Hardinge of Penshurt. Farnol had a sudden moment of doubt and wondered if he was mistaken about the intended victim of the assassination plot.

'Start right in, dear boy. It's a little early, but I think a whisky wouldn't do you any harm.'

A bearer brought in a tray, retired at once as Lathrop waved him away and poured the drink himself. Farnol sipped the whisky, let himself relax; or forced himself to. If Lathrop believed his suspicions, his responsibility was over. And, the most comforting thought of all, Sankar might no longer consider him a worthwhile target. Not with the real target so close now . . . He found he was not relaxing at all and he put down his drink and sat forward.

'George, I believe there's a plot to assassinate the King – '

Lathrop listened without interrupting. He took his monocle out and polished it with a silk handkerchief, but didn't put it back in his eye; instead, he rolled it through his fingers as he might have a coin, smudging it and cleaning it again and yet again. It was the only sign that he was troubled by what Farnol was telling him.

'Well, that's it, George. I hope you believe me?'

'Why shouldn't I, dear boy? Just because we haven't lost a monarch from assassination in five hundred years doesn't mean it hasn't been tried. There were five or six attempts to kill Queen Victoria. There's enough bloody sedition going on in this country right now . . . H.E. knows about it, but I don't think he'd dare mention it to the King. His Majesty has some pretty firm ideas of his own about how India should be run. He doesn't think much of the ICS – I gather he doesn't think much of civil servants anywhere. He's all for strengthening the powers of the princes and the hereditary rulers.'

'I wonder if Sankar knows that?'

'I don't think it would make any difference if he did. The King thinks that all that's needed is for their paternal influence to be widened. He could be right about some of the princes – in the small States, perhaps that's enough for the time being. But some of the other buggers . . . There's Baroda, for instance. H.E. won't trust him as far as he could throw him. We know he encourages the printing of seditious pamphlets – we've uncovered half a dozen presses in his State. And that missus of his, the Maharani – bloody woman should be strung up. She's always sending money to Madame Cama in Europe, helping that bitch stir up trouble for us . . .'

Madame Cama was a leading revolutionary, more dangerous perhaps than the other expatriates such as Har Dayal; but Farnol had not heard anything of her for at least a year. 'No, I believe you, Clive. The point is, where and when are they going to make the attempt?'

'I think the safest thing would be to clap the lot of them into jail till the Durbar is over.'

'We've done that with over three hundred of the worst buggers in the city. Given 'em bed and board for a couple of weeks. But one can't do that with ruling princes, old chap. What excuse would we use? Suspicion of murderous intent? I don't think the King would stand for it, for one. Even if we got Sankar out of the way, what about Mahendra and Bertie Kalanpur?'

Farnol wriggled in frustration. 'I suppose you're right. I

still haven't worked out what Savanna's part was in all this.'

'Shall we hazard a guess?' Lathrop polished his monocle again. 'He's ambitious, let's say. Or perhaps greedy. Take your pick. He wants to be comfortable in his old age, have some money – he had none at all, y'know. He thinks he can stir up trouble in Serog, get the Ranee kicked out and have Mahendra take over. We've done it ourselves for our own ends, why shouldn't he copy us? He'd move in as Mahendra's adviser, set himself up as a somebody instead of being what he's been all his life, a nobody.'

'You're not guessing all that.'

'No, dear boy. We've known about Rupert Savanna for some time. We were just giving him enough rope to hang himself – or let the Ranee hang him. She'll never let that lunatic brother of hers take over. When the time came, she'd have been in there tooth and nail and Mahendra and Savanna would have been lucky to get out alive. She's a bitch and a tyrant, but she's part of the status quo and so long as she is, we'll put up with her. Though I don't think her maternal influence is the sort the King favours . . . Politics, as they say, makes strange bedmates. An apt expression, in her case. As you possibly know.'

Farnol ignored the opportunity to boast of a conquest; he knew there were no victories in a nymphomaniac's bed. 'That doesn't explain why Savanna buzzed off to the palace at Serog as soon as I got back to Simla.'

'No, that's where the guessing starts.' Political intelligence was mostly a guessing game; which was why Lathrop enjoyed it so much. He swore obscenely, but only to get his imagination oiled. 'You tell Savanna there's a plot to assassinate the King – you have no proof, but he's heard enough rumours for your suspicions to be the final straw. He skedaddles down to Serog to see Mahendra, to ask if he knows anything about the plot. Sankar is there and he decides that Savanna has to be got rid of. But the poison, whatever it was, doesn't work as swiftly as they'd planned. So Savanna is still alive when you and the others arrive.'

'Savanna would have been against the plot to kill the King?'

Lathrop nodded. 'He was a stupid bugger, I never really

wanted him in the Service once I found out what he was like, but he'd sucked up to all the right desk-wallahs and I couldn't get rid of him. He was stupid and traitorous, too, I suppose, but he would never have had any part of a plot to kill the King. He was too middle class for that.'

Farnol smiled. 'I thought that was what we were?'

'No, dear boy. Families like ours –' The Lathrops had been in India even longer than the Farnols; the first George Lathrop had been on the staff of Thomas Pitt when that opportunist had governed Madras for the East India Company in the 1690s. 'We're classless, I think. And stateless, too, I'm afraid. When the Raj finishes here, who'll want us?'

'You think we'll have to leave India some day?' Farnol wasn't surprised by what had been said, only that it was Lathrop who said it.

'Not in my lifetime, nor perhaps in yours. But we can't rule 'em forever, Clive. This plot we're talking about – it's indicative.' He stood up. 'Go and check in with your chaps – I'll have a gharry take you over to your regiment. Your father's there – he'll be delighted to see you.'

'I've got my man Karim Singh keeping an eye on Sankar. What about the others?'

'I'll have them watched. I'll see H.E. first thing in the morning when he arrives from Bombay with the King. We've brought in an extra 4000 police and security is as tight as we can make it. But you never know . . . I'll make sure that Sankar and Bertie and Mahendra are in the procession tomorrow morning for the King. Keep 'em out in the open where we can keep an eye on them.'

'There's going to be an attempt some time, George. Sankar hasn't come all the way down here to pay his respects to His Majesty.'

On his way out Farnol stopped to be greeted by the NCOs. They were all friendly smiles, but there were questions behind the smiles: they knew something was up, they were eager to know what it was. But Farnol knew Lathrop would tell them in his own good time.

Outside, as he was about to step into the gharry that had been called, he said, 'What about Monday?'

'Let him go. I don't think Krupps would reward him for

224

being actively engaged in you know what –' Again a warning nod at the gharry driver. 'We'll let him and his wife stay for the Durbar, then we'll quietly escort him down to Bombay and put him on a ship for somewhere.'

'He's talking of Singapore.'

'Good. Let them worry about him for a while.' The Empire, if not one giant bureaucracy, had learned bureaucratic habits: if a problem couldn't be solved, pass it on to someone else. 'By the way, that newspaper gel, Miss O'Brady – is she likely to start writing any articles that could stir things up?'

'Possibly. The Americans invented something they call freedom of the Press.'

'Bloody idealists. They make it so hard to run the world properly. But they'll learn some day . . . Better keep an eye on her, too. Shouldn't be too difficult, eh, you lucky blighter?'

Farnol rode through the city of tents, marvelling at and amused by the splendour of some of the camps; the regiments appeared, like the princes, to want to out-do each other in magnificence. He saw familiar flags: Skinner's Horse, Mayne's Horse, the Bengal Lancers, the Guides: history fluttered in the breeze. Then the gharry drove in under the green, silver and gold banner of his own regiment and there was his father to greet him.

'Clive.'

Hugh Farnol was as tall as his son, but bonier; his face suggested an axe-head, he looked as if he would cleave his way through life. He struggled to overcome the emotion of the occasion. To lead the regiment before the King at the Durbar would be the climax of his life and for the past week he had felt the excitement building; but to see his only son again after six months, to have him here to ride behind him in the parade, swelled his feeling to where he felt he must burst with it. He wanted to fling his arms round Clive, hold him to him; but that would never do. Instead he tried to break his son's fingers with the strength of his handshake.

Clive saw and felt the emotion in his father, but he was equally constrained by his Englishness and just returned the strength in his father's grip. The handshake had, if nothing else, lessened the risk of hernia brought on by emotion.

4

'She's too huge for such a frock. She looks like a sequinned landslide.'

'He plays second fiddle to everyone. Rather badly, too.'

'You mean you think she sleeps with any man who asks her?'

'If the Dutch cap fits –'

There were no gossip columnists in those days; had Cholly Knickerbocker and the others been alive and working then they would have had a ball at the reception held by Farnol's Horse. I suppose it was the same virtually everywhere else that evening in the tent city of what in the future would be called New Delhi. Malice is a weapon of the bored; and there were many bored amongst the English in India. Receptions such as this were ideal for such gossips; victims were pinned against walls by phrases every bit as sharp as knives. Being a stranger, which is the best camouflage, I was still comparatively safe. I moved through the crowd and aroused nothing more than curiosity.

'Listen to them!' Colonel Farnol was flushed with disgust. 'You must think we're a dreadful lot, Miss O'Brady.'

'It's the same the world over, I'm sure. Don't be too ashamed.'

'I suppose so. My elder gel, Clive's sister Elizabeth, is married to an Australian, God save her. Met him when he came over here selling us horses. Lives up-country in New South Wales, near some small town. Says it's just the same there. I suppose women need gossip to keep 'em alive.'

Oh, he almost got a knife in his ribs then. He was saved by the approach of Mrs Farnol and Clive's other sister Penelope. It was ridiculous, but somehow I hadn't thought of Clive as being part of a family; he had seemed so self-contained, as if he had created himself. I was still feeling my way round him,

226

if that isn't too indelicate a way of putting it; belonging to a family as close as the Farnols seemed to be, somehow he seemed more human. Some women, and I am one of them, prefer not to fall in love with loners.

'We've been admiring your frock, Miss O'Brady.' Mrs Farnol might have been voluptuous if she had let herself go; but she wore the corset of respectability as well as that of fashion. 'We've been reading about the new hobble-skirt.'

'It isn't comfortable, Mrs Farnol. One could never run away from men in it.'

'Does one want to?' Penelope was nineteen, beautiful and unmarried.

'Behave yourself,' said her mother, but her smile showed she meant no rebuke. She was in her element tonight, Queen of the Regiment if not its Bride, two of her three children with her. 'Ah, here's Clive!'

As he had promised he did indeed look exotic. As did his father and all the other officers of Farnol's Horse: I had been promised peacocks and I had got them. They were not wearing their turbans, they were for outdoor parades; but the dress uniform made us women look dowdy, farmyard hens. It was an emerald green jacket with silver facings, tight gold trousers with a green stripe down the leg, the lot topped with a green-and-gold sash piped with silver. Graustark could never have looked so gorgeous as that regimental tent in Delhi that evening. True, the diplomats and the Indian Civil Service men were soberly dressed, but the soldiers had the courage of their conceit. They knew that no one but the Indian Army could look so beautiful; at least none of the Europeans present. The princes were still to arrive.

Clive took my arm and led me out of the tent on to a carpeted walk, a sort of portable terrace. There were shrubs in massive pots, thick white ropes slung between freshly painted posts, forty yards of green and gold carpet; but it all looked as impermanent as a stage set. Ever since I'd arrived in this city of canvas the impression had been growing that I was in a theatre, a summer stock show that, as soon as we all turned our backs, would have its lights turned out and its sets struck. It suddenly occurred to me that so far there had been no applause, that India was silent.

'Where have you been?' I asked. 'When you weren't here to meet me I wondered if they'd think I'd gate-crashed – '

'I was held up.' He took my hand. 'You look beautiful.'

'So do you. You also look worried.'

He hesitated, then nodded. 'I'm worried about Karim Singh. I sent him to keep an eye on Prince Sankar – Sankar was supposed to be here this evening, but he hasn't turned up. Neither has Karim – he was to meet Private Ahearn at the Red Fort in the Old City, but he didn't turn up, either.'

A small group from the regimental band was seated at the end of the walk, facing an open end of the reception tent. They finished a Gilbert and Sullivan medley, then, to show their taste was universal, they began on *Swanee River*.

'Where's Ahearn now?'

'He's gone back to the rendezvous.' I don't think I realized till then that the word was also a military term. In my world only lovers had rendezvous. I was learning . . . 'I'll join him as soon as I can get away.'

'Be careful, Clive.' Then I did something I'd never done before: I kissed a man before he kissed me.

He didn't embrace me, just continued to hold my hand while he returned my kiss. But when I took my hand out of his I could barely open my fingers.

'God, I wish we could go somewhere! Nothing but damned tents – and I'm sharing mine with three other chaps!'

He was right: a tent is no place for an assignation, except perhaps for desert sheiks, Boy Scouts and Girl Guides. Maybe it was just as well: I think I would have thrown caution – and my corsets – to the winds that night. 'What's the matter? Now you look uncomfortable.'

'Dress trousers aren't made for lovers.'

'Do you mind!' But I wasn't really shocked, I was too much of a lover.

We went back into the tent and Viola Westbrook stumbled towards us looking as if she was about to topple on her face. She was dressed in a hobble-skirted frock in a yellow that matched the trousers of the officers; it threw a ghastly hue up on to her face, highlighting all the years that face had spent in the Indian sun. She told me she had ordered the dress from Harrods in London, sending them her measurements and asking them to send her the most fashionable frock they had in the season's most fashionable colour. She hadn't bought a new frock in six years and she hadn't known that the pastel shades of the Edwardian era had given way to bright colours.

'I should have sent them my age instead of my measurements,' she said. 'But now it's here and I've paid for it, I'll damn well wear it.'

Now, swaying like a carnival tent that had collapsed about its pole, she put a hand on Clive's arm and leaned on him. 'I'd love to sit down, but there's no room in this damned tube to bend my knees. I'd have done better to have come in my old tweed skirt and my cardigan. I'll be glad when all this is over.'

'You won't, you know.' Clive smiled affectionately at her. He was one of those men who had time and regard for old women. They are rare today: *I* know. 'You'll dine out on this till the next Durbar.'

'I shan't be here for that. This King is going to be like his grandmother, live for years. Am I right?' She looked at him shrewdly, half a dozen other questions in her eyes.

'That's what we all hope.'

'What sort of answer is that?'

Then the Nawab, the Ranee and Prince Mahendra arrived, bright and beautiful as a trio of birds of paradise. Only the hen was as beautiful as the cocks.

The Ranee looked at Clive, admiration and lust in her dark eyes: I could have assassinated her on the spot. 'Darling Clive, you do India proud!'

'Thank you, Mala. But that wasn't the intention.'

Then Viola said, 'Bertie, where are your wives? I was looking forward to that chorus line of saris! Surely you're not keeping them in *purdah* on such an evening?'

'They have headaches,' said the Nawab.

'*All five of them?* That must be frustrating for you.' Viola glanced sideways, gave me a wicked grin.

'What a beautiful frock,' said the Ranee, not wanting to be overlooked while other, absent women were discussed. 'It's a little tight, isn't it? Did your dressmaker run it up *on* you?'

Nothing about the Ranee was tight except her smile. She wore a rich blue sari that flowed round her like liquid silk; her movements were so lazily graceful that one was almost hypnotized just looking at her. Only the blaze of her jewellery kept you from dozing off. Her hair was done in a single thick plait worn down one side of her head and over one of those magnificent breasts; the plait was encased in a net of diamonds. She wore a collar of emeralds and rubies and each wrist was cuffed with a bracelet of diamonds set in gold: she was a willing prisoner of her own rich vulgarity. Behind her, looking sulky, perhaps even a little mad, was Mahendra, sporting nothing but a pearl stickpin in his pink turban.

'Where's Prince Sankar?' Clive said. 'He was invited.'

'Perhaps he has a headache, too,' said Viola, carrying more knives than a fancy French butcher.

'I am not his keeper, Clive.' The Nawab lost nothing in comparison with the officers of Farnol's Horse. He wore gold breeches and a silk *achkan* in a pattern of red, gold and blue stripes; his turban was gold with a blue aigrette in which a ruby glimmered like a drunk's eye. He looked to me as if he had been splashed with egg and ketchup. He saw me looking at him and he turned away from Clive as if he were glad to be distracted. 'You see me in all my glory, Miss O'Brady. These are the MCC colours.'

'MCC?' The colours were an eyesore.

'Marylebone Cricket Club. I wore this once at Lord's and the gateman refused to let me in.'

'I'm not surprised,' said Viola. 'You'd have ruptured Jack Hobbs.'

If he was offended, he did not show it. He laughed, a little too heartily, and began to tell a boring story about when he had once batted with Jack Hobbs, who, I gathered, was a sort of Ty Cobb of cricket. The band began to play a Victor Herbert waltz and I wished there was room for dancing, so that Clive could take me in his arms.

Then a regimental orderly slipped up beside Clive. I heard him say, 'You are wanted outside, Major. There's been some trouble.'

End of extract from memoirs.

5

Private Ahearn stood in the shadow of the high wall of the Red Fort beside the main gate. He was dressed in baggy breeches, a long shirt, a leather waistcoat and a muslin turban and he felt bloody ridiculous. But Major Farnol had insisted that he had to make himself inconspicuous when he came down into the Old City to meet Karim Singh; he had even smeared dirt on his face and hands to make himself look more like a coolie. He felt like he was playing some kid's game and he was glad none of the fellers back in the Connaughts could see him. But the last few days, ever since they had left the palace at Serog, had been no game and he had done everything that the Major had told him to. He had come here at four-thirty this afternoon, expecting Karim Singh to turn up at five o'clock as arranged, and had squatted down against the wall to make himself look even less conspicuous. At six o'clock, with still no sign of Karim, he had trudged back to the camp of Farnol's Horse and, after an angry argument with a suspicious sentry, had reported to Major Farnol. Who had promptly sent him back here and told him to wait all night for Karim Singh if needs be.

He sat down with his back to the wall, careful not to prod himself with the bayonet he carried in the belt under his long shirt. It was the only weapon he had and he wished for the comfort of his Lee-Enfield. He watched the traffic passing him, going down to the bazaars. He ducked his head as four British soldiers went past on their way to the brothels; he wished he were going with them instead of sitting here; he'd rather risk a dose of the clap than what might happen here in the dark of the Fort wall. He was too uneducated, too ignorant of history, even Irish history, to appreciate the irony of a Belfast Catholic assisting to uncover a plot against the English. He was an Irish rebel, but for himself not for Ireland. He just hated the bloody Army, not the English.

But maybe things were going to be different when he got

himself into Farnol's Horse. He stirred a little, feeling the horse beneath his legs again; it was almost better than having a woman under you. He looked down the road after the soldiers who had disappeared into the darkness and all at once felt contemptuous of them. Bloody foot-sloggers. He'd been one of them himself, technically still was, but ahead of him he had more delights than those poor sods would ever find in a brothel. Karim Singh, who wasn't a bad sort for a coolie, had told him what it was like in the regiment. It sounded just the life he'd settle for: his only real ambition was to get off his poor bloody feet . . .

He stood up, stretched his arms and almost fell over with shock as Karim Singh softly called to him from the black shadow of the gateway. 'Holy Jay-sus! Where you been, boyo?'

'Come here – quick!'

Ahearn recovered, slipped into the gateway. In the darkness he could barely see Karim, but the big Sikh seemed to be pressing himself back against the stonework, an arm held across his belly.

'Where you been? Jay-sus, the Major was getting worried, yes –'

Karim was having trouble breathing. 'You've got to get me back to camp, Mick.'

Ahearn put a hand on the arm across the Sikh's belly, felt the warm blood soaking through the shirt. 'You ain't going to be able to walk that far, man. I'll go and get a gharry. What happened, for Christ's sake?'

'I followed Prince Sankar – he went to four different places – I couldn't leave him to meet you here. But some of his chaps must have been following *me* – two of them jumped on me. They knifed me –'

'What happened to the buggers?'

'I killed one. The other one got away . . . Get me back to the camp, Mick. I don't feel so bloody marvellous –'

Ahearn ran out into the road, looked wildly up and down for a gharry. The gharry-wallahs were never around when you wanted 'em . . . Then he saw one coming up the road and he ran down and jumped into it. He stood up in the ramshackle carriage, slapped the driver on the shoulder and told him to hurry. The driver, startled at being spoken to in English by a coolie, turned to argue and Ahearn belted him over the ear and told him to get going. The driver cracked his whip above his horse and the spavined animal broke into a stumbling trot.

Opposite the gate to the Fort Ahearn jumped down and ran into the blackness under the arch. For a moment he thought Karim Singh had disappeared; then he heard the moan and saw the Sikh had slipped to the ground. He picked him up, struggling under the weight of the much bigger man; he cursed, as he had all his life, at being so small. Somehow he half-carried Karim out to the gharry, pushed him into the smelly, flea-infested vehicle and scrambled in after him. Then he snapped at the driver to head north up the road towards the camp. The driver whipped his horse and again it broke into its stumbling trot and started up the road, the driver yelling for the slow-moving traffic to get out of his way. Ahearn, sitting beside the slouched Karim Singh, could hear the big man sighing with pain as the gharry rattled and swayed.

'Won't be long, boyo. We'll get you fixed up – '

Then the two men came at the gharry out of the crowd straggling down the road, one from each side. Ahearn saw the flash of a knife on either side of him and he yelled a warning to Karim and dragged his bayonet out from under his shirt. The driver, always alert for snatch-and-run robbers, slashed with his whip at the man on the left; Ahearn drove his bayonet straight into the chest of the man coming in on the right. The man fell sideways against the wheel of the gharry, clutching at the bayonet; Ahearn, not wanting to lose his own grip on his only weapon, fell out of the gharry on top of the man. He went over the top of the thug, still holding the bayonet and feeling it come loose out of the man's chest, and rolled in the dust. He came up on his knees and saw the second man coming at him with his knife. He tried to bring the bayonet up, but he was too late. The knife went into his throat and he fell backwards into the dirt of the road.

In the instant before he died it seemed that his gaze widened to take in everything about him. He saw the gharry disappearing up the road into the darkness, the horse

233

galloping now; he saw the dead thug beside him and the other man running into the crowd; and he saw the crowd, which had spread out to stand in a wide half-circle, nobody moving, everyone just staring silently at him as he died. *Holy Jay-sus, they're always there, just standing and watching . . . yes . . .*

6

Early in the morning Farnol and George Lathrop went to see Karim Singh in the camp hospital. When he had brought Karim here last night in the gharry, Farnol had insisted that the Sikh was to be kept in a section on his own and he had stayed there till Lathrop had sent down two Ghurkas who were to stand guard over Karim till further notice. The sister in charge had wanted to ask questions, but Farnol had told her this was a Political Service matter and she had had the sense and experience to ask no more. When Farnol and Lathrop got to the hospital at six in the morning another sister was in charge.

'He had a good night.' She was one of those tough-minded, cheery nurses; she would have told John the Baptist's head not to worry. 'But he's a very lucky man.'

Farnol knew that. When he had gone out of the reception tent last night and followed the orderly down to the gharry waiting outside regimental headquarters he had been expecting the worst. His fears had been confirmed, or so he thought, when he had seen Karim Singh stretched out on the seat of the gharry. Then the Sikh's eyes had opened and he had whispered, 'Go down to the Fort, sahib. Mick is there in the road —'

Farnol at once had sent a sergeant and three men down to the Old City, giving them a description of Ahearn and how he was dressed. By the time he had got back from seeing Karim admitted to the hospital, the rescue party was back at camp with Ahearn's body.

Farnol had stood looking down at the little man in the dusty, blood-stained coolie's clothes that were too big for him.

No matter how many dead men he saw he was always amazed at how even the faces of men he knew well turned into those of strangers. But this particular stranger had saved the life of Karim Singh.

'Bury him as if he was one of us, sergeant. He was going to be on our strength as from tomorrow. He was a Catholic, I think. Ask the R.C. padre to arrange a Mass for him.'

The sergeant looked puzzled. 'One of us, sir? This chap?'

'Yes!' Then Farnol realized his voice was too sharp; he softened it. 'I'm sorry, sergeant. Just take my word for it – Private Ahearn deserves to be buried as one of us. I think he'd appreciate it if he knew.'

The sergeant, though curious, was not dense. 'Yes, sir. We'll see he gets a decent burial.'

'Did he have any personal things on him when you picked up the body?'

'Nothing, sir. One of the coolies in the crowd told me he'd had a bayonet, but someone had pinched that. There was another coolie in the road, looked like he'd been stabbed by a bayonet.'

'What did you do with him?'

'Told the coolies to get rid of him, sir.'

It was so easy to dispose of the unwanted dead. He didn't ask if the sergeant had found a tattoo mark inside the elbow of the other man. He was certain it would have been there.

Now he and George Lathrop were visiting the survivor; and he felt relief and gladness that it had been Karim Singh who had escaped. He was not quite sure what anger would have made him do if Karim had been the one to die. Probably he would have sought out Sankar and tried to kill him . . .

Karim Singh, in pyjamas and without his turban, his hair pulled up in a top-knot, looked far less imposing than usual. 'I am sorry about Private Ahearn, sahib. It should not have been him who died, it had nothing to do with him – '

'What happened with Prince Sankar? Colonel Lathrop would like to know.'

Karim tried to ease himself up straighter in the bed, but Lathrop waved him down. 'Stay comfortable. We're not putting on a show here. Where did Prince Sankar go when you followed him? Was he alone?'

'He was alone, sahib. He went first to where the horses and elephants are being held. The Nawab of Kalanpur and then Prince Mahendra came to talk to him there.'

'How long were they there?'

'About half an hour, sahib.'

'Where did Prince Sankar go then?'

'To the camp of the Rajah of Batlor. He was there an hour.'

'Christ!' said Lathrop. 'He's gathering in all the hill States. Or trying to.'

'All the small ones, anyway. Go on, Karim.'

'Then Prince Sankar went down to the Old City. He went into a house off one of the bazaars and after a while a man arrived in a gharry, but I couldn't see his face, he had his turban wound down over it. But I could tell he was a very superior person the way he brushed the coolies out of his way as he went into the house. He was there an hour, then he came out and drove away. Then Prince Sankar came out and went down to Mussoorie Street and into a house there. I asked a storekeeper who lived there and he said a *sadhu*. A holy man with much influence.'

'That's all we want,' said Lathrop. 'A combination of the princes and the *sadhus*. Go on, Karim. Where did Prince Sankar go from there?'

'I don't know, sahib. That was when the men jumped on me. I was marvellously lucky to get away.'

'Indeed you were,' said Lathrop and patted the big foot sticking up under the sheet. 'Jolly good work, Karim.'

Farnol shook Karim's hand, putting the same pressure into the grip as he had when he had shaken hands with his father; he felt almost the same emotion. He would have been embarrassed to say he loved a man; but he knew he had more regard for this big cheerful Sikh than just that of the friendship between master and servant. Karim's handshake was no less firm.

The two officers went out into the pearly morning light. Dust might hang over the rest of Delhi but not here above the tent city: the water-carts were already at work. Coolies, all of them in new white trousers and shirts, the best dressed they had been since birth, were sprinkling the new lawns. A pi-dog slunk up towards a kitchen tent and was chased away as if it were a whole pack of jackals. A man wandered about with a can of white paint and a brush held at the ready, as if looking for yesterday's paint to fade or peel. India, or anyway this part of it, had never looked so immaculate. It was just unfortunate that assassins could not be laid to rest with water or paint.

'Well, now we have to think about where they're going to try and kill the King,' said Lathrop. 'I've got a motor car; and Hugh Stacey, who's in charge of security, and I are going down the line to meet the King's train. We'll talk to H.E. about it.'

'About what? Cancelling the parade from the station?'

'Can't do that. I'm sure the King wouldn't hear of it – he hasn't come all this way to deny the people a chance to see him. No, the parade will have to go ahead.'

'They could make their attempt anywhere along the route, then – ' Farnol did not know Delhi as well as he knew the hills.

'Stacey and I think the worst risk will be along the Chandni Chowk.'

Farnol did know the Chandni Chowk, the street of jewellers and gold- and silversmiths, sometimes called the richest street in the world. The houses and stores along both sides of the street were backed by alleys into which any assassin could make his escape. And the street itself would be packed with spectators, a dense crowd that would be an unwitting accomplice of the killer.

'We're going to be unpopular, but we can't take any risks along there. Stacey started moving troops and police in there at dawn – H.E. brought in 4000 extra police from outside Delhi and Stacey is using all of them. Nobody will be allowed into any house on the Chowk after six a.m., not even if he lives on the street. There'll be troops on the rooftops and there'll be a policeman at a window of every house. They should all be in place by now.'

'One feels so bloody helpless . . . With all our precautions, they could still succeed. Especially if there's a fanatic amongst them.'

'Someone like Mahendra, you mean? You've got to keep an eye on him.'

'Me? I'm not in the parade. There's only a special troop from each of the regiments – twelve men, that's all. My father couldn't put me in – there'd be a hell of a stink from the other chaps if one of them had to be put out to put me in. I've been away from the regiment too long.'

'You'll be in the parade, old chap. I've arranged that you ride as special escort to the Ranee's coach. Mahendra will be riding with her.'

'Does the Ranee know I'm to be her escort?'

'No. But I don't think she'll mind – I gather she was an old gel friend of yours.'

Farnol threw back his head and laughed, glad to let a little tension escape him. 'Some day, George, we must have a durbar of our own, just the chaps from the Political Service who've slept with Mala. We could have quite a roll-up.'

'Our sins are paying off. She won't object if you're riding behind her. Give her the eye occasionally, as if you're promising to meet her tonight.'

'I'm going to ride behind her – that'll be difficult. I'll be looking right into the eye of Mahendra.'

'Just what we want. Well, I'll see you at Salimgarh station. I'll be coming on the royal train.'

'Where will the King be in the parade? Is he riding an elephant?'

'No. He's a stubborn bugger, they tell me. But then I guess all kings are . . . H.E. wanted him on an elephant, with a gold howdah and all the trimmings. But the King insists he's going to ride a horse. He doesn't seem to appreciate that the population out here expect a ruler to look like a ruler. Their Rajahs don't lead parades on bloody nags. Give you a lift back to camp?'

'I'll walk, George. I want to think a little.'

'Don't let your train of thought get too long, Clive. That could lead you into absolute bloody despair. Keep your chin up, as they say. I've always wanted to meet the bugger who said that. Must've been some bloody desk-wallah who'd never seen strong sunlight. I lift my chin and I'm blinded.'

CHAPTER NINE

Farnol went to see Bridie before he rode into the Old City with the troop from Farnol's Horse. 'I'm sorry to be so early –'

'I've been up since six – I shouldn't want to be late for a day like this. You look even better than last night! That turban – I thought only rajahs could get away with something as swanky as that.'

The green, gold and silver turban was indeed swanky. Farnol wore it with pride and a certain *élan*: Englishmen, being Empire builders, adapt well to the costumes of the conquered. 'The trick is to remember to duck when you enter a low doorway. Will you be watching the parade?'

'Viola has arranged that. Somewhere close to the entrance to the King's camp.'

He was glad she would not be somewhere close to the Chandni Chowk. 'We'll have lunch together, then watch the polo this afternoon.'

'Are you trying to tell me you expect no trouble this morning?'

He had to be honest with her; he could feel his worry showing on his face. 'No. I'm trying to tell you I *hope* there's no trouble this morning.'

She put a hand on his arm. 'I hope so, too, Clive. Nothing would please me more than to be able to write a story that said everything went off beautifully, as planned. If it does, I already have the head for my story – The Glory of Empire.'

He smiled. 'You've changed.'

'Maybe I'm carried away by the atmosphere. My editor will probably cut my story and my father will never speak to me again if he hears of it. But –' She laughed at herself: she tingled with martial tunes, foreign tunes. 'I shall cheer for the King.'

'Save a cheer for me when I pass by.'

He climbed up on to his horse, a black charger that stood seventeen hands. She looked up at him and gasped at the beauty of him. 'Oh God!' she gasped. 'It must never come to an end!'

He knew what she meant and he knew it could never last forever. He rode away with a heavy heart, for he felt no pleasure in being a symbol.

2

In a hotel, no Ritz or Grand or Perapalas, just outside the Old City, Zoltan Monday lay beside Magda and looked at the lazily whirling fan hanging from the cracked and stained ceiling. A portrait of Queen Victoria, the glass covering it spotted with fly-dirt, hung on the wall opposite the bed. He wondered why her portrait still hung there: didn't the hotel management know there had been two monarchs since? Perhaps they had given up caring who reigned over them.

Magda stirred, opened one eye and smiled at him. Her whore's smile: it delighted him and yet hurt, a constant reminder of how they had met. Then her smile died, she scratched herself vigorously and jumped out of bed. 'There are fleas! I'm being eaten alive! Scratch my back!'

He was aware of his own discomfort; he got out of bed and stood beside her. 'Scratch mine.'

They stood there, arms round each other: it was like some sort of erotic love-play. Then he held her to him and she felt him rising against her: the fleas had left *that* alone. 'I'm not getting back into that bed, darling. I'm not going to share you with the fleas.'

'We'll move out this morning.' A stiff member was full of optimism.

'Where shall we go? There isn't a vacant room in Delhi. You must telephone Baron von Albern, ask him if he can put us up. No, I'll telephone him. I think he still has an eye for the ladies.'

'If he saw you like that –' He was raw and spotted from flea bites and love bites. But he would still have been randy if he had been suffering from tiger bites. He loved her, and still he could not quite believe his luck.

Then there was a knock at the door. They both threw on robes and he went to the door and opened it. A bearer stood there, one who looked too smart and clean to be one of the hotel staff.

'Good morning, sahib. My master, the Nawab of Kalanpur, asks can you and your memsahib come to breakfast with him before he leaves for the parade to greet the King?'

'Now? It is so early –'

'My master must leave at eight o'clock for the parade. If you could hurry, sahib –'

Fifteen minutes later the Mondays were outside the hotel getting into the gharry the Nawab had sent for them. Another gharry was hailed to carry their luggage; even if they had to camp out in the open Monday was determined they were not coming back to the hotel and its fleas. They drove at a smart clip through the already busy streets and fifteen minutes later were sitting down to breakfast in the Nawab's personal tent. The Nawab was dressed for the parade: he made breakfast look like a State banquet. He ate a boiled egg only a little larger than the ruby stuck in the aigrette of his turban. Each time he leaned forward he had to put up a hand to keep his four rows of pearls out of his buttered toast. Magda, ravenous, gorged her stomach and her eyes.

'May we talk business, Mr Monday? Does your wife mind? I am so rushed for time.'

Monday spread marmalade slowly on his toast, preparing himself. He had never expected to be doing any business with Bertie, this cricketing fool. Was the man going to offer him some price for Magda to replace the wife he had lost?

'My wife acts as my secretary, Your Highness. Please go ahead.'

'We should have had our meeting in Simla, but I was still awaiting instructions.' The Nawab smiled, wiped butter from his pearls with the napkin a servant handed him. 'I am Mr Brown.'

3

The royal train steamed into Salimgarh station, narrowly missing a pi-dog that the hundreds of troops, police, dignitaries and lackeys, all standing at attention, had not been able to prevent from intruding. Shite hawks sat on the platform roof, looking for offal amongst all the pomp, and some ravens croaked a counterpoint to the band as it struck up *God Save the King*. The royal carriage pulled up at exactly the right spot and the King and Queen stepped out on to the carpet that had been laid for them. His Excellency Lord Hardinge, the Viceroy, following on, remarked that the King stepped off into exactly the middle of the carpet. He was not a superstitious man, but he took that as a good omen for the rest of the morning.

Outside the station the parade stretched away, two or three miles of precedence. Lathrop, astride his horse immediately outside the station, kept turning his head, looking for – what? Would it be someone throwing a bomb? A sniper with a rifle? Some madman with a knife, willing to sacrifice his own life as he took the King's?

The royal party came out of the station. The Viceroy, with his long face and high forehead that only seemed to accentuate his height, towered over the monarch he represented here in India; he had the diffidence and respect to stand a little apart so that the King would never fall in his shadow. The King looked at his horse.

'It's rather small, isn't it, Hardinge?'

'We had to be sure it was one that wouldn't play up, sir. I'm told this one is an ideal mount for the occasion.'

The King mounted the horse, adjusted his plumed topee, pulled down the front of the field marshal's red jacket that made him indistinguishable from the other generals around him. Then he looked up at the tall figure of his Viceroy on a horse almost two hands taller. Perhaps he should have ridden an elephant after all.

'We're ready, Hardinge. Let's start.'

'That's the Gate of Elephants up ahead, Your Majesty. All the Moghul emperors entered Delhi through that gate.'

'Will everyone appreciate the tradition of my doing the same?'

'Of course, sir.' But Hardinge was glad he did not have to put a number to the tradition-minded.

Further down the procession, out of sight of the royal party, Farnol sat his horse beside the Ranee's coach. She looked out at him from under her cap of diamonds and smiled. 'Clive darling, we must be more discreet. What would the King say if he knew we were meeting like this?'

'Whore,' said her brother sitting opposite her.

Farnol managed not to look at Mahendra, though he knew the latter was staring at him. 'George Lathrop just felt you should be looked after.'

She smiled without being coy: coyness can disfigure some women and she would never risk that. 'You two have been exchanging memories – '

He smiled, then looked at Mahendra who was about to say *Whore* again. 'Keep your mouth shut, Bobs. You're not in Serog now.'

For a moment it looked as if Mahendra was about to spring out of the coach at him. He half-rose; then abruptly the coach started up. He fell back into his seat and half-lay there glaring back at Farnol as the latter moved his horse in behind the coach. The procession began to move, stretching itself into an immensely long concertina of pomp and vanity and privilege. The crowd stood on either side of the road and cheered, because it was the only sound they could make together. Nobody had yet taught them to jeer in chorus.

Fifty yards ahead of the Ranee, several scales up the precedence, the Nawab looked down on the multitude from his gold-plated howdah. Out of his own State he was not sure whether to smile or wave or ignore the onlookers; he would have felt more at home with the crowd at Lord's where one just waved one's bat after scoring a half-century. He was a selfish man, but he was not unkind, so long as kindness did not cost him money he could ill-afford; he hoped that these poor coolies (though he did not think of the word *poor* in its economic context) would appreciate what Sankar and he and the others were trying to do for them. It would be a better India, Sankar had insisted; and he had tried hard to believe him. The wealth would not be spread more evenly, God be thanked; but less would go to the English and what was saved might finish up being shared amongst those less rich than the princes. Or so Sankar promised, though the Nawab knew he would feel no heartburn if Sankar could not keep his promise. The only promise he wanted kept was that he himself, a prince who was poor (he used the word this time in its economic context) should have all his debts wiped out and be given further loans to enable him to go on living as a prince should. He ran a jewelled hand over the side of the gold-plated howdah, fingered the pearls that hung from his neck. It was a pity they were all mortgaged to Sankar, a man who had only contempt for such necessities.

It amused him that he was the one who had been chosen to spend the half a million pounds to buy the guns from Krupps. He had always been extravagant with money; but Sankar had known he would never attempt to embezzle any of what he had been entrusted with. Sankar would kill him if he did such a thing.

'You are necessary to us,' Sankar had told him, 'because you are one of those the English will least suspect. All your stupid devotion to their cricket and their other customs is just the camouflage we need. You are necessary, but never forget that you are expendable.'

'I don't have to listen to your threats.' He was amazed, later, at the courage he had shown for a minute or two. 'I can abdicate, let you take over Kalanpur and go and live in England.'

'What on? They won't welcome paupers at the MCC. Who at Hurlingham would lend you a string of polo ponies? The English upper classes look after their own kind, much better than we do here. But they never waste charity on outsiders.'

Of course, he was an outsider: he had known that even in the most convivial moments in London and at country houses. He was sure he had true friends there, but then saw them turn away in his mind as he put them to the test. It just wasn't cricket, he told himself petulantly, but he knew that it was life.

He had been appalled when he learned of the plot to kill the King. That had not even been mentioned in the plans of the revolutionary movement.

'Good God, you can't do that! *Why* do you have to do it?'

'We want them to know we're serious – we want *India* to know.'

'But why not the Viceroy?' He had always known that someone would have to die, though he had tried not to think about it. 'He's the symbol here, not the King.'

'No, it has to be the King, not his monkey.'

He had not been able to argue: the others had all been for the assassination. And now, this morning, Sankar was somewhere on the Chandni Chowk placing the two snipers, one on either side of the street, who were going to shoot the King. The Nawab felt sick and leaned sideways, as if the motion of the howdah had brought on landsickness and he was going to vomit over the side. The crowd on that side thought it was being greeted by this prince, whoever he was, and it raised a polite cheer. The Nawab, revived by this unexpected recognition, sat back. He consoled himself that he was so far down the scale of precedence that he would not see the assassination when it occurred.

Still further up the parade, riding just behind the King's escort, were George Lathrop and Colonel Stacey. The latter was a short, stocky man from an infantry regiment and unaccustomed to horse-riding. His attention was divided between his fractious horse and looking for possible assassins, with the horse getting most of the attention. Lathrop, on the other hand, sat his horse as if he had been born in the saddle and gave all his attention to his surroundings.

They were coming into the Chandni Chowk now. The Old City, like a barracks specially spruced up for an inspection by visiting brass, had been given a new, if temporary, face for the King. Fountains that hadn't flowed in a hundred years spouted and dribbled water from new mains; policemen stood by to discourage citizens who thought the glittering pools were public baths. The few trees had been trimmed, shrubs planted, ruins shaved of their beards of weeds; what couldn't be renewed had been dressed with a foliage of bunting and flags. It may not all have been as splendid as in the days of Shah Jehan, but then nobody, least of all King George, missed those days. The King looked with regal modesty left and right as he rode along, inwardly proud in the knowledge that he was the first English monarch to visit the East since Richard Lion-Heart eight hundred years before. He would have been disturbed if he had known that so few of those in the parade and none of the spectators beside the road knew of or cared for the fact. He was already disturbed that so few of the crowd seemed to be looking at him but were looking at Hardinge riding behind him.

'What's going on?' Stacey murmured to Lathrop. 'The reception sounds a bit lukewarm.'

'His Majesty should have taken H.E.'s advice and ridden an elephant. Nobody is recognizing him. Listen to them – ' He could hear the chatter in the crowd as they nodded at the Viceroy on his big black charger. *There is the Lord Sahib. But where is the King?*

'That may be a good thing,' said Stacey, cursing his own horse, wishing *he* were on foot or even on an elephant. 'Perhaps the assassins won't know whom to go for.'

'Where's Sankar? Is he further down the parade?'

'He didn't put in an appearance.'

'Jesus Christ!' said Lathrop and almost worked his head off his shoulders as he craned right and left to scan the rooftops along the Chowk. He could see the armed men perched on the roofs of the buildings, he looked down and saw the policemen posted like stakes every ten yards along the route; but he felt uneasy, wanted to shout to the King to put spurs to his horse and gallop full tilt out to the royal camp. Instead, he thanked God, in whom he didn't believe, that he was not a full-time equerry to the King.

In the royal coach, drawn by its six horses, the Queen put up her white parasol, spoiling the effect of the Golden Fan and the Golden State Umbrella held over her by the two *chuprassi*, in scarlet and gold uniforms, perched on the dickey of the coach. The Fan and the Umbrella were heavy and the *chuprassi* were weak-armed; the Fan and the Umbrella kept tilting backwards, giving no shade at all to the Queen. She had a proper respect for ceremony, but she was a practical woman and she was not going to get sun-burned. Beside her her Lady-in-Waiting, the Duchess of Devonshire, suffered the sun and hoped the next Coronation she attended would be in a more temperate clime.

Lord Durham, the equerry, sitting opposite the Queen, leaned forward. 'This is the Chandni Chowk, ma'am. The street of goldsmiths and silversmiths.'

'Indeed? I'd like to see some of their work.'

'Yes, ma'am.' Durham knew she would ask him again tomorrow: she never forgot a request or an order. He hoped the gold- and silversmiths would be in a generous mood.

Then the royal party was out of the Chandni Chowk and Lathrop breathed a sigh of relief. The King, safe in his ignorance of the designs on his life, rode on, irritated by the puzzling indifference of his Indian subjects.

4

Queen Mary sat in a chair in the pink-and-blue silk-lined bedroom tent of the royal suite of six tents. Lord Durham, on the way into the royal camp, had told her that it covered 85 acres and she had been pleased at what she had seen. She had done a quick tour of the royal suite because she was a good housekeeper and she liked to see that George was comfortable. She had been particularly pleased at the King's writing room with its mahogany table, beautifully carved chair, the white Bikanir carpet and the Persian rugs, though she had wondered who had put the small statue of Buddha on the mantelpiece. Probably some servant who didn't know that George was the Head of the Church of England, which was careful of displaying even statues of Christ.

She had bathed and changed into a loose robe and wished for nothing more than a few hours to herself. She never resented the duties of being George's Consort; rather, she delighted in them. But, though this was supposed to be the cool season, she was already finding India more than a little uncomfortable.

She glanced at the books that lay on the table beside her. *The Broken Road*, by A. E. W. Mason, biographies of Hastings and Dalhousie, stories by Rudyard Kipling: she had ordered the books to be packed before she left London. But she was not very interested in English life in India, though she did not think she would tell George that.

He came into the bedroom, sat down in another of the chintz-covered chairs. He wore slippers, trousers, a silk dressing-gown and a silk scarf. She loved to see him relaxed, to see him *private*; she had taught herself to separate him from the public figure. She looked at his fair brown hair, his neatly trimmed beard, his very red lips and the bright blue eyes that were his most attractive feature. Yes, she loved him dearly, even if she had loved his elder brother first.

'How do you think it went, May?' When they were alone he always called her by her private name.

'Very nicely, I thought. The crowds were so well-behaved. I don't know why, but I was afraid there might have been a disturbance or two.'

'I suppose it was worthwhile.' He disliked foreign travel, unlike his father, who had delighted in it: possibly to get away from Grandmama. He also had no real taste for grand entertainment. But it was he who had suggested, out of a sense of duty, that he should come to India to be crowned here as Emperor. Grandmama, at Disraeli's urging, had first assumed the title of Empress of India in 1877; but she would never have travelled further east than St Paul's Cathedral if it could have been avoided and certainly never to India. So he had insisted that he should come and he could not complain if the Indians had been less enthusiastic than he had expected. It seemed that when he had come here six years ago, as Prince of Wales, the reception had been much warmer. But then the crowds had been smaller and most of those English and eager for the opportunity to curtsey.

He looked at May, loving her, wondering if she should be worried by what was on his mind. She was the perfect Consort: she never meddled in affairs of State, but she was always there to support him when he was troubled. And he was troubled now. 'May – Hardinge tells me we may have a disturbance or two before we go home.'

'One shouldn't be surprised. Such a huge country – there are bound to be some malcontents. These princes do rather show off, as if they're trying to out-do each other.'

'Not princes, confound it! Sorry – I shouldn't be short-tempered. It's the heat.' He got up, went to her and kissed the top of her head. 'One or two of the princes do look like playing up. The Baroda chap for one.'

'Can't you have his invitations withdrawn?'

'I suppose so. But if we have any opposition here, we're not going to solve the problem by withdrawing invitations. That's ladies' tea party stuff.'

'Thank you, dear,' said the Queen, though she disliked tea parties.

He smiled and kissed the top of her head again. 'Remember the tea party Hyderabad gave for us the last time we were here? All those stale cakes and the sour cream. I told you he died last August. Hardinge tells me it was alcoholism. I gather quite a few of these chaps suffer from it. Hardinge thinks it's due to an excess of wives. No, he's quite serious.'

She laughed. 'Aren't you fortunate? Only me to drive you to drink.'

They held hands, loving each other dearly. It was a circle of two that their children, back in England, could never quite break into.

5

That evening Prince Sankar re-appeared at the camp he was sharing with his cousin the Nawab. If one counted every tiny fiefdom ruled by a semi-independent chieftain there were 675 States represented at the Durbar. The word *durbar*, from the Persian *darbar*, meant, besides a gathering to pay homage, a meeting for taking administrative decisions; but no one, least of all the minor chieftains, would be invited to take any decisions at Delhi. Nonetheless, every one of the rulers wanted to be at the Durbar and every one of them thought he was entitled to his own piece of turf at the gathering. But the government, careful that the Durbar would not spread out over the entire United Provinces, had doled out accommodation as it doled out honours. The seventy-three princes entitled to salutes of more than eleven guns and the prefix Highness had been allotted camps befitting their station, the largest belonging to the premier prince, the newly-ascended Nizam of Hyderabad. As the doling-out went down the line of precedence the allotments got smaller and smaller; finally the camps had been shared between related princes or at least compatible ones. The Nawab of Kalanpur and the Rajah of Pandar, neither of whom was entitled to a gun salute or even a rifle volley, and who were only called Highness as a courtesy and never at official functions, had to make do on a two-acre lot. Their horses and the Nawab's elephants were quartered in a common stabling area and the Nawab, feeling claustrophobic in such a confined space as he and Sankar had been given, had asked if he might billet out his wives in some common *zenana* area. But the Commissioner for Accommodation, a Presbyterian with one wife and she one too many, had firmly told him he should have left his wives at home. Which the Nawab, in view of the way things were going, now wished he had done.

Sankar had been back in the camp no longer than half an hour when Farnol arrived. Lathrop had had a watch posted on the camp and as soon as he had learned that Sankar had returned he sent for Farnol.

'Go down and let him know we have an eye on him, Clive.'

'I don't think that will worry him.'

'It will worry him to the extent that he may have to change his plans, whatever they are.'

'I wish to God we were up in the hills. We could arrest the lot of them and they wouldn't be missed for a week or two. Keep them prisoners in their own palaces.'

'We'll get them eventually. Once they've made their attempt, then we'll move in and grab the lot. Not just Sankar but everyone else involved.'

'You're taking an awful risk, George. Playing dice with the King's life.'

Lathrop polished his monocle. 'Don't you think I know it? I daren't tell anyone else, not even H.E. But if we can clamp down on this movement, get the whole lot of the buggers in jail on sedition charges and attempted assassination, it should set any other revolutionaries back on their arses for four or five years. By then I hope we're mobilized enough to deal with anything. I'm worried, Clive. I can hear the sound of drums, faraway ones – ' He breathed on his monocle, polished it; but no matter how clear it was, he knew he would never get better than a blurred view of the trouble brewing in Europe. 'The Kaiser is looking for war, Clive. If ever he got a toe-hold in India, we'd have trouble on our hands that would make the Mutiny look nothing more than a tiger hunt.'

'Are there any German agents operating here?'

'Probably. But they're not Germans. They're too shrewd for that. They'll be using people like Sankar. How does the Baron feel about it all?'

'He's on our side.'

'Poor old bugger. They'll never forgive him for that in Berlin. Well, go down and try and frighten the shit out of Sankar.'

Farnol smiled as he stood up. 'You've been very restrained in your language, George.'

'I've been practising, in case I put my foot in my mouth in front of the Queen. I understand the King doesn't mind a bit of language, after all he was in the Navy. But the Queen doesn't like it at all.'

So Farnol went down to see Sankar who, with the Nawab, greeted him politely if coolly. They sat in the main tent, which was so sparsely decorated, on Sankar's orders, that the Nawab felt a very much under-privileged prince. He could *never* entertain anyone here, even if Sankar would allow it, which he wouldn't.

Farnol and the Nawab were armed with whiskeys, Sankar with water. 'Colonel Lathrop sent me down, Your Highness. He wondered why you were not in the parade today. His Excellency the Viceroy is particularly keen that all the princes appear at every official occasion.'

'I was indisposed, Major.'

'I'm sorry to hear that. Did you call a doctor?'

'I do not believe in Western medicine. I prefer to be treated by one of our own men who understands the use of herbs.'

'The *sadhu* on Mussoorie Street?'

'I see you have your sources of information. Perhaps I can recommend him to you if you should fall ill.'

'I'd like to meet him, though not professionally.' Then Farnol looked at the Nawab. He could see that Sankar, despite his mystic leanings, could not deny his Indian tongue; argument was a passion with Indians and Sankar, though Farnol was certain he would be careful in what he said, was no exception. Farnol turned to the Nawab, who had the Indian tongue but would never be much good at argument. 'One of our sources of information told me, Bertie, that you had a meeting early this morning with Mr Monday and his wife.'

The whisky splashed in the Nawab's glass. He was an excellent batsman, could read the swerve and turn of a cricket ball, but he was a poor conspirator; perhaps he should have taken up some under-handed game like military manoeuvres. 'I just wanted to be sure they would have a good view of the parade. That delightful Mrs Monday only came to India to see the Durbar.'

'Were you able to arrange that they got good seats?'

'I believe they sat with the Baron.'

Sankar said, 'Are you paying as much attention to all the other princes and chieftains, Major?'

'We don't think any of the others can tell us anything about the death of Major Savanna.'

'Oh yes. My cousin told me about his unfortunate death. You think he had something to do with it?'

'Oh I say, old chap!' The Nawab didn't like being accused of murder, especially by his cousin, the real murderer. He had had nothing to do with the death of Savanna and he had been shocked by it. He was not stupid, ⋅but he had shut his mind against the thought that there would be deaths, many of them, when the revolution began. The murder of Savanna had snapped his mind wide open to the realization that people he knew were bound to die. Some whom he knew as well and liked as much as Clive Farnol.

'We know you had nothing to do with it, Bertie.' Sankar

smiled at his cousin's discomfort. 'If ever Major Farnol decides to arrest you, British justice will see that you're acquitted. Isn't that so, Major?'

'I'm glad to see you have a respect for British justice.'

'Not really. It's just an imperial tool of trade.'

The conversation went on for another five minutes and Farnol knew he had not made a dent in Sankar. He might have, as George Lathrop would have put it, scared the shit out of the Nawab; but Bertie, he had decided, was a very minor cog in the revolutionary wheel. He wondered if there would be any dividend in kidnapping the Nawab and putting him under intense interrogation; but he dismissed the idea. He was restricted by the need to appear civilized. If only they were up in the hills . . .

He went away frustrated and Sankar, suffering his own frustration but for other reasons, shook his head angrily at his cousin. 'You mustn't be so frightened. You looked ready to blab out everything –'

'I may talk too much, but I don't *blab*.' The Nawab gulped down his drink, as if defending himself had made him thirsty.

'I should never have invited you to join us. You're too – too damned *English*.'

'We all have our faults.' He did not mean to be witty. He was afraid, of his cousin, of the future. 'Where are you going?'

Sankar had stood up. 'Nowhere. I'm just going to send a messenger to tell Mahendra to come here.'

'They'll be watching us.'

'Of course they will. We'll sit outside and let them see us. But unless they are lip-readers they won't know what we're talking about.'

Mahendra arrived within ten minutes, as if he had been waiting for the summons, and the three princes went out to sit in camp chairs on the manicured newly-planted lawns. Only the Nawab appreciated that they were sitting on a symbol of England: he remembered the lawns of Oxford and the country houses, so different from the scraggly grass patches that surrounded the princely palaces of India. He looked at the passing traffic on the red road running past the camp: who were the spies amongst them? A road-sweeper went by, taking his time about keeping immaculate the already immaculate road, his broom swinging back and forth like a ragged-ended metronome. He glanced across towards the three princes; to the Nawab he looked sly and intelligent, too sharp-eyed to be a road-sweeper. But surely the English wouldn't use an Untouchable as a spy? The man went slowly on down the road and the Nawab shivered at the thought of the future. He, too, would be an Untouchable in certain places if the revolution succeeded. At Lord's, for instance . . .

'What happened this morning?' Mahendra was tense and upset, a spring that had been wound tighter and tighter all day. 'You were supposed to have done it in the Chandni Chowk. I kept waiting for the sound of the shots – '

'We couldn't get near the houses.' Sankar's day-long frustration made him sharp-tongued. 'There were police and soldiers everywhere. They must have guessed where we would choose to strike.'

'Why didn't you go to another spot?'

'Where? My men had only rifles – how could they have produced those in a crowd?'

'Bad planning,' said the Nawab; fear made him spiteful. 'You have me buying field guns and machine-guns from Mr Monday and you forget to provide your assassins with pistols as a reserve.'

'I don't want your criticisms,' said Sankar coldly. 'We shall kill the King before he leaves Delhi.'

'I don't think it's necessary,' said the Nawab stubbornly but weakly. He came of a family that had always looked for an easy way out; it had only survived because the British had protected it. There was no history of mighty warriors in Kalanpur, not like the ancestors of Sankar.

'It *is* necessary and it will be done.'

'Where?' said Mahendra.

'At the Coronation.'

'At the Coronation?' The Nawab strangled his voice, saw the road-sweeper coming back up the road on the other side, 'Good God – *how?*'

'With either a pistol or a knife.'

'But none of your men will be able to get that close!' He felt a sudden relief: the whole thing was going to collapse

254

because of its impossibility. 'The crowds are going to be kept right away – '

'*We* aren't. No one will be closer to the King than us when we are presented to him.'

The Nawab suddenly felt cold, as if winter had plunged out of the Himalayas. 'You mean *you* are going to kill him?'

'Perhaps me. Or Mahendra. Or you. It will depend on who draws the straw.'

'Whoever kills the King is sure to be killed himself,' said Mahendra.

'All in a good cause, as they say.' Sankar's wit was too cold to have any humour in it. In any case neither the Nawab nor Mahendra would have been amused.

'I am not going to kill the King!' The Nawab strangled his voice again; he could see the road-sweeper getting closer. 'No, I shan't do it!'

'You will do it if you draw the shortest straw,' said Sankar. 'If not, I shall kill you.'

The Nawab looked across the road at the sweeper: should he cry out to him for help? Have him bring Farnol running, expose the whole plot, throw himself on the mercy of British justice? But he remained silent and the sweeper went on his slow way down the road.

Mahendra said, 'What if you draw the straw, Sankar? You will be needed later – we can't afford to lose you – '

Sankar was not afraid of death: he longed to be a martyr. He would have preferred to die an elderly martyr; but if the revolution was successful there would be no call for martyrs by the time he was old. 'The deed must be done – '

'But why not one of the others?'

'How many of the others are to be presented to the King? Three, that's all. And they all have higher rank than any of us, they are all much richer, the revolution will need their money.' He hated that thought, that money could buy one safety and position in a revolution. The anarchists of Europe would laugh their heads off at the idea. 'Outside of them and us, none of the movement will be presented to the King, no one else will be able to get close to him. Don't you want to die in the cause, Bobs?' The English nickname, on his lips, was a mockery.

'Of course.' Mahendra felt something like fire race through him, his brain swirled.

Sankar suddenly regretted he had suggested the idea of the straws. If he had approached Mahendra alone, he felt sure now that the latter would have accepted nomination as the assassin. He had not had enough faith in the boy's madness.

'We'd better go inside to draw the straws.'

'*Now?*' The Nawab was horrified: decisions like that shouldn't be rushed.

'Now.'

They went into the main tent, the Nawab last to move and then like a man suddenly stricken with arthritis. He looked back as he went into the tent, saw that the road-sweeper had stopped fifty yards away, stood like a ghost in the deepening dusk as if waiting to be called. But the Nawab had no voice, no will: he went into the tent a hollow man.

Sankar sent for a broom, pulled three straws from it and dismissed the bearer who had brought it. He broke the straws into three separate lengths, closed his hand on them and offered his fist to Mahendra. He looked directly into the young man's eyes and silently told him he was the man to be honoured; it was not hypnotism, but he had learned from the mystics in the mountains the powerful persuasion the mind could wield. Mahendra did not look at the fist held out to him; he gazed into Sankar's eyes, feeling an intoxicating trance beginning to take hold of him; the killing was already done, he was dead and a hero and a martyr for India. He put out his hand and, still without looking at Sankar's fist, took the straw that was gently pushed into his fingers. Then Sankar turned, held out his fist to the Nawab, who took a straw. Finally Sankar opened his hand palm upwards and the others did the same. Mahendra had the shortest straw.

The Nawab had seen what had gone on, but he was not going to call for fair play, complain that it wasn't cricket. He had been saved and he was not going to risk his life again to save a crazed boy.

But the crazed boy was not so mad that he was impractical. There are times when there are none so sensible as the mad. He felt the fever that had possessed him die down and he said, 'I shall be honoured to do the deed. But what if Mala refuses to let me accompany her in the presentation line? She can do that if she wishes.'

'Why should she?' said the Nawab, suddenly nervous again.

'You know what she's like. If she gets out of the wrong side of the bed in the morning – anything at all can upset her mood – '

'Perhaps if she had a man in her bed the night before – ' said Sankar. 'Women are more amenable after a night's love-making. Isn't that so, Bertie? You're the expert.'

But a man with a multiple of wives always escapes in the morning from the bed of his partner; the Nawab was no expert on the daytime moods of satisfied women. 'I think Bobs should try and stay on her right side. Be nice to her.'

'Be nice in the cause of revolution? You really are absurdly English, Bertie.' But Sankar passed on the advice to Mahendra. 'Perhaps it would be best. You can be charming when you wish.'

'Really?' Even Mahendra had to smile at that; he knew his limitations and took delight in them. 'I'll try. But what happens to her when the revolution succeeds? Will you promise me you'll get rid of her?'

He had dreamed of succeeding Mala as the ruler of Serog, but that could have happened only in the context of a British India. Even then the British might have interfered; they had deposed several princes who had not fitted into their schemes. In the context of a revolutionary India he would have been a very small fish; better to die and be hailed than to live and be forgotten or overlooked. But he could not bear the thought of Mala's surviving while he was dead.

'She'll be attended to,' said Sankar. 'Just as will all the others who oppose us.'

'More killing?'

'If need be. But don't turn pale, Bertie – there won't be a blood-bath just for the sake of revenge. If those against us want to leave and live in England, we'll let them. They just won't be allowed to take their wealth with them, that's all.'

'I wasn't thinking of the English. How many of our own people must die? You have already killed my wife Ganga.'

257

'Not I. That was the stupid merchant Chand. He bungled two attempts to kill Farnol. He deserved to die himself.'

'He killed my wife.'

'I'm sorry about that. It couldn't be helped, given the circumstances.'

Suddenly he wanted to kill Sankar. Murder was there in his hands; but there wasn't enough courage in his heart. He held back the tears of rage, at himself more than at Sankar. He had loved Ganga and the only way he could revenge her death was with words.

Mahendra, insensitive to atmosphere, careless of what the Nawab might feel about his dead wife, said, 'I hope everything goes according to plan. There are all the millions we want to follow us . . . For all you know, your wife Ganga might have been on our side.'

The Nawab said nothing, wanting to kill him, too.

'Everyone will follow us.' Sankar had the blind faith of the fanatic. 'Nationalism isn't something that only *we* feel – it's in the villages, too.'

The Nawab sighed, gave up the idea of immediate murder. 'I hope you can spread the message quickly and then hold it . . . You may be killing the King too early.'

'Killing the King will be our rallying cry.'

The Nawab turned his face away, wondered if Ganga would have fled to England with him, been happy there.

CHAPTER TEN

I

During the next four days the hundreds of thousands of visitors to Delhi got everything they had hoped for. Romance, scandal, adultery, picked pockets, polo matches, tea parties and such balls as would be talked about even more than the Maharajah of Patiala's. The Nawab of Kalanpur played in a cricket match and, his mind on other things, was bowled for nought: the revolution was not going to be won on the playing fields of India. There were investitures at which honours were handed out like the cakes at the tea parties. Bridie estimated that if all the medals collected were dropped at the same moment the resulting clang would have been heard in Washington, where no medals were struck but where ex-Presidents and ex-Governors and ex-Senators held on to their titles as if they were baronies.

The King and Queen, each night, were glad to escape to the quiet of the royal tents. The King slept peacefully. The Queen tried to read the biography of Warren Hastings and dropped off to sleep before he had even set out for India. In her dreams she envied him still being in England. Only in her dreams can a queen afford to be envious. Nobody would believe it if she showed it while she was awake.

George Lathrop played cat-and-mouse with the plotters. He was sorely tempted by Farnol's suggestion that they should all be arrested and thrown into jail for the duration of the Durbar. He went to the Viceroy, told His Excellency what was known and asked for permission for the arrests; Lord Hardinge gave an adamant refusal. The King had to be protected in more ways than one.

'We can't do it, Lathrop. The King believes the princes are the cornerstone of his rule in India. He's right, of course

– but he just doesn't know how much we rule the princes. He's no fool and if I went to him and told him some of them are plotting to kill him, he'd believe me. But to arrest them – and how many do we arrest? Three, four, a dozen? You don't know how many are in the plot – that would put a cloud over his Coronation that he wouldn't like at all. He had enough trouble convincing Cabinet and the Archbishop of Canterbury that he should come out here –'

'The Archbishop of Canterbury?'

'Oh yes. Canterbury insisted that only he can crown the monarch and if he'd come out here and made it a Christian ceremony, you can imagine how the Hindus and Muslims would have felt. It's not public knowledge yet, but there's going to be no actual crowning ceremony. The King will put his crown on before he leaves his tent . . . No, Lathrop, there are too many factors to be considered. We'll have to take the risk, keep a very close eye on your plotters and see that no attempt is made on the King's life.'

'Why can't kings stay at home?' said Lathrop plaintively.

'Exactly,' said Hardinge, who did not like being Number Two in India, even to his sovereign. 'My grandfather, when he was Viceroy, said a prayer every day that Queen Victoria would never come to look at India.'

Lathrop went away, feeling proud, as he always did, at the continuity of families who had kept India together. Yet he could feel the unravelling, as in a rope left too long to the elements, in the continuity. There was enough Indian influence, if not blood, in him to make him superstitious; and he was troubled by the portent of what the King was to announce tomorrow at his coronation. Lathrop was one of only twelve men in India and an equal number in London who knew that tomorrow it would be announced that the capital of India was to be moved from Calcutta to Delhi. There would be cries of distress from the merchants of Calcutta as there had been when Simla had become the alternative capital for eight months of the year; the senior civil servants and army brass would not take readily to having to set up new establishments and new residences in a city that still had to be built. None of that worried Lathrop; as head of the Political Service he spent a good deal of his time travelling anyway. What disturbed him was the superstition, based on India's history, that any ruling power moving to Delhi was planning its own demise. Irrational ideas itch more than logic.

Bridie and Lady Westbrook went to visit Karim Singh in hospital, partly out of true concern for him and partly as a change from the entertainment that was beginning to swamp them. Bridie was surprised at her own reaction to seeing him with his hair in a top-knot: India, she decided, looked its best in a turban. Her Irish romanticism was overcoming her Irish aversion to things English: she was beginning to see only the best in the Empire, was turning a blind eye to its sins. If she stayed here long enough she would be a female Kipling.

'I'm falling for the theatre of it all,' she told Lady Westbrook.

'We've done a lot of good here, m'dear. We have well-deserved black marks against us, but all in all we've done more good than harm. Even Prince Sankar will realize that when he and his chums try to run India on their own.'

Karim Singh, a true son of Empire, was out of bed and sitting in a chair when his visitors arrived. He winced as he stood up and was sharply told by Lady Westbrook to sit down again. 'Sit down, you silly chap! What are you doing out of bed?'

'Stretching my legs, memsahib. Tomorrow I am going to see the King. The Major has arranged that I shall get a marvellous view, with a telescope and all – '

'Ridiculous! You're in no fit condition – '

'I am going to be there, memsahib.' Karim had never allowed himself to be browbeaten by a woman, not even this titled English lady. Discretion was only for serious occasions, like being shot at or stabbed. 'It is something that will never happen again and I must be able to tell it to my grandchildren.'

Lady Westbrook couldn't argue with such sentiment. She already had her grandchildren and suddenly she wished they could be here with her tomorrow. To see the theatre of Empire . . . 'Well, do be careful, Karim Singh.'

On the way back from the hospital Lady Westbrook, having just played hospital matron, assumed the role of matchmaker again. 'How is your affair with Clive progressing?'

'Am I having an affair with him?' Bridie had learned not to be offended by her bluntness.

'For want of a better word . . . Don't let's beat about the bush. I'm not asking if you've been to bed with him. But you are in love with the man and I'd hate to see you go to waste. What are his intentions?'

'Dishonourable, I think.'

'Good. That never hurts as a temporary measure. It means he's interested. But it's the long term we're interested in.'

'We?'

'Of course. I haven't known you very long, m'dear, but you have become one of my favourite people. And Clive has always been one. Nothing would please me more than to see you become the favourite of each other. You don't have much time to work in. What are your plans when the Durbar is over?'

'Clive has some leave and he is coming down to Bombay to see me on to the ship for home.'

'Then that's when you have to see he makes up his mind. Be irresistible, m'dear.'

'I'll work on it.' But Bridie wondered if being irresistible would be enough. She had come to India without a thought in her head about the future and now the future looked bleak.

For his part Farnol had more than love and his personal future on his mind. He was seeing the Baron: 'We want you to put some pressure on Herr Monday. We have intercepted two cable messages he has sent, one to Krupps and the other to DWM. They are coded, but we know they are orders for field guns, rifles and machine-guns.'

The Baron shook his huge head. He had been fortunate in securing a small camp of two tents for his own use; it had been suggested by the Commissioner for Accommodation that he should share with the Swiss Consul-General, but he had vetoed that. His own neutrality was enough of a burden without having to listen to the sanctimony of the Swiss.

'I can remember a time when gentlemen didn't read each other's mail. Whatever happened to honourable conduct, Major?'

'I think it finally disappeared round the time of Metternich, Baron.'

'You're far too cynical for a young man, Major.' He sighed, thinking how much better a world it would be if cynicism, like hardening of the arteries, were an affliction only of the aged. 'What do you want me to do with Herr Monday?'

'We don't want anything of this to get into the open. If possible, we should rather that the Mondays left of their own accord than have to deport them. We can do that if it's necessary, but His Excellency is all for everything being done as quietly and with as much decorum as possible.'

'Every inch a gentleman,' said the Baron, not meaning to sound cynical. 'One has to admire the English upper classes. They do everything so much better than we Germans do.'

Like remembering to lift the little finger as they passed the cup of poison. But Farnol, who was too worried to concern himself with scruples or decorum, was glad that H.E. was backing Lathrop and himself all the way. 'His Excellency would appreciate it, Baron, if you could give us an answer by this evening.'

'What sort of answer?'

'If you could persuade Herr Monday to send a further cable cancelling his orders – ?'

'That may be difficult, Major.' The stump of his arm ached as it had when it had first been amputated. He had been a soldier then and diplomacy had not been necessary; and pain, it seemed, had been easier to bear. 'However, I shall do my best.'

'One can't ask for more than that, Baron. No, don't get up.' The old man looked tired and spent. 'When this is all over, I should like to spend an evening with you. Perhaps you would care to tell me what life was like in Europe when you were young.'

'Simpler, Major. Much simpler.'

In another part of the tent city the Ranee of Serog was living her usual simple life of diamond-festooned lechery. Resigned to not being able to lure Clive Farnol into her bed again, she had cast an eye over what else was on offer and decided on three young subalterns, one from the Bengal Lancers, one from Mayne's Horse and, thinking of a trip to

London next year, one from the King's entourage. The young men each thought that he was the only favourite of this beautiful, depraved woman. The Bengal Lancer, living up to his name, was her particular favourite and was marked down for future use.

Mahendra, observing all this lust on the part of his half-sister, was hard put to restrain his natural prudery. But in the interests of revolution he only smiled at her assignations. This unexpected condonation troubled her and, sometimes at the wrong moment, reduced her pleasure. A woman's passion, unlike that of a man, can be cooled by suspicion.

Meanwhile Prince Sankar, playing his role as the Rajah of Pandar, went about the tent city paying his respects to other rulers. He visited no less than forty-four princes, all of them known friends of the British Raj, and Lathrop's informers, the road-sweepers, water-cart wallahs and gharry drivers, reported this social round and left Lathrop more wondering and worried than before.

'The bugger's playing games with us, Clive.'

'So long as he remains visible . . .'

'He's *too* bloody visible. It's as if he's nominated himself as the decoy.'

'Are Bertie and Mahendra being watched?'

'Twenty-four hours a day. I've been keeping an eye on Bertie myself. I think he's the weak link in their scheme. He looks sick to death with something on his mind. Perhaps we could bring him in – ?'

'He may look sick, George, but Bertie's a damn sight tougher than you think. I'm just puzzled why he's mixed up with Sankar – it can't be just a family thing.'

'It could be money. He's a profligate bugger.'

'He was talking about the expense of everything on his way down from Simla . . .' Then Farnol shook his head. 'No, surely a chap wouldn't get himself into such murderous company because of money?'

'Clive, you're naïve about money and its need by some people. History is full of buggers who needed money more than they did their friends.'

'So what do we do? Concentrate on Sankar?'

'There's no alternative. He's the ring-leader – or if he isn't, then we haven't spotted anyone else. Har Dayal, Madame Cama and the others we know about are all still out of the country. No, it's Sankar, I'm afraid.'

'Mahendra?'

'He worries me, but not that much. I was talking to Mala last night about him – ' He let his monocle drop. 'Don't jump to conclusions. It was at Jodhpur's reception – the good wife was there keeping an eye on me. Mahendra was there with Mala and she told me he was on his very best behaviour. The boy's insane, I'm sure, but perhaps he's getting over it. Maybe insanity is like epilepsy, one can grow out of it. Afraid I don't know enough about that sort of thing. Tried to read some books on the subject, but I gave up. Chaps were using terms that made *me* mad. Suppose I'm old-fashioned, but we all have a fault or two.' He put his monocle back in, smiled. 'You and I have less than most.'

Farnol smiled in agreement, left and went to take Bridie on a picnic out along the Jumna River. He had borrowed a small victoria from his father and they drove out through the hot golden morning, turned on to a side road and found themselves beside the ruins of a small temple. Behind them a market garden stretched back to the main road; across the olive-brown river a village was piled like a heap of white blocks, a decoration of flood markings showing on the walls. A caravan of camels moved in their slow-motion walk along the opposite bank, all their riders seemingly slumped in sleep. The river ran sluggishly and above it the hawks planed in lazy circles as if too enervated to look for a direction. A lone, sparsely-leafed tree stood beside the temple ruins and Farnol despatched some crows from it with a shout and spread out a rug in its thin shade.

It was not the most romantic spot: the smell from the river was stronger than Bridie's perfume. She had sprinkled it on a little more liberally than usual: she was being irresistible. The spot, as Farnol said, was not the best, but it did give them room to get closer to each other. It had been very difficult to get close to each other in the crowded reception tents where they had so far spent all their time together.

'When are you leaving Bombay?'

'The ship leaves a week from today.'

He already knew the sailing date, but lovers like a little torture. 'I think we should leave for Bombay tonight.'

She lay down on the blanket, put her head in his lap and looked up at him. 'Having a few extra days together isn't going to solve anything. I'd just feel you were spending more time with me so that you had to spend less time on your problem here. Anyway, I can't leave Delhi till the King is safely through the Durbar.'

'You think more of your editor than you do of me.'

'Darling.' She sat up, grabbed him by the ears and kissed him savagely. A Most Improper Bostonian, she wanted to tear his clothes from him, to be made love to on the banks of the Jumna.

He wanted to tear the clothes from her, make love to her; but not on the banks of the Jumna. Looking through her hair he saw the market gardener, two women and four children leaning on their hoes watching how the idle Europeans filled in their mornings. 'We have an audience, my love.'

'Damn!' She sat back, looked at the spectators, then waved to them. They shyly waved back, but didn't move away; this was better than digging up greens. Bridie straightened her hair, then burst out laughing. 'I must tell Toodles Ryan about this.'

'I want to marry you,' he said seriously.

'I want to marry you, too.' She stopped laughing, took his hand, turned her back on the market gardener and his family. 'But I could never become an army wife, darling. I've enjoyed India – well, not *enjoyed* it. I've found it fascinating. But I could never live here.'

'I know nothing else. Oh, a little of England, but not enough. I'd be completely at sea in America. What would I *do*? I'm a soldier. The U.S. cavalry wouldn't want me telling them how to fight the Indians.'

'Maybe you could work for my father as a trainee ward boss.'

He smiled. 'I think I've had enough of politics.'

'Do you have any money?' Her mother had taught her to be practical about certain matters.

'I suppose so.' He'd always had more than enough to pay his mess bills, buy his uniforms, run some polo ponies. He supposed a wife would cost a good deal more. 'I've never really thought about it.'

The market garden family had been joined by relatives and friends: a small crowd was gathering amongst the greens. A boat came across the river and two men and four women got out and stood on the bank looking up at the Europeans. Some crows came back and sat on the walls of the ruined temple. Farnol looked at the brown crumbling stone of the temple, saw the faint outline of a frieze of figures, all the heads turned towards him and Bridie. Even the gods were spectators.

'Let's go back.' He almost roughly jerked her to her feet, angry at the onlookers and the choice that lay before him. Why couldn't he have fallen in love with some colonel's daughter? But he had tried to; and with half a dozen princes' daughters. He had done his best to marry India, but always in the end he had held back. He did not want to hold back with Bridie, but was not sure he could marry America.

They rode back to New Delhi, though it was not yet called that and neither of them knew that it would be. They were quiet and unhappy, but not with each other, just with their circumstances.

2

The Baron took the glass of Krug '04 that Magda handed him. He had sent for the Mondays, ostensibly to have a drink with him, and as soon as they had arrived he had dismissed the bearer and asked Magda would she play hostess. She had been delighted, sure that all was forgiven and that Zoltan and Herr Baron were from now on to be the best of friends.

'This is marvellous champagne, Herr Baron.' She smiled and raised her glass to him.

'It is the last of a case that Baron von Wangenheim sent me from Constantinople.' He knew they knew the German ambassador to Turkey; they had probably drunk the same champagne at Wangenheim's table. 'I forget what the occasion was.'

'Champagne shouldn't be kept just for occasions,' said Magda.

'My wife would bathe in it if one could get it out of a tap.' Zoltan Monday sat back, relaxed and happy. A half-million-pound order already on the cable wire to Essen and more to come; he could see himself being moved to the very top of the line of Krupps agents, being invited to Germany to dine with the Krupp family at the Villa Hügel. But first he would take Magda south to Ootacamund for a couple of weeks and there in the tropical hills they would laze and make love. But always with an eye on the open door, to get out of the country before the bloodbath began. He had a cardinal rule: an arms salesman should never allow himself to be caught up in a war. 'I try to tell Magda that such a beautiful drink should not be wasted like that.'

The Baron looked at Magda, imagining her naked in a bath of Krug '04. It would not be such a waste. Or perhaps it would be, for he would not be able to do anything but sit and admire and regret. He put down his glass.

'Herr Monday, I am told you have sent a big order to Krupps and DWM for field guns, rifles and machine-guns.'

The champagne abruptly turned sour in Monday's mouth. 'Who told you that, Herr Baron?'

'It is of no matter. The English know all about it. I am giving you an order of my own now. You are to send a cable to Krupps and DWM that the consignment is not to be sent, that the English know of it and plan to confiscate it.'

'With all respect, Herr Baron, the English knowing about the consignment won't make any difference, at least not to Krupps and DWM. My clients are taking delivery of it outside the borders of India. What happens to it after that is no concern of ours.'

The Baron was prepared for that argument. He had sat all day counting the years past against the few still to come, weighing honour against ambition. He had none of the latter now and that made it easier for him.

'It is *my* concern, Herr Monday. The consignment must not be delivered at all, neither within the borders of India nor outside them. I do not think German firms should be party to revolution within a country with which we ourselves are not at war.' *Not yet*: but he managed not to say that.

Magda sat quietly, the champagne in her glass forgotten. She was completely amoral about business. Profit and commission were her only criteria. But she was not without compassion and she could see that the old man was as troubled as her husband.

'Herr Baron –' He looked at her suspiciously; but she knew there was only one business in which coquetry paid off. 'Have you looked at the other side of this situation? Do you think it is our right to pass judgement on the Indians' desire for freedom?'

He wanted to smile; but he had never insulted ladies. 'Madame Monday, I can assure you that Berlin is even less interested in the Indians' freedom than you or I are. I don't think we have to trouble ourselves with that moral judgement.'

'Who said anything about Berlin?'

'Your husband did, several days ago.' He looked back at Monday. 'I presume your employers will tell Berlin of your order?'

'Most certainly, Herr Baron.' Monday took another sip of champagne; it had regained its taste. 'I'm afraid that will take care of your order to me.'

'Not quite, Herr Monday. If you do not cancel your order to Krupps and DWM, then I shall call in Miss O'Brady and give her the full story of what has gone on. She can fill it in with details of everything that has happened in the past week and I'm sure it will be what I understand American newspapers call a scoop. I should imagine that every newspaper in the world, with the exception of those in the Fatherland, will pick up the story and run it on their front pages. It will be the last thing the Kaiser will want just now, while his cousin King George is being crowned here in India.'

Monday put down his glass, said quietly, 'It will be the end of your career, Herr Baron. I shall have to tell my employers why I am cancelling my orders.'

'That, Herr Monday, will be your privilege.' He picked up his glass, finished the champagne in it. 'You see, I do believe in certain freedoms.'

Magda stood up, collected the glasses, put them on the silver tray on the table against the wall. She did it with the air of a house-keeper who knew the party was over; but not quite. She said, 'Herr Baron, does this mean you won't want us to sit with you tomorrow to see the Coronation?'

The Baron looked at her in surprise. But not Zoltan: he knew she always tried to salvage something from disaster. The Baron said, 'The invitation still stands, Madame – '

'Then we shall be there.' She drew on her gloves. 'Come, sweetheart. We should just have time to get to the cable office before it closes.'

The Baron stood up. 'You are a remarkable woman, Madame Magda, I hope your husband appreciates that.'

'I do,' said Monday.

'The world hasn't come to an end, Herr Baron.' She gave him a sweet, friendly smile. She thought him old-fashioned and stupidly honourable, but she bore him no malice. 'There will be other orders from other clients.'

Ah, but the world *is* coming to an end, thought the Baron. But just bowed as the arms salesman and his wife, order books at the ready, went out.

3

'Today's the day,' said the Queen, only just awake and not yet queenly.

The King was already up, a stickler for punctuality. The Coronation was still five hours away, but he must be sure no one was late. He had already had all his equerries wakened and he hoped all his subjects, the millions of them, were up and about. Or at any rate the hundred thousand or so of them who would actually attend the Coronation.

God, being an Englishman and out of England, where even He found the weather trying, had arranged a beautiful day for the occasion. An equerry came in to tell the King so and remarked that it would please the Archbishop of Canterbury when he heard of it.

'Cousin Willy would give half of Prussia for all that's about to happen today,' said the Queen. She was not malicious, only sensible about the Kaiser. 'He loves pomp and ceremony.'

'I thought of inviting him. But in the circumstances, the way he's acting lately, Asquith thought it wasn't advisable.'

'I'm glad you didn't. It would have been showing off and that's not like you.'

But five hours later, when the King and Queen left their camp for the climax of the Durbar, any republican might have been forgiven for thinking that the Royal pair were indeed showing off. The King was wearing the special crown created by Garrards of London for his Indian Coronation; no one had thought of entrusting the task to the craftsmen of the Chandni Chowk. The cap was of purple velvet trimmed with ermine and surmounted with a band of diamonds, four large emeralds and four large sapphires; above that were four cross *pâtées* with ruby centres, alternated with four *fleurs-de-lys* with emerald centres. His Majesty wore the Imperial purple robes, a surcoat of purple, white satin breeches and stockings and the sash of the Order of the Garter. The Queen was almost as eye-catching, but modestly wore, instead of a crown, a diadem of diamonds and emeralds. The assembled princes, decked out like jewelled peacocks, felt suddenly quite drab when they saw them and one homosexual rajah swooned with envy and had to be revived with smelling salts.

The royal couple arrived at the Durbar site in their open carriage drawn by four horses; the King felt more comfortable and conspicuous than he had on his arrival in Delhi. A band struck up Schubert's *Ave Maria*, which pleased and amused Queen Mary but made the King wonder if he now had to worry about feminist-minded bandmasters. The band, as if suddenly realizing the possibility of its banishment to the distant Falkland Islands, switched abruptly to *God Save The King*.

The pavilion where the King was to be acclaimed Emperor stood in the middle of the vast concourse, topped by a golden dome and with steps leading up to it. There, the royal couple would be visible to most of the great assemblage and the King an ideal target for anyone with a high-powered rifle. But first their majesties had to receive homage from the princes and so they made their way to a tented canopy where the exalted traffic would be easier to handle as it passed before the King and Queen. The couple were preceded by Indian attendants carrying peacock fans, yaks' tails and golden maces. The escort came from the 10th Hussars and the Imperial Cadet Corps; the heavy purple trains of the royal pair were carried by ten pages, the young sons of Indian rulers. Out beyond the crowd a hundred-and-one guns boomed the royal salute; ladies in the crowd jumped at each reverberation and several princes in the waiting line sighed as they considered their own meagre gun salutes. The King, who throughout his life had occasionally been troubled by bouts of modesty, now began to be convinced of his own majesty, or at least that of his throne.

Bridie, seated with Lady Westbrook and the Farnol family, was busily scribbling notes for her story. She was thrilled by the spectacle, knew she would never see the like of it again; she made a note comparing it with the drab Inauguration of President Taft, then scratched it out. Neo-imperialists were not encouraged on the staff of the *Globe*.

'It was worth all that dreadful trip from Simla.' Lady Westbrook was wearing another new dress, one that gave her more leg-room than her hobble-skirt. She also had a new hat with a large bouquet of artificial roses on the crown, and a bright pink parasol; she blocked the view of those sitting immediately behind her but she looked so regal that no one dared to complain. She lit a cheroot, obscuring the view still further. 'I think I shall shut my mind to any memories after this. This is enough for the rest of my days.'

Bridie reached for her hand, pressed it. 'I shall never forget it, either.'

She wanted to tell Clive the same thing, but he was not in this stand with her and Lady Westbrook and his family. He was on duty with George Lathrop, wearing his uniform as an officer of Farnol's Horse but playing his role as political agent. He and Colonel Lathrop stood on the edge of a group of senior officers to one side of the canopy where the King was about to receive the princes and chieftains.

'Have you checked that all our friends are here?' said Lathrop.

'It's not possible, George. There's so much confusion down at the tail end. But I've seen Sankar – he's here.'

'There's a rumour that Baroda's up to something.'

'Good Christ, you don't think he's – ?'

'He'd never attempt what we're talking about – ' They were speaking in very low voices. The brass around them would be happier in their ignorance, the safest state of mind for generals in peacetime. Lathrop had no confidence in his superiors. 'If he's involved at all, he'll leave the actual killing to some lesser chap.'

Farnol looked around, scanning the huge crowd. The closest were the four thousand special guests and it was hardly likely that any one of them would be the assassin. But behind them were 70,000 other spectators, the middle class of India: the British, the *chee-chees* and the educated Indians who, if they did not run the country, kept it running. Still further behind them were what the journalists would describe as the populace. The *maidan* where the Durbar was being held was a great flat expanse, but mounds had been built at strategic points to give certain sections of the huge crowd a view. The mounds also provided an ideal position from which a sniper, if he could surround himself with enough accomplices as camouflage, would be able to draw a bead on the King when he mounted the steps to the gold-domed pavilion. But for the present the King was safe under his canopy where he was about to receive the ruling princes.

The line began to move forward. The new Nizam of Hyderabad, the premier ruler, was the first to pay homage. Still in mourning for his father, the man who had died of a surfeit of alcohol and wives, he wore a plain black suit but topped it with a yellow turban with a diamond aigrette. He moved on and was succeeded by other princes. Farnol, now watching the line, lost his concentration for a moment as he fell under the spell of the splendour. The spectrum of princes, even if out-shone by the King, dazzled with their magnificence; a river of silks stretched away down the long line; gems blazed as if their wearers dripped with a priceless liquid. Farnol saw the Nawab of Bhawalpore, a mere child, standing in line, shining like a glittering doll. Further down the line he could see the chieftains from Siam amd Burma, their pagoda-like head-dresses bright as twists of gold in the sun. Pride overcame worry for the moment; he was overwhelmed at being part of such an Empire. Oh God, he thought, echoing Bridie, it must never come to an end! But even in his head the echo was hollow.

'Holy Christ!' Lathrop couldn't keep his voice down; the generals looked at him as if he were some fervent chaplain. 'Look at Baroda!'

The Gaekwar of Baroda must have been missing from the line when Farnol had inspected it; or, amidst the splendour of the other princes, Farnol had missed him. The ruler of Baroda was making some sort of protest that for the moment escaped the puzzled and aghast crowd. He wore no silk and no jewellery, though he was one of the richest princes in India; he was dressed in the plain white linen dress of a Mahratta and he carried a walking stick instead of a sword. Farnol guessed at the purpose of the protest: Baroda, more than any of the other rulers, had fought for his independent authority. But he had chosen the wrong moment to protest: he had insulted the King and the protocol-minded Anglo-Indians would never forgive him.

'H.E. will kill him for that!' Lathrop had dropped his voice: it was a positive hiss now.

'Possibly,' said Farnol. 'But that eliminates him from our suspects. He wouldn't try something like that if he were in our plot. It would be too much of a link – '

Lathrop subsided, took out his monocle, which had clouded, and wiped it. He put it back in and said, 'There's Bertie.'

'We're safe,' said Farnol, watching the resplendent figure of the Nawab, his coat and turban in his MCC colours, bow before the King and Queen. 'He's never going to put a blot on those colours.'

'There's Sankar. He's the bugger to watch – '

The Rajah of Pandar, who hated ostentation, had been tempted to appear in the brown robes he wore when he made his retreats to the monasteries in the mountains. Then he had learned what Baroda planned to do and he knew, taking into account his own low precedence to that of Baroda, that his own protest would be dismissed as a cheap imitation of that of the senior prince. So he had compromised, had worn a simple *achkan* in dark blue silk and a small diamond in the aigrette that adorned his dark blue turban. His bow to the King was stiff, almost perfunctory, but it sufficed and he passed on beyond the royal couple and disappeared into the crowd behind them.

Lathrop let out a soft sigh of relief. 'That's him out of the way, thank Christ.'

Farnol was running his eye down the rest of the line, no longer aware of the magnificence of costumes and jewels, only looking for faces. 'Where's Mala?'

'She should be there – '

'She's not – ' Then he saw the tall slim figure in pale blue silk, his chest ablaze with what looked like a breast-plate of diamonds. 'Good God, look at Mahendra!'

4

Prince Mahendra had woken to the last day of his life with a drowsy feeling of elation. In her own tent his half-sister the Ranee had woken with the same feeling, though for a different reason. She had looked at the still sleeping form of the young Bengal Lancer beside her and wondered if she should have him seconded to her as an adviser on a permanent basis or at least till she grew tired of him. The Government might ask on what grounds he could possibly act as an adviser, but she knew one or two or three or four in the upper echelons and she could depend on them to put the question aside if it came up. The subaltern was a bright boy and he could be seconded to her for experience in Indian matters.

She shook him awake. 'Darling boy. You must be off – '

'Shall I see you tonight?'

She couldn't remember if she had promised tonight to Mayne's Horse or the King's entourage. Probably the equerry, it being the King's night. 'Not tonight. I am going into *purdah*.'

'Whatever for?'

'Rest, darling boy. Now be off. You must look your best when you trot past the King in the parade today.'

Mahendra, coming out of his own tent, saw the young Bengal Lancer leaving. He had known of Mala's visitors each night, but he had swallowed his disgust and anger: her punishment would come at the proper time. But this morning it was as if he were drugged, as if he were walking on a high wire stretched between dull sanity and the exultation of martyrdom. He did not think of himself as religious; he was not a mystic. This morning he burned with self-righteousness: what he was about to do today would be the beginning of the cleansing of India.

The Ranee, aware that tent flaps did not keep in the sounds of ecstasy as did thick palace doors, had dismissed the big Sikh who had been her bodyguard; the last thing she wanted guarded with her present diversions was her body. The young subaltern came out of the tent, certain that he wouldn't be observed. Then he saw Mahendra. For a moment he hesitated out of English politeness, then he scuttled away like all lovers who have to leave before the neighbours are up. Mahendra did not go after him, but strode across to the Ranee's tent and barged in. Naked, the first and only time he had seen her like that, she sat up and stared at him.

'You might have knocked, Bobs.' Which, even in her surprise at seeing him, she knew would have been difficult on a canvas flap.

'You filthy fornicating whore!'

The look in his eyes rather than his words suddenly made her pull the sheet up about her. 'Get out!'

But he was beyond taking orders from her or even from himself. His hatred of her and her libertine sexuality became itself sexual; he fell on her as a rapist might have. His hands clutched the throat that wore no jewels this morning; she fought more furiously than she had ever struggled in love-making; but he killed her in an orgasm of blind mad hatred that left him sprawled on her as a hundred lovers had been.

276

It was almost five minutes before his brain cleared and he sat up.

He looked at her coldly, as a man does who has made love without love. He was sane now; or at least sane enough to be cunningly practical. He turned the Ranee on her side, pulled the black hair down over the bruised throat, then he drew the sheet up round her shoulders. She looked as if she were asleep, which indeed she was, if the poets are to be believed.

He stood up but did not say goodbye to her even in his mind; there was no point in remembering her since he himself would soon be dead. He went out of the tent and met a bearer bringing tea in a silver pot.

'The Ranee is sleeping. She was not well during the night, but she is sleeping now and she is not to be disturbed.'

'Not even for the Durbar?'

'She will not be going to the Durbar. I shall look in on her myself later. But no one is to disturb her – tell Mohammed to see that no one goes into her tent. Just let her sleep.'

But he sat in a chair outside his own tent to make sure that no one disobeyed the instructions; he knew as well as anyone how inquisitive servants could be. Mohammed, the butler, came to enquire after his mistress's health and went away promising to keep the small camp quiet. Then it was time for Mahendra to dress for the Coronation.

He dressed alone, dismissing his personal bearer. He put the jewelled dagger into the belt beneath his *achkan*; he had decided against carrying a sword which might hinder him as he plunged towards the King. He looked at himself in the full-length mirror that had been brought from Serog; but something was missing. *He* was the ruler of Serog now, if only for another hour or two; but who would know? Then he knew what was needed to identify him.

He went across to Mala's tent, went in, loosely lacing the flap behind him in case some busybody servant tried to follow him. He did not look at the body in the bed: she no longer existed. He went to the large brass-bound jewel-case on the portable dressing-table, opened it and gazed at the treasure it contained. He had no idea of its value; his madness had never run to dreams of wealth. He rummaged through the case, spilling pearls, diamonds, rubies, emeralds, his fingers insensitive to them; Mala had handled them sensuously, as if they were sex objects. He took out the diamond breastplate, put it on and went out of the tent without even a glance at himself in the long mirror opposite Mala's bed. He was not interested in how he looked this morning. The diamond adornment, which certain people would recognize, was worn only to show that for an hour at least on this last day of his life he had taken Mala's place, was the Ruler of Serog.

He had been gone an hour, was trying to find Mala's place in the procession's order of precedence before it began to move forward towards the King, when the Ranee's maidservant, ignoring the butler's orders, went into her mistress's tent to see if she was ill enough to need a doctor. A moment later she came running out screaming.

Mohammed, the grey-haired butler, took over at once. He had served the family for fifty years; crises were part of the housekeeping. He regretted the death of the Ranee, but he had never felt any affection for her. He felt no grief or shock; when you have served a half-mad master for as long as he had served Mahendra, you come to expect the unexpected. He sent a bearer to bring the police.

Then, knowing who the murderer was and where he was at that moment, he sent another bearer to tell Major Farnol. Like all butlers he knew all the secrets of the household: or at least those between the Ranee and Mahendra; and he knew that Major Farnol, once the Ranee's lover, had had Mahendra under observation. He did not know what Prince Mahendra planned to do, but he knew the madman should not represent Serog at this morning's Coronation.

The bearer met every barrier possible except flood and fire in his efforts to get to Major Farnol. He was chased away by police, soldiers and petty officials who wore their officialdom as if it were a sword. He had no sense of urgency: the butler had just told him to tell the Major Sahib that the Ranee had been murdered. He had been shocked when told of her death, but death came to everyone and not even the Major Sahib could bring the Ranee back to life. He did not fancy Prince Mahendra as the ruling master, but one master was as good or as bad as another; all that mattered was to have a job and a roof over one's head. So he wandered along the back of the huge crowd, asking for Major Farnol and being chased away, while Mahendra moved slowly but steadily towards his destiny.

Then the bearer saw the Major Sahib's Sikh bearer, sitting in a canvas chair on a mound that was crowded with a host of spectators. The bearer would have missed him except that Karim Singh, besides being the only Sikh amongst a group of *chee-chees*, was the only one with a telescope. Desperate through irritation and exhaustion, the bearer forced his way up the mound, dodging cuffs and blows from the crowd, and literally fell on his knees in front of Karim Singh.

A hundred yards away Farnol was still puzzled by the Ranee's absence. 'She wouldn't let Mahendra take her place in something like this – '

Lathrop, too, was puzzled. But, with Prince Sankar already out of the way and the Nawab just finished his homage to the King, he was settling back with relief, convinced that the danger to the King's life was over for the moment. 'Perhaps she's not well. My chaps tell me she's been having rather a time with all her young men – I suppose it can catch up with a woman after a while – '

'George, she may be ill but she'd never let Mahendra wear that breastplate! She hoarded her jewels for herself – and that's the treasure of treasures!'

Then Karim Singh said right behind him, 'Sahib – '

He turned round. The tall Sikh was trying to stand to attention; he fought the pain for a moment, then relaxed, leaning on the hospital walking-stick. He hated the thought of embarrassing the Major so close to His Majesty the King.

'Sahib – the Ranee is dead. She has been murdered by Prince Mahendra, I think – '

'Jesus Christ!' said Lathrop. 'Then he's the one who's going to – Come on!'

'What do we do? Arrest him in front of the King?'

'Yes – you and I do! If he won't come quietly, then I'll shout for an escort. But we'll try to do it quietly – '

Mahendra was still some distance from the royal couple under their canopy. But he had reached a point where the line was single file now; only ten or twelve rulers stood between him and the King. The dagger in his belt rubbed against his side; all he had to do was undo a single button of his *achkan* and his hand would be on the hilt. He looked up ahead, to the side of the royal canopy; he could see Sankar and the Nawab standing with those who had already paid homage. He had a moment of childish vanity when he looked for approval on their faces, but they were both stiff-faced and he was too far away to see what encouragement there might be in their eyes. Then he looked over the shoulders of the princes ahead of him and saw the small figure of the King, dressed to kill.

He did not see the two officers marching smartly towards him till the last moment. Farnol and Lathrop, resplendent in dress uniforms and turbans, attracted more attention than they desired; but the watching crowd had grown tired of the splendour of princes. These two tall men were what the Durbar was all about. They were the British Raj, they represented the authority that had kept the peace ever since the Mutiny. They saw the officers separate, each one taking his place on opposite sides of a young prince in pale blue silk and a blazing diamond breastplate. Who was he? They looked at their programmes: the *Ranee* of Serog? A transvestite about to be presented?

Then suddenly the crowd's attention was diverted. The Maharajah of Denkanir, eighty years old and frail-legged, suddenly pitched forward on his knees as he bowed before the King. There was a gasp of sympathy from the crowd and attendants rushed forward to help the old man to his feet. It was that diversion, unintended though it was, that kept the next few moments out of the pages of history.

'Good morning, Mahendra,' said Lathrop. 'We'd like a word with you.'

Mahendra could *feel* the black cloud that suddenly rushed through his brain. It was a great pain in his head; he opened his mouth to scream but there was only a choking noise. Then he felt the hands grip his elbows; Farnol's tight fingers touched a nerve and one pain blew away the other. He snatched the other arm away from Lathrop's grip, tore the button off his *achkan* as he reached inside for the dagger. His hand came out and he lunged at Farnol: the King was forgotten, he had to kill this Englishman who was all Englishmen. Farnol was standing so close to Mahendra that only the prince immediately behind in the line saw what happened. The knife went into Farnol's ribs and he gasped; but he didn't bend over or fall away from Mahendra. He grasped the hand holding the knife, pulled it away from himself; the knife came out, dripping blood on the emerald-green jacket. Mahendra struggled, a low gurgling coming from his open mouth; as he tried to free the hand that held the knife, but Farnol was holding it with all his strength. Then suddenly Mahendra slumped, catching both Farnol and Lathrop off guard for just a moment. He turned the knife inwards and pushed his body on to it. It went in just below the diamond breastplate and up into his heart and in the moment before he died his brain seemed to explode.

Lathrop stepped in front of Mahendra, helping Farnol hold up the dead prince. He bent his head, as if being solicitous towards a man who had fainted; but he had softly but sharply called for four soldiers nearby to come forward. The soldiers, all Englishmen, did so briskly; they took hold of Mahendra and holding him upright carried him out of the line and through the crowd. Lathrop looked at the prince immediately behind him.

'Nothing happened, you understand, Your Highness? Prince Mahendra just had one of his attacks.'

'Of course, Colonel.' The prince would spend the next twenty years telling close friends what he thought he had seen; but for today he would be discreet, for he knew the power of the Political Service and he knew Colonel Lathrop. 'Now may I move forward? I have to pay my respects to His Majesty.'

Then Lathrop saw the blood on Farnol's jacket. 'Jesus wept! I didn't know – '

'I can walk off, George. Make no fuss.'

The two officers marched off through the crowd. Farnol later would never know how he managed to stay on his feet, let alone walk upright; he kept one arm across his ribs, doing his best to stop the blood from showing. Once beyond the crowd he stumbled and Lathrop grabbed him. Soldiers came forward and took hold of the wounded Farnol; a medical orderly, bored with attending ladies fainting from the heat, appeared out of nowhere and at once called for a stretcher and an ambulance. Lathrop bent down as Farnol was laid on the stretcher.

'I'll send your parents over to the hospital at once, old chap.'

'I'd like to see Miss O'Brady, too.'

A blanket was thrown over him, the stretcher was picked up. A crowd had gathered around, but these were Indians, the usual spectators. The Europeans and the *chee-chees* and the Indians far enough up the social ladder to be invited guests were once more engrossed in the main attraction. The homage was coming to an end and the King and Queen were about to move across to the pavilion on its dais where, the programme said, the King was to make some announcement.

'Do you think the King noticed what happened?' Farnol said.

'Possibly,' said Lathrop. 'But it won't be the last time someone will fall out of a presentation line. He'll get used to it.'

5

There was talk, of course. The law, if it is to be respected, cannot afford to be private. Two inquests were held, one for the Ranee and one for Mahendra: they were conducted by the same magistrate on the same day. It was established that the Ranee had died from strangulation by her half-brother Prince Mahendra; he, in turn, had died from a self-inflicted wound. Medical evidence was called to state that Mahendra had had a history of mental disorder; Lathrop, but not Farnol, gave evidence that he had known of threats by Mahendra on the Ranee's life. Lathrop was identified only by his rank and regiment; he was not called upon to state that he was head of the Political Service. The magistrate, given neither wink nor nod but knowing Lathrop's true role, did not ask awkward questions but gave verdicts in each case that caused little comment in the newspapers and only a little more in princely circles. The inquests had been held back till their majesties had left India and returned to England; by then no one cared what had happened at the Durbar that hadn't directly affected themselves. The course of law has to be public but it doesn't have to be advertised.

Bridie did not make it to her ship in Bombay. She sent a cable to her editor saying she was taking three months' leave of absence while she did more research in India. She sent him her story of the Durbar, making no mention of any plot or any untoward incident. Her editor replied, congratulating her on her story and saying that she could have her leave of absence but without pay.

'They don't pamper you in New England,' she said. 'So you'll either have to marry me or keep me.'

'Will you marry me?' said Farnol.

'If it's the only way I can get you into my bed . . . '

'You won't mind staying on in India?'

She put the question aside; she was still getting over the shock of learning how close he had come to being killed. Mahendra's knife had missed Farnol's heart by less than an inch. 'If I were not in India, I'd be forever worrying what was happening to you.'

'You could marry some ward boss and forget all about me.'

She leaned forward and kissed him as he lay in the hospital bed. She held his arms down, so that he wouldn't reach for her and draw her down on to his wound. 'No, I'm a romantic – I need to marry a hero. I don't think any ward boss would do what you did to protect a President – he'd be looking around for a new nominee. Is the King going to decorate you?'

'George Lathrop says I'm getting some medal or other. But the King won't know what it's for.'

'What about Sankar and the Nawab? Surely they're going to jail or something?'

'I'm afraid not. H.E. is going to read them the riot act, tell them if they step out of line just one inch they'll be deposed and some more loyal chap will be put in their place.'

'Will it work?'

'It's worked before. Bertie will do what he's told – he'll go back to being a good MCC chap, playing a straight bat. Sankar – I don't know. He could just disappear, make for some monastery in the mountains. Or he may stay on in Pandar behaving himself and perhaps he'll be there at the next Durbar for the next King, bending his hypocritical knee and, who knows, even getting a medal.'

Lady Westbrook and the Baron came to see Farnol in hospital the day after the Coronation. 'I'm going back to Simla tomorrow,' said Lady Westbrook. 'But I'll come down for the wedding. Bridie told me, Clive. I'm delighted for you both. I was beginning to think I'd lost my touch.'

'I envy you.' The Baron's arm ached with remembered feeling. 'May I come to the wedding?'

'Baron, would you be my best man?'

'I should be honoured.'

'Have the Mondays gone?'

'They left for Bombay this morning. Going back to Europe, I gather. He got a cable from Krupps recalling him. Expect I shall get one myself some day soon.' Then he smiled. He felt light-hearted, had a mad moment when he wondered if he might ask Lady Westbrook to waltz. 'Not from Krupps, though.'

'Did you see the parade?'

'It was magnificent,' said the Baron. 'I wish the Kaiser had seen it, he'd have been impressed.' In more ways than one, he wanted to say; but knew the Kaiser was too arrogant to be impressed in the proper way. 'Fifty thousand troops – it did an old soldier's heart good to see them marching and riding past. All those magnificent uniforms and banners stretching away . . .'

'It was like a sunset,' said Lady Westbrook and looked at Farnol and he nodded, understanding.

Farnol and Bridie were married and went to Kashmir for their honeymoon, where they discovered they were ideal partners in bed. When they returned Lathrop sent for Farnol. 'Got a job for you, old chap. How would you and the good wife like to take possession of the palace at Serog?'

'Am I to be the new Rajah?'

'Wouldn't be a bad idea. Brooke, that white rajah out in

Borneo, seems to do all right. No, you'll be a sort of regent, though your official title will be Political Adviser. The Ranee's family, her uncles and cousins, couldn't agree on who was to take over. H.E. called them to order and said he was appointing a youngster named Mulk as the heir – he's a second cousin of the Ranee. He's only twelve years old, so he'll need an adviser. I think you and your good wife should be very happy in that palace, just the place for an extended honeymoon. You'll run the State, of course. But discreetly.'

'Oh, of course. Always discreetly.' Then he smiled. 'It's ironic, isn't it? All Savanna wanted to do was run Serog.'

Lathrop nodded. 'It's settled, then?'

'Not quite. I haven't asked – the good wife yet.'

'Don't be foolish, old chap. What woman would refuse the opportunity to be mistress of a palace?'

So Bridie, like Lola Montez, became mistress of a palace.

CHAPTER ELEVEN

I

Extract from the memoirs of Miss Bridie O'Brady:

Clive and I lived in the palace of Serog for three years. We made trips, of course: to Bombay, Simla, Nepal; but each time we came back I felt as if we were coming home. Yet even in my happiest moments I knew it was not and never would be that: home was still America. But while Clive and I were so happy with each other I never mentioned what beckoned beyond the horizon of my mind.

Then 1914 came and the faraway drums were heard only too distinctly. I did go home then, to Boston; and Clive, recalled to duty, went first to Mesopotamia, then to Egypt and finally to France. Karim Singh went with him; he had spent the three years at Serog with us, bringing his family there. I hate to admit it even to myself, but I think both he and Clive were glad when they were able to escape from Serog and the tranquillity there.

Farnol's Horse, along with several other cavalry regiments, was held in reserve for the Battle of the Somme. Clive and another officer were attached to an infantry regiment, the Royal Fusiliers, for 'ground experience' as their orders stated. They went into action on 1 July 1916, and the experience remained with Clive for the rest of his life. Karim Singh was killed and Clive, wounded in the knee, spent the day in a shell-hole and watched men die like wildflowers scythed down in a grey, grassless meadow. Sixty thousand men were killed or wounded that one day and that was the end of the glory of war.

Clive was invalided back to Blighty, as they called England. I managed to cross the Atlantic, travelling as a newspaper correspondent going to cover the war work of

British women, and was re-united with Clive. He never went back to the front and we stayed in England for the rest of the war.

His leg improved, but for the rest of his life he had a slight limp. He made no protest when I suggested we should come to America and try to settle here. We did settle, first in Virginia, then in Kentucky, and he was happy till the day he died. He became a trainer of thoroughbreds and some of you may remember that he trained two Kentucky Derby winners. More people will remember the horses that won, but I know whom I remember.

We went back to India twice, in 1925 and 1937. We did not go in 1947 when India and Pakistan finally became independent nations. Clive for years had believed they must have their independence but he did not like the way it was fnally done. He wept when he read of what the Hindus and Muslims did to each other in those first few months: the blood-bath came, but it was not the British who died.

Clive died in 1961, two days after the Inauguration of John F. Kennedy as President. We were invited to the ceremony, as we had been to every Democratic Inauguration from President Roosevelt's onwards: it pays to have a ward boss for a father. I sat there that cold January day and thought of another celebration in another land: there was pride and celebration there under the grey Washington sky, but there was no glory, not as I remembered the Durbar of long ago. I never attempt to argue when my grandchildren tell me, in the patient tones that the polite young use when speaking to the blinkered elderly, that there is no place in today's world for Empire. I know they are right because my head, which is not as soft as they sometimes imagine, tells me so. But in that same head are memories of what I saw. I can never tell them the thrill I once felt when I looked up at a tall man in a splendid uniform on a tall black charger and cried, 'Oh God, it must never come to an end!'

Clive caught a chill at that Inauguration and died two days later and the light went out of my life.

So now I'm putting down the last words of these memoirs. We are at the beginning of another war in Vietnam; another Empire, the French, fell there and now, for reasons which

287

escape me (or perhaps I'm too old to care to fathom them out), we are becoming involved. Intelligent ears will probably always hear the sound of faraway drums, Cain is still loose in the world. All I can do is pray for my grandchildren and their children. In the meantime I put on my hat each day, still a lady from the neck up, and go out into the life I still lead; and if a man smiles and recognizes me, even though he be a stranger, I see Clive and smile back. For as Toodles Ryan, Honey Fitz's philosophical adviser, once said: memories are the dreams of the old.

End of extract from memoirs.

2

Bridget O'Brady Farnol died in Roanoke, Virginia, on 22 May 1966, aged 80, one month after the publication of her memoirs. She would have been ironically amused at the number of copies her book sold: 1911.